TWILIGHT

ALSO BY BRENDAN DuBOIS

FINAL WINTER

BETRAYED

SIX DAYS

RESURRECTION DAY

IN THE LEWIS COLE SERIES

PRIMARY STORM

BURIED DREAMS

KILLER WAVES

SHATTERED SHELL

BLACK TIDE

DEAD SAND

COLLECTIONS

THE DARK SNOW

TALES FROM THE DARK WOODS

THOMAS DUNNE BOOKS

ST. MARTIN'S MINOTAUR

NEW YORK

TWILIGHT

BRENDAN DuBOIS

THOMAS DUNNE BOOKS.
An imprint of St. Martin's Press.

www.thomasdunnebooks.com
www.minotaurbooks.com

Design by Dylan Rosal Greif

DuBois, Brendan.
[Dead of night]
Twilight / Brendan DuBois.—1st Thomas Dunne Books/St. Martin's Minotaur ed.
p. cm.
Originally published in Great Britain as Dead of night.
ISBN-13: 978-0-312-36137-2 (alk. paper)
ISBN-10: 0-312-36137-8 (alk. paper)
1. Canadians—New York (State)—Fiction. 2. United Nations—Armed Forces—Fiction. 3. War Crimes—Fiction. 4. Criminal investigation—New York (State)—New York—Fiction. 5. New York (State)—Fiction. 6. United States—Politics and government—Fiction. I. Title.
PS3554.U2564D38 2007
813'.54—dc22

2007033643

First published as *Dead of Night* in the United Kingdom by Sphere, an imprint of Little, Brown Book Group

First U.S. Edition: December 2007

10 9 8 7 6 5 4 3 2 1

To Otto Penzler, with thanks,

for opening so many doors

ACKNOWLEDGMENTS

The author wishes to once again thank his wife, Mona, for her encouragement and unerring editing eye. And speaking of encouragement, his parents, Arthur and Mary DuBois, have been there since his first days behind an old manual typewriter. Thanks, as well, to his British editors—Hilary Hale, David Shelley and Caroline Hogg—for their support and professionalism in bringing this book to life. On this side of the Atlantic, Liza Dawson and Havis Dawson offered wonderful representation, while my British agent, Antony Topping, did the same from London. Once again, Nick Austin, copyeditor extraordinaire, performed his editorial magic. And a special thanks to a special group of people, for what they do and continue to do: Colonel Amy Bouchard, U.S. Air Force; Colonel Mike McKenna, U.S. Air Force; Major David T. May, U.S. Army; and Specialist Chris Chesak, Idaho National Guard.

CHAPTER ONE

Our camp this evening was an old motel that had survived better than other buildings in the small town, though I guess that depends on your definition of survival. After a month in-country, my definition meant a roof and a high percentage of intact windows. An earlier visit by one of the UN reconstruction crews had set up a generator in the rear parking lot so at least there was running water from a nearby well and a few lights. When we got squared away, our team leader, Jean-Paul Cloutier, suggested that we build a fire. I could sense the hesitation in the other members of our group as we stood in the motel's vehicle area. The previous three nights, moving deeper into the disputed territory, a fire had been a fine idea, since I'd been sleeping on the ground under tents donated by the Belgians and we could hear the comforting growl of UN convoys moving out on a nearby two-lane highway. A fire was a bit of luxury. But tonight? So close to the inspection sites?

Jean-Paul clapped his large hands together, like an overwhelmed schoolmaster trying to impress his students. He spoke to us in English. It was the *lingua franca* of our little group. "I'm sure there is nothing to worry about, correct? Or else Charlie here would be telling us to huddle in a basement somewhere. Charlie, am I right?"

Charlie Banner smiled, kept his arms folded. He was in a camouflaged field uniform of the U.S. Marines, had a light blue beret on his head and wore a holstered pistol at his side. The UNFORUS brassard hung from his muscular right arm. "You folks go right ahead," he said. "I'm sure things will be just fine."

Jean-Paul gave a twitch of his head. "There you go, then. Let's get some firewood, eh?" He was about a half-foot taller than me and plenty wide. The top of his head was covered with black stubble and he had black-rimmed eyeglasses. Like the rest of us he wore blue jeans and heavy work boots, and he had a thin down parka that at one time had probably been yellow and had faded almost to white. On the lapels of each of our parkas was a square radiation-monitoring device called a TLD, which stood for thermoluminescent dosimeter and which measured our radiation exposure in-country. Although we were scores of kilometers away from any supposed fallout, the instrument was supposed to make us feel better that any random exposure was being monitored. Trust me, the gizmo was only working at fifty percent effectiveness: no doubt it was accurately measuring what was out there on the winds but it was failing to make us feel any better.

Technically we were civilians and we stayed in civvies as much as possible. Although we supposedly had the customary UN disdain for men in arms, I knew that all of us in this crew were happy to have Charlie with us, even if he was an American.

I reached into my coat pocket and took out a small flashlight. I maneuvered myself so that I was next to Miriam van der Pol, a doctor from Amsterdam who had long blonde hair in a ponytail, a bright smile and a cheerful way of going about our dreary business that made her just pleasant to be with, like relaxing by a cool spring brook after a heavy day of hiking. Not that I was under any misapprehensions about Miriam and whatever little interest she had in me. I was the youngest and most inexperienced member of the group and I had no illusions that she would find me attractive.

Still, I liked being with her.

Miriam saw me and laughed. "Ah, well prepared as always, Samuel."

"It's getting dark," I said. "I don't want to be stumbling around in the dark."

She nodded. "Monsters in the dark, yes."

"If we're lucky, just imaginary ones," I said. Yeah, monsters in the dark. Here and at home, and I left it at that. I didn't like the dark, never had since I was eight years old.

I took her to the edge of the parking lot where fall leaves had already drifted down, and the sight of the orange and red hues made me think of being back in Toronto. Just a brief pang, really, because I remembered only a few months ago being so eager to leave that stifling and safe and boring city, to go someplace exciting and challenging.

Like the saying goes, be careful what you wish for.

There were some pine trees with dead limbs on the lower parts of their trunks, pale white like bones, and we each snapped off an armful and made our way back to the vehicle area. From here we had a good view of the low-slung motel, the three white Toyota Land Cruisers with muddy sides that had the UN crest and UNFORUS stenciled on the side, and the hunched-over figures of our section clustered around a small fire. At the other end of the parking lot were four abandoned vehicles. A pickup truck, a Saab, a Toyota I couldn't identify and a minivan. All the tires were flat and windows had been shot out. A voice with an English accent came from our group, saying, "Get that fire going properly and I'll leave the stove in the lorry. A meal by firelight tonight, friends."

Miriam gently bumped into me and whispered, "Peter deludes himself. He thinks he can cook."

I gently bumped her back, liking the sensation. Who wouldn't? "Then we're aiding him in his delusion, by eating what he serves us."

By the side of the parking lot the empty asphalt road faded away into the distance. From the faint generator-supplied illumination from the motel I could make out the utility poles and the dead street lights, overhanging the roadway like tired sentinels. It was an eerie sight, all the dead lampposts heading into the equally dead town, and I looked back to Miriam and kept my gaze on the ground as we walked over to the fire.

Jean-Paul had started the small blaze with a cigarette lighter and Miriam and I dumped the wood in a pile, while Peter Brown, our resident Englishman and alleged cook, began unpacking small aluminum pots and pans. The other two members of our crew—Karen Tilley and Sanjay Prithan—went to the open lobby of the motel and dragged out some furniture: a small couch and four hard plastic chairs. I thought for a moment about getting onto the couch with Miriam but Jean-Paul had other ideas. He got there first and motioned Charlie to join him. Jean-Paul had a folded-over map in his thick hands and a small flashlight as well, and he started talking map talk with the Marine. I sat in one of the chairs, next to Karen, who was American like Charlie. Karen leaned over too close, her red hair tickling my face, and said in a low voice, "The hunt continues. Site A, Site A, all hail the wonders of Site A. What makes them think we'll find it?"

I stretched out my legs to the fire. "Somebody out here has to find it," I said. "Why not us?"

"Because Jean-Paul and that damn Marine move us too slow, that's why. Look, a week to go and if we don't find anything then a bunch of war criminals get set free in The Hague for lack of evidence. Guys who merrily set up a shooting zone near here where unarmed men, women and children were slaughtered. You want that to happen?"

I put my hands in my coat pockets. Karen's breath had a sour smell to it. "Right now all I want is a hot meal and a bed to sleep in."

"Sounds too basic."

"Basic is good," I said. "Hot meals are good. So are beds."

Her voice perked up. "So they are. You picked a room yet?"

I glanced over at the motel units. "One with a door and unbroken windows."

She nudged me. "Let me know which one you get. Maybe I'll need a roomie or something, if they run out of good rooms."

I looked at the fire and at Peter stirring something in the pots as he was joined by Sanjay. The firelight reflected off of Sanjay's eyeglasses, making him look almost mystical. Peter was a beefy-looking guy with short brown hair, who looked like he had gotten his muscles from tossing drunken customers out of London pubs. I said to Karen, "You're from California, right?"

"Right," she said.

"All the women like you in California?"

She laughed, nudged me again. "Some day you come out there, and I'll show you."

"OK," I said. "Some day." But I sure as hell wasn't going to hold my breath.

Miriam came out from our parked vehicles and gave me a bemused smile. Karen raised her voice. "Hey, Peter! How much longer? I'm tired of roughing it."

"Not too long, hon, not too long," he said. "Besides, this has been a marvelous trek, quite marvelous. You want to talk roughing it? Think of Rwanda. That was roughing it. Heavy jungle, roads of red mud, and the hundreds of bodies along the road, butchered with machetes and sharpened sticks . . . At least this place is relatively clean, and we've got good roads. Not like Rwanda."

Miriam was unpacking some of the metal dishes. "Or Fiji. Nothing like Fiji, either. A Pacific paradise, filled with smoke and shallow graves and reefs with broken boats on them, bodies floating around in the lagoons. Too hot in the day, too stifling at night."

Jean-Paul said something that I couldn't quite hear, something about the Congo being even worse. As they discussed such things among themselves I kept quiet and let the fire warm the base of my boots. This was my first assignment working for the UN so I didn't have any clever stories to offer. What few stories I had dealt with the university in Toronto and a former newspaper reporting job, and it seemed just too damn silly to bring it up. So I didn't.

OUR DINNER WAS a kind of stew from rations donated by the Americans—how nice of them, we all agreed—and was made somewhat more palatable by heavy seasoning. Peter looked thrilled at having successfully heated it up and I let him have that victory. We huddled in a circle around the fire and there was the talk of the mission, of Site A and of what we would find in the morning. While we talked and discussed and raised points about the search, the Marine, Charlie Banner, just kept quiet, eating his own meal, the firelight making his dark skin seem smooth and flawless. He was as big as Jean-Paul but while Jean-Paul was expansive in his movements and talk and actions, like he was always on stage, acting for us, Charlie was the exact opposite, moving slowly and methodically, trying to keep in the background. I always kept looking at his eyes. They seemed to have witnessed a lot of experiences, none of which Charlie had shared with us.

With dinner over I joined the dishwashing crew, bringing over buckets of hot water from one of the motel rooms, letting it drain from a tub spout into white plastic buckets with metal handles. Peter, apparently exhausted by his cooking efforts, sat on the fender of one of the Land Cruisers, smoking a cigarette. Sanjay joined me on one of the trips to get water. "You doing all right, Sam?"

"Samuel," I said automatically.

"Excuse me?" he asked politely.

"Samuel," I said. "My full name. Samuel Roth Simpson."

I picked up a full bucket in the small motel bathroom, looked at his cheerful face with its thick black mustache, and then said, "Sorry. Didn't mean to bark at you like that. When I was a kid I kept on being called Sammy or Sam or Sammy Simp. No good reason to keep pissing me off, but when I could, I just wanted to be called Samuel. OK?"

He smiled, picked up the water bucket. "OK. So. Are you doing all right?"

"No complaints yet," I said. But then again, the evening was young.

"May I ask a question?"

"Go ahead."

Sanjay walked with me to the door of the empty room, walking carefully, not wanting to spill the precious cargo of hot water. "It's about Karen."

"All right."

He turned, now looking sheepish. "I noted you talking to her earlier. Is there anything going on between the two of you?"

"Not a thing," I said. "Why do you ask?"

"Let's just say . . . I have an interest, that's all. And I don't want to interrupt anything you may be having. The gentlemanly way, you understand."

"Sure," I said, walking out to the parking lot. "But I thought you were married, Sanjay."

"Ah, yes," he said, smiling gently. "But New Delhi is quite far away."

"It sure the hell is," I agreed.

AS I FINISHED wiping down the metal cookware I had an odd sense of satisfaction, that I was providing some type of service to the group. When I had first joined up with the team most of them had been in-country for months and were wary of me and what few skills I apparently had to offer. The worst offender was Peter, who though he was exceedingly polite and gracious always gave me the impression that nothing would make him happier than to see me on the next chartered flight back to Canada. I had tried to say something about it earlier but he had said, "No, no, you get me wrong. No doubt the High Commissioner thinks you're important, and so you're here. It's just that I would much rather have a more, shall we say, traditionally skilled field worker with us. That's all. Now, excuse me, will you? I have real work to do."

Tonight, after the dishes had been put away and we were sitting around the dying fire, Peter was talking animatedly with Jean-Paul. Miriam leaned over to me—her hair not tickling me, I'm disappointed to report—and said, "I think Peter wants Jean-Paul's job."

"I think Jean-Paul wants Peter's stones," I said.

"Stones? Excuse me?"

My face warmed up some. "Sorry, stones. Slang for testicles."

"Oh," she said. "That was good. I'll have to remember that."

Then she left to get some firewood from the pile that had been set up near one of the Land Cruisers. Sanjay was saying something in a low voice to Karen that was making her laugh. Charlie was on his haunches by the fire, idly stirring the embers with a stick, and I was about to get up from the cold plastic chair—night dew was already beginning to form on the slick sides—when there were noises in the distance.

It went quiet all around the fire as every head swung round to face the dark horizon off to the west. Faint popping noises, like firecrackers in an ashcan, and streams of red and orange light, arcing up and then back down into the darkness. Jean-Paul cleared his throat. "Tracer fire—am I correct, Charlie?"

Charlie stood up slowly, stick still in his hand with a glowing ember at the end, a faint trail of smoke following behind. He stood there for a long moment, staring out into the distance. His body shifted and I sensed a change in his attitude, of a warrior sensing a far-off battle and wishing he was there instead of escorting a group of UN workers who sometimes needed their hands held and their noses wiped. He cleared his throat.

"Yep, tracer fire," he finally said.

Peter spoke up. "So, chum, who's doing the shooting over there?"

Charlie dropped the stick into the flickering flames. "Hard to tell. Rogue militia units up in the hills, maybe, dropping some harassing fire. Or maybe one of the UN front-line peacekeeper units that got spooked and now they're shooting at shadows."

Now it was Sanjay's turn. "Are we safe enough?"

Jean-Paul laughed. "Where in this cursed place is anybody safe? But at least you're safe enough here, right, Charlie? All the maps say this is a pacified area, and if trouble does erupt, our *bon ami* Charlie gets on his radio and calls in help. Right?"

Charlie nodded slowly, just staring some more out at the horizon where the faint red and orange of the tracers rose and fell. I crossed my legs and looked into the fire. "The maps say this is pacified, right?" I asked.

Peter said, "That's what the man said, or didn't you hear him?"

"Oh, I heard him," I said. "I'm just wondering if the militia units are using the same maps as we are, that's all."

Karen gave a quick laugh but nobody else joined her. Eventually the tracer fire died away and it went quiet again, except for the low roar of a jet going overhead, its running lights doused, part of the NATO force supporting UNFORUS, I supposed. Charlie joined Jean-Paul back at the couch and then it seemed like the fire lost its warming touch, for everything had changed in those brief moments when we saw the tracers out there in the distance. Another little reminder—as if we needed one!—of why we were here and what we were getting into. Nobody was talking to each other, save for Jean-Paul and Charlie, and then Jean-Paul doused his flashlight and said, "Time to retire, my friends. You have fifteen minutes of hot water and lights, and then we switch off the generator, fuel supplies being what they are. All right?"

One by one we got up from the salvaged furniture and went over to the motel units. As I'd told Karen, I'd found a unit with an unbroken door and windows and had claimed it as my own. Nobody called out a good night to me but I didn't feel bad, because I didn't offer a good-night salutation to anybody else either.

CONSCIOUS OF JEAN-PAUL'S warning, I took a quick shower and lit a small candle in a glass globe, which I placed on the shelf beside the bed. There were three locks to the door and I used them all, and then I placed one of the two chairs in the room underneath the door handle. The unit had twin beds, a bathroom and a low cabinet that had drawers in it. On top of the cabinet was a television set. I wondered what kind of people had come and stayed here in this room over the years, before the bombings, before the evacuations, before the fighting had broken out. At least it was clean, and at least there were walls and a roof. As I dried myself I switched on the television and got static. Most stations were still off the air after last spring's attack, but I was hopeful—one of my many bad traits, as Father would so often point out. At the rear of the television was a set of tiny rabbit ears, and after playing around with these and the channel selector, I was able to get a faint picture, flickering through the screen-snow.

I sat on the edge of the bed, watched the program. It was a UN news report, probably broadcast from across the northern border. A woman in a business-type suit was reading from something in her hands. Behind her on the set was the familiar UN crest. There was a slide barely discernible over her left shoulder, something about The Hague, but I couldn't make it out. I turned up the volume and just heard the harshness of the static. I wondered if it was due to the poor reception, or if some of the better-armed and better-equipped militia groups out there were jamming the signal. Militia. Such a soft term, I thought. "Death squads" was more harsh, more appropriate, but it was rarely used in polite conversation among the UN groups. Death squads worked in El Salvador and Serbia. They weren't supposed to be at work here. Not here.

I tried all the other channels. More static, except on one channel, where I could just about make out an old Michael J. Fox movie. *Back to the Future*, dubbed in French. I watched that for another minute or so, and then, as Jean-Paul had promised, the power went out and the room got very dark. Back to the future, indeed.

BY THE FAINT light of the candle I made sure that the sole window, overlooking the parking lot, was also locked. I drew the draperies closed and fastened them tightly with clothespins that I carried in my rucksack, and made sure that the bathroom door was wide open. In one of his few letters to me, Father had warned me that if gunfire ever broke out in the area I should roll out of bed onto the floor, crawl on my belly and get into the bathtub. Better chance of surviving in a tub if shrapnel was flying around. It was a good piece of advice, probably the best one that the old man had ever given me.

I put on a pair of shorts and laid out my sleeping roll on top of the nearest bed. Earlier, Charlie had swept the area for booby traps, land mines and other nasty surprises from the militias doing their dirty work, but I was still cautious. In one of the staging areas where I'd spent time before flying up to join Jean-Paul's group I had heard a story about another UN inspection team like this one, bedding down in an abandoned hotel, and how the sheets and blankets had been salted with ground glass.

From my rucksack I pulled out a foam pillow, one of the few luxuries I'd brought along. The shape and smell of the pillow helped relax me in the dark, especially after a long day like this one had been. Next out of the rucksack was one of the two paperback books I had brought along. The orders from the UN High Commissioner's overseer of the field teams had been explicit: I could bring only a bedroll plus one rucksack for my personal stuff and another for my professional gear. After the pillow, clothes, toiletries, assorted candies and spices, I could barely make room for two books. One was a thin paperback of old science fiction stories from the 1940s and 1950s, *The Green Hills of Earth*, by Robert A. Heinlein. I read that whenever I was in the mood to read the cheerful—and failed—predictions of humans blazing out into the solar system, going first to the moon, then to Venus, Mars and even to the moons of Jupiter and Saturn. The other book was a collection of George Orwell's essays, and I read that whenever I was in a mood to read about humans' failings and foibles. Lately, this book was all I ever read, and I read slowly, restarting it right away when I'd finished it. I found tonight, though, that I was more tired than usual, and I blew out the candle after only a few pages of George Orwell rather skillfully dissecting the saintliness of Gandhi.

It would have been fun to have my Nokia cell phone at my side, to call up some buds from my newspaper job at the *Star*, to hint at what was going on with the world's biggest story, but the UN had banned those and other handheld electronic devices for the teams. It was like being stuck on the longest goddamned airline flight ever, for the UN were spooked that these signals could be monitored and traced by the militias and their government sympathizers. So no Nintendo game, no cell phone, no iPod for listening to tunes, though in any case the cost of workable handheld electronics had skyrocketed since last spring.

So I curled up in my bedroll, thinking about Charlie out there in the darkness. I'm not sure when and how he slept, but he was always out there, on guard, and that gave me the tiniest bit of confidence to fall asleep. Two nights ago I'd had a full bladder and had made my way out of a tent in an overgrown hayfield, and there had been Charlie, sitting on the bumper of one of the Toyotas, sipping a mug of coffee, just nodding in my direction as I went out to find a tree to water.

There was another low rumbling and then another as two flights of jet aircraft passed overhead. Then all was quiet and I drifted off, in an abandoned motel in a small village in the state of New York in the troubled land that was known as the United States.

CHAPTER TWO

I woke up in the dark room with a start, wondering what had disturbed me, and then came the sound of more aircraft, now off to the far horizon. I had that half-queasy moment between sleep and awareness, where you wonder where you are and how you got there. And then the sleeping bag and the smell of the room and the sound of the aircraft brought it all together. I rubbed at my eyes, looked around. For some reason, an odd trick of light made the television screen look like it was glowing gray, as if it was about to come on by itself.

I stared at the screen.

Good old television. Able instantly to bring you news and information, no matter how dark and depressing, in a manner of seconds.

Good old television.

I stared at the screen some more.

And remembered.

A DAY LIKE any other in the *Star* newsroom, on the fifth floor in our building on Yonge Street, this past spring. I was working on a bright little feature story about the latest in ethnic restaurants to pop up in the Theater District—something called Thai/Korean fusion—when I heard one of the senior news editors at the other end of the room just shout out, "Jesus Christ! Will you look at that! Jesus fucking Christ!"

At that corner of the newsroom three television sets were suspended from the ceiling, showing CNN, MSNBC and our home-grown CBC, and right now, on this beautiful morning, they were all showing the same thing: an enormous plume of smoke rising above an urban landscape, a harbor in the foreground, little boats maneuvering away in a panic. I dropped my notebook and joined the scrum of my fellow journalists, gathered underneath the television screens, looking up, all of us now quiet, all of our mouths hanging open, like worshipers at some obscure rural church, suddenly seeing a sign of the Apocalypse appear before them, causing us to be silent, causing us to stand there, quietly trembling in terror.

The plume of smoke rose and rose and rose, obscuring the burning buildings, more and more of them now collapsing in their own pillars of smoke and flame, my thoughts going to all those office workers—what must it be like, stuck in your cubicles and offices, and the floors and ceilings all collapsing around you? Smoke was now blanking almost everything out, and the picture was jittery, the same picture coming in from all three networks, from some sort of helicopter-borne camera, and my eyes couldn't focus on the newscrawl at the bottom of the screen, and some voice, a tired male voice, said, "It's Lower Manhattan. Again."

A frantic female's voice in the crowd asked: "But . . . but . . . where? Which building?"

The same tired voice: "The whole southern end of Manhattan, that's what. They came back, even before the 9/11 memorial and that Liberty Tower building were finished . . . First report over the wires has radiation monitors off the scale. A suitcase nuke, it looks like. The bastards. They finally came back. They finally came back."

A great intake of breath, like all of us had been punched in the gut at once, and then the phones were ringing, there were shouts, and we all started scrambling back to our desks, and I knew then that I'd never write that Thai/Korean fusion story, would probably never write another silly little feature story like that ever again, and as I got to my desk there was another shout, and I and the others turned round and the picture on the screen was suddenly sideways, like the helicopter was flying on its side, out of control, and just as our shocked minds were trying to process that odd little image all three television screens went blank.

And then the lights and the power went out.

As the rest of the attack against our unfortunate neighbor to the south continued, all during that very long first day.

I UNZIPPED MY sleeping bag and got out. I was awake and felt hot and smothered. I needed some fresh air and I went to the motel-room door, carefully undid its three locks, and then opened it, just a bit. I had left the chain on and only wanted to breathe in the cool night air, but I smelled something else, the smell of tobacco. Somebody was out there, smoking, and that could only be one of two persons in our group. So I undid the chain, tossed on my coat, and stepped outside, onto the cold pavement.

Karen was there, on the paved sidewalk in front of the rooms, her face illuminated by the glow from her cigarette. She said, "Jesus, Samuel, scare the shit out of me, why don't you?"

"Sorry. Needed a bit of fresh air. You OK?"

"Sure," she said. "Needed a nicotine fix and my . . . well, let's say I was told to take it outside."

"Oh."

She smirked. "Don't look so shocked, all right?"

"It's a deal. I won't."

Karen took another puff. "How do you like our little group, Samuel?"

I shrugged, hands in my coat pocket. "Group seems fine. Just wish that . . . well, I don't know."

"Wish what?"

"Wish we were doing more than just driving around, poking and prodding. We're not talking to people, we're not really investigating. Just following leads, here and there, leads sent to us from Geneva or Albany. Not sure what kind of progress we're making."

Karen tapped some ash on the ground. "Not much, but some days it can't be helped."

"Why's that?"

"Don't forget, the people here and in the other refugee zones in my fair little country don't particularly want the UN around, asking questions and doing our job. The natives obviously wish we'd go away, and even the refugees don't want us supposedly working on their behalf, because most of them think we're just aggravating the situation. So when both sides don't want to talk to you, it's tough."

"I know . . . it's just, well, frustrating."

I saw a bit of her smile in the glow of her cigarette. "Your first assignment. How sweet. Glad to see we haven't beaten out your idealism yet, but give us time."

I smiled in return. "Thanks. I hope it takes a *long* time."

"Probably not. But even then, I thought most newspaper types were cynical. Guess you're the exception, eh?"

"Maybe so," I said. "Look. Can I ask you a question?"

"Sure."

"Why the UN?"

"Hmm?"

"Well," I said, "I thought most Americans didn't particularly like the UN. And those who wanted to do relief work, they went elsewhere. Like Oxfam, CARE, WorldVision, that sort of thing."

"Maybe I'm just the exception, then," Karen said.

I said nothing and she laughed and said, "Blame it on my grandparents."

"Your grandparents?"

"Yeah. They were in San Francisco, back in '45, when the UN was first really set up. They had minor roles in publicizing it but from what I remember them telling me it was still like being present at the creation of something grand, something wonderful. After tens of millions of people dead during the Second World War, cities obliterated, so much suffering and disease, the UN was just full of possibilities. And I guess they warped my little mind when I grew up, made me think that maybe the world could still use an organization like the UN, as battered and as bowed as she is. So there you go. Satisfied?"

"Suppose so."

So we stood there for a moment, the wind picking up just a bit. Recalling what I had been thinking just a few minutes earlier, I said, "Karen?"

"Yes?"

"Last spring . . . during the attacks . . . were you in California?"

"Mmm," she said, taking a drag. "That I was. And lucky to be there, too. I was supposed to fly out to Miami that afternoon for a conference on Caribbean development. I think my flight might have caught the south end of the Kentucky strike . . . but I had the flu and stayed home and missed my flight. Lucky me."

"Yeah, lucky."

She eyed me and said, "You were in Toronto?"

"At the newspaper. I was writing a restaurant story when we got the word about the Manhattan strike. And a couple of minutes later . . . well, us and about fifty percent of Canada lost power when the other strikes happened—took a while for us to bounce back. But we did manage to get a paper out that day, and the rest of the days. There were some backup generators that weren't affected, and pretty soon the rest of the country was able to get reconnected. Lots of power coming out of Hydro-Quebec; they were able to divert a lot of it in-country."

"Lucky you," she said.

It felt good to be out in the cold air. "And you?"

"Mmm?"

"What . . . what was it like for you?"

Karen held the cigarette in her hand for a moment, the ember glowing hot and red, before taking another defiant puff. "You trying to give me nightmares for the rest of the night, Samuel, is that it?"

"Nope," I said. "Just passing the time."

"Hah. I bet."

I thought for sure that she was going to turn around and head back to whatever room awaited her. But instead she folded her arms and said, "Nice sunny April morning. I was staying with my sister for a while. Out on the rear deck, wrapped in a comforter, trying to get some fresh ocean air into my lungs. That kind of spring morning that only southern California can put out, you know? Just sitting there, not thinking much about anything, except I was hoping that my breakfast of tea and toast would stay down. Looking out over the ocean, looking at the jets. We were north of LA, so there were always a few jets in the air . . . just part of the scenery . . . and I don't know what caught my attention . . . but I saw the jets . . . well, they weren't flying right."

Karen turned and looked at me. "Sounds so simple. They weren't flying right. There were three of them. They were losing altitude, their wings were wobbling, back and forth . . . I remember standing up. Screaming at my sister to come out and see what was going on. The jets wobbled some more, and then one after another, they rolled over and dove right into the ocean—just a big fucking splash of water and spray . . . By then I was crying, crying real hard, and my sister came out and told me that all the power was out . . . and the phones weren't working. We couldn't even get our cell phones to work. And then . . . some godawful noises from the street . . . cars sliding into each other . . . nasty crashes . . . we didn't know what the hell was going on. It took days before we heard about the balloon strikes. Days. What I saw was what happened when those six nukes were set off at altitude. All the electronics on those aircraft and scores more across the country were fried. Those lovely aircraft suddenly become nothing more than pieces of heavy metal, falling to the ocean. The crews . . . I know the passengers must have had it bad, dropping into the ocean. But I think it was the flight crews that had it worst. An aircraft that they knew, that they had trained on, had suddenly gone dark, had gone mad. I imagine those last few minutes, in those dead cockpits, must have been the very worst."

"We were luckier," I said. "The EMP effect didn't reach that far north, and we were able to get the local power grids up and running. Most of the border towns and cities got the brunt of the blackout first because of the way the power grid was set up. Still, it took a month or so before all the news made its way north, what with the border problems . . ."

And then I let that last sentence just dribble out. Still a sensitive subject back home. Did the PM do the right thing by shutting down the borders? Months later it was still a subject of controversy in Ottawa. Those who say yes said he had no other option; the hundreds of thousands of Americans streaming out of the big cities once the power went out and the water was off and the food deliveries stopped, they would have overwhelmed whatever assistance we could have provided. Those who say no, that the PM did the wrong thing, said a safe and secure Canada, with lights and power and food, could have served as a safety valve for the panicky Americans, could have softened the blow, maybe prevented the later troubles after the strike.

Something for the history books to decide, I guess, and I was thankful that Karen didn't rise to the challenge. Instead she rubbed her arms and said, "Lucky. Yeah, you were lucky all right. Everybody thinks California is a nice warm paradise, palm trees and Santa Ana winds and cocktails by the pool. Man, it can get fucking cold at night in California, especially after one night without power. Or a week. Or a month. People were breaking up patio furniture, decks, trying to burn wood for heat. Houses that had a working backup generator that wasn't fried by the EMP, they rented basements and attics for gold jewelry . . . and some houses, the rent was even higher."

"Oh."

"Yeah, safe Canadian boy," Karen said, her voice brittle. "Oh. Before the balloon strike, me and about a hundred and fifty million or so of my sisters were safe and secure in our little cocoon of feminism and twenty-first-century progress. And when some assholes set off suitcase nukes, tens of thousands of feet up in the air, we went from the twenty-first century to the eighteenth century. A rough ride. And you tell me, what does a starving feminist do when she's offered a can of Chef Boyardee beef ravioli, after she hasn't eaten for a week? Hmm?"

I didn't know what to say.

She dropped her cigarette, stubbed it out with a vicious twist of her foot. "I'll tell you what she does. She survives. That's all. She survives. Hey, gotta go."

"All right."

Karen turned and looked back for a moment. "Thanks for the company. But Samuel?"

"Yes?"

"No offense . . . but don't ask me about California again, all right? Deal?"

"Deal," I said, having gotten my quota of fresh air—and a whole hell of a lot more.

I STOOD OUTSIDE for a few minutes longer, taking some deep breaths, bothered by what Karen had told me, cursing that reporter's curiosity that made me poke and pry. I was about to head back into my room when I saw movement, off at the other end of the parking lot. I stepped back into the doorway, my heart thumping a bit harder, wondering who was out there, hoping that it was our Marine escort, and then seeing Peter, our resident Brit—and, in my humble opinion, resident jerk—come into the vehicle area. He stopped for a moment, his head swiveling around, and I had the oddest feeling that he was looking straight through me. I wondered where he had been. He had come down the main street that led into town, though there was nothing up there, nothing at all. But if he was nervous at being out there alone at night by himself he wasn't showing it.

I stood still.

He went to one of the end units of the motel, unlocked the door and went in.

I continued to stand still.

And then he popped out, to take one more glance around. I put my hands behind my back, to stop them from shaking, and when Peter went back into his room I went back into mine, resecuring all three locks, knowing that my little quest for fresh air would keep me awake for most of the long night.

CHAPTER THREE

In the morning rain had come through for a bit, and I joined the others for a stand-up breakfast in the parking lot, shivering. But at least it wasn't dark. I was tired, not having slept much after my little excursion outside my room. Karen gave me a cool glance that said it all: our conversation last night did not happen, and please don't bring it up. And Peter was Peter—when he said that he had slept like a brick, not moving once during the night, I wondered why he was lying. I also wondered why I should care.

Another hot shower sure would have been fine but Jean-Paul decided against restarting the generator because he wanted to make an early start. Not that he had put it up to a vote in the group; he had just done it, like some EU bureaucrat in Brussels, deciding on his own the proper fat content for a particular English cheese. A low mist hung over everything, the water droplets beading up on the various surfaces. While last night the parking lot of the motel had seemed almost cheerful, with our vehicles parked in a semicircle and a fire warming us up, now the place looked trashed. The ashes and logs were black and slick-wet, and the bright orange furniture that we had dragged from the motel looked out of place. This little piece of the countryside now looked worse than it had the day before, and it was our fault. And I knew that any suggestion on my part to move the furniture back and clean out the fire pit would be met with puzzled smiles. What would be the point, compared with what was already out there? And my answer would have been the only one I could come up with: to show respect. But I guess being the youngest in the group meant I still had a bit of optimism.

This morning Sanjay took over the cooking duties, which were minimal: hot tea or instant coffee, with hard rolls and orange marmalade. For Sanjay and Jean-Paul and Miriam and Peter, this seemed to be a reasonable breakfast, though I wished for something more substantial, like eggs and bacon or pancakes and sausages or even a cruller or two. I'm not sure what Charlie or Karen normally had for breakfast—Charlie probably thought breakfast was a waste of time and Karen probably had granola or fruit mix or some damn thing—but whatever we had, we ate on the wet hoods of our Land Cruisers.

Sanjay sipped noisily from his metal mug of tea, the liquid wetting the ends of his mustache. "Look over there," he said, gesturing with a shrug of his shoulder to another Land Cruiser, where Jean-Paul had a satellite phone up and working. "I think Jean-Paul is getting his marching orders from Albany, don't you?"

Jean-Paul was speaking rapidly in French, gesturing wildly with one hand. Peter was next to him, holding a map steady against the hood of the Land Cruiser. Charlie was at the end of the parking lot, looking up and down the road. Karen was next to Sanjay, and I noticed how she had gently bumped her hip against his twice when she didn't think anybody was looking. I guess New Delhi was still quite far away.

Miriam took another hard roll, split it with one hand while spooning out some more marmalade. "Jean-Paul is under a lot of pressure, as are the other teams in this area. If there is no Site A, then there is no case in The Hague. And without a case in The Hague, you know what happens next. The criminals are released and, most likely, are released back to this poor country to start up where they left off if the UN leaves as agreed. Shooting refugees for sport. We have to do what we can."

"How many teams do you think are out here?" I asked, finishing my meager breakfast and hoping against hope that tomorrow we would have something, anything, other than the chalky-tasting marmalade again.

Sanjay shrugged. "A half-dozen, maybe more. All driving around on the ground in this county, all poking around and asking questions and doing who knows what." He raised his head. "But up there . . . up there out in space are surveillance satellites, satellites that have the information we need. Archival footage to compare to real-time footage. Compare and contrast. See the trucks and the trains at work. All up there, ready to be used at a click of a mouse button. And we cannot touch it. Not even a single byte."

Karen kept silent and Miriam added, "The Americans and the Russians have the best equipment. And neither are in a position to help us. You know how it is. The Americans are still humiliated over what has happened, and the Russians don't want to piss off the Americans, in case they ever get back on the world stage like before."

Sanjay looked at Karen, as if to suggest in a way that maybe it was her fault, I don't know. Sanjay said bitterly, "I know how it is, but I don't have to like it."

I looked over and saw Jean-Paul apparently still hard at work, with Peter next to him, equally intent. Then I had a start: Charlie was talking to two people, down where the road met the parking lot. To change the subject I said, "Look there. Seems like a couple of local men have come over to say hello."

Sanjay and Karen and Miriam looked where I was pointing, and Karen said, "Look again, Samuel. The locals look like they haven't reached puberty yet."

I felt my face flush with embarrassment as I realized she was right. The two visitors were young boys and, looking again, I spotted the bicycles that they had been riding. Miriam said, "Young boys, out for a ride. How incredible. I wonder where their parents are. I don't care what the map says about pacification; if they were my boys, they would still be in a basement or a shelter. Or in Canada or Mexico."

"Life muddles along," Sanjay said. "Seems like they're telling Charlie something."

Which was true. The boys were pointing up the road and Charlie was talking back to them, nodding his head, and when it seemed like he was satisfied with whatever it was they were saying he reached into his camouflaged coat and pulled out two chocolate bars. He passed them over and in a few seconds the boys were back on their bicycles, riding back to the town. Charlie watched them for a minute or so, and then ambled back and started talking to Jean-Paul. His face was impassive and I think I knew why. It had been quite normal in the previous century for good-hearted American military men to give out candy to local children in an occupied area. But these were not normal times, not when an American Marine had to do that in his home country. Our team leader pressed the satellite phone against his chest while Charlie talked to him, and then Peter caught my eye.

"Better wrap up breakfast, folks," I said. "I think we're going to be moving out quite shortly."

Miriam smiled at me. "Samuel, you are so right."

I helped with the dishes yet again, and then Jean-Paul strolled over. By now the stubble on his face almost matched in length the stubble on the top of his head. "We have to head out immediately," he said. "Those local boys told Charlie that something bad happened at a farmhouse a few kilometers away."

"What kind of bad?" Karen asked, wiping her hands with a brown paper napkin.

"Bad enough," Jean-Paul said.

WITHIN TEN MINUTES we were on the road and I looked back at the broken-down motel, feeling a bit of regret at leaving it behind. The bed and the room had been comfortable, and maybe we would be back tonight. Then again, maybe we'd be in a field once more, shivering from the early autumn cold. It all depended where we went and what we found.

Our three Land Cruisers made a small convoy as we drove along the narrow blacktop. The first Toyota was being driven by Charlie, with Jean-Paul at his side. I was in the second vehicle, with Peter driving and with Miriam in the rear seat, leaning in front so that she could talk to us, and Sanjay and Karen were in the last vehicle. I looked back a few times, saw them laughing a lot as we drove out. It looked like Karen had found the right room last night, and that the room's occupant had helped erase memories of California after last spring's attack.

Within a few minutes of leaving the motel we passed a refugee column heading in the opposite direction. It was smaller than others I had seen before in the weeks I had officially come "in-country." This one consisted of two pickup trucks laboring under heavy loads of furniture and luggage, and two tractors pulling large flat wagons. About fifteen or twenty people, men and women, boys and girls, all ages, looked at us blankly as we sped past them. I watched them for only a moment. When I had first come here, I had wasted time examining the looks in the faces of the refugees, trying to determine on my own if these were aggressors or victims. And after a while I gave it up. I couldn't tell, speeding by in a UN vehicle. The faces of the refugees all began to look the same: the same blank stare, the same resignation, the same exhaustion that prevented them from even glancing at us as we sped by, the official representatives of what was grandly called a peacekeeping organization, traipsing around in a nation that had usually hated the UN, even during that outfit's good days. It was a hard thing to be a refugee here, especially when you had grown up thinking that refugees only lived on the other side of the world.

The road was well maintained and we stopped only once, at a crossroads where a fueling station had been set up. Three olive-green tanker trucks had pulled into a dirt parking area that looked like it had once held a farmstand that now consisted of burned wooden beams and shingles dumped in a ravine. Two armored personnel carriers guarded the approach from each direction. The familiar UNFORUS was stenciled in black on the side of each APC. The soldiers were Hungarian and were friendly enough, especially when they spotted Karen and Miriam. While only a couple of the soldiers seemed to speak any English, they managed to fuel up all three Land Cruisers within five minutes or so.

As we left, a couple of the soldiers stood out in the road, automatic weapons slung across their backs. They waved and called out, and Peter swiveled in his seat and said, "Looks like you've got a couple of potential boyfriends there, Miriam."

She laughed, rested her thin forearms on the rear of our seats. "Drive on, Peter. Just drive on. Besides, maybe they were waving at Karen."

I folded my arms, leaned back. "I think Karen is spoken for."

"By who?" Miriam asked.

"Sanjay," I said.

"Oh," she said. I couldn't figure out what she meant by that one word.

The road narrowed some and Peter concentrated more on his driving. The morning fog hadn't lifted yet and the fields and shallow valleys were still covered by the slowly moving curtains of light gray mist. Miriam rested her chin on her forearms and said, "All this beautiful country. Look at all this land. My father and grandfather, they would have been thrilled to have so much open land around them. Good land, too."

"Farmers?" I asked.

"Dairy farmers, yes," she said. "The best. But land in Holland is so expensive. My father never quite forgave my mother for giving him three daughters, and he never quite forgave his daughters for not wanting either to be farmers or marry farmers. Soon, when my parents both pass on, so will our farm. Sad."

Peter said, "Sad, sure, but at least they won't be gunned down by their neighbors because they didn't follow the crowd, or because they tried to escape to a nearby town."

"True," Miriam agreed. "Peter, your father? A police officer, as well?"

"Nope, a solicitor. Like his father before him. But the same disappointment. Didn't want his son out in the streets, getting his hands dirty dealing with the muck. Poor old boy."

Miriam chuckled. "How like me. Father and grandfather."

I folded my hands together. Miriam turned to me, gently nudged my shoulder. "And you, Samuel? Newspapermen in your family?"

"No," I said, enjoying the brief touch from Miriam but hating everything else that was now going on. "No, they were soldiers. My great-grandfather was in the trenches in the First World War. My grandfather was at Dieppe. And my father was in the Canadian Army, as well."

"Oh," Miriam said. "Well, your father, he must still be proud of you, then."

"You would think so," I said. Then the Toyota Land Cruiser in front of us braked suddenly and an arm was thrust out of the driver's-side window, windmilling excitedly.

PETER SLAMMED ON the brakes, causing Miriam to shout something out, and me to bounce up against the seat belt. Peter slammed the gear lever into reverse and backed suddenly. I turned, wondering if we were going to slam into the other Toyota, but Sanjay—surprisingly enough, considering his passenger—was paying attention and had backed up as well. Sanjay stopped about fifty meters away and we carried on reversing to stop about twenty-five meters in front of him. Then I tried to swallow.

Miriam leaned forward. "What's wrong?"

Peter swiveled around in his seat again, his eyes wide and his stare hard. "Not sure, but that was the disperse signal Charlie gave us up there. Damn it, with all this bloody fog this sure is a great place for a fucking ambush."

I was aware of just how exposed we were, and I wished that Peter had kept his mouth shut. I knew the purpose of the dispersal signal: to prevent us from lumping together and thereby making ourselves an easy and attractive target. Our Land Cruiser's engine was still rumbling in idle and I thought about how thin the metal of the doors and frame around us was. The militias were well armed. A couple of sweeping motions with a couple of automatic weapons and the UN would be out one inspection team.

Miriam said, "Jean-Paul and Charlie are stepping out."

"So they are," Peter said.

I leaned forward, saw them get out, kneel down by the side of the road. I rubbed my hands against my pants legs. Peter suddenly opened the door and said, "To hell with this, I'm not waiting here to get gut-shot. I'm going up to see what's going on."

Miriam said, "We're not supposed to move without the all-clear signal. Those are the procedures. Right, Samuel?"

I shook my head. "Sorry, I'm with Peter on this one. Let's see what's going on."

I joined up with Peter at the front of the Toyota and walked with him as we went up the road, our feet sounding loud on the pavement, loud enough that I imagined gunmen kilometers away could hear us. I swiveled my head constantly as we went up to the first vehicle. Peter just kept looking ahead of us and said, "Miriam still back there?"

"Yep."

Peter snorted. "Nice little Dutch girl. Almost as bad as the Krauts when it comes to following the rules. Karen and Sanjay moving?"

I turned again. "Nope. Still in their Toyota."

Another dismissive noise from Peter. "Probably tearing off a piece or something while we're waiting."

"You always this pleasant, or are you trying extra hard today?"

Peter just laughed, a nasal tone I couldn't stand. We got close enough to hear Jean-Paul and Charlie talking, and Peter called out, "What's going on?"

Jean-Paul stood up from the pavement, brushing at his knees. There were dark areas around each knee, where moisture from the road had soaked through. "You should be back there with your vehicle. I didn't give the all-clear signal."

"Sorry, boss. I thought I saw it. Right, Samuel?"

Jean-Paul looked at me, his gaze judging and evaluating me. I had seen that look before, many times, growing up in Father's household. "Well?" he asked.

"That's what we thought," I said. "We thought we saw the all-clear."

"Hmm," Jean-Paul said.

Charlie stood up and said, "Looks all right, Jean-Paul. Just a spoof."

Peter stepped around the side of the Toyota. "What's going on? And what sort of a spoof?"

"There," Jean-Paul said. "Charlie saw this before we ran into it."

I got closer and saw the "it." A length of heavy string or fish line, stretched across the road. My throat tightened up and I stepped back. A tripwire. I remembered a slide-show briefing for us new arrivals, weeks ago, on booby traps and their uses. The other end of the tripwire could be attached to anything from a land mine to an artillery shell to homemade napalm. They were called IEDs: Improvised Explosive Devices. Rumor had it that some were built from the firsthand knowledge of local veterans who had served in Iraq years back. Some of the photos in the slide show displayed graphically what could happen to you after a tripwire had been used and one-inch-diameter steel ball bearings had come scything at a human target at waist height. I cleared my throat and said, "Charlie, how in hell did you see that?"

Charlie smiled, rubbed at his strong chin. "Lucky for us it's been a wet morning. The dew collected on the string, so I could see it before we ran into it."

"Jesus Christ," Peter breathed.

Charlie kept on smiling. "Doesn't make much difference," he said. "Still looks like a spoof."

"Like Peter said, what kind of a spoof?" Jean-Paul asked, still with that schoolmaster's voice.

Charlie motioned us to the string and we walked to the left side of the road. One end of the tripwire was tied firmly around a sapling, and when Charlie tugged the other end I flinched and both Jean-Paul and Peter swore and backed away, like me, expecting the sudden *crump* of a booby trap going off.

But nothing happened. The string became limp in Charlie's hands, and he tossed it to the side, among the tall grass and brush. "A spoof," he said. "A fake booby trap, maybe to slow us down, maybe to give somebody amusement."

"Maybe those two boys," I offered.

Charlie nodded in my direction. "Perhaps. A spoof," he repeated.

"Fine," Peter said. "A damn joke. Can we get moving, see if that farm is for real—or is that a spoof, too?"

Charlie looked over at Jean-Paul, giving him a knowing glance. I wasn't sure what was exchanged in those looks, but Jean-Paul gave a little nod, as if something had been settled earlier. "All right, we move on. But we move on in helmets and body armor."

Peter protested. "What for? That bloody stuff's hot and heavy."

Charlie looked at Peter, and the gaze made me flinch. "Better to be hot and heavy than be on the side of the road, bleeding out, waiting for a medevac chopper to dust you off," Charlie said. "I'm the military advisor and escort to this little outfit, and right now I'm advising helmets and body armor, and your team leader's agreed with me. So. You've got a fucking problem with that? Sir?"

Peter shook his head, and I decided I liked Charlie even more. "No, no problem," our Brit said.

WE RESUMED DRIVING after about fifteen minutes or so of digging through our gear, pulling out the black body-armor vests and the light blue helmets with the white UN crest. The helmets were dented and faded, the crest depicting the globe and olive branches chipped and worn away. Miriam held up hers and shook her head. "Makes me wonder what places this helmet has traveled, what horrors it has witnessed."

Peter said, "Is it clean? Is it whole?"

"Yes—why do you ask?"

Peter smiled, showing his teeth, which needed a good brushing. "Just be glad there are no bloodstains or holes or flecks of brain matter inside. I've seen it before. Bad luck and all that."

I saw the sweat stains on the green webbing inside my helmet and thought about what Miriam had said. She was right, whatever Peter might say. These helmets had been used and re-used. With money tight for peacekeeping, allowances had to be made. I put on my helmet, tightened the chinstrap, and instantly felt ridiculous, like an impostor. My buds at the *Star* would probably wet themselves laughing at seeing me dressed like this. We helped each other with the Velcro straps of the body armor, making sure that our radiation monitors were not obstructed by the material. I was pleased when Miriam turned down Peter's offer of assistance and asked me to help.

Peter pretended that it didn't bother him when I stood behind her and gingerly pulled the straps tight against her. It seemed a special, intimate moment, and I had an urge just to stand there, my hands around her slim waist. Then Miriam turned and smiled and said, "Fine. Let's go, then."

We followed the lead Toyota again, though slower, and Peter said, "I still don't like what happened. Spoof or no spoof, someone's fucking with our heads. This place is supposed to be pacified. I don't like it, not at all."

"Maybe it was the kids," I said again, seeing how the land was beginning to rise up, fences with barbed wire and fields all around us. Some of the mist started to burn off.

"Well, maybe it was the daddies of those kids, looking to see what we do in case we spot a booby trap or obstruction in the roadway. Now they know our hand signals, how we'll disperse, the distances we aim to put between each other. Easier for them to take us out."

"So," Miriam said, trying to lean forward to talk to us without bumping her helmeted head on the roof of the Toyota. "What should we do? Go back to the hotel? Try to fill the swimming pool? Is that it?"

"No, but Jean-Paul could get on the horn there and get us some backup, besides that Marine," Peter said. "I'd feel a hell of a lot better with an APC in front of us, that's for sure."

I folded my arms, saw brake lights come on again up front. "Aren't enough to go around, you know that."

Miriam added, "Besides, this area's pacified. That's what all the maps said."

"Sure," Peter said. "But remember what Sammy here said last night. Did anybody tell the paramilitaries what kind of maps they should be using?"

Then we all shut up as the lead Toyota turned right and started going up a dirt driveway. We followed and I swung my head around, to check on the third Land Cruiser. Sanjay and Karen were back there but I didn't see any laughter, any smiles. It's hard to stay in a good mood while wearing a helmet and body armor. I saw something else I didn't like: two black mailboxes, torn from their wooden posts and flung to the ground.

The driveway went up about a hundred meters, and Peter said, "I surely do take it all back. That sure don't look like a spoof to me, mates, does it now?"

I didn't answer, just trying to take it all in. There had once been a large farmhouse here, with a barn and a couple of outbuildings. But the windows were all shattered and there were scorch marks where fires had burned. In front was a large dirt turnaround and all three Land Cruisers maneuvered so that they were facing back down the driveway, for easy escape. A tractor was on its side, and a pickup truck was on flat tires, its body rust-red from having burned some time ago. We got out and Jean-Paul motioned us to stay behind. I felt my hands quivering as Charlie went into the rear of his Toyota and came out hefting a utility belt from which hung various items of equipment. He was also holding an M-16 rifle. Unlike the rest of us, his helmet looked like it belonged on him. Karen and Sanjay joined us, standing behind the front of the Toyota where the tires and engine block might protect us if something bad were to happen.

Karen said, exasperation in her voice, "Damn it, there he goes again. A man with a gun. Ninety percent of the world's problems—and one hundred percent of our particular problems—would be eliminated if we could figure out a way to get rid of men with guns."

I think I surprised everyone there—including myself—by saying, "Don't be so quick to get rid of this particular man. He'd die fighting to protect you, Karen, so show some appreciation, why don't you?"

Karen made a dismissive noise and looked to Sanjay for something, maybe reassurance. But Sanjay was watching with the rest of us as Charlie carefully walked around the buildings, stepping in and out for a moment or three. He then went into the two-story farmhouse. The building was painted bright yellow, which made the scorch marks around the broken windows that bit more dramatic. I looked out beyond the trees, wondering if the gunmen had come from there or if they had been so blatant as to come right up the driveway.

Charlie came out of the house, the M-16 slung over his shoulder, and I realized then that my legs had relaxed—earlier they had been threatening to start shaking. Charlie met with Jean-Paul and they talked for a moment. Then Jean-Paul came over to us, shaking his head.

"No bodies, but there looks to be evidence in the barn and in the downstairs living room," he said quietly. "Time for all of us to get to work."

There. For the first time since I had joined the team I had heard those quiet words. I went with Peter and Miriam to the rear of our Toyota, where each of us pulled out our work rucksack.

CHAPTER FOUR

I wasn't sure who to follow—those going into the house or those going into the barn—but when Miriam headed to the open doorway of the barn I joined her, my heavy rucksack dangling from one hand. We stood there for a moment, letting our eyes adjust to the gloom inside. I was surprised at the concrete floor of the barn: such an expenditure wasn't to be expected in such a poor part of the country. Before us were empty stalls, bags of feed and fertilizer, and one area piled up with hay bales. One wooden wall was splintered and broken, like something had battered it fast and with great violence, and on the concrete below the wall hay had been spread around.

Miriam stood by the wall, started toeing away some of the hay. "Peter, Samuel," she said, her voice as serious as I'd ever heard it. "We've got bloodstains here."

Peter started undoing his rucksack. "And we've got impact rounds in the far wall. Looks like someone got lined up and shot."

"Yes," Miriam said.

I felt like I could not say a thing. They had been to such places before, had had experiences, had a history with each other. All I had was my own rucksack and my own pitiful tools. I spared a glance as Peter started working, examining the bullet holes in the chewed-up wall, making soft little exclamations of delight as he found empty brass casings on the concrete.

Each casing was picked up and placed inside a tiny plastic bag. Miriam worked just as diligently but much more quietly as she gently brushed away the strands of hay covering the floor. Each of them was now wearing latex gloves.

I took out my own tools: a small laptop, a digital camera and a portable satellite uplink station. I powered up everything and when the camera was ready I input the day's date and time and our coordinates—with the GPS signal they were accurate to a meter or two. Then I got to work also, photographing Miriam and Peter, and then photographing the evidence as well. It was quiet in the large barn as we worked, and I tried not to let my imagination take hold of me. I concentrated on the documentation that was required of me. Miriam was a forensic pathologist, Peter was a forensic analyst, and I was a former newspaper reporter, just trying to keep records of what had happened here. And all of us were UN employees. Not much in the way of peacekeeping, but it was something that had to be done. Peter and Miriam had their own laptops out and talked cryptically to each other about blood spatters, tissue samples, angles of trajectory and round sizes. I tried to stay out of their way and document as much as I could, letting everything exist only within the tiny screen of the camera. Somehow it made matters just a little bit easier.

Twice I stopped and went over to the laptop and uplink station. There I downloaded the images from my camera, sorted them out and made sure that the correct captions were attached. Then they were uploaded and I got a reply within a minute, saying the photos had been successfully received in Geneva. I wiped the sweat that had collected on my brow, underneath the brim of the helmet. The latest in digital and transmission technology, recording for all time—as long as things were recorded in bits and bytes—a type of massacre that had happened on this planet for millennia. I imagined some sour little Swiss bureaucrat in a cubicle somewhere in Geneva, idly looking at what I had submitted and then placing it in some file or e-mail attachment to The Hague. One more atrocity among thousands. We sure as hell still didn't know how to prevent war crimes, but at least we were experts at recording them.

Charlie came over, his M-16 slung over his shoulder. "Break time," he announced. "Jean-Paul says it's time for lunch and some debriefing."

Miriam said nothing but Peter was on his knees with a small flashlight, looking for more shell casings underneath a piece of farm machinery. "We're rather busy here, Charles. Perhaps later."

Charlie grinned. "Nope. It's now, sir. Like the good man said. Lunch and a debrief."

After spending time in the barn with the blood and bullet holes and the scent of decay, I couldn't imagine being hungry, but Jean-Paul had taken control of lunch and had cooked up some sort of broth, with hard rolls and cheese to accompany it. Maybe it was something to do with his unerring ability not to let the job get in the way of being fed. Someone had placed a canvas tarp on the ground and we leaned up against the sides of our vehicles, eating quietly. Overhead a flock of ravens flew to the south, croaking and calling, and Sanjay said, "I hate the birds in this country. They are all so fat."

Karen said, "It's no wonder. There's so much to eat out in the open now."

Miriam moved to take off her helmet and Charlie said, "Sorry, ma'am. Body armor stays on."

"But this place is quiet," she said. "Nobody is here. Nothing."

Charlie nodded, his weapon at his side. "Nothing we can *see*, ma'am. It's the stuff we can't see that worries me. The helmets and body armor stay on."

Peter said, "How much longer do we stay here, Jean-Paul?"

Our team leader wiped some broth out of his metal bowl with a piece of bread. "We stay until the job is done."

Peter said impatiently, his eyes flashing, "I know that. But how much longer?" He waved a hand. "Not meaning to sound crude, but this is one more farmhouse, one more dead family, in a very long and sad list of other farmhouses and dead families in this state and other states. So sorry and all that, but it's not Site A. Not by a long shot."

Jean-Paul munched on his bread, stood up. "We stay until the job is done. Site A will take care of itself. Samuel?"

"Yes?" I said, stepping up quickly.

"We need you now in the farmhouse, if that is all right with you."

"That'll be fine," I said. Peter looked glumly up at me, like the former British police officer he was, being overruled by a superior he didn't respect. I walked away.

I FOUND IT harder going in the house. In the barn one could distance oneself from what had happened, what horrible things had gone on in there among the hay and tools and machinery. Nonetheless, it was a different kind of place, a place for animals and tools. It wasn't a home. But inside the house there was no barrier, no distancing, nothing that could act as a buffer for what I saw. Among the couches and kitchen tables and bookshelves and television sets, among the day-to-day comforting items of reasonable and safe life, madness had broken in. Madness that had ripped everything asunder, that had left broken dishes and torn furniture and piles of clothing and shattered photos and twisted toys. Some spray-painted slogans had been left on the walls, some of the letters dripping into fresh bullet holes in the plaster, other letters oozing into the spatter of dried blood. The paint was black and the blood spatter was now a dark brown. I paused, holding my digital camera in my hands. Where to start? Where to even begin? Sanjay was by the wall, measuring the distance between the bullet holes. I think he sensed my hesitation, for he looked over at me.

"I know how it is," he said softly. "You see this home and you wonder who they were. You wonder what kind of man the father was, you wonder how the mother treated their children. You wonder how old the children were, what kind of games they played, how they lived here. You wonder what it was like when the men with guns broke in. Who they were. Angry refugees from one of the cities? Or angry neighbors, upset that this family had given aid and comfort to those now considered enemies, outsiders? Then you wonder what happened. Was the mother raped in front of the children? Was the father killed first? Were the children taken away? You wonder how men could do this to people who were fellow citizens of their country, who were civilians, simple farmers. Fellow Americans, as they would say. Samuel, you are wondering all this, and you cannot let it happen."

My words sounded like they were being strangled in my throat before I uttered them. "How? How do you do that?"

Sanjay looked around him, looking so serious and proper, even though he was still wearing his helmet and body armor. "By doing what we are doing. By remembering them, by paying witness. You do your job as best as you can, but you don't dwell on what you can't see. You cannot let your imagination take over. You have to do your job with what is there. Trust me, that is more than enough."

I just nodded, picked up my camera. Like before, in the barn, I took photos of the living room and the blood spatters and the bullet holes. I went to the other rooms as well, a children's room and a bedroom for the parents upstairs, where the fires had been set and had sputtered out. The smell of burned wood was nauseating. I made a special point of taking photographs of the few framed pictures I could find: photos of weddings, of school graduations, of family celebrations. I tried to heed Sanjay's advice not to dwell on the implications of what I was taking shots of. I just made sure that the photos were in focus and were framed properly and had the correct captions. In a narrow hallway I moved between Jean-Paul and Karen in mid-conversation, with Jean-Paul being his usual pompous self:

". . . Agree with Peter, we can't spend all this time here with no bodies, no additional evidence. Site A is supposed to have more than a hundred bodies and the evidence . . ."

". . . Won't ignore this site. So, sorry, Karen, but that's the way it's going to be . . ."

Back in the living room Sanjay was processing some of his own information in his laptop, while I took additional photographs of the bloody clothing that had been left behind. These photographs would go in specially bound books prepared by the International Red Cross. With many records being destroyed in villages and towns here in New York and other places as well, especially those in the immediate footprint of the EMPs from the airborne nukes, these books were often the best source of information left. Sometime, somewhere, some trembling survivors would leaf through these photos and find a baby sock or a man's shoe or a woman's frock that they could identify, and one poor family's fate would be transferred from "identified" to "identified." Again, not much of a peacekeeping function, but as record keepers we could not be beat.

Then I found myself alone on the front steps of the house, having downloaded and uplinked the latest photographs and captions. I found I could not spend another second in that dead place. My hands were threatening to shake so I clasped them in my lap. Outside, Charlie was leaning against the fender of one of the Toyota Land Cruisers, sipping yet another cup of coffee. He looked over at me and then went back to his coffee. Behind me the door swung open and Jean-Paul sat down next to me.

"So," he said. "Taking a quick break, eh?"

I just nodded, fearful that if I opened my mouth I might throw up. Not a way to impress one's supervisor, even if it was just Jean-Paul.

He reached under his parka, took out a packet of Gauloise cigarettes. He lit one and asked, "A smoke, Samuel?"

"No, thank you," I said, grateful that I could get those words out without choking on them.

The smell of the harsh French tobacco was almost comforting and Jean-Paul clasped both his large hands together, holding the cigarette in his rubber-gloved fingers. He said, "The first time is always the worst. Always. No matter what you see in the future, this will be the worst of the lot. That should give you some comfort."

"It doesn't," I said.

"Don't blame yourself, then."

"Sorry, I do," I said, my voice getting stronger. "Hell, there aren't even any bodies in there, but I still feel like puking on my feet. And some of my photos suck, because my hands are shaking so much that the pictures come out blurry. A hell of a thing to be doing. And compared to what you guys do . . ."

Jean-Paul took a puff of his cigarette. "We have you, and that is fine. And still, despite everything you've said, here you are."

"Yeah, well, I don't think I'm doing shit."

"No, that's not true," he said. "What you are doing is important. What we all do here is important, but you are the record keeper. Months and years from now, our reports with their formal and stale language about bullet holes and decomposed bodies and clothing identifications will be forgotten. But your photos and your reports and your journals will be read forever, to show the world what has happened here."

"Why? So it doesn't happen again? Faint damn chance of that, and you know it."

Another puff of his cigarette. "If there is to be any progress, we cannot ignore what has happened. Sometimes we can prevent the atrocities, and sometimes we cannot. And when we cannot, we comfort the survivors and prosecute the criminals. A little thing, perhaps, but better than doing nothing at all. We are not a perfect organization, the UN. We never have been. But we are a start."

"True . . . but this is different. I've been in the States, many times. To come here like this, to see them like this . . ."

"I know. In some ways it is the hardest, eh? As so-called civilized men, we believe in 'the other'. That only bad things can happen in certain backward places. In the Sudan. In the Balkans. Not the Adirondacks. But under pressure—after the spring bombings—even the most advanced places can collapse."

I rubbed my hands together, not sure what to say next, and Jean-Paul said, "I know your father. How is he?"

"All right, I suppose. Where did you know him from?"

"In Mogadishu."

"Oh," I said, not wanting to say any more.

Jean-Paul dropped the cigarette butt on the brown grass, ground it out with his boot heel. "If you write to him, tell him I said hello, will you?"

"If I write, I will."

"Another thing—but not to be mentioned in any letter to him."

"All right," I said.

"The thing that happened to him after Mogadishu . . . Not his fault. For what it's worth, I think what happened to him was unfair. All right?"

"Sure," I said. "But you'll excuse me if I don't agree with you. It was his fault. From start to finish. He was the CO. Period."

"And that will have to be discussed at another time," Jean-Paul said, opening the door. "Look. Take some more time off. Go for a little walk. Keep in view of the farmhouse and Charlie and don't go into the woods. But clear your head some, all right?"

"Sure," I said, and when the door slammed behind him, I looked out again to the little dirt driveway and Charlie still standing there, our coffee-drinking sentinel.

I FOLLOWED JEAN-PAUL'S suggestion and got up and walked around the muddy yard, looking at the empty clotheslines, the thin ropes moving slightly in the breeze, and at an overturned tricycle, and a picnic table with peeling green paint. The woods were mostly pine, about fifty meters away from the rear of the house, and it just seemed right to me that the men with guns had come out of these woods sometime during the night, for that was when they preferred to work. At night, when everything was dark and everything was permissible, especially if you were from far away, you were hungry, and you wanted to take what you didn't have.

I went behind the barn and saw that the fog had burned off so much that I could make out a rise in the land, some distance away, and two other farmhouses on the crest of the ridge. Woodsmoke eddied up from chimneys at each of the houses, and I wondered who was in those two homes. Were they local refugees, back home now because of the accord and because of the UN force? Or were they survivors of what had happened, only now emerging from root cellars and hidden shelters in the forest, having been terrorized here after fleeing one of the big cities?

Or maybe they were collaborators or former members of the militias, who had kept watch on their neighbors all these years so that when the night fell after last spring's attack and the knives and guns came out they could so efficiently do their work. How could they still be there, I thought, just hundreds of meters away from this massacre site? Hadn't they seen the men with guns come across the fields, or drive up in pickup trucks and cars? Hadn't they heard the shouts, the screams, the gunshots? Hadn't they seen the muzzle flash of gunfire, the flames coming out of the windows, the smoke billowing from the house?

Hadn't they noticed a damn thing?

Out behind the barn the tilled earth stretched away, and I walked for a while in the muddy soil, remembering again the farms back home in Ontario, farms larger and better maintained than this one. But, even then, I felt a pang of homesickness as I trudged across the field, trying to clear my head. My fingers ached from working my equipment and my head ached from the helmet and my shoulders and back ached from the body armor, and for about the thousandth time since I came in-country I wondered why in hell I had volunteered.

Then I tripped and fell into the mud.

I stood up. "Moron," I said to myself, and I looked down, wondering what I had tripped over. Something in the dirt. I nudged it with the edge of my boot.

A woman's shoe.

I stepped back as if the damn thing was electrified. I looked around this part of the field and saw that something was wrong, very wrong.

The dirt didn't make sense.

All across the field were muddy furrows, running straight and true from the rear of the barn to the nearest fence. But in this place, where I had tripped, the dirt was different.

It had been disturbed, and recently.

I turned and ran back to the farmhouse. Halfway there my chinstrap came loose and I had to hold on to my helmet with a free hand while the mud stuck to my racing feet.

PETER FROWNED AS he moved the thin metal probe up and down in the dirt. "Looks like we've got something here, Jean-Paul. Dirt's moving around easy enough, and I'm getting soft resistance at the other end."

Jean-Paul had another cigarette between his fingers. "Good. Miriam?"

She was on her knees in the mud, gently probing with a flexible thin hose that she dipped in and out of the dirt. The clear plastic tube ran back to a small open case, which she examined. There were dials and digital readouts and I stood there, still breathing heavily from my burdened run back to the farmhouse. Karen and Sanjay and even Charlie were standing nearby, in a semicircle. Karen and Sanjay looked angry. Only Charlie looked calm, but with him I would never think that I could guess what was going on behind those quiet eyes.

"Decomposition gases," Miriam said. "There's decaying flesh under here. Less than a meter, I'd guess."

Another nod from Jean-Paul. "Very good. Peter, are there shovels in that barn over there?"

Peter stood there, the probe resting on his shoulder. He was staring down at where Miriam was working.

"Peter?" Jean-Paul asked. "Did you not hear me?"

At first Peter's voice was so quiet that I almost didn't hear him. ". . . Difference does it make, Jean-Paul? You know why we're here, why another half-dozen teams are out wandering the countryside. Looking for Site A. Does this look like Site A? Does it?"

Jean-Paul took a drag from his cigarette. "No, it is not Site A. But it is something. We will do what we are tasked to do, and continue our work."

"But it's a waste of time!" Peter said, and I could make out Karen and Sanjay nodding in agreement. "We've got a week to find Site A, and we shouldn't be wasting our resources here."

Jean-Paul's voice was quiet and firm. "You'll have us leave them here, forgotten and in the muck?"

Karen spoke up in Peter's defense. "No, we won't forget them. Make a report and list this site for further excavation. We should leave here and get to work on finding Site A. This is just one more farm family, Jean-Paul. You know how important Site A is to the High Commissioner."

Jean-Paul looked at all of us through his black-rimmed glasses. "Yes, I do. Perhaps better than the rest of you. And if any of you are someday assigned to supervise a field team, then you can do as you please. But *this* field team is under *my* direction. And I direct that we begin the excavation. Now. Understood? No more time for questions. No more time for back talk. Or you will be relieved of your duties and will be sent out on the next chartered flight to your respective home country. Understood?"

I wasn't sure but I think Charlie was enjoying this little demonstration of the UN in action, for he turned away for a moment, as if to hide the amusement on his face. Peter muttered something under his breath, jammed the thin metal probe back into the ground, and strode over to the barn. After a minute or two he came back, carrying two shovels under his arm. He tossed one at me—which I caught, thankfully—and glared at me.

"You found this spot," he said. "Least you could do is start digging."

I said nothing, just took the shovel and got to work. A few seconds later Peter joined me.

THE DIGGING WAS hard going, even though it was clear that the soil had been freshly turned over. The earth was thick and muddy and wet, and large chunks of it stuck to the shovel blade. I found that after just a few minutes of work I was sweating underneath the body armor and my helmet. My hands began to get sore, and the sounds—the sickening squishing and plopping noises as chunks of mud were piled up to the side—were obscene. As Peter and I dug we kept quiet. Then Karen and Sanjay went to one of the Toyota Land Cruisers and came back, each carrying a long dark object, which they unrolled on the wet ground, speaking not a word. Rubberized body bags, in two sizes, for adults or children. How thoughtful.

I dug and dug, my wrists and hands aching, and I wished for a break. But I wasn't about to give Peter the satisfaction of seeing me give up first, so I concentrated on the digging and every now and then raised my eyes to see what was going on around us. I saw Karen and Sanjay laying out the body bags. I saw Miriam looking at the readouts on her black box. I saw Jean-Paul and Charlie talking to each other in low voices. I saw another flock of ravens going overhead, croaking at us as they flew to sit in the nearby pine trees, to watch what we were uncovering for them.

"Time for a break," Peter gasped, and I shoveled two more loads of muck out before agreeing.

"Sure," I said, feeling good that I had outlasted our moody Brit. "Time for a break."

Peter got out of the hole, walked to the side of the barn and leaned back against the dark wood. I stayed in the hole, toying with the soil. Miriam came over and said, "How are you doing, Samuel?"

"I've had better days," I said.

"Look, you see that?" she asked.

"What?"

"Those white streaks, in the soil. Not good, not good at all."

"What do you mean?"

She shivered and then hugged herself. "Lime. Helps speed up decomposition. The militias do that to hide the evidence."

I suppose I should have waited for Peter to return, but Miriam was looking at me and I felt like I had to do something. I started digging again and then it was as though the earth beneath me belched, for something foul and sour started wafting up. I gagged and clambered out of the trench, and Miriam called out, "Jean-Paul, we're getting close now, very close."

She reached into her coat pocket, took out a small container of a white salve. She unscrewed the top and said, "Over here, Samuel. Just for a moment. For the smell."

Miriam delicately inserted her index finger into the open jar and pulled out a dollop of the salve on the end of her finger. She gingerly smeared the gunk on my upper lip, right under both nostrils, and a blast of peppermint seemed to roar right through my nose and into my head. I looked at the jar. Vicks VapoRub. She managed a smile and I smiled back at her, standing in a muddy field with the odor of decaying flesh now all around us, and the moment was so intimate that I wished I didn't have to move.

But now Jean-Paul was there and he said, "Peter! Please join us."

I grabbed the shovel and went back into the hole, feeling emboldened now. I didn't know who I was going to uncover, what I would find or how I would react, but Miriam was there, Miriam had prepped me. It would be all right. I carried on digging, the stench now trying to overpower the peppermint still wafting through my nostrils, and then I winced and my stomach heaved as the shovel struck something soft and yielding.

Now Peter was there, saying, "Hold on, try this," as he passed down a long-handled spade. Everyone was clustered around the hole, blocking most of the light, but I didn't care. I was the center of attention, I was doing something real, doing more than just record words or images, and I kept those thoughts in the forefront of my mind as I moved the spade around carefully, scraping away more of the dirt. I silently said a prayer for whoever I was uncovering, and I pledged the pledge of the young and innocent, that I would help make the guilty pay for what they had done to the people in this little farmhouse.

"I've got a head here," I said. "Give me some more light, please."

The crew backed away and I felt an irrational sense of accomplishment, because they were doing as I requested. I worked on as painstakingly as I could, uncovering the eyes, the long heavy nose, the rest of the short-bearded face, and—

I said something loud, dropped the spade and recoiled, trying to get out of the hole. I fell back into the mud. The crew clustered around, looking at what I had uncovered as Peter grinned down at me.

"Congrats, Sammy," he said in a sarcastic tone that I didn't like. "You've dug up a bloody cow."

CHAPTER FIVE

We made our camp that night in the dirt turnaround in front of the burned-out farmhouse. By the time we had gotten out of that muddy field and had cleaned up and established what was really there—two dead cows and a calf—dusk had come, chilling the air. Charlie told us it was too dangerous to ride back to the motel and we were too tired to complain that much. Sanjay said, "I thought this area had been pacified," but Charlie, who was cleaning his weapon on the hood of one of the Land Cruisers, replied, "Daylight you can pretend all you want about how safe things are out here, but I don't like the dark. We start out now, we'll be in darkness in less than five minutes, going back with headlights and taillights bright and shiny, telling the world our business. Sorry, Sanjay, that ain't gonna happen."

So we moved the vehicles around so that they were in a triangular formation, to provide some semblance of protection, and the tents and mattresses and sleeping bags were brought out. Nobody suggested spending the night inside the farmhouse or the barn, and I didn't find that surprising. While we were unpacking one of the Land Cruisers, Peter leaned in and said, "We could have had proper beds and hot water tonight if it hadn't been for you and your bloody dead cows." I pretended not to hear him and took out a bundle of aluminum tent poles.

The tents were set up near the Land Cruisers and dinner was a quiet affair, with Peter muttering about how bloody unfair it was to have to cook supper when he had been digging out three stinking cows just a few hours earlier. His attitude was reflected in the food: sticky pasta and lukewarm tomato sauce, eaten off metal plates. I sat by myself, leaning up against one of the Land Cruiser's tires, exhausted. My back ached, my wrists throbbed and it hurt even to move my fingers. A small fire was set up in the middle of our little camp, and Charlie was in charge of it tonight, making sure it didn't get too large, too bright. It was nothing like the cheerful blaze we'd had the night before in the motel parking lot. It was a tentative, frightened fire that didn't do much except light up the immediate surroundings.

Jean-Paul broke away from the group, came over to me and sat down. He passed me a small metal cup and I sipped it, and started coughing. "What the—"

"Some cognac, that is all," he said. His voice had a touch of humor in it. "Everyone gets some cognac tonight, no matter what the High Commissioner thinks about consuming alcohol while we are working. We worked pretty hard today, especially you."

"Thanks—I think."

"What do you mean, 'think'?"

"I'm not sure if you're being sarcastic, that's all," I said. "Peter and the rest of the team look like they'd get me on the next airplane to Toronto if they had their choice. All that work this afternoon, over three dead cows. And to top it off we get to spend the night here, instead of at the motel."

Jean-Paul said, "We had no way of knowing what was in that gravesite. We would have been remiss to drive away and leave it. And don't be so sure that we would have gone back to the motel. Charlie might not have allowed it. So we were doing our job here today, and doing it well. You have no reason to feel bad. Tomorrow we will keep on working."

"Site A, am I right?"

I could sense his shoulders shrug. "Among other things. We will look for Site A, sure, but we will do other work as well. We should not flit from village to village, town to town, without having better information. And the information we have about Site A is nearly nil. But unfortunately there is plenty of work to be done up here. Just be grateful we are not down south in Manhattan, eh?"

I shivered, thinking of what had happened there. "You're right. I'm glad I'm not in Manhattan."

"So true," Jean-Paul said. "It is so bad down south that it is said you can smell the bodies from many kilometers away, even before you get to the new Ground Zero. Be thankful you are here. At least the air is clean, for the most part."

I finished off the cup of cognac and passed it back to Jean-Paul. "Thanks."

"You are so very welcome."

SLEEPING ARRANGEMENTS THAT night were standard, as when we'd camped out before. Miriam and Karen shared a tent, while Sanjay and I shared another one. Peter and Jean-Paul shared the third one, while Charlie made do on his own, like he always did. As far as tent-mates went, Sanjay was all right. He didn't snore, though sometimes his legs did kick around a bit as if he was restless at night—dreaming, I guess, about far-off India or nearby Karen. He had an irritating habit of getting up early, murmuring to himself and then getting dressed in his sleeping bag before barreling out of the tent as though he was late for a train. But tonight we both crawled into our sleeping bags and murmured a "good night" to each other without saying much else. I curled up on my side on the thin mattress pad and tried to sleep, still wearing my pants and shirt and socks. The sleeping bag was clammy and cold, and I curled up, trying to warm myself, knowing that the darkness was out there, like it always was.

But I was too tired to sleep. My body ached and my back and my hands and my neck were stiff. All I could see in my mind was the face of that poor dumb cow, slaughtered for who knew what reason, and then probably buried by some kind neighbors who were tired of seeing the bloated bodies slowly decompose in the field. As for the people who lived here, who knew? Perhaps the documentation work that I had done today would end up helping some family in some other country, looking through the pictures of the house and the clothing, to determine what had happened to their loved ones.

I turned over in my bag, stared at the blank tent wall. I blinked my eyes and tried to think of back home, safe and cool Toronto, tried to think of something that would soothe my mind and ease me into sleep, but that didn't work either. I wanted to think about the *Star* and my buds there and the nightlife on the weekends and clubbing in the John Richmond district. But instead Father barreled into my thoughts, and in my mind's eye I saw the red face, the white handlebar mustache and gray-stubbled head, and heard the comment, always the same comment: "Screwed up again, eh, boy? Not going far in this world if you keep screwin' up like that." Good old Father, who had wanted his son to join the family business—the Canadian military—but the boy had disappointed him by entering journalism instead.

Sanjay moved again, then there came the stealthy noise of him trying to unzip his sleeping bag. I stayed motionless, not wanting him to know that I wasn't asleep. With the sleeping bag undone, he loosened the tent flap and a blast of cold air blew in as he went outside. I stayed there, curled up, wondering if he was finding a tree to water or going to get something to drink. But why move so quietly? To be considerate of his tent-mate? Not likely.

Then, from the tent nearby, came the low sound of laughter, followed by a giggle. Oh. But why not? Even in the midst of death and destruction, life—such as it was—went on. I rolled over and got a small battery-powered lantern, which I switched on. It emitted a small beam of light, just enough to read by, and I felt around in my rucksack for one of my two books. Not being in the mood to read Orwell's essays about the foibles of mankind, I decided to read instead about humanity's adventurous spirit and found myself flipping through the pages of *The Green Hills of Earth*.

Just after I'd finished a short story about a couple from Luna City who decided to return to Earth to live—with disastrous results as they reacquainted themselves with smog, overcrowding and poor plumbing—the tent flap suddenly opened and a woman's voice said, "Samuel? Still awake?"

I dropped the book, moved the lantern about. There was Miriam, her hair hanging loose, wearing a blue down vest and red flannel nightgown, on her hands and knees.

"Sure," I said, sitting up. "What's going on?"

"Can I come in?"

"Of course."

She said something in Dutch and came in on all fours. I glanced sheepishly away from her suddenly exposed cleavage, and then she rolled over and laid down. "There. Sorry, Samuel, I am a grumpy woman tonight, that's what's going on."

"What's . . . oh, I'm sorry."

Miriam rested the back of her head on her hands and looked up at the ceiling of the tent. "Working with such a small team, when you're one of just two women, you try to look out for each other. Men have different ways of working, different ways of looking at things. So if you're one of a pair of women, you help each other out and do little favors for each other. Do you understand?"

"Yeah, I do," I said. "Like asking you to be out of your tent for a while, so that . . . well, so that someone can come by for a visit."

Miriam laughed. "That's a polite way of saying it. A Canadian way, perhaps. Coming by for a visit. No mind, for what you said is true. Earlier Karen had asked if I would leave the tent at a certain time, for bathroom functions perhaps, so that she could entertain a guest. But now he has been there for over an hour, and I'm cold and tired and I think they've fallen asleep in there, and I'll be damned if I'll go knock on that tent to ask permission to go back in to my own bed."

"Then why don't you stay here and take his bed?" I said.

She rolled over. "Thank you. I was hoping you'd say that."

So Miriam threw open Sanjay's sleeping bag and rolled herself in, and when I was sure she was settled I put my book away and switched off the lantern. I lay still there in the darkness, listening to her breathing, so close to me. I wondered what her hair would feel like in my fingers, what her flesh would taste like against my mouth. Miriam stirred and said, "It was a long day today, wasn't it?"

"That it was," I said.

She sighed. "You think we'd be happy, finding three dead cows in a field and not a mother and a father and their children. But no, we're not happy. A hell of a thing, isn't it, to hope to find dead human bodies in the mud? But that's what we do. Even here, in this place. This is what we do."

"So far, it doesn't seem like we're doing much."

"True. But we do what we can."

It was comforting to lie there in the darkness, talking to Miriam. "To what end? To deter future gunmen from slaughtering their neighbors during bad times? It hasn't happened yet, either in this century or the last. And if it can happen here, in the homeland of the sole superpower . . ."

There was a rustling noise as she rolled over on her side. "Ah, but how do you know? True, there have been killing fields aplenty these past decades, from Cambodia to the Congo to here. But if we hadn't taken the time to prosecute the criminals, identify and bury the dead, and comfort the living, perhaps more gunmen would have risen up to kill their neighbors. In England. In France. Perhaps in my own country."

"Perhaps," I said. "But sometimes it just seems futile."

Another sigh. "You're getting too cynical, Samuel. Too cynical for such a young man."

"I'm not that young."

Another rustle of cloth. "You're right. You are not too young, chronologically. But in everything else, compared to what I and the others have seen, you are still a young man."

It was my turn to shift in my sleeping bag. "Give me time. I'll grow up."

"Ah, this is true. You will grow up here, so fast. So fast."

Then she yawned. "Thank you for allowing me in here. Please, I have to get to sleep, all right?"

"That's fine, Miriam. Just fine."

Then I was surprised by her touch, just a feather glance with her fingers across my brow, as she whispered, "Good night." I wish they had reached a few inches lower, to touch my lips at least, but luck or whatever wasn't with me tonight. I wanted so much to return the favor, maybe by gently stroking her cheek, but the events of the day crowded in upon me and I could all too easily imagine reaching out and poking her in her eye or ear. So I lay still.

I wished I could say that the rest of the night was magical, that Miriam's scent and gentle breathing relaxed and quietened me, but that didn't happen. Dear Miriam was an even more restless sleeper than Sanjay, and she snored loudly for most of the night.

But I didn't think of leaving the tent, not once.

IN THE MORNING the lousy weather returned, penetrating drizzle accompanied by another heavy fog. By some unspoken agreement we stayed out of the house and the barn again, and ate breakfast standing up, wearing our yellow rain slickers, except for Charlie who was dressed in his Marine camouflage gear. Karen and Sanjay made a point of ignoring each other as we ate the hard rolls and drank the lukewarm tea. Peter stood beside me and said, "Who the hell do they think they are fooling?"

"Each other, maybe," I said.

"Hah." He slurped noisily from the metal teacup and said, "I think people up on the ridge heard those two, they rutted so much."

"Yeah," I said, wishing that Peter would just go away.

Then he said, "Hey, I saw who tumbled out of your tent this morning. Good on you. Just sleeping, or something more?"

I tossed the tea on the ground, as close as I could make it to his feet without looking too obvious. "Piss off, will you?" I grunted and walked over to the tiny fire to try and warm up some, as Peter's laughter followed me.

Within minutes of our sparse breakfast Jean-Paul was on the satellite phone again, speaking in low tones in French to whoever was on the other end, either at the UN compound down south or to Geneva. I was impressed by how refreshed he looked. The rest of us, with the exception of Charlie, looked like we had spent a week hitchhiking along the Trans-Canadian Highway in the middle of a thunderstorm. But Jean-Paul looked like he had gotten a solid eight hours of sleep and a hot shower. He talked and smoked and waved his hands about as the rest of us packed away the gear, and I wondered how come his tent-mate Peter looked so much like us and not like him.

As I slung my rucksack into the rear of our white Toyota Land Cruiser, I looked again at the house and thought that I hadn't taken a photograph of the entire farm. I had taken dozens and dozens of photos of bloodstains and bullet holes and clothing and even of some dead cows, but not a single one showing this farmhouse and its buildings standing alone. I got my digital camera out of my bag and was setting up the shot when Peter's voice called out, sounding strained: "Charlie, we've got visitors, coming up the driveway."

I turned and saw Charlie standing by the hood of one of the Land Cruisers, his M-16 in his hands, looking down at the driveway. A black pickup truck was grinding its way up, its tires and sides muddy. Karen, who was at my side, whispered, "Oh, shit, this doesn't look good, doesn't look good at all. That's a militia truck if I ever saw one."

I saw what she meant. The truck had a powerful engine and fat tires with thick treads and the windshield was gone, as were the side windows, the easier to fire weapons from inside the cab. Three guys were in the front of the cab, all wearing clear-glass goggles to protect themselves from the wind while driving fast. Four other guys were in the back of the truck, leaning out to look up at us, all of them with their own goggles pushed back up on their foreheads. They seemed to be in their twenties or early thirties, they had on blue jeans and fatigue coats, and the only thing that reassured me—besides the presence of Charlie—was the fact that there were no weapons visible.

Sanjay stood behind Karen, looking over her shoulder. "I thought this place was pacified. What are they doing out in the open? Don't they know Charlie could call in some helicopters, some backup?"

I said, "Weather's too bad for helicopters, and they know that. Maybe they're just on a scouting trip. Maybe they're—"

"Jean-Paul," Charlie said, keeping his voice even and his gaze focused on the truck. "Get your crew behind some cover. Now. And why don't you get on the horn and start talking to your people?"

For once, Peter didn't argue, and for once, Jean-Paul didn't have to repeat Charlie's orders. We all scattered but I stayed close to Charlie, who was still keeping his gaze directed down toward the driveway. Karen was whispering something to Sanjay and I looked over to see that Jean-Paul had the satellite phone in his lap, talking low and urgently. I couldn't see where Peter and Miriam were. There was a faint *click* and I wondered what the noise was. Then I clasped my hands together as I realized it was Charlie, switching off the safety on his M-16. His voice still low and casual, he said, "That you, Samuel?"

"Yes."

"Think you can get in the rear seat of this Land Cruiser, without raising your head, and get something for me?"

"Sure I can," I said, feeling reassured just a bit, like I was contributing something.

"Good. On the floor there's two black duffel bags. Bring me the largest of the two, all right? That's very important. The largest of the two."

"You got it," I said, and I crab-walked back to the door and opened it up. I looked inside, at the jumble of gear and bags and equipment, and saw the two duffel bags. But which one was the largest? It was impossible to tell from where they were situated. I looked at them, trying to decipher which one was largest, when Charlie said, "I need that bag now, Samuel. And I'm not fooling."

Shit. I pulled the bags out, both of them heavy, and saw instantly which one was the largest, I dragged it over to Charlie. He stepped away and said, "Unzip the top, will you?"

I pulled back the heavy zipper and said, "It's open."

"Great," he said. I gaped in awe at how fast he moved now, plunging down, one hand holding the M-16, the other burrowing deep into the bag and coming out with a small satchel and a tubular weapon with a handle, both of which he threw on top of the hood of the Land Cruiser. His hands moved in a quick blur as he opened up the satchel, brought out a metal cylinder about the size of a small egg and slid it into the now open weapon, which I had finally recognized as a grenade launcher.

Then whatever sense of professionalism I had kicked in. This wasn't the time to keep an eye on Charlie; it was time for something else. Keeping low, I scuttled back to where I had started and picked up my Sony camera. I went to the rear of the Land Cruiser, still staying close to the ground, and I ignored the whispers of my teammates. I got down on the cold dirt, crawled past the left rear tire and looked down the driveway. I got the viewfinder up to my face and started taking photographs of the pickup truck as it finally slowed down. The guys in the vehicle were talking to each other and I zoomed in a bit with the camera, catching all their faces. *Click, click, click.* I took the pictures as fast as my fingers would allow. I started out with a group shot of the truck and its passengers, focusing first on the three men in the cab and then on the four guys in the rear. Then I took close-up shots of each individual face.

I tried not to think too hard as I was taking the photos. But still, I was struck by the similarity of the faces, how they looked like they were all related and had come out of the same polluted gene pool. They all had raggedy beards or mustaches, their complexions were rough and scarred, and when they smiled I saw plenty of signs of poor dentistry. I saw them talking among themselves, some of them laughing and smiling, and it seemed like the guy in the center of the cab was in charge. He talked first to the driver and then to the guy closest to the passenger-side door. Then he turned back and said something through an opening in the rear cab window.

Voices. No, just a voice. Charlie murmuring, "Just a bit closer, darlin's, and I'll show you some serious fucking hurt."

I pulled my face away from the camera and looked over at Charlie who was now leaning across the hood of the Land Cruiser, the grenade launcher looking tiny in his big hands. I went back to my camera work and took yet another set of group photos. Then I paused as my breath caught and my hands suddenly started shaking. The driver of the pickup truck had said something to the guy in the center, who now seemed to be looking right at me. He laughed and held up a hand, waved in my direction, then raised his middle finger in the classic gesture of insult and threat. I could not take another photo. I could not move. The only thing I could do was to understand the terror a small creature feels when faced with a snake slithering up to eat him. This man was a member of one of the local militias, no doubt about it, pacified zone or not. I knew down to the frozen marrow of my bones that only a handful of meters separated the two of us and if he got close enough he would shoot me or stab me or bludgeon me with about the same amount of emotion that I would have about swatting an irritating mosquito that had come into my tent. Death squad, I thought. This was a death squad. "Militia" was just too bland a term.

I was frozen. I was terrified. My breath was coming in quick gasps and the camera was shaking in my hands so much that I had to move it away from my vulnerable eye sockets. Then the truck stopped, its engine grumbling.

Charlie murmured something and waved at the men, making sure they could see the grenade launcher. There was a quick confab among the group. I had the feeling that Charlie had just upset their plans, that in the rear of the truck, hidden under an old bedspread or a piece of canvas, were their weapons. But now they had to think. They had to gamble. And the gamble was whether they could pull out their guns fast enough to stop Charlie popping off a round from the grenade launcher.

I found that my breathing was beginning to ease. The equation had suddenly changed once the militia group had noticed Charlie. Now the camera wasn't shaking as much in my hands and I could imagine what could happen. An ill-advised movement by the militiamen and then a loud *pop* from the grenade launcher and a loud *bang!* as the round found its target, a nice blossom of orange and red fire and black smoke. Then Charlie would probably pick up his M-16 and hose them down, shoot at them all, shoot at these militiamen who hadn't expected to come up against a real soldier, nope, probably all the practice they'd had was shooting farmers and shopkeepers and businessmen and businesswomen and dads and wives and children.

I was surprised at how much I enjoyed that little fantasy of seeing these young men gunned down. They had ruled this piece of the country like their own little feudal kingdom, stealing whatever they wanted, murdering whomever they wanted, and raping anything female, from eight to eighty, that came across their path. I wanted them to be hurt. I wanted them to be scared. I wanted . . .

I wiped my face against a coat sleeve. I wanted to throw up, and I trembled. I imagined my father's blood coursing through my veins right now, the temper, the violence, the easy way to settle things, either through fists or knives or bullets. It wasn't a nice feeling.

Another quiet comment from Charlie: "C'mon, you fuckers, what you got going?"

I looked at the truck again and then put the camera back up to my face, used the zoom function once more. There was some serious talking going on among the three men in the truck's cab, and then it seemed like the center guy—who, I now noticed, had a goatee—made a decision. Some of his companions in the rear seemed to complain, but he said something sharp and that was that. The pickup truck began to back down the driveway, and then the center guy looked back in our direction and made an expansive shrugging motion with his hands and shoulders, like he was saying, "Oops, got me, maybe next time."

Sure. Maybe next time. I carried on taking photos until the truck disappeared into the thick fog. Then I put the camera down on the ground and sat up, wiped my hands on the side of my coat.

Charlie turned to me and grinned. "Guess I earned my salary today, huh?"

I just nodded.

CHAPTER SIX

There was a lot of talking and arguing and discussion after the truck left. Charlie just smiled at me and broke down his grenade launcher. I smiled nervously in return, and also felt an odd sense that he and I had shared something when I had passed the weapon over to him. It was like he'd had confidence that I could help him with something so important, and I felt good, even though a minute or two earlier my hands had been trembling with fear.

Peter was yammering away at Jean-Paul, who in turn was talking loudly into the satellite phone, while Karen and Sanjay were standing close to each other, trying to make sure that their voices were heard as well. Miriam, on the other hand, was standing by an open door of one of the Toyota Land Cruisers, eating a piece of German chocolate.

". . . Tell the bloody UN that we won't move any more unless we get a proper armed escort, damn it . . ."

". . . If this place is so pacified, what were those militiamen doing, out in the open like that . . . ?"

". . . Head back to California if this happy crap holds up . . ."

Charlie whistled a little tune as he put everything away. I went over to him. "That was a great job you did, Charlie, a very great job," I said.

Even though his words were calm, I could tell he was pleased by what I said. "Wasn't much of anything, Samuel. Guys like that, they feel important and on top of the world when they've got the weapons and nobody else has. When the roles are reversed they just scatter away, like when you turn on a kitchen light at night and the cockroaches head for shelter."

Having been fortunate enough in some ways not to have grown up in an environment like that, I said, "What would you have done if they had kept on coming up the driveway?"

"What do you think I would have done?" he asked, zipping closed the duffel bag with the grenade launcher inside.

I thought for a moment as the conversation continued around the besieged figure of Jean-Paul, still talking loudly and rapidly into his satellite phone, speaking French.

". . . Nothing against Charlie here, but I'd feel a hell of a lot better with a couple of APCs at our disposal . . ."

". . . Can't trust what the UN says about this area, we should just pack up and get the hell out . . ."

". . . Agree with Sanjay, this is ridiculous . . ."

Charlie was waiting for a reply, so I said, "I'm not sure what you would have done. All I know is, I'd have hated to be in your position. I mean, standing here, evaluating the threat, wondering if they were just some local toughs, out exploring and looking to steal something. That'd be a hell of a thing, if you had done something and it turned out they were unarmed."

"Yeah, you're right," Charlie said. "That *would* have been a hell of a thing. So, Samuel, you still haven't answered the question. What do you think I would have done?"

"I think you would have done the right thing, that's what."

He didn't say anything in reply, but his smile was wide. Then I looked over at Miriam, who carefully folded up the chocolate wrapper and placed it in a pocket of her down vest. She smiled and winked at me, and I smiled back, thinking then and there that I was falling in love with her. It would have been so simple for her to have let the wrapper fall to the ground but no, she was showing respect and she wasn't about to trash this destroyed family farm.

"*Bien, bien*," Jean-Paul said, hanging up the phone and then rubbing a large hand across the top of his head. His face was red and when he turned away from the phone everyone who had been talking fell silent. I was suddenly glad that I had kept my mouth shut, for he looked like he was one sharp comment away from blowing up. That might have been amusing to watch, but my amusement meter was pegged pretty low after what had just occurred.

"All right, my friends, this is what's happening," he started out. "I've contacted the military liaison. There's a quick-reaction force coming here shortly. We are to stay here until they arrive. Charlie, you have my gratitude and that of our little crew here. That was spectacular, what you did, facing them down. Truly spectacular."

Sanjay interrupted, "We should be doing something more, Jean-Paul. We should make sure that the reaction force knows what they're looking for. Those men and that truck should be taken off the streets—"

Peter interrupted in turn, "Yeah, and what kind of bloody description can we give them? A bunch of men in a black pickup truck? You know how many of the towns and villages around here have pickup trucks?"

Charlie spoke up, quieting everyone with his strong voice. "Talk to Samuel, why don't you?"

All faces were turned in my direction, and Jean-Paul said, "All right, let's talk to Samuel, then."

Charlie was smiling again in my direction, and I said, "I've got photos."

Karen said, "Photos? You've got photos?"

"Sure he does," Charlie said. "While the rest of you were hunkered down, Samuel here was doing his job. He got nice photos of those bad boys—am I right, Samuel? *Lots* of nice photos."

I turned to Jean-Paul and said, "I've probably got a couple dozen or so. Group and individual pics of the truck and its occupants."

Finally, Jean-Paul grinned, came over to me and slapped me on the shoulder. "Very good. Here, while we're waiting for the reaction force to arrive, we'll uplink your photos to Geneva. Very good, Samuel, very good."

So I got back to work, with words of congratulation from everyone else in the group—except Peter, who was busy checking on what we had available for lunch later. Which was fine by me, for Miriam had slipped me another piece of her German chocolate, and that was worth much more than any words from Peter.

BY THE TIME we had uplinked my photos of the militiamen—using, at his request, Jean-Paul's data system, which was much more high-powered and encrypted than mine—the quick-reaction force had arrived: four APCs with big black tires and machine guns and grenade launchers mounted on a turret on top. All four had UNFORUS painted on the side and the flags they were flying from radio whip antennas on the rear were Ukrainian. Three of the APCs took up positions on the road, while the lead unit came up the driveway and the unit commander—wearing camouflaged clothing and the blue beret of the UN—spoke in fairly passable English to Jean-Paul. At the time I was standing next to Charlie. I thought he might amble over and talk to the Ukrainian army officer, as one professional to another, but he didn't. He had a grim look on his face and when Karen said something about him going over and explaining what had happened, he said no, he wasn't going to do that.

"That's Jean-Paul's job," Charlie said.

"Well," Karen said, "don't you think it might be helpful—"

Charlie walked away, shaking his head. "Ukrainians—can you believe it? In my fucking country."

And I knew why Charlie had stood still. Foreigners under arms, in his country, doing his job. To Charlie, no doubt, that was disgraceful. Me, I was just glad to see the extra firepower.

With the photos uplinked and my gear back in the Land Cruiser, Sanjay came over to me and said, "Good job again, getting those photos."

"That's my job," I said.

"Still . . ." Sanjay looked around him and leaned toward me, speaking softly, so that Karen wouldn't hear him, I suppose. "That was a brave thing to do, to take such pictures of the militiamen when they were so close to us. Me, I don't even pretend to have such bravery. I went to medical school and learned all there is to know about human bodies and the creative ways men devise to hurt them and destroy them. But I cannot handle dealing with the living—their fears, their wishes, their demands, their families. I prefer the dead, for what is the worst you can do to a dead man?"

"Not a hell of a lot, I guess," I said.

"So true. And I cannot even handle my family, who felt disgraced that I would lower myself to working with the dead. So the coward's game again: here I am, with the UN, far away from my home."

I nodded toward the APCs. "Hell of a place for a coward."

He smiled widely. "We take what we can, don't we?"

"That we do."

Eventually the APCs backed down the dirt driveway, their engines burbling loudly, the yellow and blue flags flapping in the breeze. I got into a Land Cruiser with Peter and Miriam, Miriam this time sitting in the front seat. She said, "Jean-Paul told me that one of the Ukrainian APCs will be with us for a while. Isn't that good news?"

Peter shook his head. "Bloody soldiers will ask us to feed them, just you wait."

I said, "Having protection like that should be worth a meal or two."

"Fine," Peter said. "Then you can cook for them."

Miriam glanced back at me as we bumped down the driveway, and I leaned over the rear of the seat.

"OK," I said. "I guess I can maintain your high standards of cuisine."

Miriam smiled and Peter said nothing else. I was feeling pretty good, until I looked back and remembered that I hadn't taken the photo of the farm, the one I had wanted so much to.

IT TURNED OUT to be a long day as we tracked down two possible locations for the elusive Site A. The first place was an athletic field for a regional elementary school. We parked the Land Cruisers in a paved lot at the rear of the school and the APC parked there as well. Without any prompting from Jean-Paul we put on our helmets and protective vests again, and we gathered around a wooden picnic table that had its footings set into concrete. The school was brick and one-story, with lots of windows—and with most of them shattered. What few windows weren't broken had children's drawings and paintings on paper taped to the glass. New grass had grown in the field and at both ends what looked like soccer nets stood sentinel, their netting torn and flapping in the breeze.

Jean-Paul said, "We received two pieces of intelligence saying that bodies have been buried here, in this field. Air surveillance last week proved inconclusive. So now it's our turn."

Sanjay turned and shielded his eyes from the sun with his hand. "That's bad intelligence, and you know it, Jean-Paul. Look at that grass. Nothing's been disturbed here, nothing at all."

"True," Peter said sharply. "But we follow orders, don't we? The word comes down from on high that we search this field, and that's what we're going to do. Right, Jean-Paul?"

Jean-Paul folded up his map and didn't take the bait. He said, "So glad you agree, Peter. So let's get to work."

It was rather dull work. The Ukrainian soldiers stayed in their APC, keeping its hatches open, and Charlie sat on the ground by one of the Land Cruisers, his M-16 across his lap. It looked like the Ukrainians wanted to spend some time with Charlie but our Marine would have none of it. Foreign troops in his country. I could hardly imagine the humiliation he must have felt. We stretched across the field in a line, maybe five or six meters long, carrying thin metal probes. I had the feeling that if Peter had been in charge we would have finished this search in ten minutes or less. But Jean-Paul was doing things by the book and he set a slow pace as we marched across the field, looking for mounds of earth, for any fresh disturbances, poking and prodding at the ground with our metal probes.

By now the sun was higher up in the sky and with our helmets and protective vests on we got hot indeed, even though the calendar said it was fall. Since our line was so short, we had to trek up and down the field four times, finding absolutely nothing except on our third pass, when we found the remnants of a parachute flare. We gathered around it and Peter rolled over the heavy cardboard canister, saw the RAF markings. Part of the NATO contingent that had first come here after the troubles.

"A postcard from home," he said, smiling. "How brilliant. How about a picture, Sammy?"

I looked at Jean-Paul, who gave a small shake of his head. "Sorry. My gear's back in one of the Toyotas. Maybe later."

Peter nodded and turned back, and we returned to work. I imagined a school band out here, playing for the students: it was spookier than hell, looking over at the school building, wondering where the children were, where they had all gone. Despite what the PM had ordered last spring, lots of families here and elsewhere had snuck across the border into my home country while so many others had just hidden out with families or relatives in the basements of their homes. The streets were almost always empty, and it was that emptiness that sometimes creeped me out most of all.

LUNCH WAS AT the picnic tables at the rear of the school, near where some swing sets and other play gear was set up. The Ukrainians surprised us all by not only having their own food but by sharing what they had with us. There were four of them and only their officer could speak English, but that didn't stop the other three from flirting with Karen and Miriam. They laughed a lot and eventually so did Miriam and Karen. They had loaves of chewy black bread and some sort of meat paste and cheese gunk in tubes, which they spread on torn-off chunks of bread. Peter, however, made do with a couple of hard rolls and a jar of peanut butter from South Africa. Charlie, as usual, ate by himself, still sitting on the ground, ignoring the Ukrainians.

When we were done, Jean-Paul made a brief report over his satellite phone, and then we drove out of the schoolyard. In front of the school was a white flagpole, and a dark flag hanging from it flapped in the breeze. Miriam looked up and said, "That flag is black. Completely black. What does it mean?"

I waited for Peter to say something and was pleased when he didn't know the answer, which I supplied. "Anarchists," I said. "The black flag is the flag of anarchists."

Miriam asked, "What do they want?"

"Anarchy," I said.

"Goody for them," Peter said, as we turned and got onto the road, the APC leading the way. "At least somebody's got what they want."

WE DROVE ABOUT three kilometers to another site. The roadway passed through a cluster of small homes, each of which had been burned. The houses were smaller than what I had been used to when I'd been growing up in peaceful and prosperous Canada, but the yards were neat and well-maintained, with stone or wire fences separating them from their neighbors. Miriam shook her head as we proceeded, saying, "So sad, oh, how sad."

"Maybe so, but it's just real estate," Peter said.

"Excuse me?" I said.

Peter said, "Look at all those houses. You see anything missing from the driveways?"

I looked out the side window, saw what Peter was driving at. "Yeah," I said. "There's no cars or trucks."

"Right," he said. "So that means whoever lived here got a fair amount of warning and bailed out, probably heading east or up north, to the border, before the refugee streams got here and the locals started shooting. So what got left behind got stolen and burned by either the refugees or the townies. Sad enough, but I don't consider that a war crime. Site A, where two hundred-plus people from a refugee column got disappeared over a weekend, that's a war crime. Not a burned-out block of shitty houses."

I said sharply, "I can see why you joined the UN, Peter. You've got one hell of a humanitarian streak inside you."

The back of his neck got bright red. "Bugger off, youngster," he said softly. "I was working the East End for the Metropolitan Police before you learned to wank off. I've seen bodies pulled from the Thames, swollen up and ready to burst. I've seen women and children burned and stabbed and bludgeoned, lying dead in flats where the rats thought they owned the place. That there is crimes, what's done against females and kids and innocent men. Property is property. So bloody what? It gets burned or destroyed, it's nothing. Rebuild, rebuy, go on somewhere else. At least you're alive. This shit here doesn't impress me. Site A impresses me, and if our Froggy leader doesn't stop wasting time we're never going to find it and a fair number of criminals are going to be set free from The Hague before the week is out."

The road descended some and then ran by the side of a river. Across the river were open fields and a tent city, with the dark green and white canvas of the tents stretching for what seemed to be a kilometer at least. Flags were fluttering from some poles stuck in the dirt across the river but we couldn't see what nationality they represented. Some of the white tents, though, had big red crosses on their roofs.

"There," Peter said, motioning with a free hand. "That's where we'll find Site A. By going in there and talking to people in the area, people who had a hand in the rounding-up and the killing and burying. You can bet not all of them have fled the neighborhood. Some of them are right over there, feeding and sleeping on the world's generosity, while we make do with half-arsed tips and stories."

I was trying to think of what to say when the column ahead of us braked and slowed. We headed to the second inspection site.

PAST THE SMALL neighborhood of homes this site was part of an industrial facility of some sort, dominated by a large brick warehouse with small windows that was three stories tall. Graffiti scrawled on the side in white paint said *RED RULES!* Two other buildings, wood-framed, had been burned to a collection of rubble, scorched beams and black shingles. We pulled into a poorly paved parking lot on the other side of which were six trailers for tractor-trailer trucks. All of them were burned and split open. Still wearing our vests and helmets, we got out and looked at the warehouse. It seemed to be fairly intact. Jean-Paul, shaking his head, had his laptop and data gear on the hood of one of the Land Cruisers.

"This site matches what was sent us," he said, looking up at the red-brick building. "But I don't know . . ."

Karen and Miriam stood together, looking as well, their arms folded. Beyond the land that belonged to the warehouse was a chainlink fence and a wood. The APC stood to the side of the Land Cruisers, its engine rumbling. The APC commander came out of the hatch, stumbled a bit on the lip of the opening, and came over to Jean-Paul. My hands felt itchy. Sanjay and Peter were talking to each other and I didn't like the feel of the whole thing. The air felt like the heaviness you get just before a thunderstorm roars through, when the air is thick and moves slowly and there's a sense of force in the air, an electrical force ready to be unleashed.

The Ukrainian commander shook his head after talking with Jean-Paul and went back to his APC. Then Charlie came over to Jean-Paul, his M-16 slung across his back. "Sorry to tell you this, Jean-Paul, but you can't be going in that warehouse," he said.

"And why's that?"

Charlie gave him a look like he was saying, Are you so dumb that you can't see it? He went on, "Jean-Paul, that place is an ambush waiting to happen. Old warehouse like that, no power, lots of corridors and rooms and doors. You could place tripwires, motion detectors, even cut holes in the flooring and cover it with tar paper so you'd fall in. Man, it would take a platoon of Marines and three or four more UN teams like yours before I'd even think of going into a place like that."

Jean-Paul said stubbornly, "We have intelligence. We have information that there are bodies in that warehouse."

"Maybe so, but you're not going in," Charlie said.

"This team is under my command."

"And the security and safety of this team are my responsibility," Charlie went on calmly. "You know that, just as well as I do, and I'm not going to get your people hurt or killed. Call for backup, call for reinforcements, I don't care, but that place is too big and spooky for me to let you guys go in."

By now the others had joined in and Jean-Paul's face was reddening up, like he was ready to let loose a good one. But there was a *clang!* as a side hatch of the Ukrainian APC came open and its commander strode back. He had a piece of paper in his right hand and said, "Monsieur, if you please, I have message for you."

Jean-Paul was surprised. "A message for me? Through your comm net?"

"Please, message," the Ukrainian soldier insisted. "Look at right now, please."

I looked over Jean-Paul's shoulder as he read the message, which was handwritten in block letters and which caused my legs to start trembling:

MONSIEUR UN—
OUR THERMAL DEVICE IN TANK SHOWS MANY
BODIES IN BUILDING.
BODIES ALIVE, NOT DEAD.
WE LEAVE NOW.

Karen put her hand to her face as Jean-Paul folded the piece of paper and said quietly, "We don't do anything drastic. We just move away, quietly and smoothly. Don't raise your voices, don't stare at the warehouse. Just get in the vehicles and get out."

We all did just that. I couldn't help myself, though, and I did spare a look at the warehouse. Its windows seemed to mock us all, this little group of international visitors, ready to go in and do good. The building seemed haunted—possessed, even—and I thought of that message again from the

Ukrainian APC commander. *Bodies alive, not dead. We leave now.* We sure as hell do. I'd been spooked when Charlie had talked about the booby traps that could be in that dark building—tripwires and concealed holes in the flooring—and the thought of men with guns and knives, just waiting for us to clamber inside, full of earnestness and good intentions, with them ready to tear us apart, made me want to stand behind Charlie and ask for his help.

But Charlie was busy, his eyes flickering back and forth, looking at the entrance, at the many blackened windows. I got inside our Land Cruiser with Peter and Miriam, and then everybody else was in the other Land Cruisers as well, with Charlie bringing up the rear, being the last one in. Peter was muttering something and his face was mottled red and white, and Miriam seemed to hunker down in the front seat as though she was trying to present a smaller target. All three Land Cruisers backed out of the parking lot, their reverse gears making a high-pitched whining that made my teeth ache, and then the APC backed away as well, all its hatches clamped shut, the turret with the grenade launcher and machine gun moving from side to side like a hunting dog looking for a scent.

CHAPTER SEVEN

From the warehouse we headed north, passing over a small bridge that spanned a swollen river, the water rushing by so fast that little spumes of spray rose up as if a pod of whales had hidden themselves there. After the bridge we passed through another deserted village, the buildings closed and locked, and took refuge at the top of a small hillside park a couple of kilometers away from the warehouse. Here there were a set of picnic tables and a monument to a couple of past wars, plus a white flagpole that wasn't flying anything.

There was a dirt path that was meant for walkers only, but our group wasn't in the mood for conforming to such niceties so all four vehicles clambered their way up, led by the APC. It was late afternoon and I felt nervous and strangely tingly and alive when I stepped out of the Land Cruiser. I stripped off my helmet and the protective vest and threw them both back inside the vehicle. Karen said, "Don't you think you should keep that stuff on?"

And I said, "If it stays on any longer, I'm going to die of heat stroke, and what's the point then, right?"

Maybe I was too sharp for her, but I didn't care. Some pine trees shaded the area of the war monument and Sanjay was leaning against it, cleaning his glasses with his handkerchief. The monument had been defaced with black paint and it looked as though someone had taken a hammer and chisel to some of the names, hacking them out. "Rewriting history," I said to Sanjay. "Just like the ancient Egyptians."

"Excuse me?" he asked.

I gestured to the place on the monument where the bronze names had been hacked out. "When a Pharaoh passed on, his name—his cartouche—was cut in stone throughout the empire, to symbolize that his memory would last forever. But sometimes dead pharaohs passed out of favor due to some religious or political struggle. So then their names would be gouged from the stone, to erase the memory that they had even existed."

Sanjay looked at the stone he was leaning on. "So that's what happened here. Rewrite history, destroy your enemies. They kill the living, bury their bodies, and then obliterate the names of their ancestors from the old stone. This is a blood-drenched country, you know that? Ever notice how many monuments and statues and plaques they have dedicated to their wars? Every village, every crossroad, every marketplace or town square has a monument to death." He put his glasses back on. "No wonder what happened here took place, with such a bloody people, after the spring bombings."

I said, "Don't throw stones."

"I'm sorry, what did you say?"

I looked at him calmly. "You and I both know the history of your own country, from the 1947 partition on, all the millions dead on both sides, up to and including the present day. There's a saying: people who live in glass houses shouldn't throw stones."

Sanjay's gaze back at me was just as calm. "Are you excusing what has happened here?"

"No, I'm not. Just asking you to adopt some perspective."

"Young man, I'm not in the mood for lectures," he said.

"I don't think I'm that young, and I wasn't offering a lecture."

"Yes, you were. I come from a place with thousands of years of proud history, millennia of art and architecture and poetry that still sings to us . . . and you are from a frozen wasteland that offers hockey and beer. Grow up, why don't you? And stop lecturing."

"Sure. One of these days."

"I won't wait for you," Sanjay said dismissively. "Now, if you'll excuse me, before you start yammering about Kashmir . . ."

He moved away from the stone and walked down to one of the Land Cruisers, while I looked again at the monument, which had listed the names of the sons and fathers from this village who had fought in the Second World War. I rubbed both hands through my sweaty scalp, thought of the hate and energy that it had taken to do this, to climb up this hill with hammer and chisel and try to obliterate the past because someone's descendants had done something wrong, like feeding or sheltering some of the many people who had deserted the cities when the power had gone off. With all that had gone on in this country, making this final gesture of destroying the past seemed as dark and as despicable an act as spitting into an open grave.

Maybe I was wrong. Maybe I shouldn't have raised my voice in defense of the people who lived here, for all I had just accomplished was to piss off a teammate, and that would matter more to me in the long run.

I reached out, touched the sharp edges of the monument, and went back to join the others.

KAREN WAS TALKING to Peter about the warehouse. She said, "We didn't have to run away like that, like scared rabbits. We had those Ukrainians. We had Charlie. Hell, a call from Jean-Paul to the regional headquarters could have gotten us some backup. For all we know, that warehouse could have been holding some refugees. A hell of a thing, don't you think, that we'd be running away from refugees?"

Peter said, "Yes, a hell of a thing. Here, want to see another hell of a thing?"

With that, he grabbed her upper arm and roughly pulled her to the rear of the mud-spattered Ukrainian APC, where two of the soldiers—neither of whom spoke English—were gathered around the rear hatchway. Peter pointed out something to her.

"See? See that?" he demanded.

Karen broke free from his grasp, strands of her hair falling free from underneath her blue helmet. "See what, you jerk?"

"Look, right there," he said. "Here and there."

I saw what Peter was pointing at. Two little dents, pock holes about the size of the tip of a finger, where the dark green paint had flecked free. The two Ukrainians had fallen silent. Something cold and squishy was now roiling around in my chest.

"Now do you see it, you silly woman?" Peter said. "Impact sites, from gunshots. The Ukrainians heard them strike just as we were leaving the warehouse. A little farewell message from whoever was in there, in that warehouse you were so eager to search."

Karen brushed her hair back, looked at me and Peter and the Ukrainians, and then stalked away to a stand of bushes near a metal and concrete barbecue pit. Peter looked at me and said bitterly, "Amateurs. Bloody fucking amateurs." Then he walked away as well. The Ukrainians started talking among themselves, and I went back to the Land Cruiser that held my rucksack.

I SAT AT a picnic table with Jean-Paul, who was calmly smoking another of his Gauloises. His eyes looked tired behind his black-rimmed glasses. We gazed at the three Land Cruisers parked in a triangle, with the Ukrainian APC positioned just a bit beyond, down the side of the hill so that it could provide covering fire. Jean-Paul took a long drag on his cigarette and said, "How are you doing, Samuel?"

"I'm doing fine," I said. "The question is, how are *we* doing?"

"Hmm," he said, and then fell quiet.

I went on. "The past couple of days have been lousy. I mean no disrespect, Jean-Paul, but what have we accomplished? From those two kids to the militiamen who came to the farm to the lousy intelligence that sent us to that schoolyard and then the warehouse . . . It seems like we're being set up, or at least sent around in circles. We're no closer to Site A than when we first came out here."

"True," he said, inhaling again.

"Again, no disrespect, Jean-Paul, and I'm not trying to act like Peter, but it just doesn't seem right. We've been lucky so far, but I don't know how long this luck is going to last. This part of the countryside is supposed to have been pacified and it's nowhere near that. Look at the warehouse, the paramilitaries back at the farm. This place isn't pacified, and we all know it."

He slowly nodded, took another puff at his cigarette. "Pacified. A good word. Decades after the bloodiest war in history and after setting up the UN, one would think that this planet *would* be pacified, would at least have peace, that people would eventually have learned to get along with each other. But we're not even close to that dream, my friend Samuel. Can I tell you a secret?"

"Certainly," I said.

Jean-Paul smiled faintly. "Not much of a secret, but here it goes. We're losing, Samuel, and losing rather badly. What we're doing here is probably pointless, at best."

I felt like I had just heard the parish priest speak about the attractive qualities of a demon called Satan. "I disagree. That is one hell of a secret. Go on."

A Gallic shrug, then he said, "Karen said something a day or two ago, about men with guns, and the heartbreak and terror they cause. A bit simplistic, but she had a point. There was a time some years ago when we could make a difference, could keep warring countries or factions or other groups of men with guns apart. That was the era of the copper phone line and the telegraph and black-and-white television. In those days we had the luxury of time."

In the distance, over the horizon, I thought I heard the murmur of helicopters on patrol. Jean-Paul looked up with me and continued. "But then the world got wired, got connected, so that extremists in Idaho could communicate with their brethren in Berlin, so that mujahedin in Afghanistan could give real-time lectures to their comrades in the Philippines, and so that women-haters in Iran could get support from those in the United States who wanted to put women under the lash. All this connectivity, so that the brushfires and incidents and little wars could happen, right after another, sometimes in a planned fashion. We're like a fire department in a small village that has one little fire engine, and we're racing from blaze to blaze, trying to put the fires out, and being very, very lucky if we can just contain them. Well," he said, waving a hand to the village we had passed through, "our luck's not holding."

"But what we're doing—you can't mean it when you said we're not making a difference, that what we're doing is pointless."

Jean-Paul leaned to the right and gently nudged me. "My dear young man, what difference are we making, eh? Tell me the truth: what are we doing?"

"We're documenting war crimes," I said. "Preserving evidence, for use in future trials. To show others that, even when something criminal happens in a nation like this, there are consequences."

"Are we preventing any bloodshed?"

"Maybe," I said. "Maybe the fact that we're here, collecting evidence, will prevent future outbreaks."

"Aaahh, yes," he said. "The old argument. Used in Kampuchea, in Rwanda, the Congo, Sierra Leone, Fiji and now here. The world community did nothing and let the bodies pile up. And when the shooting and the hacking is complete, now we will go in and count the dead and feed the living, and try to track down the criminals. And how much bloodshed has been avoided, how many lives have been saved by this process of ours?"

"Who knows?" I said stubbornly. "But something still has to be done."

"Indeed, you are correct, something must still be done," Jean-Paul said, smiling, tapping the ash from his cigarette onto the ground. "That's what I thought, back when I was your age. That I would do something important. I was a lawyer in a small village in the south of France, and I thought I should do more besides prepare land-deed transfers and wills for elderly widows. I had a hunger to see the world, to do more. The curse of the French, you know. We feel we have to share our superiority with everyone." He laughed and even I smiled along. It was good to see him laugh, especially after the days we had been having.

He continued. "Like you, I think, my father is one who—"

"Please," I said. "I really don't want to bring my father into this."

Jean-Paul eyed me coolly. "You must not continue to blame him for what happened in Mogadishu. It was not his fault."

"He was in command. Everything in his command was his responsibility. Including the deaths that occurred. Sorry, Jean-Paul, it *was* his fault. So can we drop the matter, all right?"

"Very well," he said, rubbing his hands together, keeping the cigarette held at the ends of his fingers. "I will talk, then, about *my* father. A tall, dour man who married my mother when he was in his fifties. He was a lawyer as well, but he always kept quiet concerning what he had done as a young man, before he started his own practice. Only after he passed on did I learn the truth about what my father did as a lawyer. You see, Samuel, during a certain time in the 1940s he was employed by the French government in a small city just north of our village, a place called Vichy."

"Oh," I said.

"Yes, 'oh'," Jean-Paul said. "He was young and had no real power, but what little power he had aided the Nazis and their Gestapo to round up Jews in the south of France and send them to places like Treblinka and Auschwitz and Theresienstadt. That was what my father did. When I learned that, within a week I had quit my position and applied to the UN in Geneva. So here I am."

"You and me and everybody else," I said. "Your village—where is it?"

"Ah, it is in Provence, a place of warmth and beauty and fine food and wine. A place where even today you can see monuments from the Roman Empire. The arenas, the memorial arches, the old roads."

The sound of the helicopters grew louder and I scanned the horizon, still not seeing a thing. Routine patrol, perhaps. One hoped.

"I was there once, on a college trip," I said. "I'm sorry to say that I think the food was overrated, except for the desserts. But the landscapes were amazing."

"Ah, of course, quite beautiful, like this land we are in now," Jean-Paul said. "But this place is still bloody, with lots of bloody memories. The early colonists. The French and Indian wars. The Civil War. So forth and so on. And my memories begin with relics of the ancient Romans. Ironic, isn't it, that we owe so much to the Romans and their concepts of law and government. The Senate, the voice of the people, ideas and ideals handed down over thousands of years. But the Romans also gave us their legacy of slavery, of conquering other nations, of killing your enemies for sport in the arena. An odd balance, when we cherish the good and try to overlook the bad."

He finished his cigarette, dropped it to the ground and ground it out with his heel. "And while we try to balance this, even to this day, the barbarians are out there, beyond the gates, beyond the pale, preparing their weapons, preparing to kill us all. Samuel, my apologies."

"Excuse me—apologies for what?" I asked.

"Apologies for giving you a lecture as if you were a schoolboy. No more lectures today." Jean-Paul stood up and said, "You are right. We have done nothing these past days but go in circles, and each time we have been in the line of fire, in some sort of danger. No longer. This afternoon, we will—"

We both turned at the sound of an engine revving up, and I saw a black cloud of diesel smoke rise up from the Ukrainian APC. The rear hatch was open and the APC commander was waving frantically at Jean-Paul, who trotted down the hill with me following right behind him. The Ukrainian shouted over the noise of the APC engine: "Monsieur, so sorry, but we must leave! Two of our comrades, they are under fire, some distance away. We must go help!"

Jean-Paul yelled back, "But we need you here, we need—"

The Ukrainian smiled and gave a thumbs-up, as if he couldn't hear or didn't care what Jean-Paul was saying. He ducked back into the APC and slammed the hatch shut. Jean-Paul cursed in French, leaned over and pounded his fists against the APC's side, but the engine revved up again and the armored vehicle bounced its way down the hillside, its fat black tires sinking into the soft soil and grass. Jean-Paul stood there, fists now at his side, and slowly the other people in our team came over, not saying a word. It felt horribly vulnerable up there on the hill, and I knew that if probing or curious eyes were looking us over they'd just seen our main line of defense leave. I thought Charlie was wonderful and superb in what he had done for us, but he was just one man. Just one man with weapons, against the entire countryside.

Jean-Paul turned to us and said, "Samuel?"

"Yes?"

"Please be so kind as to put on your vest and helmet. All right?"

"Certainly," I said, glad that he wasn't raising his voice, wasn't expressing disappointment, though Karen—still clad in her own helmet and vest—smiled with satisfaction at seeing me rebuked.

"*Messieurs et medames*," Jean-Paul said. "We are finished here for the day. We are going to head back whence we came, and we're not going any further into this area without better support."

Karen, Miriam and Sanjay were smiling, and Peter said, "Where are we headed, then?"

Jean-Paul said, "I think we all agree that the motel from a couple of days ago was in a safe place. That's where we will return. And we will not leave it until we have better assistance. When we get to the motel, I will be in contact with the Commissioner's field office. Peter, is that agreeable to you?"

I wondered why Jean-Paul had asked Peter's opinion about anything. Maybe he was seeking reassurance, maybe he was just trying to confuse Peter. If so, he was succeeding.

"Agreeable?" Peter asked. "It sure as hell is agreeable."

Jean-Paul folded his arms. "But you know that it puts us behind in our quest for Site A."

Peter grinned. "Hell, Jean-Paul, I said I wanted to *find* Site A. I sure as hell don't want to become *part of* Site A."

That caused some smiles among us—with one notable exception: our borrowed Marine, Charlie. He had his M-16 slung over his back and was looking down the hill at the slowly dissipating cloud of dust that had been left behind by the APC rattling away from us. He shook his head.

"Damn Ukrainians," he said.

PACKING UP TOOK only a few minutes and with the Land Crusiers' engines idling Jean-Paul gathered us together and said, "Charlie and I will take the lead. This will be a straight sprint, driving as fast as we can to get back to the motel. I've radioed ahead and there'll be a contingent of Peter's countrymen waiting for us."

"Paratroopers?" Peter asked.

"The same," Jean-Paul said.

Peter grinned, and for once I didn't mind that mocking smile. "How fucking brilliant. Best news I've heard all day."

Jean-Paul said, "We drive fast and we drive safe. We don't stop for anyone. I don't care if we even see some young lads holding up a sign, eh, that says, 'This Way to Site A.' We just go on and make our way back to the motel."

He looked at each of us individually. "I know you are disappointed. I know you are frightened. But you're a good crew, and I am happy to be with you. And one more thing. I was told that the power will be back on tonight at the motel. So. Hot showers—does that sound good?"

Karen said, "It sounds excellent, Jean-Paul."
"*Bien*," Jean-Paul said. "We go now."
Which we did.

I SAT IN front this time, next to Peter. Miriam made as if to protest and I said, "Please, Miriam. You're safer in the rear, with the gear and the supplies."

"I don't like it," she said. "I don't like being treated as though I'm weak and—"

"Oh, shut up, will you?" Peter said. "Or I'll sit in the back and you both can sit in the front. We've got to get moving before it gets dark."

So we bounced down the hillside, seat belts secure, our helmeted heads striking the roof of the Land Crusier. Peter laughed maniacally as we reached pavement and started speeding west, heading back to that motel, the precious dumpy little motel that had seemed so dreary a couple of days ago and was now scrubbed and cleaned in our minds to make a little slice of paradise.

"Oh, this is it, this is fine," Peter said, grinning widely, handling the steering wheel with aplomb. "None of this putt-putting along. We're making time, friends, we're making good time, and there's hot showers tonight!"

"Real beds," I said, actually enjoying Peter's exuberance. "Real beds with mattresses."

Miriam laughed as well. "Electric lights. I do love electric lights."

We stayed close behind the lead Toyota, with Karen and Sanjay keeping close behind us. I looked at the sun heading toward the horizon, saw a line of low-lying clouds moving in. It would be twilight soon, and then dark, but if we were lucky we'd be back at the motel, in the comforting presence of British paras, before the sun completely disappeared. The road went through the small village, past a town green with a monument to a past war—and I pledged then to apologize to Sanjay when the moment arrived—and past stores and buildings, their windows either broken or covered up by old plywood boards. Scraps of paper and cardboard blew by as the lead Toyota, driven by Jean-Paul and with Charlie riding shotgun, powered ahead.

When we were through the village, Peter exhaled loudly and said, "OK, that was good. No snipers, nobody outdoors. Hate small towns like that. Plenty of hiding places. One last thing, we go like a fucking bat out of hell past that warehouse, and we'll be free and clear. Just you see."

I laughed. Miriam squeezed my shoulder and said, "What's so funny?"

"Just thinking about when I was in high school, sneaking out before the day was over," I said. "Couple of us would pile into someone's car and then drive out of the school parking lot. Other kids who would try it got caught, and we figured that was because they moved too slowly. We'd drive fast and bounce over the speed bumps, and because we moved quick we made it out without being caught."

Miriam squeezed my shoulder again and Peter said, "Speed, that's what it takes, speed, and—Bugger!"

The taillights ahead of us flashed red. Peter slammed on the brakes, slewed us to the right, and there was a *bang!* as the third Land Cruiser clipped our rear. Our vehicle bumped up and down, grinding to a halt as Miriam yelped and I said, "What the hell—"

The lead Land Cruiser was making a bumpy U-turn and the driver's-side window was down, Jean-Paul waving at us frantically. Charlie was leaning through his window, the M-16 poking out alongside his head. Peter swore, backed up, looked over and saw the third Toyota, its front right fender and headlight smashed, backing down the road. He yelled out after Sanjay, "Fucking wog, can't you fucking drive?"

Miriam was saying something, trying to calm Peter down, I think, but the third Toyota was now turning around, leaving us, as Peter rocked us up and out of a shallow drainage ditch that had almost trapped us. On both sides of the road was flat pastureland, one small factor in our favor because we had a clear view all around and could see that no one was coming toward us.

I swiveled my head and saw what had happened, where it had all started.

Just ahead was the small bridge that spanned a river, one we had crossed just a couple of hours before. But now it was blocked. Someone had parked a yellow school bus directly across the road, blocking both lanes of the bridge, and the tires were flattened. I knew there was no way we could get through that mess, especially if the people who had moved it were still around, of which there was a pretty good chance. Peter slammed on the brakes, backed us up and made a quick turn. I turned and said, "Miriam, duck down, right now."

Much to my surprise, she did just that. I tasted something salty, wiped at my lip, and saw blood. I winced as the pain started.

"Speed," Peter muttered, punching the accelerator to the floor. "Bloody speed."

CHAPTER EIGHT

We didn't have much of a choice, so we ended up back on the hill with the little park, picnic tables and desecrated war memorial. We parked in a triangular formation again and Peter bailed out after setting the parking brake. He went to the rear of the Toyota, started swearing again. "Samuel, how about you getting a tool, maybe a tire iron or something? Look here, will you?"

In the fading light I saw what he was pointing out. Where we'd been struck by the third Toyota the rear fender had crumpled in, and a jagged piece of metal was only an inch or so away from our left rear tire. Peter muttered something and said, "If that fool had been going just a bit faster we'd still be there by that bridge, waiting to get our throats slit or our brains blown out."

I said nothing, opened up the rear door and found the tire iron below our first-aid kit and flare-gun case. I handed it over to Peter, who started to lever back the piece of metal. Hesitantly, Sanjay came over and said, "Is . . . is everyone all right?"

Peter didn't even look up. "Back away there, friend, unless you want this rod shoved up your Indian arse."

Karen was next to Sanjay and she said, "It was an accident, that's all! We didn't see you brake! It was just an accident."

The metal bent back and Peter stepped aside, looking at his work. Then he shot a gaze over at Karen. "What was going on back there in that truck, love? Hmm? A little kissy-kissy? A little hand job for your boyfriend? Was that why you almost tossed us into a ditch?"

Karen strode forward, "You limey son of a bitch, why don't you—"

Miriam grabbed her arms, tugged her away, and Peter went back to work, pulling free another twisted piece of metal. By now the light was getting dim and Peter was breathing hard. Then he stopped, dropped the tire rod and leaned back against the dirty fender of the Toyota. He folded his arms and looked over at me, shook his head.

"It's going to be one long night, just you see," he said.

I nodded. Despite my dislike of Peter, I had to admit that having an ex-cop and an active-duty Marine with us tonight was going to be the best news we could expect.

I WAS SITTING by myself on top of one of the picnic tables, getting a drink of water, when I saw Jean-Paul talking to Sanjay, Peter and Karen separately, and then to all of them as a group.

I couldn't hear what was going on and was glad. I wasn't in the mood tonight for what passed as diplomacy. The water tasted good, even coming from a plastic canteen. It made me think of how much water we had left, how much food we had left. Hot showers, hot food, an actual bed to sleep in—they seemed further away than ever. Peter had been right. It was going to be a long night. And I didn't like long nights. Another gift from my father.

Someone broke free of the group and came up to me. Our Marine escort, Charlie. His M-16 was slung over his shoulder, and he was carrying a black duffel bag, presumably the same one that contained his grenade launcher. He sat down next to me on the picnic table and said, "Hey."

"Hey yourself," I said. "Want a drink?"

"Sure," he said. I passed the canteen over. He took a long swig and handed it back to me, and I took another swig myself, just sitting there on the table, feeling a cool breeze come up the hill.

Charlie said, "We're in trouble, you know."

"Yeah, I figured that out."

"It's going to be a long night."

"So I've been told," I said.

"Jean-Paul, he put a call out to the field office," Charlie said. "There's low-lying clouds and fog moving in. About the only way we'd get off this hill *is* by helicopter, and that ain't gonna happen with the weather turning bad."

"They have equipment that lets them fly at night and in bad weather, don't they?"

"Yep," he said. "But they only said they would come if we was under attack, with gunfire and all that good stuff. Then—maybe—they'd risk an extraction. Otherwise, here we stay, on our own."

"If you're trying to scare the shit out of me, you're succeeding."

Charlie scraped mud from one of his boots, using the toe of the other one. "Wondering if I could count on your help tonight."

From somewhere I remembered my training from months ago and an admonishment that as civilian UN workers we shouldn't offer assistance to any military member that might jeopardize our status. That kind of training emphasized that the only way we could be above the conflicts in this troubled land was if we didn't show that we favored our armed escorts. I promptly forgot that part of my training.

"Go ahead," I said. "What do you need?"

Charlie chuckled. "What I need is some sleep. I get a feeling that you nice folks think I'm just a living, breathing military machine. Well, that ain't true."

I said, "I've never thought that."

"Well, it's nice that you said that, but you're lying," he said. "Which I don't care about right now. What I *do* care about is doing my job, which is protecting you and your partners, and I can't do that right if I'm nodding off. So here's what I'm asking: can I count on you to spell me a bit during the night—to keep watch?"

The thought that I would be responsible for everybody's safety while our armed protector dozed terrified me. But what else could I say? "Sure, you can count on me. How about the others?"

"What others?" he asked.

"You know, Jean-Paul, Peter, Sanjay . . . even Miriam."

Charlie shook his head. "Nope."

"Why not?"

" 'Cause they're too UN-blue, that's why," he said. "And you're not. You showed me that the other day, when you got my grenade launcher for me. Anybody else there, in the dirt, would have rolled over on his or her back and started lecturing me about what they could or couldn't do. You didn't pull that crap on me. You did what had to be done. Which is why I'm going to trust you to do the right thing if something happens tonight."

"Jean-Paul won't like it," I said. "He'll have to clear it."

Charlie grinned. "Jean-Paul's gonna love it, 'cause he may be true UN-blue but he wants to wake up tomorrow morning with his head on his shoulders. Just you see."

"OK," I said. Charlie got up from the picnic table and ambled down to the squabbling group.

I took another swallow of water.

IT WAS TIGHT quarters, what with the vehicles parked in a close triangle. Before Peter started our evening meal Charlie walked around and made sure that whatever dim light was shown didn't make it out from the cover of the three four-by-fours. There was no fire, just a little flame from the gas stove. Peter, usually a grumbling sort when it came to cooking our dinner, managed to cook some sort of fettuccine dish—that, along with water and hard rolls, was our evening meal—without saying more than a fistful of words. There was no wine, no cognac, no pep talk from Jean-Paul. Miriam sat by herself and Karen sat beside Sanjay, shivering and looking out blankly into the darkness around her, while Peter shoveled his food in so quick it was like he had been starved for days. I don't even think I tasted anything, anything at all.

When Peter made a move to start cleaning up the dishes, Charlie stopped him with a shake of his head. "No, not at all," he said. "We're in bandit country. No more lights tonight, even if you have to go to the bathroom. If that happens, just walk a few yards out beyond the Land Cruisers and do your business in the dark."

Karen cleared her throat. "Do you think they know we're here?"

Peter said loudly, "Of course, you stupid cow, of course they know we're here. We've practically set up a searchlight, inviting them to come and pay us a visit. We've been driving around in circles, and they left a little calling card for us with that school bus. Or did you think they were offering to take us out on a field trip?"

I think Sanjay was going to say something but Jean-Paul beat him to it. "That's enough, Peter. Quite enough. I think we've all had a long enough day. Let's try to get some sleep, eh?"

Miriam said, "I think that's a good idea."

I just kept my mouth shut.

THERE WAS A little scene later on when Karen said that she was damned if she was going to sleep in a tent, not with all the bad guys out there: she was going to sleep in one of the Land Cruisers. Jean-Paul gently explained to her that there wasn't enough room, and she said something like "Fuck it, I'll *make* the room." And in her tone of voice I caught a hint of what it must have been like back in California when the lights and the power went away. So she and Sanjay emptied the rear of one of the Land Cruisers and let down the rear seat, and both of them crawled in there together. Peter muttered something about hoping that the bloody thing wouldn't be rocking later on, waking us all up. Then he put up a tent for himself and Jean-Paul. I got my sleeping gear and one of my duffel bags together and thought about what Karen had said. I inflated my air mattress and took up residence near one of the Land Cruisers which was riding high because of the way it had been parked.

Jean-Paul came over to me and said, "It might rain tonight."

"It might. But I'll feel better sleeping outside. Besides, when Charlie comes and gets me I'd rather be out in the open."

He nodded. "That's another thing . . . thank you for volunteering to assist Charlie."

"Not a problem."

"If you could volunteer another thing . . ."

"Sure."

"In your official recording of what is going on, it will be appreciated if you don't let on that you helped Charlie with our defense. It would make trouble for us in Geneva, when we're done here."

I was going to say something about how we might well and truly be done here if a couple of dozen militiamen who hadn't been disarmed rolled over us during the night. But I kept my mouth shut.

"We're in enough of a jam as it is," I said. "I'll do my best to minimize any additional trouble."

I ASKED CHARLIE to check on something for me, which he did quickly, so I was able to sit up against one of the Land Cruiser's tires and do a little work on my laptop to ease up my nerves some. Charlie had made sure that I wasn't letting any light escape but even so Miriam found me. She was carrying her own sleeping bag and mattress pad.

"You have another reason for being outside, don't you?" she asked.

"I do."

"Which is why I'm here," she said. "I'd like to know what it is."

"You sure?"

"Yes," she said.

I closed the lid of my laptop and Miriam sat down next to me. A breeze was coming up and she said, "You're not really dressed for sleep, are you?"

"I take it you're pointing out that I'm still wearing my flak vest, and that my helmet is right next to me," I said.

"Yes," she said.

Despite the windbreak protection of the parked vehicles, my fingers had already started to chill from the slight breeze. "First of all, I'm doing something tonight that is against my contract with the UN."

"Helping out Charlie—I know that," Miriam said quietly. "But still . . ."

"What I'm going to say will sound cowardly," I said.

"I doubt that, but go on."

I tried to think of what was out there, down the sides of the hills, in the trees and the burned homes and the empty streets of the village we had just driven through. "It's like this. Karen was just a little bit right when she refused to get inside a tent. I don't like the idea of people coming up here when I'm in a sleeping bag, zipped up, and inside a tent that's also still zipped up. I might as well be hanging off a tree branch, strung up by my ankles, waiting for them to do what they want."

Miriam said, "Then why are Peter and Jean-Paul in tents, do you think? Are they being stupid?"

"I don't know," I said. "All I know is what I feel like tonight, which is being outside."

"What about Karen and Sanjay?"

"As far as I'm concerned, they're still zipped up, if you know what I mean," I said. "They're stuck inside a vehicle. They may think they're protected, but rifle rounds or mortar shrapnel can punch through that kind of metal easily enough."

"So you're outside," Miriam said.

"So I am," I said. "And that's where the cowardly part comes in. If something happens and there's bullets and shrapnel flying, then I don't want to be restricted. I want freedom of movement."

"Why is that cowardly?"

"Obvious, isn't it? Instead of worrying about my teammates, I'm worried about myself. I should have talked to Jean-Paul, told him what I thought. Instead, here I am."

"Correction," Miriam said, unrolling her mattress and bedding. "Here we are. You do not mind if I spend the night here next to you?"

"If I did, I'd be an idiot."

Miriam laughed, but though it was nice to have her next to me I remembered the last time we'd slept close to each other and how her snoring had kept me awake all night long. I hoped she wasn't going to repeat her nocturnal noises because I needed some sleep.

But Miriam wasn't in the mood for sleeping, not yet. She maneuvered herself up closer to me and said, "I've always liked Canadians."

"Always?" I asked. "Why's that?"

I put my laptop down on the ground, moved so that I was closer to her.

There were murmuring sounds coming from the tent and the rear of the Toyota Land Cruiser. Charlie was nowhere in sight, but I didn't care where he was. All I cared about was that he was doing his job.

Miriam said, "You Canadians played a crucial part in the liberation of my country, that's why. Oh, there were plenty of other Allied troops who fought the Germans in Holland, but a hell of a lot of the fighting was done by Canadians. Didn't you say your grandfather was in the army during the Second World War?"

"Yes," I said. "He was at the Dieppe landing, in 1942, in France. A total disaster. He was wounded in the leg, mustered out. So I'm sorry to say he wasn't there to liberate your homeland."

"And your father? He was in your army, was he not?"

"Yep."

She said, "You don't speak much of him, Samuel. I guess you don't like him."

"You guessed right."

"Why?"

Good question. I really didn't have too many hours to explain to Miriam all the miserable ins and outs of my relationship with my father so I said, "Another reason I'm out here is because of him."

"How is that?"

"I'm afraid of the dark. Have been since I was quite young. Maybe eight or nine."

"Bad dreams?"

"Oh, yes—bad dreams. Night after night. Waking up screaming. Not sure why I got them. Just happened. But my father . . . he thought he could cure me. So one night he forced me outside in the rear yard, with a pillow and a couple of blankets, and locked the door. Said that once I saw there was nothing out there that could hurt me, then I'd be fine."

"What happened?"

"Sat frozen, near a cellar doorway, and practically screamed every time a branch broke or a bird called. Didn't sleep a bit all through that long night. Next night I was back in the house, but I still had nightmares. But I learned to stay quiet. And that's that. And years later I'm still afraid of the dark—and I don't like my father very much."

"I can see why. He doesn't sound very likable."

I tried to lighten the mood. "Which, of course, *is* our proudest Canadian trait. Likability."

Miriam laughed and moved even closer to me. "See, I knew there was a reason I still have affection for you Canadians."

I turned to her, seeing her very well, even in the darkness. "And I've always had affection for the Dutch."

"Really? For how long?"

"For a month or so, that's how long," I said.

She laughed again and I leaned forward and we kissed, and that was that. No fireworks, no tingling expressions, no grappling on the ground. Just a soft, almost chaste kiss. I could sense her smile and she said, "Sleep well, Samuel."

"I'll try," I said.

BUT I COULDN'T, not yet, so I went back to my laptop as Miriam rolled over. I checked the battery power and found that I had at least four hours left before a recharge would be needed and I was almost finished for the night. I checked the news headlines and felt depressed at what was going on in the rest of the world. As I flipped through the different screens on my browser, the screen would sometimes go black for an instant and then recover. I thought that maybe something was wrong with the machine but a quick diagnostics test showed that everything was fine. Which in turn made me wonder if the militias were out there again, jamming incoming signals from the satellite traffic that the UN had leased for this particular mission. I remembered reading somewhere that this type of jamming was impossible, but some of the militia units were smart, had lots of money, and probably derived a great deal of pleasure from making our mission difficult, so I guessed it was possible after all.

I checked my personal e-mail account—empty, save for a travel agency that wanted to send me on a trip to Bermuda—and then my UN account. There, lined up in little blue icons, were the e-mail receipts from Geneva, stating that all the files I had sent earlier from the farmhouse had been retrieved and documented. Good. At least something was working right.

Still . . . I went back and checked the timestamps for my outgoing messages and then the receipts. Less than ten minutes' gap between the two. Yet there were no receipts from the messages that Jean-Paul had sent for me, the ones containing the photographs of those suspected paramilitaries who had come up the dirt driveway, until they'd spotted Charlie.

Not a one, though plenty of time had passed.

Odd.

Of course, maybe all the receipts had gone straight to Jean-Paul on his own account, since he had sent them on to Geneva on his own laptop. That must have been what had happened. I had made sure that I had cc'd the receipt tool, to make sure I got copies of any receipts sent back, but maybe Jean-Paul had an encryption system on his machine that had stripped my receipt request away even before the files arrived in Geneva.

I powered down the machine and closed the lid. Whatever. Too little battery time and sleep time to worry about it any more.

I crawled deeper into my sleeping bag, hearing the soft wheezing from Miriam next to me. I tried to get comfortable, found it hard to do, out on this hilltop. Miriam was slumbering and I thought about Charlie, out there on watch, and that managed to calm me down enough so that eventually I did fall asleep. But not before I gently touched my tongue to my lips and imagined I could taste Miriam there.

THE SOUND OF footsteps woke me and I rolled over and sat up as Charlie leaned down next to me. "You awake, Samuel?"

"Yep."

"Good," he said, a large bulk in the darkness. "Come along with me—watch your step."

I threw the sleeping bag open, sat up, and immediately started shivering. I put my boots on, wincing as the cold material snapped against my feet. Charlie stood there by the Land Cruiser, patient and waiting. I got up, remembering to grab my helmet, and staggered some. I yawned. It felt like I'd had a glorious ten or fifteen minutes of sleep.

"Let's go, OK?"

Charlie moved out of the triangle of parked vehicles and I followed him as closely as possible as we went up the hill some, to an outcropping of rock that sat on a little knoll. There was a picnic table there and we both sat down on top of it.

I rubbed at my face and listened to Charlie. "OK, you've got a good three-sixty up here. I'll be down there in that little group of trees. Anything goes on, anybody comes up this way, you just quietly come down and get me. All right? And don't come up close and shake me awake. You might get hurt. Just come down and gently tap me on the foot."

"OK," I said, still shivering.

"Here," he said, handing something over. "Night-vision scope. It's got a nice long battery life, so I've left it on for you. Doesn't make sense for you to try to learn it all in one night. Hold it up to your eyes, give it a shot."

The scopes were lightweight, with a foam eyepiece. I blinked and looked across the landscape, now illuminated in a ghostly shade of green. I could make out the hill and the rocks and the saplings, the distant road we'd driven up and even the small buildings of the nearby village.

"Pretty slick," I said.

"That it is," Charlie said. "But don't spend the whole night with the scope up against your eyes. It's good but it has lousy peripheral vision. You could be staring down at the road, watching something move, while a dozen guys sneak up behind you and take you down. So just pop it up every now and then, keep a view on."

I let the night-vision scope drop away from my face. "Ask you a question?"

"Sure."

"These guys who might come up and take me down . . . just who the hell are they?"

Charlie grunted. "You serious? Thought you had all those briefings and shit."

"Of course, but I want to hear it from you. Who *are* those guys?"

Charlie seemed to hesitate, as though he really wanted to get to sleep instead of yapping to his young charge, and he said, "They're just guys, really. I mean . . . well, look. Towns and cities, they have peace 'cause the cops are around. Right? But lots of cops . . . they're in the Guard or Reserve, and they've been called up for Iraq and other places. So the cops are stretched tight, and if there's widespread problems they can't do their jobs. So, thing is, if the cops get into too much trouble, then the governors, they can call up the National Guard to keep order. But suppose your National Guard unit, instead of being home, is out in Kirkuk or Tehran? What do you do then when the troubles start?"

"I don't know. Keep your head down?"

"Maybe, but this little country of ours . . . guys with guns know other guys with guns. And if there's trouble, they're gonna fight. Maybe they'll do it singly, maybe in a little group, maybe in a county organization they call a militia. And if they think all the local troubles are due to a bunch of refugees rolling in from the big bad cities, then they're gonna kill 'em."

"Sounds cold."

"It *is* cold, and the problem is that these militia types have always been underestimated. Always. Lots of people forgot, bunch of years ago, it was just a couple of militiamen who took down a government building in Oklahoma City and killed nearly two hundred. Some forgot. Others didn't."

I put the night-vision scope back up to my eyes. Nothing. I brought it down and said, "If you don't mind . . . Charlie, where were you during the attacks last spring?"

"Me?" he said quietly. "At home in South Carolina. Camp Lejeune. Doing some work—checking pallets of ammunition, make sure they were stacked right. Funny, huh? Something as boring and as simple as that. Then we got word of the Manhattan strike . . . and, hate to tell you, that wasn't much of a surprise. Poor old New York City has always been target number one. And then the balloon strikes . . . Jesus, what a mess. Lucky we had pretty secure communications and backup power supplies. Didn't affect us too much, in the beginning."

"Bet the balloon strikes were a surprise, then."

And then the surprise was on me when Charlie shook his head and said, "No, sir. Not at all . . . Oh, the delivery system was a surprise, using modified weather balloons to raise up the suitcase nukes to a high enough altitude to cause damage with the EMPs. Simple and imaginative delivery system. Everybody thought the suitcase nukes would be placed in the cities but, except for Manhattan, they weren't. Still, that's the lessons of war. Always surprises. Pearl Harbor. Tet. Second World Trade Center attack. But you wanna know what the real surprise was?"

"Sure."

Charlie leaned in a bit. "Surprise was—we still don't know who did it. We got the usual and customary blowhards. Islamic Sword of Justice, the Sword of Justice from Islam, neo-Nazi creeps—standard crap like that. But no, none of 'em. Oh, we know where the suitcase nukes came from. Our smart boys can actually analyze the fissile materials and determine their source—like a DNA analysis—and those bad boys came from an old Soviet Union storage facility that secretly got raided years ago. By using the right contacts and the right amount of money, almost anybody could have bought them on the black market."

"Yeah," I said, not knowing much more what to say.

"And that created another problem," he said. "After the balloon strikes, you had all that death, all that destruction, all the cell phones, computers and even car engines fried, airliners crashing in your backyard, so people are pissed. They're angry. They want to strike back. And if you can't strike back at who did this to you, well, you strike back at whatever's convenient. And if that happens to be refugees who roll into your village or town from some urban center and demand food and shelter and whatnot, well, there you go. A better recipe for disaster you probably couldn't come up with."

We stood there then, a bit quiet, and I said, "One more thing? To change the subject?"

"Yeah?" Charlie asked.

"Do you want to leave a weapon with me? A gun or something?"

He chuckled. "When's the last time you fired a weapon, young man?"

It felt cooler. "Couple of years ago. Did a story about the RCMP, the new weapons they were being issued. Ten-millimeter Glocks, I think. I got to fire off a few rounds at a firing range. Before that, some rifle shooting with my dad. That's it."

Charlie tapped me on the shoulder. "Well, you're ahead of everybody else in the crew 'cept for me and maybe Peter, and I'm still not letting you have anything you can shoot. You're doing well up here with the scope. Just keep an eye on things and come get me if you see anything. All right?"

"You've got it," I said. "You go catch up on some sleep. When do you want to get up?"

"You let me decide that, if you don't mind."

"Sure," I said.

Charlie started to move down the hill. Then he stopped. "Oh. And one more thing."

"Yes?"

"We're depending on you," he said. "Don't fall asleep on the job."

I shivered again, hugged myself, felt like the whole world was out there, watching me.

"No problem of that," I said.

"OK," Charlie said, and in a few seconds I was alone up on top of the hill.

And pretty much scared shitless.

CHAPTER NINE

For the first few minutes I kept myself occupied, sitting on the table, checking out the scenery, looking for any movement, anything at all. But soon I got a feeling for our surroundings, out there beyond our little sanctuary. The parked Land Cruisers were behind me, hidden by tree cover, and I could see fairly well over the tops of the trees. All around the hill the slopes fell away either to a treeline or to the road. I did as Charlie instructed, raising the scope to my eyes every few minutes, feeling a bit of power in my grasp as the nightscape came alive in the green glow of the instrument.

But after a while the novelty of using the night-vision scope began to wear off, and I became conscious of how cold and hard the picnic table felt against my butt, and I felt the breeze that chilled my arms and legs. I wished that I had thought earlier of bringing up a blanket to keep myself warm, but that might have made me sleepy and I had promised Charlie that I would stay awake. No falling asleep on the job. But something else in the nether regions below my waist was demanding my attention so I got up from the table and walked down the far slope for a minute or two until I came to a low clump of bushes. I undid my pants and let loose, the stream of water arcing out into the foliage, and I felt such a sense of relief.

As I did my pants up I heard the low roar of jets flying overhead, and I looked up and saw nothing but blackness. No stars, no moon, nothing but the cloud level that prevented an extraction by helicopter. We'd been warned when we'd started that we would have few friends or allies out here in the countryside; nobody had told us that the weather would be against us as well.

I started back up the hill, walking carefully, feeling the darkness all around me, and I wished I had brought the night-vision scope with me. But soon enough I banged my knee against the table and got back up on top. The scope came up, my hands grew colder—and then I saw movement, down there in the field, about a hundred meters or so from where I had been relieving myself.

I moved to get off the table and to go get Charlie, but hesitated. Movement, all right, there was movement. But what kind of movement?

I put the scope back up, saw shapes down there, moving around. I felt along the side of the scope and found a little knob, and by experimenting with it I learned that it was a zoom-feature control. I moved it slowly, focusing in on the group of shapes, and let out a breath as I saw it was a pack of dogs, running and chasing around. I watched them as they played, as they fought each other over something, and then the lead dog ran away with something in its jaws. It looked like a tree branch. I *hoped* it was a tree branch. In my neighborhood in Toronto, dogs were cheerful little critters, kept under control by their human masters. In this particular bleak district, these dogs were out on their own. And I tried to shake off the image of that dog, with something large in its jaws, remembering a story that Karen had told about her service in Rwanda, where packs of dogs would haunt the roadways and alleyways of destroyed villages, devouring and gnawing at the human bodies heaped up in bloody piles.

I dropped the night-vision scope in my lap, rubbed my hands. Another flight of jets went overhead, and I envied the pilots up there, warm and safe and secure, far away from the ground and the animals that feasted on the dead.

ONCE AGAIN DURING the night I went into the bushes for relief, knowing it was the stress of being up here, responsible for everyone, that had made my bladder overactive. The sounds kept me jumpy too—the few insects out there, the sound of night birds on the prowl—and other things as well: the growl of jets overhead, another engine of some sort—an APC? a truck?—from beyond the line of trees, and once, the far-off thump of an explosion. In some ways I was flashing back to when I was eight, not believing that my own father had forced me outside and had locked the door after me.

I checked my watch, saw that nearly three hours had passed. I was tempted to go down and wake up Charlie but he'd said he would get me when it was time. And I should let the poor guy sleep. He was right: he wasn't some robotic Rambo, out here protecting us with only an oil change and a dusting-off every three thousand kilometers or so. I could sleep during the day, maybe, if we did get back to the motel by a different route. And Charlie? He'd be on the job, like he was all the time.

So I sat, shivering occasionally from the cold, and then I raised the night-vision scope for a scan of our neighborhood. Still nothing.

Then, when I lowered the scope one more time, I noticed a lightening of the overhead cloud cover. It seemed as though dawn was approaching. I could make out the planks of the picnic table, the thin grass cover on the ground and even the clump of bushes that I had used as a urinal. I rubbed my hands, thinking that my job was nearing its end. Charlie would probably be up soon and then I could come off the top of this damn hill and let somebody else worry about safety for a while. I didn't much care what was for breakfast; I knew that we had enough tea and coffee for something hot to drink, and that was all I cared about.

I brought the scope up to my eyes again, and then my hands began to shake. Something was going on, down by the road. I lowered the scope, rubbed at my eyes, and then looked again. The damn light was giving me a problem, for with the approach of day the image was fading. I focused as tightly as I could without losing the definition and I wished I had thought of bringing my own photo gear up here. I moistened my dry lips and continued looking. I only had them in view for a few moments. There was a line of people walking along the side of the road. There looked to be about six or seven men and women bunched together in the middle of the column. Nothing unusual, except I could tell that the men leading the group and those following it had weapons. And the central group itself moved oddly—even in the lousy image I was getting through the scope I could tell that they were bound together. A line of prisoners, moving along in the dawn, their captors secure in the knowledge that the cloud cover was preventing any surveillance.

Damn them, damn them all.

They disappeared around a curve in the road. I lowered the scope for the last time as birds began chirping and moving about. I heard a rustle and turned to see Charlie coming up the faint trail, his assault rifle slung over his back. He was yawning but he looked good, and in his hand he had two metal cups, steaming. He came up to me, passed one over, and said, "How was the night?"

"Quiet," I said, the cup shaking in my hands.

Charlie raised his own cup to drink and then paused. "What's wrong?"

"I just saw something."

"Nearby?"

"No, down there on the road. It's gone now."

"What was it?"

"It . . . it was . . ." I paused, swallowed, conscious that no matter how upset I was it sure felt good holding that warm mug of coffee in my cold hands. "Damn it, Charlie, I think I just witnessed a war crime."

Charlie nodded, sat up on the table next to me.

"Considering where we are, that sure makes sense," he said. "Anything's possible in the dead of night."

WE WENT DOWN and talked to Jean-Paul. He called in my sighting and didn't say much else as he and Charlie looked at a map spread out over the hood of one of the Land Cruisers. There was a frightened feeling to the group that was beginning almost to ache through my bones. I remembered the first time we had gone out, a few weeks ago, and how at that time nothing would have stopped us from doing our job. Back then, if I had come down with a sighting of some prisoners being led along the roadside we would have roared out after them, no matter what. We would have depended on our brashness, on our confidence that we were on the side of right, to do what had to be done. But not this morning. Jean-Paul just called it in and stayed there by the Land Cruiser, cup of coffee at his elbow, while he and Charlie looked over our options on the map. Their conversation seemed depressing enough, so I didn't stick around.

I yawned a couple of times and joined Miriam who was leaning against the door of the closest Toyota. She smiled at me, warming me right up. "You do OK?" she asked.

"I did," I said. "Quiet night, except for what I saw just before daybreak. A line of people, being led off. It looked like they were under armed escort."

Miriam's face looked white in the early morning light. "Does Jean-Paul know?"

"Yep. And so does the regional office. So here we sit, all of us, while those people are being led away."

"We can't do everything, Samuel. You know that."

"Yes, I do," I said, feeling an urge to yawn again. "But I hate it when people keep on reminding me about it. It sounds so—"

Karen came up from the trail that led to the road, buckling on her helmet with shaking fingers. "There's a white van, coming up the trail. Looks like it's full of men."

Jean-Paul looked up from the hood of the Toyota. Charlie moved away and grabbed his binoculars and M-16. "Stay here," he commanded. We obeyed him for about a second or two and then we followed him. The van coming up the road slewed from side to side on the dirt path. It was white but, like our own vehicles, it was filthy with mud along the sides. Charlie looked back at us, shook his head in apparent amazement that none of us could follow directions, and then raised his binoculars to his eyes.

Karen stood next to Sanjay, and Peter was with Jean-Paul. Miriam was behind me and I felt an odd protective urge, making sure that I was in front of her. Karen said, "Who are they, Charlie? UN? Local people? Militiamen?"

Charlie lowered his binoculars and said slowly, "Well, none of the above. How's about that?"

Sanjay said, "Is it good? Or bad? Can you tell us that?"

Charlie shrugged. "Up to you to decide if it's good or bad. It's the press, that's who. Television."

Which was true, we realized as the van slowed to a halt on the slope of the hill and the sliding door on one side opened up.

WE CAME DOWN to meet them, and the mood of our little group instantly changed. After all the dark events these past couple of days, seeing the press was a good thing. It meant contact with someone from the civilized outside, someone who wouldn't take a shot at us because we were the wrong religion, ethnicity, political party—or because we were from the UN. We soon learned that the television crew consisted of an older cameraman, a female producer and a polished young man who was apparently the "talent." On the windshield and side windows of the van the words AUSSIE TV were displayed with letters made from masking tape, and even the radio antenna flew a small Australian flag.

They seemed as short on sleep as we were, stumbling out of the van. The cameraman seemed to be in his fifties, with a thick beard and a red nose that looked like it had been rearranged a couple of times in a barroom brawl or two. He carried his camera in one beefy hand. The woman producer was about twenty years younger than the cameraman, and seemed to be the same age as the on-air talent. She had on tight blue jeans, knee-high leather boots and a thick red down vest, and she had a clipboard in her hands. The talent yawned and rubbed at the back of his head. He had on dress shoes, dark slacks and one of those thigh-length trench coats that foreign correspondents must be issued with each time they get their passport stamped. There was a flurry of introductions and though I'm bad at names—I often forget them the moment I've heard them—I remembered that the cameraman's name was Mick, the woman producer was Alice and the talent was John. Alice and John started to talk to Jean-Paul and Charlie, while Mick stayed behind, scratching at his beard.

Karen said, "How long have you been out? Did you see anything this morning? Is it safe?"

Mick grinned at her. "And g'mornin' to you, luv. Let's see. We've been out in this countryside for about a week now. What did we see this morning? Whole lotta nothing. Is it safe? Christ on a crutch, is anything safe in this country? Hmmm? All I know is that we're Aussies, and so far nobody out in these woods has got a beef against Aussies."

"What are you doing out here?" I asked. "Looking for Site A?"

Mick laughed, gestured to his two companions who were still talking loudly to Jean-Paul and Charlie. "Maybe *they* are, but you want to know a big secret? We're lost. We've been lost for days, rumbling around all these deserted roads and little hamlets. Site A, Site B—who friggin' cares? All those two care about is a good story, and we've had diddly these past few days. It's like everybody either moved east or north, crossing the border. You boys and girls up to anything interesting?"

Peter, with his arms crossed against his chest, said dryly, "Well, we found a couple of dead cows the other day."

I thought about what I had just done these past several hours, and the photos I had taken of those militiamen driving up to that farmhouse. I said, looking right at Peter, "And besides that we've been eating some swill, day after day, that someone claims to be food. You got anything good to eat in the van?"

I saw Miriam cover her smiling mouth with her hand as Peter's face turned red, and then he strolled away. Sanjay said, "Samuel's telling the truth. You've got any food in there? We're running kind of low."

"Sorry, mate, all we've got left is oatmeal and instant coffee," Mick said. "I think we was hoping we could—Oops, time to get to work. Hold on."

Curious, I followed Mick as he went over to the producer and the correspondent. With a practiced move, Mick tossed the camera up and balanced it on his shoulder, and like magic, Alice, the producer, passed over a wireless microphone to John who held it under Jean-Paul's chin. The microphone had the logo of their Australian television network, ABC, on one side. John looked over to Mick and said, "Ready?"

"Yep. Count off, will you?"

"Sure," he said. "Three, two, one . . . All right, your name, please."

"Jean-Paul Cloutier."

"Could you spell your last name, please?"

"Certainly. C-L-O-U-T-I-E-R."

"Your position?"

"Section leader, war crimes investigative unit four, United Nations Force in the United States. UNFORUS."

By now all of us were grouped in a semicircle, watching Jean-Paul and the Australian television crew at work. The correspondent said, "Mister Cloutier, have you had any success in locating Site A?"

"No, not yet," Jean-Paul said. "Though we are confident that we will be able to find this particular war-crimes site."

"Before the deadline in a few days, when the current batch of war criminals in the dock are due to be released from The Hague?"

"If not us, then someone else," Jean-Paul said.

Beside me Sanjay hid a smirk, and even Peter shook his head in disbelief at what Jean-Paul was saying. I think we were all feeling like we were having trouble finding our asses with our hands, and here he was, making a ridiculous prediction like that. What respect I had for Jean-Paul just took a little hit—like finding out your high-school biology teacher believed in creationism.

The correspondent said, "What have you found so far, in this part of the country?"

Jean-Paul shrugged. "The aftermath of a systematic slaughter by one armed group of Americans against their unarmed neighbors, that's what. People seized, murdered, their bodies hidden, because of who they are, because of where they had fled from. That's what we have found. Just like other UN investigation teams, I am sure."

"But no hard evidence of Site A."

"Not yet," Jean-Paul said.

"Mister Cloutier, could it be that you haven't found Site A because the UN doesn't want you to?"

"Excuse me?" Jean-Paul asked, his voice rising. "What do you mean by that?"

John pressed on. "There have been rumors that some members of UNFORUS, either through bribery or intimidation, aren't doing quite as thorough a job as they could. That turncoats within your own organization have sabotaged the investigations. Have you heard any of these rumors?"

It looked like Jean-Paul was struggling to control his temper. "No."

"Do you have any comment on these rumors?"

"No."

"Anything else you would like to add?"

"One more thing—if you promise that it will air on your network."

Now it was time for John to shrug. "I can't promise that, but I'll see what we can do."

"Fine," Jean-Paul said. "Then this is my last comment. We are here in this country to see that justice is done. That is all. We are not on any witch hunt, nor are we on any mission to undercut the legitimately elected governments of the USA and its individual member states. In fact, the President of the United States has not opposed our entry here, and in his position as Commander in Chief has ordered the U.S. armed forces' cooperation with the UN teams in those states affected."

John added, "But you know, of course, that the President is in seclusion, at his rest area. Camp David. He's not said a word in public for several weeks."

Jean-Paul said, "I have nothing to say about the President of this country. All I can say is that we have a mandate from the UN Security Council to perform this work, and no matter the obstacles we will continue to comfort the injured, to aid the homeless, and to seek justice against those who committed these crimes. That is all."

"Great," John said, pulling the microphone away. "Mick? Alice?"

They both chimed in. "Fine, just fine."

Mick lowered the camera and I saw Jean-Paul relax a bit. John said to Mick, "Little while, maybe we can do a stand-up for today. Find some burned-out school or farmhouse."

"Well, we've sure got our share of those to pick," Mick said. He looked up at the low-hanging clouds. "Wish the weather would improve, though."

I said, "Us, too."

Alice spoke up. "Excuse me, do you mind if we follow you for a bit? We seem to have gotten misdirected, and we're not quite sure where we are."

John interrupted. "We certainly would know our location if only you two would listen to me, if we'd taken that turn back at the crossroads."

Alice looked slightly embarrassed, as though she didn't like the rest of us seeing what she probably had to put up with, day after day. "In any event, we'd like to spend some time with you, if it's all right. Whatever the case may be, we do appear to be, um . . ."

"Lost?" Karen asked.

Mick agreed. "More lost than a joey on a bender."

Karen laughed. "Then good luck to you, 'cause we're lost as well, and we can't seem to find our way back."

WELL, JEAN-PAUL SEEMED to bristle at that remark, and he said, "Come along, we have good maps. The challenge is to find equally good roads to go along with them."

So we went back up to our little campsite where Mick produced a thin cigar, which he lit up. Karen wrinkled her nose and walked away. Mick looked at me for an explanation and I said, "From southern California. You know how it is. Wants a no-smoking area for everywhere, from restaurants to hilltops."

"Considering what's been burning out here, I'm surprised she'd even care," he said. "You been doing this long?"

"No, not at all," I said. "Less than a month. Does it show?"

Mick laughed, took a deep drag on his cigar. "Oh, yeah, it does. You look tired, a bit dirty, but you've still got that innocent eagerness you get on a puppy's face. You know? Young and smooth and full of energy. No worry lines. No thousand-yard stares. Like you haven't been out in the bush that long. No offense."

"*You* look like someone who's been out in the bush for a very long time," I said.

Another drag on his cigar as he carried the camera easily enough in one hand. "You got that right, mate. Nearly twenty years humping this camera gear, from one bloody hot spot to the next. Africa, Fiji, South America and now here. All the time recording for posterity the unique ways men have come up with to kill other men, women and children. Car bombs, hanging, knives, rocks and every type of firearm imaginable. That's the joy of what I do, you know. In the old times the stories of this kind of butchery were told in oral or written tales, passed down from generation to generation. All cleaned up and proper, with heroes and villains. Now here I am, with color film and sound, ready to bring it into your living room while you're cooking dinner, reading the newspaper or scratching your dog's arse. Not too many heroes, way too many villains. And you know what I've learned?"

"A lot, I'm sure."

"Yeah, but here's the important one," he said, pointing the stub of his cigar at me for emphasis. "Real living is having enough to eat, a warm and dry place to sleep, and regular bowels. Everything else is extra. They teach you that at UN school?"

"Didn't teach us much at UN school," I said. "Wasn't much of a school."

Now Jean-Paul was in a huddle with Charlie, Peter and the two Australians, John and Alice.

Mick said, "The hell you say."

"The hell I do, I guess," I said. "The UN expected you to come along with your own set of skills, and so here I am."

"What kind of skills? Investigator? Pathologist?"

"Journalist."

This made Mick laugh so hard that I thought cigar smoke was going to come out of his ears. "Go on, you're pulling my leg. A reporter? Where?"

"In Toronto. For the *Star*."

"What kind of stories?"

I wished I could have said politics, or courts, or even the crime beat. But Mick seemed to be a guy who had a sensitive bullshit detector built in.

"Feature stories," I said. "Human-interest stuff. What they call soft news."

This brought forth another burst of laughter. On this remote hilltop and considering everything I'd seen so far, what I'd just said sounded so ridiculous that I joined in, laughing with him. Mick paused and said, "Then what the hell are you doing out here? Writing cheery stories for the papers back home?"

"Nope, doing something like you folks are," I said. "Recording what's happening for posterity—except this posterity is at The Hague."

"Oh, got it now. Documenting war crimes."

"Yep."

Mick shook his head, just as Jean-Paul and the group broke up. "Tell you what, mate, I could have saved you lots of time. Tape library I got back home shows the same thing. The orphans, the burned homes, the corpses decaying in fields. All you had to do was borrow the tapes and just change the captions. That's all. Would have saved you lots of time."

I started walking away, to where Peter and Miriam were waiting for me, up by one of the Land Cruisers. "Thanks for the offer, but I prefer to see it firsthand."

Mick tossed his cigar away. "If I see you in a month, I'll see if you've changed your mind."

"Deal," I said.

CHAPTER TEN

In order to make time and get going, we skipped breakfast—except for whatever tea and coffee had already been brewed—and came down the hill, with the Australian television van following us. Once again we were in second place in the procession of vehicles, and Peter said, "Look behind us, why don't you? That idiot Sanjay's almost a klick away. Guess he doesn't want to run up my arse again, huh?"

I folded my arms, decided not to ask him to turn up the heat. "Who would, Peter?"

Behind me Miriam didn't say anything, but she did gently stroke the back of my neck, just a little touch, I guess to let me know that she was there. I remembered that kiss last night, a chaste kiss between a maiden and a smelly knight errant who was terrified and hungry and tired. I turned quickly and gave her a smile, and she said, "I don't know why but I just feel happier, having that TV crew with us. And Aussies, to boot. They weren't part of the intervention, they're not taking part in any peacekeeping. It just seems like they're a good thing to have with us."

Peter said, "What? You think having a van like that is going to prevent some rogue militia unit from lobbing a couple of hand grenades at us?"

"Maybe not," I said. "But it might buy us some time."

Peter shook his head. "Dreamers. I'm surrounded by bloody dreamers."

Miriam leaned up to him so close that I was horrified she was going to kiss him. But no, she was looking down between the two of us, at a map on the car seat. "Tell me again: where is Jean-Paul leading us?"

"Well, he's been leading us around in circles all this time, so I'm hoping his luck will change," Peter said. "We're heading to a major north-south highway, just three or four klicks to the east. There's an on-ramp from this road that enters the highway, and that gives us two options. Either head south, where there's a major UN resettlement area, or just hang in there, wait for a UN convoy to stroll by, and catch a ride with them."

"Nice options," I said.

"Nice to have them, for a change," Peter said.

Miriam, still leaning in between us, said, "What do you think about that TV crew, what that reporter said?"

Peter scratched at the side of his face. "You mean that stupid git with the perfect teeth? What about him? Sounded like the usual newsie nonsense."

I said, "I think Miriam's talking about what he said about the UN inspection teams being sabotaged."

"You mean, like this one?" Peter asked. "How we've gone round in circles, not knowing where we were going, and how we haven't found a bloody thing? Except for—" He spared me a quick glance. "No offense, except for some dead cows. Sure, maybe we've been sabotaged, or maybe we've had some bad luck, or bad leadership. Trust me, if there was some serious sabotage going on we wouldn't be breathing. No, sir, not at all."

Peter looked down at the map, looked up again. "Brilliant. Here we go. That access road should be here, right above this rise."

I had my hands clasped in my lap and was still enjoying having Miriam between the two of us. It seemed to me—perhaps I was being irrational—that she was leaning in my direction. I looked ahead and saw the road curve up and to the right, and the brake lights of the lead Land Cruiser. In the distance below us, off to the left and right, I could make out a four-lane highway, just like the map had indicated.

But there was still one problem.

The overpass, which should have led us to an on-ramp or some other sort of entrance to the highway, was gone.

Peter swore, and I just kept my hands still.

THE THREE LAND Cruisers and the Australian television van parked in a row at the crest of the rise. We all got out and stood, in front of the parked vehicles, and I had a sudden vision of some men with guns rising up and cutting us down with one wide sweep of their weapons. It would have been so easy to do, so easy to kill us all in a matter of moments.

In shocked silence I looked below where we were standing, saw where the overpass had ended up. Right across the highway. It seemed silly, seeing how a large piece of precision engineering consisting of tons of concrete and steel beams and pillars was now lying across the highway. It was too odd, it wasn't right, and it made one think of looking around to see if a camera crew was on hand, some camera crew from a motion-picture studio, for something so huge and dramatic could only be some sort of special effect. That couldn't be concrete and steel resting there. It had to be plywood and plaster and plastic.

I had my hands in my pockets, and said, "Bombing raid."

"Excuse me?" Sanjay said.

"NATO bombing raid, before the cease-fire," I said. "Smart bombs from three or four thousand meters up—must have dropped this overpass right across the highway. Do it right and you've managed to blockade a major resupply route, or a roadway that the militias were using to truck out refugee prisoners to the execution sites."

Jean-Paul turned to our silent Marine escort. "Charlie?"

Charlie didn't look too pleased but he answered anyway. "Could be. See down there, on the other side, the other ridge? Looks like some of it's been cleared away. So at least the UN is using part of the highway now."

Charlie was right. On the other side of the roadway, piles of crumpled concrete and twisted rebar had been bulldozed away, clearing part of one highway lane. Just our luck, though, that it was on the other side, and not nearby.

Peter kicked at a chunk of pavement. "Damn NATO was too efficient," he said. "See how chewed-up the hill is? They must have come in with another load of bombs, taken out the exit ramps to the highway and pounded up the hill. Tornadoes."

"What? What do you mean, tornadoes?" Karen demanded. "I thought bombs did this, right?"

Peter didn't say anything and I felt sorry for Karen, so I said, "Peter meant a type of aircraft. Tornadoes. And if I'm right, they carry a type of munitions that is used to cut airfields and roads in half. Correct, Peter?"

"Uh-huh," he said.

"Who the hell flies Tornadoes?"

I decided I liked the sour look on Peter's face. "That's where the irony comes in. Tornadoes are mostly flown by the British. Am I right, Peter?"

"Or the Germans," Miriam said. "I've seen them at an air show, outside Rotterdam."

"Well," said the sharp voice of John, the Australian reporter. "This is all bloody well and nice, enjoying the view up here, but what the hell are we going to do about it? Mister Cloutier?"

Jean-Paul seemed lost in thought, standing there with the folded-over map under his arm. "Yes, what is it?"

"I said, what in hell are we going to do? Just sit up here?"

"It's an idea," Jean-Paul said.

"An idea, the man says!" John said, turning to us all, talking in that cultured television voice. "His sole idea is to have us sit on our arses up on this bloody hill all morning!"

If the comment bothered Jean-Paul he sure didn't show it. Instead, he said, "Yes, an idea. This is a highway used by UN forces. We stay up here long enough, a convoy or column will show up."

"And if the militias see us out here in the open, then we're all dead, right?"

Sanjay's turn. "We could move back down the road, find a wooded area. One or two of us could stay up here and keep watch."

Peter had a smile at that suggestion, and I knew what he was thinking: Sanjay wouldn't mind being up here alone with just Karen to keep him company. But the Australian correspondent wasn't having any of it.

"Look, Cloutier," John said, walking over to him, his correspondent coat flapping around his legs. "You've got four-wheel-drive vehicles there, right? Let's all pile in and go down this hill, and then hook up with the road. OK?"

Jean-Paul said, "Charlie?"

But Charlie wasn't rising to the bait. So I said, "Unexploded munitions."

John turned on me. "What did you say, kid?"

"Unexploded munitions," I said, seeing how the guy's face was getting more red. "Look at the access ramp. Look at the hillside. Has to have been a number of air strikes here. Which always means a number of unexploded munitions. Chances are, we start barreling down that hillside in our vehicles, we'll set something off."

"Hell, that's a chance I'm willing to take," John said. Alice came up to him, tugging at his arm, and he brushed her off angrily. Mick was standing there, silent, with his camera at his feet like an obedient dog curled up before its master, and Peter leaned across and said, "Guess nobody else wants to take this chance."

John said, "Well, hell, there should be another way of getting onto this highway, and we're gonna take it. Alice, Mick, let's saddle up."

Mick looked over at me, shaking his head just slightly, and grabbed his camera. Alice, however, grabbed at John again and dragged him away a few feet. From that distance, I could only make out snatches of their conversation, which fast deteriorated into an argument:

"... Why can't we just wait with these folks ..."

"... You heard what they said, they're gonna wait all day ..."

"... Where's the problem with that, we've been lost since we got here ..."

"... You've been lost, Alice, not me. If you let me drive ..."

"... The rush? We stay here and ..."

"... Miss a big story. We're not staying. We're moving out ..."

"... Safer here with them, John, and you ..."

"... That's it, right. You're scared. Right? Should have asked Don to come ..."

"... OK, I'm scared. I want to see my two-year-old again. Is that a crime ..."

"... Done with this and done with you ..."

John broke free from Alice, nodded in Mick's direction, and they started walking back to the white van. Alice stood there, clipboard hanging from her hand, looking at them and then looking back at us. Her face was pale and she was trembling, and I did not want to think of what was going through her mind. Should she stay with us or go along with her crew? Possible safety with us and certain career disaster. Or maybe a few uncomfortable moments in the van, and then finding a way onto the highway, and sharing some funny stories with other television crews at the UN refugee camp, less than an hour away. What a choice. Karen whispered something and I thought maybe Alice heard her, and then the van started up, with John driving. He honked the horn and Alice brought a hand up to her face, turned around and walked to the van.

Sanjay said, his voice shaking a bit, "Oh, they'll be all right. You'll see."

"Sure," Karen said. But I couldn't agree with him, not at all. The van backed down the road, made a reverse U-turn, and then was gone, the little Australian flag flapping bravely in the wind from the radio antenna.

WE STAYED UP there by the blasted on-ramp for most of the morning, and, surprisingly enough, Jean-Paul accepted Sanjay's suggestion about keeping watch on the highway. We brought the Land Cruisers down and found a place to park them, behind a high stone wall, and while Karen and Sanjay took the first watch, we waited. And waited. A slight mist was forming and for a while I sat in one of the Toyotas, playing cribbage with Miriam. Then I decided I had to walk around. Besides the fact that Miriam beat me, four games to nil, I felt enclosed and trapped inside the vehicle. Charlie was out on a high point of the perimeter, keeping watch, and he was wearing a black wool watchcap instead of his usual UN blue beret. Jean-Paul was sitting on a tarp, leaning back against the stone wall, working on his own laptop. When he spotted me he said, "Samuel?"

"Yes?"

"A moment, if you please."

I came over and he said, "Peter went down the hill a couple of minutes ago, for a bathroom break. If you don't mind, it's time for Karen and Sanjay to get relieved. I'd like to send Peter and you up there."

"I'd rather go with Miriam."

"Yes, and I'd rather be in Marseilles having a wonderful hot bowl of fish soup, but that's not going to happen, now, is it? Now. Please run along and get Peter. He went down that trail, over by the far Land Cruiser."

So I went, droplets of mist dripping down on me from the trees. Miriam was inside the Land Cruiser I had just left, reading a paperback. She waved at me and I waved back.

THE TRAIL WAS wet and covered with grass and patches of soft mud, so I didn't make much noise as I went into the woods. Peter and me, keeping an eye on the highway. What fun. I shivered from the cold and remembered that wonderful motel we had stayed at, what now seemed ages ago. A roof and electricity for a while, and even a hot shower. Paradise. The woods I was in were a mix of hardwood and pine, but there weren't many leaves on the ground. I felt sure it was different back home in Ontario. All the leaves would have fallen by now.

I went in a few meters and was going to call out for Peter when I heard a voice. I stopped, waited, and then walked some more, slowly. Yes, a voice all right, muttering something at a rapid pace. I crept forward a bit, listened. The wind shifted and I could make out individual words, but not enough to make sense. But it was enough to determine that the voice belonged to Peter. But was he talking to himself?

Another couple of steps. No, he was talking to someone, it seemed like, for there would be a pause, a reply and then another pause.

The voice sounded closer. I went off the trail and into the woods, walking as slow as possible. There was a shape, crouched by the trunk of an evergreen tree that had fallen. The wood was beginning to rot, falling away from the trunk in chunks of gray and brown. And there was Peter, on his knees, talking into his hands. The wind seemed to shift and I heard the word "grace." It struck me as odd: could he be praying before a meal? Peter?

I watched and saw him move his head. Then I noticed the little plastic earpiece, snug in his right ear, with a wire running down to something clasped in his hands.

Radio. Peter was talking, all right, but not to himself. And who was he talking to, and why?

Well, that was a puzzler, and I sure as hell wasn't going to find the answer now. Maybe Charlie could have gone in there, demanding to know what was what, or maybe Jean-Paul. But not me. I had a creepy spine-tickling feeling that if I went in right there and confronted Peter about what he was doing, then something quite bad would happen. To me. And Peter would amble back up alone to Jean-Paul, and I would be missing, and would remain missing, and my father would hear from the UN in a month or so that I had disappeared, and he would harrumph and say, "Figures." And that would be that.

So I crept away back onto the trail, and then moved a couple more yards further away. I called out, "Peter! Hey, Peter! You around here?"

Then Peter came crashing through the underbrush, zipping up the front of his blue jeans.

"Yeah?"

"Jean-Paul's looking for you," I said. "He wants us to relieve Karen and Sanjay, up on the rise."

"Lucky me," he said, finishing his business.

"My thoughts exactly," I said.

He grunted and looked at me, and I avoided his gaze. I don't know. It just seemed that if he kept on looking at me, then he could figure out that I had been observing him earlier, speaking into a radio, doing God knows what. Or maybe he'd reckon I'd been watching him that other night, in the motel parking lot, when he had come back alone as though he had been somewhere secret. I remembered the stand-up interview with the Australian television crew earlier today. Saboteurs at work, making sure that none of the UN groups working out here would ever find out anything about Site A.

Saboteurs.

"Well?" Peter demanded.

"Excuse me?"

"Let's get back up there, unless you want the group thinking you and I are doing what Karen and Sanjay are no doubt doing."

"There's a thought," I said, and my back tingled again, looking at those big hands of his. "Tell you what, after you."

"Whatever," he said, and I felt just a bit safer, following him instead of having him follow me.

Just a bit.

WE WENT THROUGH the area where the vehicles were parked, and this time Miriam didn't see me, her head still buried in her paperback. Charlie and Jean-Paul were still at their same stations, hard at work, Jean-Paul on his laptop, Charlie with his binoculars, weapon and hunter's eye. We got back on the road and Peter had his hands in his pockets, whistling a little tune I didn't recognize. Our boots sounded loud on the asphalt, and up ahead, by a pine tree on the right, I could see Karen and Sanjay, keeping watch on the quiet highway below them.

"Beautiful sight, isn't it?" Peter said. "Woman from California, married man from India. Finding true love in the service of the United Nations, investigating war crimes."

"I guess a poet would say you love where you can find it," I said.

Peter looked over at me, the light catching the stubble on his face. "Poetry? You're going to start quoting poetry at me?"

"I wasn't thinking about it."

"Good."

"But," I went on, "if it seems to tick you off so much, maybe I will, after all."

"Hah," he said.

I looked around at the countryside, at the bare trees and falling oak leaves, thought about Halloween coming up. One of my favorite holidays as a child. Going out trick-or-treating, deciding what kind of costume to wear. Talking to schoolmates, learning which homes gave out the best candy, and which homes should be avoided because they gave out apples or—shudder!—granola bars. I was going to ask Peter if he had ever trick-or-treated as a youngster, and decided not to. I couldn't imagine this sour man having a childhood, not at all, and I was still flustered at having seen him earlier, talking low into a radio.

"Christ," Peter said, "if something doesn't come by on that highway in . . ."

I heard something, but Peter was still yammering; and I said, "Hey, shut up for a sec, will you?"

That surprised him into silence. I thought he was going to snap back at me when maybe he heard something as well. We both turned and looked down the road. Nothing.

"Well?" he asked.

"I thought I heard something," I said.

"Some*thing* or some*one*?"

I shrugged. "Not sure. Hold on."

So we did. A breeze came up, blowing dead leaves across the equally dead road. From behind us I could make out the voices of our two comrades, up by the tree.

"Come on," Peter said, "We've got to get to Karen and Sanjay."

"Wait," I said, seeing something move along the side of the road. "There's something there."

"Jesus," he said, turning away from me. "You can stand here and just wait. I'll go on and relieve those two."

I didn't say anything. Peter took a step, and then stopped. I held my breath, thinking maybe I would lose focus otherwise. Then the shape took form. It was a man. Walking slowly up the road as if he was an old man who'd been freed from a rest home or a hospital, moving with great dignity and purpose, but slow, all the same. His hair was a mess but his clothes were good, nice pair of slacks and a trench coat that came down to his—

"Damn it, that's the Aussie TV guy," I said. "It's John."

Peter didn't say anything but he followed me as I started walking toward the slowly moving man. He walked right up the middle of the road, and he looked tired, like he had been walking quite a distance. Breakdown, I thought. Their van must have broken down and he was coming back here for help. That was all. Just walking back for help.

He slowed down, looked up and saw us. He gave us a weak wave.

"Peter, it's—"

"I know who it is," Peter said. "I've got eyes, haven't I?"

John slowed even more and began to weave some, as though he had been drinking. I started walking toward him and then speeded up. Peter was behind me. More voices could be heard as Karen and Sanjay finally spotted us.

"John," I called out. "You OK? Where's the rest of your crew? Where's Mick and Alice?"

He managed a smile. But just as I got close enough to see the chalky color of his face he collapsed on his knees and said weakly, "There's trouble."

Then John fell forward full-length onto the ground before I could catch him. I knelt down beside him, looking at him, looking at the blood covering the back of his coat.

CHAPTER ELEVEN

Remembering my training, I rolled John over onto his side to check his breathing. But Peter pulled me away and then Karen was there, speaking crisply and professionally, saying, "Sanjay. Our vehicle, my tan leather pouch. Bring that and the first-aid kit. Get Miriam over here, too. And tell Charlie there's bad guys in the area. Tell Jean-Paul as well."

I stood up and stepped back, my hands sticky, saw that they were covered with John's blood. His breathing was coming in low, rattling gasps. Karen and Peter were working together, Karen examining the newsman's back while Peter cradled his head in his lap. Peter's voice now had a soothing tone, a type of voice I had never heard from him before, and I had to look at him twice to make sure it was the same Peter. "OK, John, try to relax, try to take it easy. Where's your people? Where's the van? Who did this to you?"

I could see John's lips moving, saw Peter bend down and listen. "Louder," Peter asked, but not in a demanding way. "Please, John. Tell me louder."

"Here," Karen said to me. "Help me with his coat."

I knelt back down on the pavement, helped Karen to undo John's coat. It was hard going because John was lying on his side, holding the coat down. Peter said, "Samuel, my inside coat pocket. There's a folding knife. Get it."

I reached into the open coat, conscious that John's blood was now smearing Peter's shirt. But neither of us cared. I got the knife and snapped it open, passed it over to Karen. Then I heard John moan again and barely audibly say, "Go right . . . Go right . . ."

"OK, John," Peter murmured. "We hear you, we hear you."

Karen said, "Ah, shit, where is everybody? Here, start pulling away the coat while I start cutting."

She went to work with the knife, her hand moving swiftly and surely, the blade cutting away the fabric of the expensive coat. I pulled away the pieces of cloth, nausea rising up in my stomach, seeing the shirt now soaked completely through with John's blood. I held something heavy in my hands. The man's wallet. I flipped it open quickly, saw the glassine photo pages inside, his driver's license, press identification, picture of him on a beach, holding the hand of a woman and a young child, nice family portrait, back in warm and safe and sunny Australia. I closed the wallet and let it fall to the ground, along with the remnants of his coat. John was now shivering and Peter said, "He's going into shock, Karen."

"No shit," she said, her hands now completely stained. "OK, I've got at least three entry wounds in his back. Peter, you got anything up front?"

"No."

"Damn it, he got chewed up really bad—Christ, finally."

Lots of voices, trotting figures, all carrying something in their hands. It quickly became even more chaotic as Charlie demanded in a loud voice where the bad guys were, while Jean-Paul kept on asking information on where John's companions were, and Miriam and Sanjay and Karen talked among themselves, ignoring everybody else. Except once, when Karen spoke up sharply and said, "Charlie and Jean-Paul, shut the fuck up, will you? We'll be lucky enough to stabilize him for a medevac chopper, if those assholes feel like flying today."

Peter was still there as well, talking quietly to John, using that soothing voice that probably came in so handy when he was working the mean streets of London, comforting the injured or the bereaved. Sanjay said, "Samuel, make yourself useful! Hold up this IV bag!"

I stepped forward, dropped a piece of John's coat that I had been holding. I grabbed the soft plastic bag and held it up, while Sanjay slipped the needle at the end of the tubing into an exposed forearm. A thin Mylar space blanket covered most of John in an attempt to keep him warm, and the area around him was messy with his blood and with empty plastic containers and bandage wrappings. A small green oxygen bottle was near his head, and Peter slipped a clear plastic oxygen mask over his nose and mouth. Miriam was working side by side with Karen and they were speaking to each other in technical phrases and acronyms, none of which I could understand or follow. Their hands moved like those of two concert pianists. Charlie looked almost frantic, squatting down and sweeping the area with binoculars, M-16 at his side. Jean-Paul was talking again into his satellite phone, trying to arrange a medevac, trying to reach somebody, and what little French I knew told me that he was having problems communicating with the regional headquarters.

I stood there, my legs tired, holding the IV bag still, not daring to move it, fearful that I might pull the needle out or do something else to make the situation worse. Karen and Miriam were tending John's back, and Sanjay was at his front, running his hands up and down his chest and abdomen, looking for exit wounds. From my vantage point I was looking down at John, his face gray-white, his eyes wide and staring up at me. I smiled down at him in my most reassuring way, as if to let him know that a dedicated group of men and women were doing their damnedest to help him live, to bandage him up so that he could get to a real hospital, where he would recover and get back to Sydney or Melbourne or wherever, with a prizewinning story of how he had almost ended it all on the world's latest killing fields.

I kept smiling at him all the time until he closed his eyes and died.

WE SAT AT the side of the road, exhausted. Karen was weepy and Sanjay had his arm around her, while Miriam looked despondent. I sat down next to her and she leaned against me and said, "Oh, Samuel."

I held her hand and she squeezed it back.

Peter and Charlie had moved John's body to the side of the road, placing it in a hollow by an outcropping of two boulders. They had carefully stretched the Mylar blanket over him, securing it with small rocks so that the breeze wouldn't catch it and blow it away. Now they were talking to Jean-Paul, and while I expected a lot of shouting and arm-waving and red faces it didn't happen. The three of them were standing in a circle, looking solemn, motioning every now and then toward us and then to the covered body of John. Miriam said, "We have to go look for the others."

"I know."

"Charlie won't like it," she said. "I'm not sure Peter will like it either, but we have to look for the others. And right now. We shouldn't be waiting around."

I squeezed her hand. "You're absolutely right."

And I got up and walked over to them.

CHARLIE SAW ME first as I came closer. "Yes?"

I looked over to Jean-Paul, who still held on to his useless satellite phone as if he was expecting an apologetic message to come through at any moment. "Why are we still here?"

Now all three of them looked at me like I had come over and had just ordered a pizza or something. I carried on and said, "John's dead. But we don't know what happened to the rest of his crew. Why are we still here? We should be looking for them."

Charlie said something about the terrain being dangerous and Jean-Paul said something about trying to regain communication with the regional UN office. But Peter shook his head and spoke over them, saying, "He's right, you know."

I wasn't sure who was more shocked, me or the other two.

"Say what?" Charlie said.

Peter said angrily, "The kid's right. We're sitting around here on our arses while John's getting colder and colder, and we don't know where the rest of his crew are. We should go look for them. John mentioned where they might be, just before he died."

Charlie said, "Jean-Paul, there are hostiles out there. I don't really think it's—"

Jean-Paul put the receiver back on his satellite phone. "I must be getting old, or getting less bold. Peter and Samuel are right. We cannot forget those two. No matter what. Helmets and flak jackets on. Let's get going."

A FEW MINUTES later, the three Land Cruisers were back on the road, engines idling. Peter had a map in his hands and was talking to Sanjay and Jean-Paul. Charlie shot me a dark look and I guessed he wasn't my best buddy any more, which was something I could live with. While that was going on I got into the nearest Land Cruiser and took out my duffel bag. I went over to the side of the road, to the place where the Mylar blanket was. I unzipped my bag and took out my Sony digital camera. I took a number of photographs and then knelt down and removed the rocks securing the blanket. I pulled it back to reveal the gray-white features of John. His face and name were probably familiar to hundreds of thousands of viewers back in the land Down Under, but right here and now he was just another statistic, another little checkmark. I centered his face in my camera's viewfinder and took one picture. Then another. And then another.

After I put the blanket back Karen was there, brushing her hair back away from her tear-stained face. "What the hell are you doing here? Taking souvenirs?"

"No, I'm not," I said, gingerly placing the stones back around the edges of the blanket. "I'm just doing my job."

"Job? What do you mean, your job?"

I looked up at her angry expression. "What the UN pays me for. To document war crimes. And it's just my luck I got to cover a fresh one."

Karen shook her head and walked away. A moment later I followed her.

PETER LED THE way, driving one of our vehicles, and I sat up front with him and Miriam was in the rear. We headed down the slope, away from the highway that had once promised us a way out. Riding once more unto the breach, in the dirty and crowded and now smelly Toyota Land Cruisers. I was becoming heartily sick of being inside them. The other Land Cruisers were right behind us and we sped down the road, coming to an intersection. As we blew right through it, I yelled out, "Hey, what the hell are you doing?!"

"What's your problem?" Peter said.

"Stop the car, stop it—you're passing the intersection!"

Peter said, "So what?"

Maybe it was the time of day or what had just happened, but I reached over with my left foot, plunged it past his legs and punched the brake. Peter flailed at me with his right hand, and Miriam was saying something, and I punched the brake again and again, and finally the Land Cruiser slid to a halt. There was another thump as we were struck again from the rear. Miriam said, "Oh, damn, I hope that wasn't Sanjay."

I reached over, turned off the ignition, grabbed the keys and got outside. Peter scrambled right after me, swearing, his London accent now very thick. "You bastard, you stupid bastard, I'm going to fucking nail you!"

Jean-Paul and Charlie came up to us, the Marine with his weapon in his hand. Jean-Paul said, "What's wrong? What's wrong?"

Peter grabbed the front of my coat with one hand while Miriam held back his other arm. He said, "Damn fool stopped us for no reason."

I held the keys behind me, like we were in a schoolyard brawl, and said, "He passed the turnoff."

"What turnoff, you idiot?" Peter said, tugging at me, his face scarlet. "What fucking turnoff?"

Jean-Paul pulled him off me. Karen was now out with us but Sanjay was still in the other Land Cruiser, the one that had rammed us, probably happy that I was getting the brunt of Peter's anger. I said, "Go right. That's what John said. He said go right."

Jean-Paul said, "Is that true?"

"Bloody fuckwit, no, it's not true," Peter said. "He said go *straight*. That's what he said."

"Karen?" Jean-Paul asked.

"Shit, I don't know," she said, folding her arms. "I was too busy trying to keep the poor guy alive."

I said, "I know what I heard. He said go right. That's what he said."

"Bloody Canuck, that was his Aussie accent you were hearing. He said go straight. That's what he said. He didn't say go right."

Jean-Paul started saying something and Charlie said, "Well, shit, let's take a right, see where that goes. If it doesn't look promising, then we go back."

Jean-Paul nodded. "Makes sense."

Peter stalked off. "Well, you drive with the little shit, then. Fucked if I will."

I suppose I should have said something about what I had seen earlier, the quiet moment in the woods when Peter had been talking with radio gear to someone. But then I thought about Mick and Alice, the producer who wanted to go back and see her children. So I got into the Land Cruiser, driving for the first time since I had been here, and Charlie joined us, sitting up front. That made me feel better.

WE TOOK THE right, like I was sure John had said, and we'd driven down the road a couple of klicks, past abandoned farmland and areas of woodland, when Charlie said, "Slow down, Samuel. Slow down."

"What's going on?" I asked, and Miriam said, "Oh. To the left."

I slowed down and stopped, and we all got out. Charlie stood there, weapon at the ready, and he said, "By the side of the car. Now."

The other Land Cruisers stopped. Our little group assembled behind Charlie and I saw what he had noticed. The brush and grass on the left side of the road had been disturbed and there were fresh tire tracks. I sniffed the air and said, "I smell smoke."

"So do I," Miriam said.

Jean-Paul came up and said, "Charlie?"

"I think we might find something, if you give me a minute," he said.

"All right," Jean-Paul said.

Of course, Charlie wanted all of us to stay behind but none of us were listening to him. We straggled after him, our pathetic little parade following our armed Grand Marshal, and then Miriam grabbed my hand again as we all spotted the rear end of a white van. An attempt had been made to burn it but whatever fire there had been had since died out. But the van was still smoldering, the windows were shattered, and the side door was open. The stench of burned plastic and scorched metal was stronger now. Charlie motioned us back with his free hand, but we kept walking forward. Bullet holes had perforated the side and front of the van. I circled around and saw a shape in the front seat, slumped over. Charlie went over to check and then Sanjay was there, saying, "Is he wounded? Is there something we can do?"

Charlie shook his head. "Don't think medical science knows how to fix blown-off heads, now, does it?"

I stepped closer, recognizing the shape and clothing of Mick, the cameraman, and nothing else. He was slumped over the steering wheel, his arms dangling down, and something in my stomach did a queasy flip-flop as I noticed the pulped mass of bone and brain and blood and hair that had once been his head. Just a few hours ago, this combination of muscle and tissue and ligament had been breathing and living, talking to me about being a cameraman in the service of journalism. Now it was all dead flesh, growing colder and colder with every passing minute.

Peter finally spoke, saying, "Anybody see the producer woman? Alice?"

"No," I said. "Not yet. Maybe she went straight, like you thought."

If Peter heard me, he didn't say anything. He started going through the brush and bramble, and then Karen yelled out, "Over here! Over here!"

We ran up the side of a small hill, to a place where the grass hadn't grown up as much. The woman called Alice was lying there, eyes staring up blankly, legs spread wide open. Her arms had been staked to the ground. Her slacks were gone and a pair of white cotton panties was tangled around one ankle. Her blouse had been torn and it looked like someone—or several someones—had worked on her torso with knives. The area around her had been trampled and disturbed, and there were empty bottles of Budweiser beer scattered about.

"The bastards," Karen whispered. "The filthy, murdering bastards."

Sanjay whispered back, "What about the cease-fire agreement? What about the truce?"

"Guess somebody didn't get the word," I said.

Jean-Paul slowly walked up to join us. He was carrying several satchels and dropped them on the ground. "Charlie?"

"Yeah," he said.

"Is this place relatively secure?"

Charlie looked up at him as though Jean-Paul had just announced that he intended to flap his wings and fly to the moon. "That's a hell of a word, 'relatively'," he said. "You want my advice, we all get back in our wheels and head back to the highway. This place is going to the shits pretty quick, and I can't defend a crew like you by myself."

"True," Jean-Paul said, kneeling down on the dirt and unzipping the bags. "But we have work to do, right here. And we cannot leave. Peter? Miriam? Karen? Samuel?"

I looked at the group. Peter was stolid, not showing any emotion, but the others looked like the poor producer woman had, a few hours ago. Terrified and wanting to go someplace safe, someplace away from this madness. I took a breath, walked over to my own bag. I took out my Sony and said, "I'm ready to go to work."

Miriam joined me. "So am I."

Karen said, "Oh, fuck. I guess I am, too."

HOURS LATER, AS we were cleaning up, I stood next to Miriam and said, "I have a proposition for you."

"That sounds interesting," she said, wiping her hands dry with a dirty towel.

"Would you care to share my tent tonight?" I asked.

She smiled and nudged me with her elbow. "Do you have something naughty planned?"

I coughed and took the soiled towel from her. "I wish I could say that. But I don't want to be with Sanjay tonight and have him play musical tents again, and Peter is about ready to strangle me, and the other two . . . Well, Miriam, you went right to the top of the list."

I winced as I dried off my own hands. The fingers and palms were blistered from having dug three shallow graves for the Australian television crew. Karen and Sanjay and Peter and Miriam had gotten tissue samples, swabs and even some latent fingerprints from the burned-out and shot-up van. I had done my own work with camera and computer, but I'd had no success when I'd tried later to upload the information. Either the satellite uplink was malfunctioning or maybe the jamming from the militias was active again. Working with the camera this time, I was grateful for having the viewfinder between my eyes and what was on the ground before me. The burned-out van, the shattered body of Mick and the brutalized and violated body of Alice seemed only to exist in the space beyond the camera, and I found that comforting.

Now we were parked under an oak tree, a number of klicks away from the shooting site. We were drawn up in the by now familiar triangular formation. After maneuvering our way into some woods, Charlie had gone out with us and directed us to drag branches and pieces of brush around to hide the fact that we had gone in among the trees. We had a cold dinner of cheese, bread and water, and a cold wash-up, and by then I was exhausted.

Miriam nudged me again. "All right. That's a deal, then. I'll share your tent tonight."

"Thanks."

Miriam smiled. "My pleasure."

I wanted to believe her.

JEAN-PAUL GATHERED US together and said, "I . . . I am tired, as are all of you. We will be here tonight, and tomorrow we make our way back to the highway. I . . . I . . ."

I stood there, hands in my coat pocket, shivering, wishing we could have built a fire. But there would be no fire tonight, not even something hot to heat up water. We were standing in a loose semicircle, Sanjay holding a cupped flashlight, throwing off just a little illumination. Then my throat tightened as I saw that Jean-Paul's eyes were filling with tears. I felt bad for a moment, about all the times I had thought poorly of him. Poor guy was just overwhelmed. He coughed into his hand, rocked back and forth on his heels for a moment, and then went on. "I . . . I am very proud of you, all of you. Get a good night's sleep."

We went back to the tents, one beside each Land Cruiser. Sanjay was heading toward the closest one. "Not so fast," I said.

"What do you mean?" he asked.

"What I mean is that I've already made other arrangements," I said. "My tent-mate tonight is Miriam."

"Oh . . . really?"

"Yep."

"Then where am I to sleep?"

I was very tired and wanted to end this quickly. "Shit, Sanjay, sleep on a rock for all I care. Go crawl in with Karen."

He shook his head. "That may not be possible. We had a fight earlier."

"Well, there might be some people in New Delhi who'd be happy with that—wouldn't they?"

Sanjay muttered something and stalked off. I wish I could say I felt bad about it, but sometimes wishes just don't come true. All in all, I felt pretty good, considering.

CHAPTER TWELVE

Miriam climbed into the tent soon after I got settled in. I aided her with my own small flashlight, cupping the beam with my hand to keep the glow down. Her blonde hair was loose and her cotton nightgown was dark green, and when she was in I shut the light off.

"Samuel?"

"Still here," I said.

I felt her body shaking beside me. "It's damn cold."

"It sure is."

"Can we do something about it?"

In the darkness I smiled. "To quote someone you know quite well, do you plan something naughty?"

"Not at this moment," she said.

So we went back and forth for a bit, and unzipped our bags and tossed them together, and Miriam cuddled up against me, putting her head on my chest. Her fine hair tickled my nose and I inhaled the scent, feeling a knot of tension at the base of my skull start to loosen up. I thought about other women, mostly college women I had known, from York University or the University of Toronto. And Pamela, a copy editor at the features desk back at the *Star*. Right now they all blended together in one flash of memory. Lots of laughs, lots of giggles, cell phone numbers exchanged and quick couplings in a rented flat somewhere. Nothing like now. Nothing like Miriam. Nothing at all.

"It gets quite cold back home," she said.

"Uh-huh," I said.

"I love skating, especially on the canals," she said. "It's flat and beautiful, and you can skate for hours and hours. There are warming shacks and little restaurants where you can get hot cocoa or spiced wine to drink . . . Oh, I do miss that . . . You must skate, am I right?"

"What makes you think that?"

Miriam laughed. "You're Canadian. I thought all Canadians skated."

I gently squeezed her shoulder. "Well, you got me. You're right. I *do* skate, though it's been a while. But no canal skating. Just frozen ponds and lakes."

"Did you play ice hockey?"

"Didn't have the coordination," I said. "I can skate a fair piece, but trying to skate while holding a stick, chasing a puck, when other people on skates are getting in your way . . . nope, I just loved skating. Being out there, gliding, enjoying the breeze in my face."

"Me, too," she said, and we lay there for a while, just breathing. I felt her move and then her chin was resting on my chest. "Samuel . . ."

"Mmm?"

"You did something brave today."

"You sure?"

"Yes. I . . . I think we were all waiting for someone to say something, something about leaving, but you followed Jean-Paul. You said we should stay and do our job. You were the first one to say that. And I found that very brave."

I didn't know what to say. I touched her hair with my free hand and then moved down to the smoothness of her cheek. She gave a slight intake of breath as my hand reached her lips and my forefinger gently stroked the skin beneath her nose. Her mouth opened slightly. I felt the touch of her tongue and I leaned up and kissed her. It was a miracle, moving in the darkness like that, but our lips met, gently for a moment or two, and then, with a sudden intensity that I think surprised us both, we gasped and embraced, our arms and legs entwined.

"Oh, please . . ." she said.

"Miriam. Whatever you want. Whatever."

She kissed me again. "Stop talking. Please."

"Yes."

Miriam pressed harder against me, now lying on top of me, supporting herself on her elbows, breathing more harshly, her hair falling about me.

I held her head with one hand and with the other moved up her side, cupping a breast, feeling the nipple stiffen. I gently pinched and rubbed, and then started unbuttoning her nightgown. In turn, she tugged down my pajama bottoms, freeing me, and I gasped as her hand held me tight. There was more confused tumbling around as she eased off her panties and then she said, "Samuel, Samuel," and slid down upon me. I gasped at the sensation, feeling the cold staleness of the tent air and the sleeping bags around me, and how it contrasted with the sweet, wet and hot delight of Miriam's inner warmth. She rocked back and forth, moaning and whispering to me, and I whispered back, holding her tight as both of us forgot everything that was going on, save for within those few safe feet inside the tent.

"Miriam . . ."

"Shhh," she said. "Just don't stop. Please."

"Of course."

LATER SHE WAS cuddled up with me again, idly scratching my neck and chin. Her bare breasts were pressed pleasantly against my chest, and she said, "That was a delight."

"It was the best."

"Not too naughty?"

I bent to kiss the top of her head.

"No, not too naughty, not at all."

"Mmm," she said. "Ask you a question?"

"Go ahead."

"Jean-Paul mentioned something earlier, about you and your father. He said he knew your father. Is that true?"

Talk about killing the moment. *Thanks, Dad.* "Yes, it is true."

"So is that why you are here? Because of your father?"

"Partially true," I said, trying to remember everything Miriam and I had just done a few minutes earlier, trying to recall each taste, each scent, each sensation. Nothing like the other few women in my life. Not even close.

She started scratching my ear. "How is that? Partially, I mean."

"I guess I joined up because of what he did and what he didn't do."

"Somalia," she said simply.

"Yep."

"Would you like to tell me about it?"

"Not really," I said.

"Ah," Miriam said, now gently tugging at my ear. "But will you anyway?"

I licked my lips, tasting the subtle essence of her. "All right—I guess. He was in Somalia. He was in the Canadian Army, in charge of the Canadian peacekeepers, in a neighborhood of Mogadishu. These Canadians were supposed to be the very best, the elite. And they were, which made the scandal later so much harder to accept."

"What scandal?" she asked quietly.

I took a breath. "The compound where the Canadians were staying was hit every night by thieves. Petty thievery, mostly. Food and clothing. But the army guys got upset. They captured a couple of the offenders. Kids, really. The army guys were furious. They tortured them with knives and then took them out to a dump and shot them. The thievery quieted right down. It took months before the story came out. A videotape of the soldiers brutalizing the Somalis turned up. But my dad . . . he knew all about it."

"Samuel," she whispered.

"And then he tried to cover it up, and then he tried to defend what the troops did. In the end a couple of the soldiers were dismissed and did quiet jail time. My dad was allowed to resign quietly, and that was that. My dad. And that was the military he wanted me to join. To keep up the family tradition. Some family. Some tradition."

"So why are you here? To make amends?"

I squeezed Miriam's bare shoulder. "Maybe a pop psychologist would say so. I don't know. All I know is that I felt I had to come here, to make a contribution, to do more than just write stories about the latest club opening, or the wives of the Blue Jays raising money for American refugees. That's all, and that's why."

"And your mother?"

"Mom . . . well, she left my dad a few years back, when I was in college. She's living in Florida, I think, at some seaside community. Finding herself after all these years. Pretty safe—the strike last spring didn't affect her or her friends that much."

"Mmm," Miriam said, her breathing slowing down some.

I held her like that for a while, and said, "Miriam?"

"Mmm?" came the questioning tone.

"I need to tell you something," I said. "About Peter. I think he's working for somebody else, somebody else besides the UN. I caught him this morning, talking to someone over a concealed radio. He didn't see me but I saw him. Do you know anything about that?"

No answer.

"Miriam?"

Her breathing was regular and slow so I decided to let her sleep. I closed my eyes, shifted her weight some, and kissed the top of her head. I squeezed her tight. She murmured something and we stayed like that, all the night through.

WHEN MORNING CAME Miriam had rolled away from me and was sleeping deeply. I crawled out of the tent, carrying my clothes, coat and shoes in my hand, and in the dew-wet cold morning I got dressed, shivering. It was still and quiet in this early part of the day. The dirty Land Cruisers were streaked with dew, as were the tents. There was a cough and Charlie approached, weapon slung over his shoulder.

"Nice show," he said.

"Glad I could help."

He rubbed his hands together and said, "A long night."

"Anything going on?"

Charlie turned his head up to the gray sky. "Jets overhead, twice during the night. Some ordnance was dropped, up to the north."

"Think the cease-fire's over?"

He said, "What we saw yesterday, sure as hell looks like somebody's decided to toss away the agreement. Damn, it's cold!"

I said, "Why don't I get coffee going?"

Charlie said, "Don't tempt me, Samuel. You know I don't want an unshielded flame. Some of these militias, they have thermal-imaging devices they've stolen from the Reserves or National Guard."

I motioned to a trail that led past the oak tree we were parked under. "Down there, there's a little rocky hollow. Saw it when I went on a bathroom break before hitting the sack. I could get the gas stove there, heat up a bucket of water. Won't take long and I'm sure you and everybody else could use something hot."

Charlie smiled. "OK, against my better judgment. Just don't take too long."

"I won't."

CHARLIE HELPED ME get the stove and some water out of the cluttered rear of one of the Land Cruisers and I walked the short distance away from the campsite. As I walked away, Miriam emerged, yawning, and blew a kiss in my direction. I waved and felt warm and tingly inside. A damn good feeling.

Along the narrow trail there was a rock outcropping, behind which was a little hollow. I set up the stove and lit it. It hissed into life quickly. I put an empty metal coffee pot over the stove, filled it with water from a plastic jug, and sat down to wait. I drew my knees up to my chin and wrapped my arms around my legs, shivered, and watched the stove do its work. I closed my eyes and was delightfully rocked again by the memory of last night, recalling the sounds and tastes and sensations of Miriam, dear Miriam. I kept my eyes closed, imagining us getting out to the highway in an hour or so, getting picked up by a UN convoy, and maybe, just maybe, getting back in time to take Miriam out to a real dinner at a real restaurant. No more cold meals, no more reconstituted stew or mystery meat. A real meal, complete with tablecloth and silverware.

I opened my eyes, heard the rustle of creatures in the leaves and the harsh call of a blue jay. Steam was rising from the top of the coffee pot, the lid rattling softly in the stillness of the rocky area. I turned the stove off and picked up the coffee pot with a folded-over handkerchief. It felt hot through the cloth, and I knew that in a couple of minutes our little group would have coffee with our meager breakfast. A nice thought, and I would make sure Miriam got the first cup.

I went around the rock outcropping, out onto the trail—and damn near slammed into the back of a line of armed men.

THEIR UNIFORMS WERE torn and muddy and had no UN crests on the shoulders or sleeves, and I noticed right away that everybody was carrying a different kind of weapon. Militia, I thought, about a dozen of them, heading up to our campsite. Just then the guy at the rear of the line noticed me. He started turning toward me, ready to yell out a warning to his comrades, his rifle swinging round with him.

I tossed the hot water in his face, dropped the coffee pot and ran like hell into the woods.

He screamed. There was the harsh crack of a rifleshot, then another and then a whole fucking chorus of gunfire as I ran into the woods, hunched down, my back suddenly feeling exposed and extremely itchy as I cursed myself for leaving my flak vest and helmet back at the tent. I swung to the right, past the trunks of some pine trees. There were snapping sounds and thunking noises as the fatal pieces of metal traveling toward me at thousands of feet per second struck branches or tree trunks instead.

I ran and ran, thinking I should head up to the left to warn the others. But then there was more gunfire, and the flat, heavy sound of an explosion. Charlie. Charlie was fighting back.

I stopped, leaned back against a birch tree, breathing hard. More gunfire. Another explosion. Distant yells. A gunshot or two. And then . . .

Car engines. Starting up. Revving up. Now moving off, now fading away, now quiet.

I clenched my fists, waiting. More quiet.

I was alone.

FOR AN HOUR or so I stayed in a hidey-hole where a tangle of tree trunks had fallen together near a swampy area. I crawled in and waited, trying to calm my harsh breathing, trying to quiet the thumping in my chest. I closed my eyes for a moment, just a second, really, trying to remember last night and Miriam. But all I saw was that line of armed militiamen, heading up to our campsite. I crouched as low as I could, trying to stop moving, trying to stop the rustling of leaves and branches. I waited, my throat dry and my chest tight. I looked up overhead at a tiny patch of gray, where the clouds still blocked the sky. I blinked and waited some more.

Some more gunshots, up on the hill where we had just been.

I waited some more. I coughed and rubbed my face.

The wind rose, rattling some branches, making me think that people were out there, waiting for me. I kept watch on the faint patch of gray.

I checked my coat. The pockets were empty. No hat. No gloves. No food. No water.

I eased back out of the hidey-hole, looked around. Poplars, bare blueberry bushes, dead swamp grass. Nothing else. I stood up, still breathing hard. I rubbed at cramps in my legs, tried to gauge where the sun was, up there beyond the clouds. The smart thing would be to start moving, moving real slowly, taking my time, heading out to the highway. Hide there by the roadway, wait for a UN convoy to come by. That would be the smart thing.

I rubbed my face again, looked at where I had come through, and gauged something else: where our campsite had been.

I didn't feel very smart.

But I did feel right.

I moved in that direction.

IT WAS SLOW going, pausing and waiting. I remembered a time when I was twelve or thirteen, going on a disastrous deer hunt with my father. One of those father-son bonding rituals that are supposed to bring one closer to one's dad or son, and which usually did exactly the opposite with us. I learned a lot of things back then—how I hated being cold and wet, how I hated getting up early and standing among the dark trees, and how I hated seeing an innocent deer being blown away by riflefire—but I also learned how to move through the woods. I learned to move as quietly as possible, pausing every now and then to look at the trees and brush and openings. I learned to look for shapes that didn't belong, that marred the background, because usually it meant that Man or his works were nearby. And the particular examples of Man and his works crawling around here this fine day were bent on slaughtering me and my workmates.

In any event, my caution meant that a fifteen-minute stroll back to our campsite took almost two hours, and that was no problem at all.

I came to a point where the trail emerged into the tiny clearing and I waited, kneeling behind a tree trunk, fists clenched on my thighs. One of the Land Cruisers was there, resting on flattened tires, windshield glass blown out and its white sides peppered with shrapnel and bullet holes. A couple of collapsed tents were strewn around, along with bits of clothing and other belongings.

But that wasn't what was bothering me.

The body beyond the Land Cruiser was bothering me.

I looked around, trying to see if anybody could be there, watching the scene. I knew I was balancing a couple of possibilities: possibility one was that a couple of the militiamen were hanging back, to see if I or any other UN worker was returning. Possibility two—the one I was gambling on—was that having completed their ambush they were now on the move, on the chance that a UN rapid-response force was riding to a belated rescue.

The body was still there.

I got up again and walked into the campsite, right up to the body near the shot-up Land Cruiser. I felt terribly exposed, like a naked Christian dumped in the middle of the Colosseum, and I wasn't sure if any lions or gladiators were around. But still, there was that body.

I got closer, looked down.

Sanjay Prith stared up at me, his eyes open and sightless.

I knelt down, automatically touched his throat, though the torn-up condition of his abdomen and lower legs told the story. Blood had caked and pooled around him. I hoped he had died quickly. His skin was dry and cold to the touch.

"Sorry, Sanjay," I said. "Sorry you had to end up here, so far from home."

I closed his eyes with my hand, tears starting to form in my own eyes. I moved closer to him, whispering, "If I'm ever contacted by anybody from New Delhi I'll tell them you were a hero, a true gentleman who did everything by the book. And I'll mean every word of that."

I STAYED ONLY a few minutes longer. A thought came to me that I should dig a grave for Sanjay, or at least cover him up, but a colder part of me took over. No, it could not be done. I didn't want to leave any evidence that I had been here.

The Land Cruiser was a charred hulk. The upholstery had burned away and the exposed bare springs of the seats looked odd. Among the debris of the campsite, I could see that our tents had been shot through and sliced by bayonets, as had the sleeping bags. I sniffed, and became nauseous as I saw that the attackers had relieved themselves on the scraps of the tents and sleeping bags, shitting and pissing everywhere. There was no food, no water, nothing I could take away with me. Just the soiled cloth and empty brass casings of cartridges, their dull brass color looking icy.

I also saw some blood trails leading back into the woods, and that colder part of me came back. I hoped that Charlie had charged a hefty toll before leaving.

I went back to my own tent, saw that my gear had been trashed as well. My Heinlein book was soaked through and its pages had been torn, but the Orwell book had survived. I stuffed it in an inside coat pocket—and then I saw something else that made my hands start shaking again.

A green flannel nightgown, torn and bloody.

Miriam.

I brought it up to my face. Then I let the cloth drop, and walked away from the campsite, not looking back once.

IT WAS A long afternoon. I headed away from the campsite, staying away from the road, moving at my own pace through the woods. I kept going at a constant rate, taking the time to scan around me as I tried to head toward the highway. As I moved I strained my ears to pick up any sound from the forest around me, waiting to hear a faint voice, a branch snapping or the sound of a rifle bolt being slammed home. And as I moved my thoughts whirled around in two separate vortices: anger and fear at the ambush I had survived, and anger and fear at having been abandoned. I knew the latter emotions made no sense at all. What could I have expected? That Charlie and the others would stay there, hoping I would make a triumphant return? Hell, no, they made the right decision, hard as it was. Leave me and the body of Sanjay behind. No doubt Charlie had taken control, and had made the tough and right decisions.

Still, I didn't like the feeling.

As the light started to fade I smelled something familiar, the stink of something that had burned. Then I saw spaces among the trees opening up and I noticed that a whole swath of birch and pine had burned away. Another battle site? I came closer, intrigued despite myself, and saw that large areas of earth had been churned up by chunks of metal. I stopped, looked around and up and saw how branches and trunks had been ripped down.

I looked back at the pieces of metal, saw the remains of an airplane engine.

Aircraft-debris field, a rational part of me observed. A jet had crashed here.

I walked around the crash site, sniffing again the old odor of fuel and plastic and metal, burned and crumpled and destroyed. Movies and television shows always depicted aircraft crash sites as being neat, with fuselage and other parts readily identifiable. But everything here was so charred and mixed up that it was hard to tell what the hell each item had once been. And just when I was ready to give up I came across a piece of wing. It had been charred along most of one side but I made out a national emblem: a black Maltese cross.

German, then, I realized as I looked down on the wing fragment. And I remembered that overpass, how it had been dropped and how the freeway on-ramps had been chewed up. A German Tornado, on a NATO mission to bomb that overpass—a mission that hadn't ended well.

I kept on moving, heading toward where I hoped the highway was.

CHAPTER THIRTEEN

About an hour after I found the crash site I stopped at the bank of a river, the water rushing past, rapids spewing up sprays of foam. I knelt down and took a swig of water, using both hands to form a cup, and then sat back against a moss-covered boulder. I took a deep breath, wiped my cold wet hands against my coat. It was getting dark and I had no idea where I was. I guessed that the highway was on the other side of the river, but with the light fading I didn't want to try to cross that surging torrent without a better idea of the surroundings. One misstep and a month or so later my father would get an interesting letter from the UN.

"Well, Boy Scout Samuel," I said out loud. "Time to find some shelter."

I went deeper into the woods so that the sounds of the river faded away some. I knew I was going to have a hard time sleeping tonight; I didn't want the noise of the rushing water back there to keep me even more awake. As I moved, I kept to the same pace that had kept me alive during the afternoon, pausing and looking about me, listening again to any sounds out there.

But so far everything had been fairly quiet, with just the chattering of the birds and the sounds of tree limbs knocking against each other every time the breeze came up. I walked for another ten minutes or so until I found a place where an evergreen was growing out of the side of a small rise. Earth had fallen away from around some of the roots, and by carefully digging a hole into the base of the root system I made a tiny cave. Working slowly and diligently—I didn't want to leave freshly disturbed piles of leaves or dirt lying about—I filled the little cave with leaves and boughs from another evergreen tree. It started to get even darker and I crawled into my little shelter, my head hitting the rough surface of its ceiling. Some earth trickled down the back of my neck. I coughed and managed to pull in a few additional boughs to block the narrow entrance. I lay back, pulled my collar up and put my hands inside the coat pockets. I listened, but all I could hear was my own breathing, labored and still frightened.

I shifted in the darkness, the leaves that I was lying on sounding very loud as I moved. My stomach rumbled with hunger and I licked my dry lips, wishing that I had drunk more back at the river. Of course, who knew what the hell was in the water I had just drunk, but I didn't care. I shivered some, crossed my legs, and stared up into the darkness.

I remembered being eight. I remembered my mother sitting with displeasure in the den, my father grabbing my hand and saying that he was going to break me of my fear of the dark, right then and there. I remembered being sent out into the rear yard, carrying blankets and a pillow. It had been a warm night. There was a quarter-moon up. It hadn't made a difference. I remembered this eight-year-old boy going from the front door to the rear one, trying to open them but finding both doors locked. I remembered the eight-year-old boy crying for his daddy, crying for his mommy, refusing to believe they weren't coming to get him. I remembered the eight-year-old boy being terrified at seeing all the lights in the house out, nothing there but a dark house, knowing that his mommy and daddy were asleep, ignoring their boy outside. I remembered the eight-year-old boy, huddled by the cellar door, blankets wrapped around him, shivering all night long, hearing the night noises, waiting and waiting for the sun to rise.

I remembered.

I shifted in my hole.

It promised to be a long night.

I AWOKE WITH a start, wondering why the tent was so cold and my damn sleeping bag was so lumpy. I moved some and listened to the noise of the leaves that cushioned me. Then I remembered, remembered everything, and my legs started trembling as I recalled the gunfire, the dirty and unshaven faces of the militia members, the bloody campsite and the body of

Sanjay lying there in the cold, so far away from his home in India. And, of course, the torn green flannel nightgown that belonged to Miriam, that had sweetly enclosed her body and had kept her warm, and was now a bloody and torn rag. I could not bear to think of what might have happened to her.

I shifted about some more and then froze. I heard voices, out there in the woods. I waited and tried to stay still. The voices were low and barely audible, and I couldn't even make out an individual word. Then there came the sound of a dog barking, and then another, and I shivered some more. Searchers, maybe, looking for that lone UN observer who had gotten away after scalding one of the militiamen. A dog barked again.

Hold on, the rational part of me observed. It didn't make sense that they would be looking for me, not at night, not in the woods. Too much trouble with flashlights and stumbling along the trails and such. No, it didn't make sense, not at all. Maybe there was a militia unit out there, maneuvering around, but it didn't mean they were looking for me. The rational part of my brain said, *Look, that doesn't make sense, not at all.*

I crossed my legs, tried to ease the shivering. It didn't work. The irrational part of my brain—which was in full control this dark night—was saying that it made perfect sense. Considering everything that had gone on before and the search for Site A and what I had seen, it made perfect sense that the hunters would be on the prowl.

I kept as still as possible. The voices faded away. There was one more bark from a dog, and then silence.

I stayed there, breathing evenly and slowly, waiting for the voices and the dogs to return.

ANOTHER START AS I woke up again, and there was no missing what had disturbed me: a flight of jets, low over the valley, their engine noise extremely loud. I turned on my side as the sound of the planes faded, and then there came several hollow-sounding *booms!* as the bombers dropped their ordnance some distance away.

Some cease-fire. Some armistice.

And another thing: during the much-censured bombing campaign that had finally brought about the armistice, NATO had been criticized for doing their job from so high up, at altitudes of five or ten thousand meters. Too many civilians had been killed in that pleasant euphemism known as "collateral damage," but since most NATO countries really didn't want to be here they sure as hell weren't going to expose their pilots to shootdowns, like the poor German pilot from that Tornado wreckage I had come across yesterday. But if what I had heard just now was any indication, the days of high-altitude bombing were over. These jets were low and their aim was definitely more accurate. Something had changed.

I shifted again, tired of hearing the leaves rustling. I remembered how much I had disliked being in that tent and sleeping bag—all right, before Miriam had come along, let's be real—but in the cold and damp and dirt I was now living in I would gladly have agreed to spend the rest of my life living in a tent in the common area of my apartment block back in Toronto—if only I could get out alive.

Out alive.

What a phrase. What joy in those two little words.

More jets overhead, and it was starting to make sense. I was able now to work it out from everything that had gone on these past few days. It was plain to see that the agreement had collapsed, that UN communications were being jammed, and any UN forces in-country were being hunted down and picked off, one by one, by the militia. Or by the death squads, if one was being impolite.

I sure hope Charlie was on the ball yesterday, I thought. Good ol' Charlie. Put in an impossible position to do an impossible job, and he had done well. It looked like everybody else had got out—leaving just me and Sanjay—and I hoped they had made it past the cease-fire lines.

Still more jets. I tried to ignore the thirst in my throat, the hunger in my belly and the cold everywhere.

MORNING, FINALLY. I stumbled out of my hidey-hole, stretched some and felt muscles and ligaments pop and creak. I watered a nearby tree, then went back to my hiding place and carefully covered it up. It had been a good location and if I couldn't make it across the river, or if something bad was going on—another euphemism for so many bloody possibilities—it was good to know that I had somewhere to hide out. I went back to the river, falling into the earlier routine of moving slowly, and I wondered whether, if I ever got back home, I would at least be able to talk to my father about how I had made my way through the woods and survived. Maybe he would appreciate what I had done. Maybe we would finally bond in that magical way that real fathers and sons supposedly share. Or maybe he would growl and grunt and go on for an hour about how I could have done everything better. Knowing my father, that would be the most likely possibility.

Back at the river I grabbed another sip of water, splashed some on my face, and then kept on heading downstream.

AND IT DIDN'T take long, much to my joy. After about ten minutes' worth of walking, the river widened some and slowed down, and there was an area of exposed rocks and sandbars that made it easy for me to get across to the other side. The gray clouds that had been overhead all the time during these past days had finally dispersed and it felt good to see the blue sky overhead. If Charlie and Jean-Paul and Miriam and Karen and, yes, even Peter were in a safe area, having clear skies would make extracting them by helicopter that much easier. Even if the communications gear was still being jammed, all they would need would be an exposed area of land, the sound of a patrolling NATO helicopter overhead and one shot from a flare gun.

Then—maybe—somebody would come looking for me.

In the meantime, I still had to find that damn highway. How hard could it possibly be?

Now I was on the other side of the river, I made it through some low areas of brush and bramble, actually eating some blueberries that had managed to hang on. But instead of quieting the hunger in my stomach, they made it worse. It was as if some ravenous beast inside my belly was now fully awake and on the rampage, demanding something to eat. My mouth watered as I remembered Tico's Place, a coffee shop about a block away from my old job at the Toronto *Star*, and how I could easily spend an hour there, eating my way through crullers, eggs—scrambled, over easy, any which way you wanted—and back bacon and sausage and—

I finally stopped drooling over my memories of food. The slope I'd been toiling up had flattened out—and I had found a road.

A damn road.

I knelt down and looked up and down it. It wasn't much of a road, just dirt and gravel, but it sure had been churned up some by heavy vehicles. I glanced again. Nothing. Just a dirt road, almost parallel to the river. I got up. Which way? Left or right? Just like that old short story, the lady and the tiger. Which door would be the right one? Which one would lead to death?

If I'd had a coin I would have flipped it. Instead, I turned left and started walking, if for no other reason than that if I headed to the right I would be going back to where the ambush had taken place. And that was unappealing, for so many reasons.

I WALKED SLOW but sure and after a while I came across something of an oddity: twice I noted a place at the side of the road where a wooden post had been sawed off. That's all. A wooden post, about the width of one's hand, sawed off by a chainsaw, it looked like. The second time I noticed it I searched the area to see if a signpost or something else had been taken down. But if it had, whoever had done the work had taken away the sign.

After about another ten minutes of walking, I found another signpost. But not one made of wood.

The road had curved to the right, and as I rounded the bend I saw something hanging from a tree. I ducked back into the brush on the side of the road, waiting. Nothing. Not a sound, not a movement. I waited some more, and then started walking through the brush, my feet sinking into wet soil. What I had noticed became clearer. It looked at first like a tangle of wires, as if someone had dumped some telephone cable in a tree. But then I saw something flapping there like a large banner, moving slightly with the wind. I walked closer, stopped, and then saw the shape.

I didn't move. I just stood there, fists clenched in my coat pocket.

I thought, just for a moment, about turning around and going back. I didn't want to see what was ahead.

But all that time, all that distance covered . . .

I shook my head and stepped out onto the road again, finally recognizing what I had seen. I stepped closer, now hearing the faint billowing sounds of the parachute flapping in the breeze. What I had thought were telephone wires were actually parachute cables. And dangling from them, like a store mannequin or some college mascot, was the body of a pilot. I came up to him, saw him hanging there about two or three meters up from the road. He had been dead a while, and somebody had stripped him of his boots and helmet. His dark green flight suit was intact, save for some rips, and his face was blackened and had shrunk some from exposure to the elements. It looked like he'd had a moustache. It was hard to tell. His hands too were black, as though they had turned to leather from being exposed. I looked closer, wanting to see if he had a name stripe on his flight suit, but most of his chest was obscured by a cardboard sign. The sign had been made from a flattened six-pack Budweiser beer carton, and had been fastened around his neck by a thick string. Written in thick letters on the sign was this:

THE REAL WAR CRIMINAL

I kept on looking at him, trying to think of what it must have been like, hanging up here exposed like this. This had to have been the Tornado pilot, the wreckage of whose plane I had found the day before. Shot down by the local militias who'd been using stolen Reserve or Guard munitions, he finds himself hanging in a tree. Maybe he's unconscious or semiconscious. All he wants is to get down to the ground safely. A few minutes earlier he had been emperor of his own little universe, safe and secure in his cockpit, an elite pilot in an elite force, with ego and attitude to match. Flying to save the urban civilians of this frightened nation, urban civilians emptying out from the cities, looking for food, looking for safety, looking for shelter. Then, in a blur of noise and pain and shock, he's ejected from that safe world and is now on the ground, the deadly ground. He's there, dangling, probably injured, unable to move much. And then the men come, the men who he hopes are his rescuers. But no, they're not his rescuers. It's worse than that, much worse. They're the people who live here, who have been bombed and strafed and targeted by him and others who have traveled thousands of kilometers to wage war on this country, and the people who live here aren't interested in rescue. They're interested in revenge, pure and simple.

God, I hoped it had been quick for him.

There was a faint creaking noise from the branch as he swung back and forth. Again, I thought that I should at least do the right and noble and civilized thing, which would have been to cut him down and bury him. But I chose the coward's route, yet again. If I did that, it would tell every death squad in the area that a stranger was around, someone who didn't belong, someone who himself should be hunted down. I couldn't take that chance.

I reached up—I wasn't sure why—to touch one of his bare feet, but he was too high off the ground. I resumed my lonely walk and after a minute looked back. I wished I hadn't: in the interim a crow or raven had perched on the dead pilot's shoulder, and had gone to work on his face with its sharp beak.

I kept on walking, and didn't look back again.

ANOTHER HUNDRED METERS, another signpost, but whoever had chopped this one down hadn't done a thorough job. Scattered in a drainage ditch were some color brochures of the kind handed out to advertise tourist attractions, and I pulled one free from the mud. Days of soaking and exposure had faded most of the photos and lettering, but what was visible told me where the road led—or had led—to, somewhere called Bronson's Works. I wasn't sure who Bronson was and what kind of work he did, but I probably had a fifty-fifty chance of finding out, depending where the dirt road ended up. The only other readable lettering was on the bottom side of the reverse of the brochure, in small letters:

NEW YORK PARKS COMMISSION
H. Lewis Tolman, Governor

I dropped the brochure and continued on my way. As it turned out, I didn't have that far to go.

THE DIRT ROADWAY widened some before it was abruptly blocked. Somebody had plowed up the surface into a thick earthen berm, and then, in a creative burst of landscaping, had covered it with shrubbery and other small trees. I climbed up the berm, pushed my way through the thick growth, and then stumbled and fell down the other side. I got up, brushed off my hands and clothes, and walked a little further before I came out onto pavement.

A real road, this time.

I looked back the way I had come. It was easy to see, close up, the work that had gone into making the berm, but to a truck or other vehicle speeding by, the dirt roadway would have been fairly well hidden. Bronson's Works or whatever was back there was no longer open for business. I rubbed my cold hands together, looked over my options. There weren't many. I turned to the right, started walking again. I felt exposed, out there in the open and in plain view, but I was tired of creeping through trees and brush, walking slowly, pausing every now and then to see if I was being hunted. It had been more than a full day since the attack on our campsite. Remembering what Jean-Paul and Charlie had said, I recalled that the militias didn't like to stay in one spot for too long: too many chances of being spotted and arrested or attacked. So the little group that had killed Sanjay and had sent me running was probably far away on the other side of the county by now.

Still, I kept my ears and eyes open, always looking behind me, ready to duck into the side brush and drainage ditch if I heard a vehicle. But there was nothing. It was all fairly silent, save for the sound of my feet on the cracked pavement. My hair felt greasy, my face was dirty and covered with stubble, and I was tired and still horrified at what had happened yesterday. But I was on the move, heading—I hoped!—to where the highway ran. And before I took too many more steps, I tugged off my TLD and tossed it into the ditch. No need to advertise that I wasn't from around here; the locals didn't carry such dosimetry. And worrying about radiation exposure at a time like this seemed to make as much sense as worrying about my *Star* retirement plan.

Twice I passed farmhouses set far back from the road. Both times I saw woodsmoke coming up from the chimneys. So families were still here, still living. Each time I considered going up to the house and perhaps wheedling some breakfast or directions. But each driveway had been blocked by a metal fence hung with signs that said NO TRESPASSING and NO SOLICITATIONS. Perhaps the signs were there just for show. Perhaps. But I kept walking.

Then the road climbed up some, and on the left-hand side I saw a large two-story frame building, with a porch and gas pumps out front. COOPER GENERAL STORE, said the black-and-white sign hanging over the steps leading up to the entrance. Out behind the store was a wire enclosure where a woman in jeans and a gray sweatshirt was feeding some chickens, scattering feed from a metal plate. She finished what she was doing and then entered the rear of the store, the door slamming hard behind her. I stopped, took in this domestic rural scene. The wind shifted—and then my stomach started grumbling, making a noise so loud that I'm sure farmers kilometers away could have heard me, for I had smelled fresh bread cooking. I started salivating so much that I had to spit on the ground, and I resumed walking. The store had rakes and shovels and other tools on the porch, and the two gas pumps had signs hanging from them, one saying NO GAS and the other saying DON'T EVEN BOTHER ASKING.

I stopped in front of the store, my need to keep moving running right up against my need to get something to eat and drink before I fainted. I licked my lips, looked up at the store and the door leading in. Yet another sign said OPEN.

Unbelievable. OPEN.

I checked my pockets. Empty. But in my wallet was a Canadian five-dollar note and some UN-issued scrip. I didn't want to try using either in this store. But there were credit cards in my wallet, MasterCard and Visa, and those little credit-card signs were snuggled up on the door, right next to the OPEN sign, meaning that this general store out in the middle of nowhere accepted credit cards.

OPEN.

I headed up to the entrance. After all, not only might I get something to eat—if I was lucky—I just might be able to get directions to the highway as well. It couldn't be that far to walk. And it'd be easier to walk on a full stomach, full of energy.

It made sense. It made good sense.

I walked up the porch, opened the door, and walked in.

A little bell over the door jingled as I entered, and I blinked my eyes, for the room was fairly dark. There were shelves of merchandise off to the right, mostly dry goods but some canned food, the cans lined up to make the shelves look full. The floors were wide and wooden, and had been worn down from years of use. To the left was a lunch counter, with a half-dozen stools lined up in front. Little metal napkin dispensers were each flanked by a menu and bottle of ketchup or mustard. It looked so damn homey and safe that it almost made me cry.

The woman I had seen earlier, out feeding the chickens, was behind the counter, working on a ledger. She looked up, curious. She seemed to be in her early fifties, face worn but pleasant, black hair streaked with gray pulled to one side.

"Help you with something?" she asked.

My legs started shaking, just from the sheer pleasure of someone asking me that. The sheer joy. "Yes," I said. "I was wondering if I could get something to eat. Some breakfast."

She shrugged. "If you're not looking for fancy, sure. But I gotta warn you. I haven't had meat in a while. So no ham, bacon or sausage. Or orange juice, either. Can cook you almost anything else with eggs, if you'd like."

My mouth started watering again. It had been more than a day since I had eaten. I cleared my throat and said, "Well, that would be great. But I have a little problem."

The woman turned a page of her ledger. "Problems in this county come by the bucketful. What's yours?"

I shrugged and said, "My car broke down, a couple of . . . a couple of miles down the road. Thing is, I left my cash back there, in the glove compartment. The only way I can pay for breakfast is through a credit card. Is that OK?"

She smiled slightly. "Mister, last year at this time I'd have told you that no, it wouldn't be OK. I'd have said that my policy was that only the store goods could be paid for by credit card. I wouldn't let anybody—and I don't care if they was my neighbors—I wouldn't let anybody pay for breakfast by credit card. But you know what? Like they say, shit happens. Sure. Have a seat."

I sat down and she got up, saying, "One more thing, though. You seem to be a nice enough lookin' fella and all, but I want to run that credit card through first. All right?"

"Sure," I said, opening up my wallet and passing over a Visa card.

She took it and said, "Thing is, if the phone lines are down, like most days, then you get a free ride no matter what."

"All right," I said, sitting there patiently, hands folded in front of me.

The woman went over to the cash register and ran my Visa card through one of those little machines that rule your credit rating. "Hah," she said. "I've got a dial tone. Then it's gonna be a good day. Took some rebuilding but the phone lines are back, some of the computers, and most days we got power for a while. Guess those assholes who nuked us won't keep us down long, right?"

I smiled and just nodded.

After some beeps and buzzes she smiled and came back and handed over the card. "You're good to go. What would you like?"

I smiled, hoping that drool wasn't running down my chin. "Sure. How about some scrambled eggs and toast?"

She nodded. "Two eggs OK?"

"Could I get four?" I asked.

The woman smiled. "My, you must have walked far. Sure. Four it is, though I'll have to charge you extra."

"That's fine."

"Extra toast?"

"Yes, please."

"I've got milk and coffee, though I can only give you one cup of coffee."

Hot coffee, I thought. Hot coffee and real eggs, not eggs served from a plastic pouch and made whole again with cold water.

She started working at the grill as things started heating up and sizzling. She slapped down a mug of milk and coffee in front of me and I put two sugars in the coffee and took a long, hot swallow. I wiggled my cold toes. Soon I'd be fueled up and ready to go. I asked, "Is the highway far from here?"

The woman's back was to me as she worked on the grill. "Oh, just up the hill and over to the right. There's an access road that hooks up to the interstate. You hopin' to hitch a ride or something?"

"I'm thinking about it," I said.

She turned, passing the plate of eggs and toast over to me. "Might be your best bet. If you're broke down like you said, Jake in town might be able to give you a tow, but I don't know if he's got any gas. Here, eat up, 'fore it gets cold."

I sprinkled salt over the scrambled eggs and ate two or three forkfuls so fast that I don't think I even tasted them. But my taste glands kicked in right away and I looked over at her and said, "Heavenly ambrosia. The best eggs I've ever eaten."

The woman seemed to blush. "Well, there's something to be said for farm-fresh eggs and homemade bread. Look, would you like some raspberry jam for your toast? No extra charge?"

"Only if it's no trouble," I said.

She waved a hand at me. "No, no trouble at all. It's back at the house."

"No, really, you don't have to," I said.

"Bah," she said, wiping her hands on a towel. "I've got to bring some over anyway. You just hold on."

I just smiled, my mouth full of food, and went back to eating as the woman went out the rear of the store. I carried on eating the scrambled eggs but forced myself to slow down—I didn't want to show my appreciation for this nice lady by suddenly getting sick and puking up on her country-store floor. I took a last bite of toast—real butter, strong and flavorful, nothing like the margarine grease I had been used to. Then the door at the rear opened up and she came back in.

But her hands were empty.

"Oh," I said. I was going to add that it was OK, I didn't need any raspberry jam at all, when three men came in behind her. They wore jeans and fatigue jackets, and had rifles slung over their shoulders.

I put the fork down slowly.

The main door to the store opened up and two other men came in, dressed like the first three. Muddy boots, jeans and slung weapons. Patches of some sort or other were sewn on the sides of their jackets, along with tiny American flags.

I swallowed the last of my breakfast.

CHAPTER FOURTEEN

My gracious host and cook was no longer smiling. "He gave me a credit card. It's from some bank in Toronto."

A little voice spoke up in my head, and it sounded distinctly like my father's. *Fool, fool, fool.*

The oldest man, heavyset and with a beard that came to the middle of his chest, looked at me. "Is that true?"

"Yes," I said.

"What's your name?"

"Samuel Simpson."

A man behind me said, "So. You from Toronto?"

"Yes."

"What the hell are you doing here?"

I looked down longingly at my empty plate. "Having breakfast."

A couple of the guys laughed, and then a hand fell on my shoulder. I kept on looking at the heavyset bearded man. "Not bad, mister," he said. "I'll give you that. But any more smart answers and Tom here's gonna whack you one. All right?"

"All right."

"What are you doing here?"

I sighed, looked at their faces, wondering if this was anything like what my grandfather had felt when the raid on Dieppe had gone so drastically wrong.

"Just walking around, checking things out," I said. "A tourist whose car broke down, that's all."

The bearded man nodded slowly. "Look, it'd be easier if you just gave it up, pal. I don't want no blood on Beth's floor here. That wouldn't be polite, now, would it?"

"No," I said, knowing the various forms of UN identification that were in my wallet. "It wouldn't be polite at all."

"The truth, then."

"Truth? The truth is, I'm assigned to an investigation unit with UNFORUS. I've gotten separated from my group, and I'm just here, having breakfast, and then I'm going to the highway."

I saw their faces change, all of them, as expressions darkened and eyes narrowed. Then the bearded guy said, "All right, then. You can finish your breakfast."

I wiped my face slowly with a napkin. "I already have," I said. "Just as well—I've lost my appetite."

The bearded man exchanged a look with the guy behind me who was holding on to my shoulder. Then the bearded man said, "Fine. You're now under arrest."

And then my arms were pulled back, and a hood was pulled over my head.

EVEN THEN, I was surprised at how polite they were. Two men helped me to my feet as another one finished binding my arms. My arms were tied together at the wrist, but not tight enough to cut off my circulation. The hood smelled of hay, and I was flanked on either side as two of the militiamen each grasped an elbow. They walked me to the store, opened the door and led me out, one of them saying, "Steps coming up, lower your foot down, there you go."

Behind me, the woman said, "Well, who's gonna pay for breakfast, then?"

A male voice: ". . . Got his goddamn credit card, now, don't you? Use that . . ."

I stood still, trying to calm my breathing, trying not to think of too much, except I was attempting to grasp what the bearded guy had said: I was under arrest. He didn't say I was going to be taken into the woods and shot, or out to a gravel pit and shot, or to the town square and shot. Not that these options weren't open to me—and to my captors—but I was hoping for a little wiggle room. "Where am I going?" I asked.

A nudge to the ribs. "No talking. And if you keep talking, you'll get the shit kicked out of you. OK?"

I didn't say a word, just stood there. Another—and sharper—nudge to the ribs. "Hey! I asked you a question. You understand?"

"I do understand," I said, letting impatience slip into my voice. "And you said no talking. So I kept my mouth shut."

The other guy laughed. "He got you there, Frank."

"Smart-ass fucker," Frank said. "You just keep quiet."

Through the hood I made out the sound of a truck engine, and then I was grasped again by the elbows. "OK," not-Frank said. "Up you go. The back of a pickup truck."

It was awkward, trying to ease my way up onto the bed of the truck with my hands tied behind me. Frank swore at me as I flailed around, but not-Frank gave me a boost. "Move it back, move it back," came a voice, and I slid my butt back against the metal bed until I bumped up against some canvas bags of something. There was the clump of boots and doors were slammed, and then we were off, bumping along the road. Something dull pressed against the back of my neck.

"Listen well, UN man," Frank said, "I've taken down a lot of fuckers like you without losing a wink of sleep, so do me a favor: try to escape. I'll blow your fucking head off, right here."

Not-Frank said, "Oh, calm down."

I didn't say a thing.

The truck swung around and we started going down the road. There had been movies and poorly made television shows that I'd seen in the past where the bound and blindfolded hero kept track of his progress by listening to passing sounds, by measuring the thumps of the tires against potholes and by gauging through some internal compass how many lefts and rights he took to his place of captivity.

I never said I was a hero. The only thing I could gauge was when we left the paved road for a dirt road. We traveled for a bit until we stopped, and Frank said, "George, c'mon, time for a search."

So George—previously not-Frank—helped me off and I stood by the side of the road, hearing the truck engine rumbling in front of me. Frank undid the ropes on my wrists and nudged me. "Strip," he said.

"Excuse me?" I asked.

"Strip. Take off your clothes. Remove everything you've got on, except for the hood."

I took a breath from inside the hood. "No."

George played good cop. "C'mon, guy, don't make a fuss. We don't have that much time."

"Nope."

Though I was expecting it, the blow to the back of my shoulders still stunned me. I fell to the ground, and then there were a few kicks before Frank, voice laboring from his exertions, said, "*Will* you take off your fucking clothes, huh?"

I gasped. "No. Take them off yourself if you're in such a fucking hurry."

Which was what they did—after a few more blows. In a couple of minutes I was standing there, swaying back and forth, naked in the cold except for the hood. I could hear Frank and George murmuring and then my clothes and boots were dumped at my feet. "Here. Dress yourself. But keep the damn hood on or we'll shoot you."

It was hard going, but I managed. As I struggled to finally get my boots on, I said, "What was that all about?"

Frank didn't say anything. But George, again seemingly playing good cop, said, "You look like a smart guy, all things considered. I'm sure you can figure it out."

I got everything back on and said, "My watch?"

"Sorry," Frank said, laughing. "Confiscated. Hey, George, you want the book?"

George said, "Nah. I've got plenty of books. Orwell, huh? I remember reading one of his books back in high school. *Nineteen Eighty-Four*, it was called."

Frank said, "Was it any good?"

"Shit, I don't know. Couldn't finish it. Cribbed from *Cliff's Notes* for the term paper I had to write. Here you go." George stuffed the book back inside my coat and I was led back to the truck. As George was helping me up, I muttered, "Tracking device."

"Huh?"

I raised my voice. "You're looking to see if I'm carrying some sort of tracking device. Am I right?"

George said nothing, but Frank said, "Yeah, I guess you're a smart one. Yep, looking for a tracking device. Just in case you were a plant, being sent to infiltrate one of our base camps. Set up a homing signal for some of those fuckers to bomb us."

Another nudge. "Just be glad you don't have any fresh scars, you know? Heard from some militia groups in Idaho, by shortwave, that some UN guys were infiltrating their base camps with tracking devices that had been surgically implanted. So. Like I said. Be glad you don't have any fresh scars."

"And why is that?"

George sounded apologetic. "We would have shot you at the side of the road."

Though they didn't ask me to, I kept quiet for the entire rest of the trip.

ABOUT FIFTEEN OR so minutes later we passed through two checkpoints, the truck having slowed down considerably. I could make out a variety of sounds—people talking, machinery, other vehicle engines—and the smell of woodsmoke. The truck came to a stop and once again I was helped off. My hands were untied and the hood was removed, and I stood there blinking, taking it all in. We were in a wooded area that had been cleared of brush and saplings, so only the taller evergreens shaded us from overhead. In front of me was an old school bus up on cement blocks, its yellow paint faded away almost to a dull white, the tires rotting in places, parts of the sides rusting away. The bearded guy who seemed in charge came up to me. "Here's the rules. In there—" he motioned to the school bus "—is your new home. You go in there and stay still until we come for you. There's a potty in the rear. You come out the door, you look out the windshield or windows, and you're a dead man. Understood?"

"Yes," I said. "Can I ask a question?"

"Sure," the bearded man said.

"You said I was under arrest," I said. "What's the charge?"

"Crimes against humanity," the bearded man said, without a trace of humor.

I WENT INTO the school bus, recalling all the times that I had climbed these same types of metal steps on my way to school when I was younger, dumber and sure as hell a lot happier. But I had never been in a bus like this before. It had been adapted for its new use: most of the seats had been unbolted and taken out. I walked down the aisle, past soiled mattresses lying on the metal. The floor creaked as I went to the rear where a green wool blanket hung, concealing a chemical toilet. Someone had come in earlier, painting the windows and the windshield black, and tiny white light bulbs, looking like they came from a Christmas tree, provided a little illumination. I sat down on one of the surviving seats, rubbed my wrists and my hands and face, and waited. The bus smelled of grease, old clothes and stale air, and fear. Especially fear.

There were faint noises coming in from outside, and still I sat there, waiting. Not good, not good at all. But at least I had been arrested. I had been arrested for something—nutty as it sounded—so at any rate I was still breathing.

But until when? Nobody at the UN knew I was alive. Nobody at the UN knew where I was. And, judging by how stealthily these militiamen had brought me in, I doubted that the UN knew the location of this particular camp.

I shifted around, thought about all the children who might have ridden in these very same seats; wondered if they had grown up and were now busily slaughtering their long-distance neighbors who were coming up here for help. I looked at the window, saw something. I went closer and saw that somebody had carefully scraped away a bit of the black paint, allowing a tiny peephole to the outside. I remembered the warning—look out the windshield or the windows, you're a dead man—but I couldn't see how I could be caught.

But still . . .

I hesitated only for a moment. Had my grandfather hesitated at Dieppe? I looked closer out the window, saw the campsite. The grounds had been cleared of underbrush and other barriers, leaving tall evergreens and other trees. Camouflaged netting had been stretched between the tree trunks, hiding the complex from prying eyes overhead. If the militiamen could keep their machinery and fires under control, then thermal detection could be thwarted. Sure, maybe a spy satellite could peer through almost everything—I knew that some of the American satellites had wide-range radar that could penetrate the overhead netting—but since the Russians weren't cooperating in this UN mission and the American satellites obviously weren't available, I could see how this camp had remained hidden.

In front of me were mobile trailers, tents, pickup trucks and groups of armed men who were moving about, eating, talking among themselves or cleaning their weapons. There were even a dozen or so horses, off to the left, grazing peacefully from oatbags hung around their necks. I got up and went to the other side of the bus. The same type of peephole had been scraped away, but the view here was not as interesting: just a cleared lane of dirt and a woodline a few meters away, and a few strands of rusting barbed wire stretching away on both sides. That was all. Below the window someone had carved a message into the paint. I looked closer, felt a chill as I saw a Star of David, and below that, in tiny letters: *S. Steinberg, please remember me*. I went back to the seat, sat still for a moment and then looked at my wrist. No watch, of course. Confiscated earlier. I reached into my coat pocket, took out my book of Orwell essays, and settled down to read.

There was nothing else I could do.

LOST IN THOUGHT after reading an essay about Orwell's experiences in the Spanish Civil War, I jumped as the door up forward slammed open and a younger militiaman came in. His face was shadowed with stubble and his head was almost fully covered with a black wool cap.

"Come along," he said.

I kept the book open, not knowing why I was doing what I was doing, only that it felt right. "You didn't say the magic word."

The militiaman looked confused. "What do you mean, 'the magic word'?"

"Please," I said. "*That*'s the magic word."

He shrugged, reached under his coat, pulled out a pistol. "Here's my fucking magic words: Smith and Wesson. How about that?"

I closed my book, put it back in my jacket. "They'll do."

I got up and headed to the front of the bus, the floor creaking again under my weight. Outside, two more militia members flanked me and I fell in with them. Again, this is the place in the movie where the hero overpowers the armed militiamen, hot-wires a pickup truck with a paper clip and a snappy quip, and then roars away to safety. But this particular hero just shivered and looked around at the campsite. It looked like nearly a hundred people were living there, under the trees and in the trailers and tents. I saw a number of women and children as well as the men I'd already noticed. If there was any particular uniform, it was blue jeans or camouflage pants plus military-surplus jackets. Almost every person I saw was carrying a weapon, even the women and some of the children. Two of the kids, young boys about nine or ten, pointed guns at me and made shooting noises. I flinched, making one of my escorts laugh. "Don't worry, UN man," he said. "Those guns are just plastic."

"For now," the other one said.

I kept quiet.

At the nearest trailer, a militiaman standing guard opened the door and I went in. I noticed something odd on the side of the trailer, two words painted in red. *RED RULES!* This trailer looked like it had once been a residential home, but the chairs and couches had been taken away. The small room, with thick soiled carpeting, had a wooden desk in the center, and behind the desk was the same bearded man who had arrested me back at the general store. At each side of the desk stood an American flag and another flag sporting a blue ensign and seal that I couldn't recognize. In front of the desk was an empty chair, straight-backed and wooden. My escorts stayed behind at the door. The bearded man looked up at me and said, "Have a seat."

"All right, I will," I said, taking the empty chair.

The bearded man picked up a pen and prepared to write on a yellow legal pad. "The name is Saunders. Royal Saunders. I'm colonel-in-chief of the Free Columbia Militia. Your name?"

"Simpson. Samuel Simpson."

"Where are you from?"

"Toronto, Ontario."

"Age?" Saunders asked.

"Twenty-six."

The pen moved rather delicately, considering how large Saunders's hand was. If I had been a prisoner of war I guess I could have gotten away with name, rank and serial number. But I'd been told in my training—which seemed like a lifetime ago!—that if captured one should cooperate as much as possible. What would be the point otherwise?

"Occupation?"

"Current or prior?"

"Let's start with prior," Saunders said.

"A reporter with the Toronto *Star*."

"And currently?"

I looked at that calm bearded face, a face that wouldn't have looked out of place anywhere in Toronto, at the CN Tower or the Astrodome, the face of a man who was judging my fate. I cleared my throat. "Special investigator, UNFORUS."

Somebody behind me muttered something. Saunders motioned with his free hand. "For those of us who don't know acronyms, could you explain what 'UNFORUS' stands for?"

I had a feeling that he was playing with me, but I went along with the game anyway. "United Nations Force in the United States."

"Where did you train?"

"Ottawa, to start. Then here in Albany, where I was assigned to my unit."

"Uh-huh," Saunders said. "And who invited this force into our country?"

I didn't answer.

Saunders looked up from the legal pad. "I asked you a question, Samuel. Who invited this force into our country?"

"I think you know who."

A slight smirk. "Since I'm the one asking the questions, I want the answers from *you*. So, Samuel, who invited this force into our country?"

Third time lucky. "A Security Council resolution, which authorized UNFORUS after the terrorist attack on New York City and the balloon strikes last spring resulting in the . . . disorders and riots in certain states. You know that's why the UN came in."

"A resolution. A piece of paper. And it gave you and everybody else reason to invade us, is that right?"

"The Security Council authorized the force, because of the . . . the disturbances taking place here. That's why. Even the American ambassador to the UN didn't vote against the resolution. He abstained. Even your President didn't come out directly to oppose it. Some of your senators and congressmen were even in favor of the intervention. Which enabled the resolution to pass, which in turn authorized the creation of UNFORUS."

"And how long did that traitorous ambassador live after that vote? One week? Two weeks? Even with him being in Geneva and all?"

"I don't recall."

"And why did you join this force?"

I shrugged. "You wouldn't believe me if I told you."

"Try me."

"I like the States. Always have. And when the troubles started, well, I wanted to do my part to help out. I was bored with my reporting job. I thought I could make a difference by signing up with the UN."

"By spying against us?" Saunders asked sharply.

"I wasn't spying."

More murmuring behind me. Saunders talked lower and slower, like he was trying to make a point. "You're a foreigner. You're in this country illegally. You and the rest of your crew have high-tech surveillance and tracking equipment. We don't care what you say about why you're here. We know your real mission. You're identifying targets, identifying areas to strike, for the next round of attacks, to weaken us even further."

"I wasn't spying."

Saunders went on as though he hadn't heard me. "Bad enough that you and the other UN folks snuck in after the bombings and the balloon strikes, killing more of us and forcing us to accept your intervention. Now you're setting us up for the next round of attacks, even worse than before. Take away our sovereignty. Take away our flag. Take away our guns."

"Sure," I said. "That's our secret plan. Take away your guns. You see, we have this funny little idea about men and guns. We think it's a bad thing when men with guns start killing their neighbors, start raping their women, slaughtering their children, shooting them in hotels or buses or cars. We think it's a bad thing when—for whatever reason—the local, state and federal governments seem incapable of preventing such slaughter. That's why we're here. To stop the killing and document what happened—and to prosecute the guilty."

Someone behind me whispered, "See? They admit it. They're here to take everything away from us."

I rubbed at my eyes. "Listen, do you folks know anything about sarcasm? Do you?"

Saunders stared right at me. "We know a lot of things. We also know that you and your kind don't belong here."

"There's been an agreement, an armistice."

He made a motion with his hands. Then, in a blur of activity, I was grabbed and wrenched back as the chair was pulled away. I fell on my butt and then the kicking started as I turned over and tried to protect my head with my hands and arms. I rolled around the floor, screeching and hollering, remembering my earlier training: if you're ever attacked, make a lot of noise. It'll either attract help or it will satisfy your attackers that they are doing enough damage.

No help was likely anytime soon, but I guess the second part worked because the kicking didn't last that long. They stopped and I lay there as Saunders leaned over his desk and said, "Can you sit up?"

"I think so."

"Then do it."

I sat up, my ears ringing. The inside of my cheek hurt where a kick had slammed it against my teeth. I looked behind me at the two militiamen, who were breathing hard, faces red, looking pretty satisfied with themselves. Then I stood up, weaving back and forth, and limped over to the chair, where I sat down.

Saunders also sat back down. "You asked me earlier if I knew anything about sarcasm. I'll tell you what I know. 'Sarcasm' is in the dictionary, just before 'shithead.' Understand?"

I gingerly touched the edge of my jaw. "Yeah, I do."

"Good," Saunders said. "Samuel, this was a lousy interrogation. You should think of doing better next time. Or else we're gonna start by breaking your fingers. All right?"

I just looked at him, said nothing. Saunders said, "Fine. Take him back to the bus. And in case you haven't figured it out, the armistice is over."

I guessed it was.

CHAPTER FIFTEEN

Back in the bus, I went to the rear and used the chemical toilet, where the shakes started and where I vomited into the filthy plastic bowl. I rinsed out the bowl. There was a bucket of water by the toilet and I used it to wash my hands and face. Then I went back to the main part of the bus. A plastic shopping bag that said PRICE CHOPPER on the side was on one of the seats. I opened it up and found a hard stick of salami, some bottled water and a piece of cheese. The seal around the water bottle was unbroken, and it looked like the salami and cheese were also firmly sealed.

So what?

If they wanted me dead, I doubted that poisoning would be their method of choice. I sat on the seat and ate the meal, the salami's saltiness making the wound in my cheek sting. I sipped at the water and saved half the bottle. The tiny bulbs were still burning, and I began to appreciate the ridiculousness of having Christmas lights illuminating this deceptively peaceful and actually deadly little scene. I found the green wool blanket and wrapped myself up. It was getting colder, and it didn't look like there was a stove or a heater in here. I pulled out my trusty Orwell and started reading. Then I put the book down. There was a commotion of some sort going on outside. I moved over to the other side of the bus, went up to the little peephole. Out under the trees there was a cluster of militiamen, and when they moved I saw that they were escorting four or five men. In the lengthening shadows it was hard to see who they were, but as they got closer I saw that they were all dressed in uniforms. Their arms were bound in front of them, they were barefoot, and on two of them I glimpsed blue brassards on their shoulders. UN forces. Irish, British, Canadian, Hungarian, Egyptian . . . who could tell?

But they were prisoners now, that was easy to see.

Then things got hellish, quite quickly.

One of the prisoners at the end of the line suddenly spun around and made a run for it to the woodline. "Jesus," I said out loud. "Don't do it."

There were shouts and the other prisoners fell flat on their faces. After another couple of shouts one of the militiamen raised his rifle and popped off three or four rounds, the muzzle flashes very bright. The soldier trying to make a run for it flopped to the ground without making a sound. More shouting, and the militiamen kicked at the prisoners lying in the dirt as if it was their fault. A couple more militiamen and some militia women came up and examined the shot prisoner, and he was dragged away. His comrades were kicked again, then dragged to their feet and they started shuffling away once more. Not one of them looked back at the body being dragged away. Not one.

I moved away from the window and then stretched out on the mattress. I stared up at the metal ceiling of the school bus, trying not to think about anything much. Later the lights slowly dimmed until they were barely glowing and I kept on staring up, still trying not to think. I got up and looked outside for one last time and saw that almost all the lights in the camp were dimmed as well.

Night had fallen.

LATER IN THE night there was the sound of helicopters, low overhead. I rolled off the mattress and went to the window again, my heart thumping. A UN raiding party, maybe—God, wouldn't that be wonderful. A quick search-and-rescue, and I could be out of here in a matter of minutes.

But no rescue arrived. I looked out the window into blackness. All the lights were off, not a single one showing. Damn, the militia were good. The faintest sound of something overhead, and everything went dark. The noise of the helicopters grew louder and louder until I could almost imagine them overhead, searching. If I'd had matches or a flare or something, I think even I would have had the stones to break out and make some sort of signal. But all I had were my empty hands, clenched in frustration, as the helicopter-engine noise started to fade away.

I stepped back from the window and then was startled so much that I almost banged my head on the school-bus ceiling as the front door scissored open and cold air came in, along with a flashlight beam. I remembered the warning I had received earlier about staying away from the window, and I thought this was it, I had been spotted. I'd be dragged out and shot, just like that UN soldier earlier.

"Hey!" came a voice. "Back away—show me your hands!"

I did just that. There was some confusion up front and a man stumbled forward and slumped onto his knees. A militiaman was behind him, holding a flashlight, the same young guy who had showed me his Smith and Wesson.

"Hope there's room at the inn, 'cause you've got to share quarters," he said, stepping back outside. "And remember the rules. No looking out or sneaking out, or you're dead men."

The door squeaked shut and the man in front of me moaned some, and then rolled over and sat up. The side of his face was covered with dirt and looked bruised. He seemed a few years older than me and was dressed in khaki slacks and a dark blue sweater and sneakers. His hair was dark and he had a nicely trimmed beard. He rubbed at the side of his head and looked over at me.

"Who are you?" he asked.

"Since I've been here longer, I think you should start," I said.

"Ouch," he said, pulling his fingers away from his head. "The name is Gary Nealon. And yours?"

"Samuel Simpson."

"Uh-huh," he said. "And why are you the guest of our fair county militia this fall evening?"

"I'm from Canada," I said.

Gary shook his head. "If you were from France, I could understand. But why Canada?"

I folded my arms. "Because I was in the employ of the United Nations, that's why. And you? What's your story?"

He leaned up against one of the few remaining bolted seats. "Ah, I'm here because of a very nasty and dastardly crime," he said.

"Which was what?"

"Being a schoolteacher and teaching the truth," Gary said.

"Oh."

He shook his head, managed a smile. "Doesn't sound like much, but in this time and place I'm afraid it's now a capital crime. Tell me, could I bother you for some water?"

I thought about going back and picking up the plastic bucket at the rear, but looking at what had just happened to him and what he had said,

I handed over my bottle of water. He examined it and said, "Your last water?"

"Back behind the blanket there's a chemical toilet and a bucket for washing up that has some water."

He started to get up. "Then I'll use that . . ."

I pushed him down gently. "No, it's fine. Drink from the bottle. I'm sure we'll get some more supplies in the morning."

Gary undid the cap and said, "Then you're a romantic, aren't you?"

"So I've been accused."

He took just a couple of sips, and then passed the bottle back. He said, "Been here long?"

"Just about a day."

"And what were you doing for the UN?"

"Investigating war crimes."

"Oh. Sounds very serious."

"It *was* very serious," I said, "though it seemed like most of the time we drove around in circles, finding a whole lot of nothing. Until just the other day, when we came upon a TV crew from Australia that then got ambushed."

"Prying eyes," Gary said. "The first rule of authority. Keep prying eyes away."

"They sure seem to be doing a good job."

"What are you? A lawyer? A coroner? A forensics investigator?"

I took a sip of my own and then put the bottle down. "I used to be a newspaper reporter. Now . . . well, my job with the UN was to document what we were finding. That's what I was doing."

He nodded. "How did you get captured?"

"By being stupid."

"Ah, well, most people don't get captured by being smart."

I laughed. "Good answer. Well, truth is, I had been separated from my unit and was trying to make my way to the interstate, hitch a ride on a UN convoy. I was almost there, about a day and a half without eating, when I stopped at a general store to get some breakfast. Then I was captured at the end of my meal."

"Cooper General Store?"

"Yep."

"Ah, the folk who run that are the Saunders family. Very tight with the local politics and militia. Your bad luck to go there."

"Sure, bad luck. Beats blaming the people on the ground, right?"

Gary grinned and said, "Blame? Samuel, there's so much blame to go around that we'd need a convoy of tractor-trailer trucks to do the job right. But do you know who I blame? Do you?"

"I have a feeling you're going to tell me, no matter what I say."

"Doctor Stanley Milgram of Yale University, more than fifty years ago. There's your man."

"Excuse me?"

Gary kept the smile on his face, like he was enjoying being back in a classroom, even a classroom that was a prison. "Oh, I'm sure the name doesn't mean much to you, but I'm equally sure his experiments do. He was the gentleman who decided to see how far people would go in following orders, no matter how distasteful those orders might be. His studies were so controversial that he was almost forced out of teaching, and his contemporaries—instead of plumbing into what he had discovered and its implications—spent their time criticizing his research and his theories."

I half-remembered a dull day at an introductory psych course, back in college. "Electroshock, am I right?"

If he'd been in the mood to clap his hands, I'm sure Gary would have done just that. "Yes, exactly. Electroshock. The active participants in the study were told that their job was to assist in an intelligence-testing session. But the supposedly passive study members had electrodes hooked up to them, and the purpose was to give them an electric shock each time they got an answer wrong."

"But it was a fake, right? Nothing was hooked up. The 'passive' study members weren't being shocked at all."

Another eager nod. "Yes, you're right. But the real point of the experiment was to see how far the active participants would go in shocking a perfect stranger, somebody they had never even met before. They were told that each subsequent shock would be stronger than the previous one, and they could even hear the subjects on the receiving end screaming, and you know what? Most of them kept going, all the way to when it looked like the subjects were going to be severely injured. Or even killed."

"A hell of an experiment," I said.

"Yes, yes, a hell of an experiment," Gary said, now looking around the school bus. "Which brings me to my current state, I'm afraid. I was using Doctor Milgram's research in my high-school class, and discussed another set of parameters, about another even larger experiment, based partially on his research. The bottom line, of course, is what people will do when they are just following orders, when they don't see another human being as a real person but only as an object. I even used some materials from the Iraqi prison scandal of a few years back when our soldiers—our brave, wonderful soldiers—were attacking Iraqi prisoners with German shepherd dogs."

From outside I could hear some yelling, which then stopped. "I take it your teaching was a bit more contemporary."

"Oh, yes, very current," Gary said, his smile fading now. "All I had to do was to mention what happened last spring. The attack on Lower Manhattan, followed by the balloon attacks themselves. The electromagnetic pulses wiped out most electronic devices in a good chunk of the nation. In the major metropolitan areas, people started to stream out when there was no more food, no more running water, when the ATMs and the gas stations wouldn't work. Police were overwhelmed. Governors whose National Guard units were overseas . . . they threw up their hands as well. Remember the chaos some years ago from that Hurricane Katrina that struck Louisiana and Mississippi? Imagine a thousand Katrinas, all at once, all across a good portion of this country, with no federal help coming. None."

I just nodded, remembering that day and the grim weeks and months that followed, watching the developing news from my safe home in Toronto, watching the horrors unfold, feeling like a helpless neighbor watching the house up the street get destroyed by fire.

Gary sighed, rubbed his pants legs. "Oh, how quickly it all fell apart that week, Samuel. With no official news, no official word of what had happened, rumors spread . . . and, of course, one thing that made it worse was that nobody took credit for the attacks. There were the usual nut-jobs who did . . . but even today we don't know who did it. We just know *what* they did . . ."

"Rough times," I said.

"Oh, yes, rough times indeed," he said. "Imagine you're living in a small rural town . . . say, in upstate New York. Your phones don't work, there's no television and no internet, and what news you do get is spotty. Some sort of nuclear strike against the nation . . . that's it. And the attending chaos. And you, in this small town, you think you can make it. It'll be a struggle, but you and your neighbors, you and your small farms and businesses, you can make it by stretching things, by working hard, by muddling through."

I rubbed my cold hands. "Then the refugees show up."

"Exactly," Gary said. "Thousands of people from the big city arrive . . . people who don't know where milk comes from, where meat comes from, where almost everything else comes from. They just know they're frightened, tired, hungry and thirsty. And there's thousands of them, on all the roads leading away from the big cities . . . hell, even from some of the mid-size cities. And you, in this little town, you're overwhelmed. You don't know what to do. Instead of love thy neighbor, you quickly learn to ignore thy neighbor, move thy neighbor along to the other town, and, soon enough, hate thy neighbor. With cops outnumbered and the National Guard overseas, volunteer militias spring up all across the affected areas. And then the killings begin."

I looked at this teacher under arrest. "You actually went out and taught that? All of that?"

"Pretty stupid, huh?" he asked.

"Or pretty brave," I said. "Though teaching the truth has often got people into trouble, over the years."

"Ain't that right." Gary drew his legs up and hugged his knees. "I've told you the truth as I saw it, as I taught it. Here's the other side of the coin, from the patriotic folks who've put us in these charming accommodations. It's not their fault that the bombs went off. It's not their fault that big cities couldn't protect their own. And it's not their fault that they had to organize, reach for their own weapons, when no one else could help them. They had to protect their families and their neighbors, and as rough as what happened was, they did what they could . . . until the dreaded UN showed up."

"Hell of a thing, still, what happened here," I said.

The little Christmas lights in the school bus flickered once, tossing odd shadows around the interior. Gary said, "We have a tradition here in this fine little country of settling our disputes with firearms. You being from Canada, I'm sure you're aware of that."

"True," I said. "It's been said that in your country you *conquered* your West. In Canada, we *negotiated*. Hey, I've got a question."

"Go ahead."

"I saw something painted on the side of a trailer. *Red Rules!* Saw the same sign a couple of days ago, painted on the side of a house. What does that mean?"

Gary said, "You don't know? Honestly?"

"Honestly."

His face looked mournful now. "*Red rules*. The motto of the ruling political class. The one overruling symbol of what happened after the bombings. Ready for another lecture, student?"

I said, "We've got time, I guess. Go on."

"All right. Look, years and years ago, when presidential elections were held the news anchors had maps that showed each state. Whenever a candidate won a state, that state would go either red or blue. Pretty soon it was almost a joke: red state versus blue state. People in one state would make jokes about the others, about them being godless fag-lovers or right-wing gun nuts. Then the smart boys who ran elections figured you could break it down even more. Red county versus blue county. But why stop there, right?"

"Sure," I said. "Success breeds success."

Gary nodded. "They got it down to red town versus blue town . . . still more insults, still more hate, still more rough words. Then the attacks . . . and when the people from blue cities show up in red towns, looking for food, they find well-armed red-town residents, who don't want to help. Red rules, my friend, at least around here, and don't forget it."

"I won't."

"OK. I answered your question. Now it's my turn."

"Fair enough."

He shifted his legs. "Tell me about your work here. Is it really on the up-and-up?"

"Excuse me?"

Gary shrugged. "This is a time when rumors—either on the internet or on the radio—are the most popular form of news. Rumors are that the UN crews in-country are doing more than just administering the armistice and hunting down war criminals."

I was getting cold so I took one of the green wool blankets and wrapped it around my shoulders. "Well, everything I've done since I've been here has been on the up-and-up. My unit was investigating war crimes, that's all. We chased down leads and carried out investigations."

"Find anything?"

"Just recently," I said sharply. "Like I said, we ran into an Australian television crew that was later murdered. And just before I got separated from my unit one of my co-workers was shot and killed. So, yeah, you can say we've found some things."

"Hmm," Gary said. "But the news I heard is that most of the UN units in this area are hunting down mass graves, right? Something called Site A. There's some sort of deadline coming up at The Hague, and if that Site A is not found the New York militia commanders at The Hague will be cut loose."

"True."

Gary smiled. "Well, good luck, then, in finding it."

"I don't think I'll be finding it tonight."

"Of course. And if not you, then good luck to your comrades. I would love to see those militiamen out there get what they deserve."

"Who wouldn't?"

Another shake of the head. "It'll take a lot of work on your part, you know. Even with the violence . . . people still have suspicions about you and your friends. In war, truth is the first casualty. The stories are about mass graves being chased down by nice folks like yourselves, running around in circles. Which is where the rumors start, about what some people think your real mission is."

"And what kind of rumors are those?"

"The usual. That having you in here is payback for all the times that UN and U.S. inspection teams have gone poking around in other countries. That Russia, Iraq, Iran, China, Serbia . . . Well, you get the idea: all those countries love the idea of coming in here and lording it over these poor Americans. That you're actually performing intelligence-gathering, identifying National Guard or Reserve armories, as well as militia strongholds. Hell, there are even rumors in some bases the UN crews are confiscating nuclear weapons. Disarming the last world superpower—which is also a rogue nation that ignores world opinion—and finally bringing it to heel."

"One-world government, right?"

Gary laughed. "Yeah, crazy shit like that. For fifty or so years, among the paranoia class, there's always been a fear that the UN—which most years is in debt and can't do much more than design a nice Christmas stamp—would come in and set up a one-world government under control from Geneva. Like the bureaucrats in Brussels overseeing Europe. And so here you are, a little late but running around with your blue berets and blue helmets. Hard not to understand why some people would see it like that."

Even though I was enjoying the conversation, I was getting tired. "Look. We're not spies for one-worlders in Geneva. We're just here to help stop the killing of innocent people, and help arrest and convict those who did. That's all. And that's what I'm going to tell that militia leader the next time he interrogates me."

"Interrogate? Really?"

"Yes," I said. "Interrogate. Why are you surprised?"

Gary managed a weak smile. "I'm envious more than I'm surprised. That means they think you're important enough to keep around for a while. Me? Well, it's a different story."

I pulled my blanket tighter around me. "What do you mean?"

"They already know my story, know my background. They have no interest in interrogating me. You see, Samuel, I've already been found guilty. Of treason, among other things. And the sentence for that is death."

WE TALKED FOR a little bit more, and then set up our sleeping arrangements. We both took a mattress and a single wool blanket, and stretched out on the soiled material. I lay there in the semi-darkness, waiting, shivering, knowing it would take an Act of God to get me to sleep this night. A few feet from me, Gary the schoolteacher lay still as well. I could not imagine what was going on in his mind this night. I had become irritated by his endless talking and lecturing earlier, wanting just to lie down and get some sleep, but now I knew why he had been gabbing so much: he was terrified, and needed someone to talk to. That was all.

I rolled over on my mattress, heard some sounds coming from Gary. He moaned and kicked—kicked out so far, in fact, that he actually struck my mattress. I got up gingerly and moved it further toward the side wall of the school bus, near the hump where the left rear wheel was. I gasped as my fingers struck a piece of rusted metal that was sticking up from the floor. I felt my fingers but didn't feel the telltale warm stickiness of blood so I stretched out on the mattress again, pulled the musty blanket over me, and listened to Gary have his nightmares.

A NUDGE. I woke up. Gary was standing over me. "You should come see this. Hurry up."

I got up from my mattress, rubbed at the crust in my eyes. My mouth tasted awful and I needed to pee, but Gary's face was white with shock. "Hurry up—back here. I saw it while I was using the toilet."

He sure had been using the toilet, for the stench was so strong that I had to breathe through my mouth. Gary said, "Take a look—over there on the left."

The rear window of the school bus had received the same paint job as the other windows and, just as before, someone had scraped a little patch clear for a peephole. "Look," Gary said. "Look there."

I bent down and placed my face near the glass. I had not seen this view of the camp before. The tents were thinned out, and I could see a clump of men and what looked like an open pit. One of the men was dragged from the group by some militiamen and then forced onto his knees. I rubbed at my eyes, not wanting to see what was going to happen next but knowing full well that I *had* to see it. It was my job. No matter my circumstances or where I was, it was my job.

The man kneeling down by the pit was suddenly left alone by the militiamen. Then another guy came over, placed a pistol to the back of the kneeling man's head, and fired one shot. The man pitched forward into the hole, helped along by a kick from the gunman, and then another man was dragged over. By now I saw both victims wore uniforms, and that they were from among the prisoners who had been brought in the day before. I stepped back and stood up, not minding the stench at all now. Gary was looking at me, his face gray, his legs trembling. From outside we both heard the sharp report of another gunshot.

"Welcome to America," Gary said.

CHAPTER SIXTEEN

Breakfast was a quick opening of the door and a bag tossed into the bus. Gary and I went forward and I grabbed the bag, took out our meal for the morning: two plastic bottles of water and two plain doughnuts. We ate in silence, sitting across from each other on mattresses. When we were finished Gary said, "You married?"

"Nope."

"Neither am I," he said wistfully. "Was going out with a local woman, very nice. Worked in the admin office of the school district. Carol Ramirez. Oh, I miss her."

"What happened?"

He shrugged, though it seemed as though his shoulders were weighed down with cement. "She's dead."

"Oh. I'm sorry. The militia?"

"No," Gary said. "Carol was in a convoy, being evacuated up north. She spoke Spanish and had volunteered to be an interpreter for this large group that had made its way up here from Spanish Harlem, if you can believe it. I wanted her to stay but no, she wanted to help out. The Canadian Red Cross had chartered some buses, and they were heading up north to Ontario. She . . . well, the convoy got mixed up with a militia unit. It was night. The militia unit was leaving them alone. They were all just heading north along the highway. It was night . . . Oh, I said that, right? Sorry.

Um, there they were and they were spotted by the intervention force. So they were bombed. A couple of aircraft—British, maybe, or even Dutch or Canadian, who knows?—did their job very well. The lead vehicle and the last one in the column were destroyed, blocking the passage of other vehicles, and then they just bombed and strafed everything else. You see, some of the militia units, they stole buses to move their forces at night, and with a couple of armored vehicles in the convoy . . . mistakes were made, right? In war or intervention to save lives or peacekeeping, mistakes always get made . . ."

I could not look at Gary, I could not look at that weary face. I just murmured "sorry" again, and cleaned up the remains of our little breakfast. Then I went to the rear of the bus to use the chemical toilet. The stench was back, even worse than before, and I wished that I could open a window or do something, anything, to get some fresh air into this little prison. I risked another look out the rear window, saw that the group of men had dispersed, though one man was still at the pit, shoveling in dirt and white powder from large paper sacks. Quicklime, to aid in the decomposition of the dead. But why bury the bodies here, so close to their base camp? Why?

Because it made sense, that was why. To keep on hiding the evidence, the evidence that something horrible was happening here.

As I came back into the main body of the bus, I saw that the front door had opened and two militiamen were standing there, pistols in their hands, looking at me and at Gary. We both stood there, silent, both of us wondering, I'm sure, who was being summoned. But at least we didn't have long to wait.

The lead militiaman looked straight at me. He needed a shave. He motioned with the pistol. "UN man, your turn."

SAME TRAILER, SAME room, same interrogator and two militiamen behind me. The bearded man who called himself Colonel Saunders. He was sipping from a mug of coffee, and he looked up at me as I sat down.

"Coffee?"

"No," I said.

"Freshly made."

"That's fine. I don't want any."

Saunders said, "You could be a bit more gracious, Samuel."

"Tell you what: you set me free, you let me get back to a UN unit, and I'll send you a thank-you note."

The colonel grinned, not a very pleasing sight. "That might be a problem.

There seem to be fewer and fewer of you UN folks in-country with every passing day."

I was going to say something sharp back to him, about what I had seen earlier that morning—the killing of the prisoners—but I stopped myself just in time. I wasn't supposed to have been looking out of the school bus. I wasn't supposed to have seen anything going on. Not a thing. But still . . .

"I heard some gunshots this morning, toward the rear of the school bus," I asked. "Target practice?"

One of the two guards behind me chuckled and I felt nauseous, that the thought of killing bound men on their knees would cause such humor. Saunders raised his coffee mug. "Target practice. Yeah, I guess you could say that."

He put the mug down, picked up a pen and a legal pad. "This is going to be your second interrogation, Samuel. And your last. Do you understand? I want to hear some better answers from you today, or it's not going to end well for you. Do I make myself clear?"

I clasped my hands, not wanting Saunders to see them shake. "Yes, you make yourself clear."

"Good. Let's begin."

And he did, right from the beginning. Name, age, address, occupation. How long had I been in the United States? What were my political views?

I hesitated on that one. "I'm sorry, I don't understand the question."

"I said, what's your politics? How did you vote? Liberal or Conservative?"

"Moderate, I guess."

Saunders glared. "Not a good answer."

"Well, that's what we have up in Canada. Mostly moderate parties."

"And which one have you supported?"

I looked at him and lied. "The Conservative Party, of course."

There was a pause, and then he wrote something down on the pad. I tried to keep my expression as neutral as possible. The party I usually vote for is the Liberal Party, but I didn't want to use that loaded adjective—liberal—with these armed men. And since they were typical Americans, I'm sure they didn't know one Canadian political party from another. Hell, for all I knew, they probably thought Bloc Quebecois was run from Paris.

"Let's talk about your training," Saunders said.

"All right."

"What kind of weapons training did you receive?"

"I'm sorry, I don't understand the question."

He glared at me again. "Weapons training. Did you receive qualifications for handling pistols, semi-auto rifles, explosives?"

I laughed. "Of course not!"

He raised an eyebrow, and I gasped as someone slapped the back of my head. Saunders said, "The question wasn't a joke, Samuel. So here we go again. What kind of weapons training did you receive?"

The back of my head was still stinging, but I kept my hands still, not wanting to give my captors back there any satisfaction. "All right," I said. "No joking. I received no weapons training."

"None?"

"None," I said.

"You're telling me you don't know how to use a firearm, of any kind?" Saunders asked.

"No, I didn't say that," I said.

"Hmm," he said, a hint of triumph in his tone. "Tell me what you're qualified with, then."

I felt the impulse to laugh again, but this time I kept it under control. "I've fired a .22 caliber bolt-action rifle a few times, back when I was a youngster. I'm not sure of the make or model. I also fired a bolt-action .308 once or twice, when I was twelve. My father wanted me to learn how to hunt deer with him. The lesson didn't take. I've also fired a pistol a few times, as part of a story I was working on in Toronto."

Saunders didn't look as triumphant. "I think you're lying."

"I'm sorry, but I'm not responsible for what you're thinking. I'm telling you the truth. That's all I know."

"Then weapons-identification training. You've certainly received that, haven't you?"

"Identification of what?"

"Armored vehicles, artillery pieces, mortars. How to recognize them in the field."

I shook my head. "No. The only training I received was the use of my recording gear, some basic first aid, some tips on working in a hostile environment and the protocol of working with an investigative unit."

Saunders scrawled some more. "Your investigative unit. Who was there?"

"Forensic pathologists, former police detectives, medical experts."

"Any military units?"

"One Marine escort, supplied under the terms of the armistice."

A voice muttered behind me, "Fucking traitor . . ."

"I want names, please."

I thought of Charlie and Karen, both American citizens, both serving the UN and now considered traitors by the militia. "No, I can't tell you that."

Saunders looked up. "That's not a request. It's an order."

"I'm sorry," I said. "I don't work for you. I'm not a member of your militia. I'm not even a citizen of this country."

"Shut up," Saunders said.

But I got up and approached his desk. "And I'm here under the authority of Security Council Resolution—"

I was going to go on and give the resolution number, and mention how many congressmen and senators from his own country welcomed our intervention, as well as how most of the major newspapers and media outlets had managed to get back to work after the attacks. But my plan was interrupted when the two men toward the rear pulled me down and started kicking and punching me.

This time it went on for a long while.

WHEN THEY WERE done, I was half-dragged, half-carried back to the school bus, where the militiamen dumped me on the steps leading up to the interior. Gary the schoolteacher was there and he helped me up inside, where I lay down on one of the mattresses. "Jesus Christ," Gary whispered. "They sure as hell worked you over."

"You . . . you should see the other guys," I managed to say.

Gary tried to let some water dribble into my mouth, and I winced as the cold liquid struck my lips. "Why? Did you get some punches in?" he asked.

"Not hardly," I said, trying not to cough. "But I do think I managed to stain some of their boots with my blood."

That got a laugh from Gary, and he tried to give me some more water, which this time I was at least able to swallow. He said, "They brought in another lunch. I could give you some of the bread, if I soften it with some water."

"OK."

He rustled around in a plastic shopping bag. "There's some soft cheese, which should be all right for eating, even with a sore mouth. You up to eating?"

I closed my eyes, wanting to just sit there, just lie on the softness of the mattress, no matter how soiled and stained. "No, not yet. I just want to stay here. How about you?"

"Oh, I'll wait," Gary said. "I'll wait. Any particular reason they beat on you, or are they just in a foul mood?"

"I guess they didn't like my answers to their questions," I said, keeping my eyes closed.

"Uh-huh," he said. "What kind of questions were they asking you?"

"Crazy stuff, about weapons training, about identifying makes and types of military vehicles, my politics . . ."

"And did you answer them?"

I coughed, feeling blood and spittle drool down my chin. "Yeah—but I didn't give any names."

Gary didn't say anything. I opened my eyes. He sat there, once more with his arms folded around his knees. He said, "Samuel, you saw what happened this morning, didn't you? You saw those prisoners get shot, right?"

I let my tongue move gingerly around my teeth. "I've just spent the morning with a bunch of thugs who think I'm an idiot . . . please don't insult me by saying the same thing . . ."

"I'm not insulting you. I'm telling you what's up. And what's up is that these guys are playing for keeps. Shit, there's a whole frigging pit full of dead people over there that shows just how real they are. So tell them what they want to hear."

I coughed up some blood again. "But I don't have anything to tell them . . . Christ, I told them everything, except the names of my colleagues . . ."

Gary said, "Tell them a story, then. Anything to stop the beatings."

I rolled over, trying to ease the pain in the ribs on my left side. "I'm sorry. I can't do that."

"Then you should try. It'd be for the best. If you confirm what they believe . . . well, they might go easy on you."

"And what do you think they believe?"

Gary looked over at the far bulkhead of the school bus. "They believe they've been wronged. They believe this country has done so much for the world and hasn't been appreciated. And when bad times happened . . . you folks took advantage of us. Of course, we're not the same country any more. For the first time in nearly two hundred years we have foreign troops on our soil. We're still in shock because of having our first city attacked with an atomic device and because of the other atomic devices that were exploded over our territory and that temporarily knocked us back to the nineteenth century. So when the UN is crawling around the countryside, reporting to who knows who, and some of these UN inspectors—we know for a fact—are ex-military or ex-intelligence from their countries of origin, it's not hard to believe that they're doing more than just setting up tent cities and stopping the shooting and investigating war crimes."

I wiped at my chin. "You say that's what they think. What do *you* think?"

Gary turned and looked at me. "I think you should tell them something different the next time they question you. And I think you should get something to eat."

I was tired of talking. I just nodded and Gary came over and helped feed me some bread and cheese and water.

AFTER OUR LUNCH, Gary said, "Man, I wish I had packed a deck of cards. Or a book. Or something to pass the time. No offense, Samuel, but this waiting is driving my head up a wall."

"I've got a book," I said.

"Really?" he said, his eyes shiny with anticipation, like a kid on Christmas morning. "What kind?"

"A collection of essays by George Orwell. Hold on."

I rolled myself up into a sitting position and freed the book from an inside pocket of my coat. Gary held out both his hands and said, "Oh, this is great, this is great."

"Tell you what," I said. "I'll rest my eyes and you can do some reading."

"Are you sure? I don't want to hog your book. I mean . . . man, a book."

"No, go right ahead," I said. One of the last things I remember about Gary was how happy he looked, sitting up against the bulkhead, a blanket over his legs. I managed to find a comfortable spot, pulled my own smelly blanket up to my chin, closed my eyes and fell asleep to the sound of Gary flipping through the pages of the Orwell book.

I AWOKE TO the sound of vehicle engines. Gary was kneeling on one of the seats, looking out through a small scratch on one of the painted-over windows. I sat up and drank some water from a nearby plastic bottle.

"What's up?" I asked.

"More militiamen coming in," he said. "A couple of trucks and a car. Maybe a dozen or more men. Looks like they're bulking up their numbers for something."

"Like what?"

Gary kept looking out the window. "Maybe an offensive, now that the armistice is over. Who knows?"

"But they're militia, guys with guns in just a handful of states . . . how can they keep on fighting against professional UN troops?"

Gary turned around and sat back down in the seat. "You forget who those people are out there. Their ancestors fought in the snows at Valley Forge, ate bread made from acorns during the Civil War, whipped the

Germans in the mud twice last century. They've fought in swamps and deserts, on and under the ocean, and in the air. If they think their home turf has been invaded, they'll fight forever. Forever, Samuel. Till the end of time."

I was going to say something funny about the end of time coming quicker than one might think when the door at the front of the bus opened up. Two militiamen came in, both holding pistols in their hands. One of them had a plastic bag, which he tossed on the floor. He grinned, revealing yellow teeth. "Only one supper assigned to this prison bus," he said. "Care to guess what that means?"

I didn't have to guess. My hands and feet and gut suddenly felt cold and clammy, and Gary couldn't even bear to look at the militiamen. We waited, all four of us frozen in some ghastly tableau, until the second militiaman waved his gun and said, "You. The teacher. Come along—it's time."

Gary managed to nod, his lips pursed. He got up, handed my book back to me, and said, "Thanks for the book. I really enjoyed the past couple of hours. It's the best couple of hours I've had in a month."

"You're welcome," I said. "Look, is there—"

He held up his hand. "No, it's OK. Samuel, I've enjoyed meeting you. Honestly. Hope you get home one of these days."

The second gunman said, "Jesus, will you stop yapping and get a move on?"

Gary brushed past me, went to the front of the bus, and paused at the top of the steps that led outside.

"Thanks again, Samuel. Thanks," he said.

I just nodded, and he walked down the steps.

If I had been a bit more brave, I think I would have made a fuss, or at least got up and gone to the seat and the window. But I couldn't move. I just lay back on the mattress and wrapped myself up in the blanket. I flinched when I heard the report of a solitary gunshot.

A gunshot that seemed to echo for a very long time.

CHAPTER SEVENTEEN

Eventually hunger managed to get me off the mattress. I got up and pawed weakly through the plastic bag, finding a hard roll and a can of corned-beef hash. There were no utensils but I was lucky that the can of hash was a single-serve one which had a snap top. No can opener necessary. I snapped the cover off and scooped the hash out with my fingers, eating it cold. It was greasy and salty and stringy and the potato chunks were tiny—and it tasted delicious. I drank some of the water and then I softened a torn-off piece of the hard roll and used it to wipe the can's interior clean.

When I was done I wiped my fingers on my pants and sat up, wincing at the pain in my side. My ribs seemed better, but not by much. I looked around the dirty and smelly interior of the school bus, and shuddered. With Gary gone, it seemed so empty. The few hours we had spent together had seemed like a month. All the talking and discussion and questions and now . . . the poor guy was now in a pit, his body cooling down, everything about him—the jokes and the tales and his love for his woman who'd been killed by a NATO air strike—gone into emptiness.

I yawned. God, I was tired. I'd never thought I could get this tired and still function. The lights around me started to dim as the power was turned down in the militia camp. I got up, went to the window, looked out through the peephole and saw just a few dim lights. It seemed like the camp was getting ready to bed down. But I was sure that somebody out there was keeping an eye on the door of the bus. These militia types seemed to be efficient at keeping their prisoners locked up. Prisoner. I thought about one of the last things Gary had said to me before he'd been led away. *Tell them what they want to hear.*

I rubbed my hands together. I had been successful during the last session in not mentioning the names of Karen and Charlie—but how long could I hold out during another interrogation like that? I had been brave once but I was sure that my body wouldn't let me be brave again, especially if my interrogators decided to graduate from boots and fists to something like knives and propane torches.

It was getting darker. But maybe I would have a respite, a night to sleep and gain some energy. Maybe I would have a night off. Maybe . . . But if these militia guys were smart—and they obviously *were* smart in a guerrilla-style way, having held off domestic police forces and the NATO military intervention for so long—they would follow the path so thoughtfully mapped out for them by interrogators from the old Soviet Union. Those guys had been expert at grabbing prisoners at odd times and shaking their nerve and composure, so a good night's sleep was probably out of the question. Especially if I could expect to be beaten up again.

Still, it would be sensible to try and catch some sleep. I went back and lay down on the mattress. I rolled over and pulled up a blanket. My hand brushed against the metal floor of the bus and again I felt the bite of sharp metal. I pushed back, irritated. Something snapped, and I felt cool air against my fingers. Great, just great, I thought. I'm trying to get some sleep, and I just poked a hole in the floor of the bus, letting in a draft—

Letting in a draft.

Try "opening up a hole," moron, I told myself.

I got off the mattress, pulled it away, felt the floor again with my hands. Rusted and rotten metal, near the left rear tire. I touched the hole I had made, felt more pieces of rusted metal snap away in my hand.

"I'll be damned," I whispered.

I got up, not feeling quite as achy and sore as I'd felt earlier. The string of Christmas-tree lights was held up by duct tape. I pulled it free with a satisfying sound of tape ripping, and brought a few of the lights down to the hole. It was about the size of my fist, and I could look down and see the ground beneath the bus. Unbelievable.

I taped the lights closer to the hole and went to work. The first few pieces of floor went easily enough, snapping and cracking away, and then it got tougher as the rusted stuff gave way to uncorroded metal. I paused, breathing hard, my hands grazed and cold. I now had a hole the size of a dinner plate.

"Just a little wider," I murmured. "Just a little wider."

I began working on the sides of the hole, back and forth, back and forth, widening it up. Once there was a piercing screech as one piece of metal scraped against another and I froze, shaking, wondering if anybody outside could have heard it. I waited, listening intently but hearing only the sound of the wind coming through the hole. I brought the lights closer, still breathing hard. Close. It would be pretty close.

Noise. From outside. Some laughter, some drunken shouts.

I got up from where I was working and went to the window. I looked through the scraped-out peephole and saw that a muddy pickup truck had pulled up, near the trailer where I had been interrogated. There was a group of men gathered around the truck, and flashlights were being played around the people and the vehicle. I blinked, thinking that one of the shapes looked familiar. I tried to keep my breathing even, tried not to move my face from the window. There. The shape I recognized had a couple of lights shone in his face—a very familiar face.

One Peter Brown, formerly of the Metropolitan Police in Great Britain, and currently a special investigator with UNFORUS.

Captured? Like me?

Then I saw him laugh with another militiaman, and then Colonel Saunders, the colonel-in-chief of the militia, came out of the trailer, almost stumbling down the steps. Saunders seemed to be drunk but he also looked happy to see Peter, who went forward with a grin on his face and offered his hand. There were some hearty handshakes and back-pounding and then the two of them went up into the trailer, like best buddies—or best bastards or something.

Now the radio gear I'd seen Peter with made sense. He had set us up. And that Australian television crew had been right, lethally so. There were indeed traitors within the UN groups operating in-country. Hell, maybe Peter had even met with some of them, the night I'd seen him outside the motel.

More laughter and some loud voices came from the trailer. Then it got quiet again.

Jesus. Peter. I glanced back at the hole I had just made.

"Think," I murmured. "Have to think this through."

I looked around the floor, gathered up the rusted and broken chunks of metal, and tossed them into the hole. Then I rolled up two blankets and tied them together with a kind of rope that I'd fashioned from the torn-up plastic bags. Then I took the water bottle, filled it from the bucket in the rear, and went back to the opening. I dropped the water bottle and blankets down the hole, and then lowered myself into it. The jagged rim reached my waistband before my feet touched the dirt. I leaned forward, grabbed the mattress, and tugged it toward me. Then I squeezed down—the metal edge of the hole scratching at my hands, neck and head—and tried not to gasp from the pain. Now I was underneath the bus. I reached up, grabbed hold of the mattress again, and pulled it over the hole. Darkness engulfed me but I thought it was worth it. Might as well make them wonder how I might have gotten out. It might only work for just a while, but just a while was all I needed.

And Peter? Damn that man, damn him to hell. If I ever got back to the UN lines I'd make sure that the son of a bitch ended up in the dock at The Hague, along with his bloody-minded fellow bastards.

But no time for that, not right now. It was time to get moving.

In the darkness I crouched down and by touch gathered up the water bottle and blankets. I crawled toward the rear of the bus, scraping the back of my head on the undercarriage and exhaust system, and then stopped, taking in everything that I could see in the illumination available. In front of me and to the left were the dim lights of the encampment and to the right were the woods. I waited until my night vision improved before I moved toward the trees, passing gingerly through the strands of barbed wire and making sure it didn't catch on my clothing. I moved quietly and deliberately and slowly. But, by God, I sure as hell moved.

IT WAS SLOW going all through that long night, but I did all right, stumbling and tripping only a few times. The first half-hour or so I was terrified that I'd hear the sounds of tracker dogs or of men beating through the brush, but I heard only the whispers of the wind and the cries of night animals as I plodded along. A half-moon was up in the clear sky, so I could at least get some idea of where I was going. Even then, I often bumped into low-hanging branches that made me wince and shudder at the fresh pain coursing through my old bruises and wounds. I tried to keep to a steady pace and to travel in a straight line. I didn't want to be thrashing around in circles.

The woods I was in began to thin out. I forded a small stream, the water looking almost silver from the light of the half-moon overhead. I paused there and filled the water bottle, drank as much as I could, and then refilled the container. My blanket roll stayed on my shoulders, heavy though it was. I resumed my walk, trying to hold to a straight line, keeping the half-moon in view.

Eventually I came upon a drainage ditch, which I jumped over easily enough. I had no idea how long I had been walking, but I was hopeful that I had put a number of klicks between myself and the militia camp. I wished I had a better idea where that camp was—I hadn't paid much attention to the peacekeeper and policing aspects of my training. But I still wanted to give an extensive debrief and memory dump to whatever NATO forces were still active in this region and provide them with the information they'd need to blast that wooded hidden area with everything they had, from cluster bombs to napalm bursts.

I climbed a small rise and found myself on a paved road. I paused, breathing hard, looking around me. On both sides of the road were farmers' fields, going off into the distance and punctuated here and there by stands of trees. I looked around in a circle, trying to determine where I should go. There. Off to the west, if I was correct, was a hazy glow, rising up from the horizon. Perhaps a village. Perhaps a highway. Or a UN encampment of some sort. In any event, it looked like a lot of lights, which meant some kind of operating authority. The militia groups liked to stay small and operate without being too obvious. That glow on the horizon was as good a target for me as any, I decided.

I started moving toward it.

I WAS PLEASED with myself for finding the road, though I guess I shouldn't have been too cocky. After all, I had only stumbled over the damn thing. Still, it seemed like I was making good time, though I had to rest every few minutes or so, shifting my bundle of blankets from one shoulder to the next. I drank fully of the water, remembering my father telling me once, a long while ago, that while you could live for a long time on an empty stomach you couldn't last long without water. Thanks, Dad, for that at least, you otherwise miserable bastard.

About the fourth or fifth time I took a break, I was sitting on a stone wall when from overhead came the noise of jets again. It sounded like they were flying over the area I'd recently left. I looked up but, of course, there were no running lights. It was strange, tracking the planes' movement only from the sound, but then I thought I caught a glimpse of their deadly shapes, briefly blocking out the stars. I waited on the stone wall, my blanket roll on my lap, and soon I saw a trickle of sparks descending, orange and red and yellow, little round globes of color. Then the horizon lit up like a distant thunderstorm. I heard a series of shuddering booms and even felt them through my feet, resting on the asphalt. I actually laughed, rocking back and forth.

"Oh, I hope they got you all," I whispered. "Every single one of you, every one of you who hit me and who killed your neighbors. And Peter . . . boy oh boy, I sure hope they got you as well . . . blow you right back to where you started . . . I hope they got all of you good . . ."

I guess I had violated some of my UN training with that little rant, but I didn't care. I stood up. The night sky off to the east was beginning to turn gray. Dawn was coming. I looked around the fields on either side of me and clambered over the stone wall. Out there, to the north, the field I was in rose up at a slight angle, and on the crest of a rise was a collection of boulders, probably too big and massive for the early farmers here to have cleared them out after exhausting themselves killing the Indians who'd been here before them. I climbed up the muddy field, very tired now. As I got closer I saw that saplings and some brush had grown up around the rocks. Perfect. I fought my way through some brambles and found a reasonably flat area that was roughly my size. I undid one blanket—saying a short prayer of thanks to the memory of the schoolteacher Gary, who had once used it—and lay down on the rocky ground. I pulled the other blanket over me and stared up at the tangle of branches and twigs overhead. I thought I saw a star but I might have been mistaken. I was surprised at how warm I was, and though the ground was hard and unyielding it sure as hell was ten times better than that soiled mattress back at the school bus.

Once I thought about a certain eight-year-old boy and then I started shivering, until the sounds of jets overhead, one right after another, drove those thoughts away. I think I fell asleep to their beautiful sounds of destruction, death and revenge.

SOMETHING PUSHED AT my foot. I pushed back, woke up and found that a dog was looking at me with soulful brown eyes. An English springer spaniel, white and brown, its stub of a tale wagging madly. In his mouth he had a dirty green tennis ball, which he dropped on my blankets. He gave a little muffled woof, and then nudged the ball with his nose.

"Sorry, pal," I said, sitting up and wincing at the pain in my back. "Not in the mood for playing much."

A voice from beyond the rocks: "Sorry, that's all that damn dog wants to do sometimes."

"Really?" I said.

"Truly," the voice said.

Some of the saplings and brush were pulled away, and an older man with a thick white beard, black coat and overalls was peering into my little resting place. A boy of about seven or eight was next to him, rubbing at a red nose that was dribbling snot. The boy's hands were empty, but the older man had a shotgun, which at least wasn't pointing in my direction.

The man said, "The dog's called Tucker. My name's Stewart Carr, and this is my grandson Jerry."

"Hello to all of you," I said. "The name is Simpson, Samuel Simpson. If this is your property, I'm sorry I trespassed and slept here."

"That's OK," Stewart said. "At least you weren't partying or driving across my fields or shooting a cow and thinking it was a deer." Then the English springer spaniel woofed again and started to worry at the ball. "Tucker . . . You see, the thing is, the dog just purely loves to play. You could spend hours just tossing that damn ball back and forth, and he won't get tired. But *we* get tired after a while, which is why he likes to find strangers to play with. He picked up your scent and saw a potential playmate."

"Makes sense to me," I said. "Look, if you don't—"

"Where you from, Samuel?"

The boy was sniffling some, still rubbing at his nose. He had on a red wool cap with a blue pom-pom that seemed about three sizes too big for him. I looked back at his grandfather and said, "Toronto. Canada."

Stewart nodded. "I know where Toronto is. You lost?"

"Surely am."

"Where you headed?"

"To the nearest highway."

Another nod. "UN, am I right?"

The dog's tail was wagging and drool was actually running down his chin, he looked so excited at the prospect of playing with me or anybody else. I said quietly, not raising my voice, "Stewart, if you're going to turn me over to your militia, then send your grandkid away and go ahead and shoot me. Because I'm not going. I've already spent some time with them and I'm not going back."

The boy's eyes were wide and Stewart spat on the ground. "Do I look like a monster?"

"Not particularly."

"Who did you have a run-in with?"

"The county militia. Headed by a guy named Saunders."

"Saunders? Fat and with a beard and not enough sense to pour piss out of a boot, even if the instructions were printed on the heel?"

"Sure sounds like him," I said.

"Bah," Stewart said. " 'Fore everything started going to the shits he ran a lube-oil place, where you go in, get your oil changed, and then leave after twenty minutes or so. Then he got some surplus army gear, a few weapons and some friends as dimwitted as he is, and poof! Now he's a colonel in a county militia. Well, shit, son, just 'cause my name's in a phone book, it don't make me a telephone repairman. I don't have nothing to do with him or his friends. But come along up from there, we'll get you fed and on your way."

I got up slowly, started rolling up my blankets. Stewart nudged the young boy and said, "Crawl in there and give 'im a hand."

So Jerry came in and said his first word since I'd met him—"Tucker!"—and pushed the dog away. He helped me roll up the blankets and I tied them off with the plastic strips. Then Stewart helped me out, back onto the field. It felt good to be standing and I said, "You don't have to feed me. Just point me in the direction of the highway and—"

Stewart interrupted. "The radio said a lot of crap is going on, so I don't think you want to be walking anywhere out in the open right now. And what's the problem? You ain't hungry?"

I think he could've heard my stomach grumble at the mere mention of food. I said, "I'm hungry, sure, but I do want to make some time. And no offense, the last time I got something to eat the woman feeding me turned me over to the militia."

"Where was that?"

"A general store. The Cooper General Store."

Stewart nodded and started walking, and I went with him. "She's another one. Sweet Jesus, Samuel, you sure had a run of bad luck, hooking up with her. Look. If you're dead set on making your own way, fine. I'll point you there. But your face is all cut up and you look like you could use a wash and a meal. Then you can get going. The choice is yours."

By now the muddy field had joined up with a dry and unkempt lawn. In front of us was a two-story farmhouse, with an attached barn and a couple of outbuildings. A dented red pickup truck was parked in a dirt turnabout. I coughed and looked over at Stewart and his grandson. "That's a nice offer. Really it is. I'm just gun-shy, that's all."

A firm nod. "'Course you are."

I shifted the blanket roll in my hands. "Why, then?"

"Why, what?"

"Why are you feeding me, a stranger and trespasser? I mean, you could have just sent me on my way and I would have been happy with that."

Stewart slung his shotgun across his back, slapped me on the shoulder. "'Cause that's a neighborly thing to do, that's why. Something a lot of us forgot last spring. Now let's get going."

I walked a couple more steps and then the dog cut in front of me, dropping the tennis ball again at my feet. I picked up the ball, warm and slimy with dog drool, and tossed it down the gravel driveway. The dog raced after it, moving almost at an angle, before snapping it up and then trotting back proudly with it in his mouth.

"Tucker," the boy said.

The dog dropped the ball at my feet, and Stewart laughed and kicked it away. "You get caught up in that, you'll be here till suppertime. Come along, Tucker. Jerry, get the leash and bring that damn dog in."

"OK," I said.

"OK," Jerry said.

Then we went into the house.

THE KITCHEN WAS cluttered and had a big range and a refrigerator that had drawings secured to it with little magnets. I apologized for tracking mud in with my soiled boots but Stewart just waved me off, putting his shotgun down in the corner next to a collection of boots, shoes and half-chewed dog toys. Tucker came in, gulped down some water from a dish and then collapsed on a blanket by the refrigerator, breathing hard, tongue hanging out. Stewart pointed out an adjacent bathroom and I went in and used a real flush toilet for the first time in a long while. I washed up with hot water and soap and examined my face. I was about another week away from having a serious beard—which was probably for the best—to cover up the bruises and scrapes along my forehead and left cheek. I scrubbed my face, winced a couple of times, and then dried myself on a towel that proudly stated it was from the Buffalo Hyatt Hotel.

Back in the kitchen, waiting for me at the table, there was a mug of tea, which I sipped, enjoying the strong taste. My stomach was now wide awake with the smells of wonderful things cooking. Stewart said, " 'Bout another ten minutes or so, we'll have something good to eat, just you wait."

"Thanks," I said. "I don't know how to pay you, but—"

Stewart moved his bulk over to the refrigerator, popped open the door and bent down, coming back up with a fistful of eggs. "You get back to the UN, you just might say that not all people out here are killers. You think you could do that?"

"Sure," I said.

"Then you'll have paid me back," he said, returning to the stove.

I took another sip from the tea. Jerry was on the other side of the table, tongue sticking out from his mouth at an angle, drawing something on paper. I said to Stewart, "You mentioned something about the radio. What's going on?"

"Depends on what station you listen to. The local stations, most of 'em run by the militia or their friends, say the UN and NATO violated the armistice agreement and it is now defunct. Now, defunct. That's a hell of a word. Didn't think most militia types could use such a word. The local stations, run by what's left of the state government and the UN, they don't say much. Just to stay in your homes and listen to the responsible authorities. But when the weather's right I get the BBC World Service, late at night."

I rubbed the tea mug, enjoying the warmth on my fingers. "What does the BBC say?"

Stewart reached up to a cabinet door, opened it and took out three thick white plates. "The BBC—and, man, I do like hearing their voices, they sound so civilized—anyhow, the BBC says that the armistice with the militia units has broken down in some counties in Michigan, New York, Vermont and New Hampshire but seems to be holding on in Texas, Idaho, New Mexico, Kentucky and Tennessee. Most other states are still quiet, the ones not really hurt by the bombings. And nobody's too sure when the armistice might be up and running again."

From outside I could hear a thrumming noise, which seemed to get louder and louder. Helicopters. Stewart stopped his work and looked up, a spatula in his large hand. Jerry stopped drawing and his eyes grew wide as he looked up at the ceiling. In the corner Tucker even whimpered some. The vibration from the helicopters' engines made the dishware rattle as they flew overhead. I thought briefly of racing outside and waving a dish towel or something to attract their attention but I knew how fast they flew: they'd be over the horizon by the time I found the door.

Then the sound drained away. Jerry picked up his pen and Stewart looked over at me.

"I guess the armistice won't be up and running again today," I said.

"I guess you're right," Stewart said.

CHAPTER EIGHTEEN

The late breakfast was eventually served: scrambled eggs again—and I sure as hell wasn't complaining—with a sausage link apiece and toast made from homemade bread. We ate quickly and Stewart raised his voice only once, when Jerry tried to give a piece of his solitary sausage to the dog.

"Jerry, that sausage is special. It's been in the freezer for months, and I'll be goddamned if a dog is going to eat it, even if it is Tucker," Stewart said. "Now, you go ahead and eat, so you can grow up and be strong. And don't pout."

And the little guy didn't pout, just held on to his fork with a pudgy fist and kept on eating. His eyes were shiny and I had a feeling that he and his grandfather had this dog-eating-from-the-table discussion on a regular basis.

The food was hot and went down quickly. I had another cup of tea and when we were finished eating Stewart said quietly, "Now, you go and clean up, and go into the living room. All right?"

Jerry looked over his empty plate. "Can I watch TV?"

"Only if you turn on the VCR and run a tape," Stewart said.

"Which one?"

"How about *The Jungle Book?*"

Jerry nodded enthusiastically. "Yep. I'd like that."

He got up, cleared the dishes and placed them by the sink. When he was done, he said, "Tucker," and the English springer spaniel followed him. Stewart leaned back in his chair to catch what was going on in the living room. He lowered his voice. "Just want to make sure he's watching a tape," he explained. "I don't want him watching the tube in case one of the militias is running things for a day or so on one of the local cable stations. The crap they put out over the airwaves . . . You know, racist warfare, the Protocols of the Elders of Zion, white power, red state versus blue state . . . Bad enough things are happening on the ground, then the clowns who seize the television stations have to pollute the airwaves again."

"I see," I said, sipping from the tea mug.

"You do, do you?" Stewart asked skeptically. "Tell me, Toronto man, what exactly were you doing, working for the UN?"

I tried to gauge his expression, what was going on in his mind, and decided to hell with it. "I was assigned to an investigation unit, looking into war-crime sites. We were investigating allegations around this county and others."

"Find much?"

"A little," I said.

"Bah, whole place is one whole war crime, if you ask me. So, Canadian man that you are, what do you think of our poor misguided country?"

I said, "I'm not sure I can really answer that."

"Oh, give it a try," Stewart said. "I read the papers, watch the news. I know that you nice folks up north have always had a strange relationship with us Yanks. Who could blame you? Here we are, overbearing and powerful and full of ourselves, and there you were, peaceful and trying to choose a path that didn't involve our rough-and-tumble way of doing things. Bad enough to have our kind of nation as a neighbor. When that terrorist attack hit Manhattan late last year and then came the follow-up balloon bombings . . . it was the tipping point. Hard to believe that one coordinated strike would cause all this chaos, even with that damn EMP effect . . ."

"Up north, although we didn't get zapped like you people did, it was hard to understand what was going on," I said. "The news coverage was spotty and all we heard were the worst of the stories. Exodus from the cities . . . lack of food and fuel . . . refugees being shot at by the militias . . ."

Stewart looked like he wanted to slam a fist on the table. "Damn it, we had years of warning. We should have been prepared for all types of attacks, but we never are. Never prepared for a boatful of explosives motoring its way up to a moored warship. Or some guys armed with box-cutters and knives, flying planes into buildings. Or some group stealing suitcase nukes and detonating them to fry all our electronics. The population looks to its leaders and their leaders fail them, and then the poor, scared, frightened people take matters into their owns hands. But then again, people . . . sometimes they get the government they deserve, you know?"

"That's what I've heard," I said.

He gave me a wry smile. "You see, a few years back I worked on the planning board for our little town here. I'd retired from a machine shop and thought I'd give something back to the community. You know? And you know what happened after that?"

I rubbed a finger around the rim of the tea mug. "What's been said before: 'No good deed goes unpunished.' "

A firm nod. "Absolutely right, Samuel. A little job like the planning board, making sure any new construction comes in and follows the rules. And you'd have thought I was wearing jackboots and a peaked hat with a goddamn swastika on top. We had people coming into meetings, screaming and yelling, I got hate mail and I got phone calls at midnight, wanting to know why I was giving my neighbors a hard time about what they could or couldn't do with their property. I mean, shit, some people thought owning a piece of land gave 'em the right to store drums of toxic waste on the back forty. So what if it leaked into the ground water, or seeped into a stream that went into a reservoir? Man's home is his castle, et cetera, and all that crap. So I gave it up, after one term. I'm getting older and I don't need the aggravation."

"Why so much anger?" I asked.

"Who knows?" Stewart said. "This isn't a bad place. Not very rich, mind you, but it was peaceful enough before the troubles. Hell, even had a nice little state park on the other side of the county. Bronson's Iron Works, one of the earliest mine and iron forges in the state. But when people started dropping out and not caring, when government becomes something to be hated and feared, and when rumors and half-truths are believed, over and over again, well, that's when the bad times come. And when the bad times come people want to hate somebody, and when those somebodies are poor refugees from the cities, trying to get some food and a place to sleep, it's easy to do."

From the living room came some boyish laughter, as I heard the rollicking tunes from *The Jungle Book*. Stewart saw that I was paying attention and said, "Thank God for VCRs. I'd hate to try to take him into town now to see a movie."

I said, "A couple of days ago I saw a road overpass that had been taken out by a bombing raid. That sure looked like something that came from the movies."

"Yeah, and you know what? Even with the killing that was going on, lots of us were humiliated when the UN approved the intervention and when NATO came in. I know they had their reasons. From state to state, you didn't know what the hell was going to happen. Some states didn't have any militias, any trouble, and their governors just used any National Guard units that weren't overseas to take care of any problems from the refugees. Other states fell apart and couldn't hold back the militias once they started gunning. And with our power and our nuclear weapons, it didn't take much to see that the world didn't want another Russia out there, a country with nukes falling apart, you know? But still, the hell of it, being bombed and strafed by countries who were supposed to be friendly to us. Not that some of the militia units didn't deserve it, but a lot of innocent civilians, in Idaho and Texas and Kentucky and Tennessee and here, they were killed by those raids, before the armistice."

I remembered the schoolteacher Gary, and what had happened to his fiancée. "But when the news footage came out, showing homes being burned and so many people being killed and hurt, and some of the rioters raiding National Guard armories and some other military bases, there was a lot of pressure to intervene. It was a bad choice, but I think sitting back would have been an even worse one."

"Yeah, I know," Stewart said, finishing off his own mug of tea. "Even now, even with that humiliation, I wish you guys had come in earlier. It could have made a big difference."

"I know," I said.

His eyes flashed at me. "No, you *don't* know. I don't mean to get pissy, but you *don't* know."

I just nodded. "Yes, you're right. I don't know."

"Ah," he said, leaning over again to look at his grandson in the living room. "I can't help it; I'm sorry. You see, it all has to do with little Jerry over there."

Something cold started tickling the back of my throat. "His parents?"

"Yes," Stewart said quietly. "My daughter, Kelly. And her husband, Ralph. She went to school in Manhattan, learning about sculpture. Met up with a nice fella named Ralph Powell. Got married and came back here, opened up a little studio. He worked on-line for some brokerage firm, got to work out of the house. Beautiful little house, beautiful little boy."

I kept silent, letting him tell the story. He took a breath. "They've been missing ever since the troubles. I keep telling Jerry, don't worry, your mom and dad, they're on vacation. They'll come back when they can. But I don't know how much longer I can keep telling him that. I . . . I just don't think it's going to end right. And you want to know why?"

"Tell me," I said.

"Because in some people's eyes what Kelly did was a crime. And her crime was to marry a black man from New York City and to have a child with him. And in those people's eyes that's a crime worth being killed for."

I HELPED STEWART wash up the dishes and then we went out to the living room, where Jerry was enraptured, staring up at the colors on the television screen. Tucker was on a dog bed of sorts, snoring fitfully. Stewart said, "You OK, kiddo?"

Jerry still stared up at the screen. "Yep."

"Tucker OK?"

"Yep."

Stewart said, "We're going upstairs for a couple of minutes, so you stay down here, right? And remember, stay away from the windows."

" 'K, Grandpa."

Stewart managed a smile, glanced at me and said, "Come along. Let's go upstairs and see what's going on in the world. Maybe then we can figure if it's safe to get you out of here."

"How's that?"

"You'll see."

I followed Stewart up the narrow wooden staircase, past little framed sketches of skiers hanging on the right-hand wall. At the top we went straight through to a small room filled with radio gear. A quick glance to the left and the right showed a bedroom on either side. With my UN-trained investigative know-how I figured which one belonged to Stewart's grandchild by the toys on the floor. In the small room were three metal tables, each set against a wall. There were a couple of amateur radios set up on two of the tables, and in front of them was an old office swivel chair, its back repaired with some gray duct tape. There were maps on the wall as well, ranging from one of the world to some that depicted the several counties in this part of New York state. Stewart flipped a few switches and sat down. I perched myself on a corner of a desk and watched closely.

"Nice old stuff, huh?" Stewart said. "That's what saved it, when the balloon strikes came. Old electronics could muddle through better than the newer stuff. That's how some of the militia units communicated with each other at the start, when they started setting up roadblocks and such. The old gear still worked, while the newer stuff—belonging to the cops and National Guard units—got fried."

"There doesn't seem to be a microphone," I said.

"Don't need one," he said, rotating a dial slowly. "You see, Samuel, I don't particularly care to talk to people. I'm just a goddamn big snoop, that's all. Used to be I'd get a kick from catching some obscure regional station in China, or an American task force in the Persian Gulf, but fortunately—or unfortunately—the really interesting stuff now is nearby. So I don't have to worry about getting a weak signal. The thing today is, I take a gander at what's going on out there, then I can get an idea of how safe it might be before you start walking."

"All I need to know is how to reach the highway," I said. "If I get there, then I'll just hang tight until a UN convoy comes by."

Stewart turned in his chair, looked up at me. "Where the hell have you been the past few days? Under a rock?"

"No," I said. "I've been running through the woods, being chased by your gun-toting neighbors. And I spent a couple of days at a militia camp, held prisoner, seeing lots of nice touristy things. Like men being shot in the back of the head for the crime of being in this country without your militia's permission. So I haven't really been up on the news."

"Well, bully for you, sport, 'cause things have really gone to the shits for you UN folks these past few days," he said. "Like I said, the armistice has collapsed here and in a few other states. Which means some of the resettlement camps are under siege, your UN investigators have scurried back to their base camps, and the open highways—like the one nearby that you're so goddamned keen to visit—have been closed."

"What broke the armistice?" I asked.

"Some militia leader in another county—probably a used-car salesman in his previous life—was captured by one of the arrest squads working for the War Crimes Tribunal," Stewart said, adjusting a dial on one of the consoles. "Thing is, his militia unit was under the impression that he was traveling under some sort of protection. Like a get-out-of-jail-free card. So they shot up a UN convoy. Then some other militia units, not particularly liking the armistice in the first place, decided to get in on the action."

I shook my head. "NATO units and arrest squads versus the militias. Doesn't seem to be a fair fight."

"You're right, but for the wrong reason," Stewart said. "The militias don't think it's a fair fight either. But the way they see it, if they keep on sniping and harassing the UN, sending body bags back to Europe and New Zealand and elsewhere, then the home governments will get tired and bring their boys home. Then the militias can get back to what they do best: killing their neighbors who just wanted some help. All right, let's see what we've got here."

Stewart looked at a small open notebook, made another adjustment.

"I like to keep track of the stations I'm listening to. OK, here's the first one. A militia station, a few towns over."

He turned up the volume and I leaned forward, listening to a man's hurried voice.

". . . Heavy casualties at Bremerton. This message is for the Second New York Activists. I repeat, the Second New York Activists. Your message is as follows: Tango, Tango, Bravo, Foxtrot, Charlie. Repeating again, this is for the Second New York Activists: Tango, Tango, Bravo, Foxtrot, Charlie."

Stewart turned his head my way. "Get a lot of messages like that. Code."

"Yeah," I said. "These guys are organized, aren't they? They set up codes, already in place, just in case. That way, they can communicate without worrying about being monitored."

"Shhh," he said, "they're still yapping."

He boosted the volume again and the voice said, "Another warning to our brethren near the Finger Lakes district. Armored units are reportedly moving in your direction. Repeating for the Finger Lakes district. Armored units, possibly Polish, are moving in your direction. We've got word that these units are sticking to back roads, avoiding the main state highways. All right. And a report in from Vanson's Volunteers: they successfully ambushed a UN convoy heading along Highway Fourteen. Congratulations to Vanson's Volunteers. And I'm Lieutenant Henry, reporting to you on Radio Free USA. Pass the news along, patriots, pass the news along . . ."

Stewart pursed his lips, moved the dial and said quietly, "Not good, hearing those clowns. Let's see what the UN has to offer."

A woman's voice, more modulated and professional than her competition: ". . . Food-distribution centers at Hopkinton, New Canaan and Riley have been temporarily closed. Please stay tuned to Radio Pax, Albany, for additional information. At the top of the hour today, Radio Pax will again broadcast those areas under safe UN control. If you are not in one of these safe areas, please be assured that the UN Force in the United States will reach you and your family. In the meantime, if you are under some type of threat or hostility, remain calm. Help will be coming to your vicinity. Retreat to a basement or a secure room. Stay away from windows. Do not travel. Listen to this station for further information. Again, this is Radio Pax, Albany . . ."

Stewart gave a snort of disgust, flipped through the dials again. "Not to worry, the woman says. Chaos is set loose upon the countryside, and neighbors are killing each other because of their place of origin. Help will get there eventually."

As the nearest UN representative, I kept my mouth shut. I knew the history of peacekeepers and peacemakers over the years, from Rwanda to Liberia to Bosnia and now the United States. Most times the UN were just like overworked police: by the time they got to you, the best they could do was bury the bodies and tidy up the countryside. But Stewart was leaving me alone. He just went back to his radio consoles.

"Ah, first real good bit of information" he said, moving the dial slowly with his thick fingers. "Hear that?"

I strained to listen but could only make out the hiss of static. "No. I don't hear a thing. Just white noise, that's all."

Stewart grinned. "Yeah, and that's good. One of the worst militia stations was broadcasting on this frequency, inciting people to rise up in arms and fight the oppressor, whoever the oppressor of the hour happened to be. They went off the air during the armistice but came right back again a few days ago. Real vile stuff—I'm just glad to hear them silenced. Gives me the idea that maybe somebody saner is gaining the upper hand."

"Where were they located?" I asked.

He kept fiddling with the dial. "About three miles down the road. So maybe things are clearing up. OK, just one more station, for the hell of it. Let's hear some of your countrymen."

And then came a cultured voice that I recognized from one of the morning news shows on the Canadian Broadcasting Corporation. Hearing that older gentleman's voice on the boring and bland and wonderful CBC suddenly made me so homesick that I wished I had never even heard of the UN or UNFORUS.

". . . UN headquarters in Geneva is reporting that the general armistice has been successfully reestablished in the states of Michigan and New Hampshire, and that negotiations are continuing in the states of New York, Vermont, Kentucky, Tennessee and Texas. Scattered outbreaks of violence among militia units and supporters of the UN intervention are also continuing in those states, sources said. Meanwhile, hearings on the UN intervention and the terrorist attack on Lower Manhattan and the aerial bombardments last spring are continuing at the American Congress on Capitol Hill, while the President of the United States continues to remain in seclusion at the presidential retreat at Camp David. In national news, the Prime Minister stated today that Canadian military units will remain on duty at all border crossings to the United States for the foreseeable future. The opposition leader, Mister MacDonald, stated that—"

Stewart switched off the station and said, "Well, I think things are about as good as they can be right now. Having the armistice take effect again in Michigan and New Hampshire is good news. Hopefully, they can straighten out the mess here in a few days or so. Even if our glorious President sits on his hands and says and does nothing."

"Based on what you're hearing, when would be a good time to leave?" I asked.

"How does dusk sound?"

"Not any earlier?"

Stewart started fiddling with other switches on the radios. "The militias like to split their activities between daylight and darkness. I've found out that around dusk and dawn is when they're on the move, getting ready to go home. That gives you more opportunities to slip through and make it to the highway—if that's where you want to go."

I shifted my weight on the table. "Yeah, I'm still looking at the highway. Eventually the UN's going to have to regain some sort of control, and the interstates are their best transport operation."

"All right," Stewart said. "Like I told you, the interstate is about—"

A phone rang, startling me. Stewart turned in his chair. The phone rang three times, and then stopped.

"Who could that—"

He held up his hand so I kept my mouth shut. The phone rang again, five times, before stopping. And then it rang five times again. Stewart's face seemed to turn gray and his body also seemed to sag in the chair.

"Coded call, right?" I said.

"Yeah."

"So the militias aren't the only ones using codes," I said. "Who's calling you?"

"A friend who, like me, isn't associated with the militias."

I asked, "What does this code mean?"

Stewart rubbed at his beard. "It means two things. The first is that you've got to get going."

I knew I should have stood up but I felt frozen to the chair. "And what's the second meaning of that call?"

Stewart looked right at me. "It means a militia unit is heading right here, right now."

CHAPTER NINETEEN

Stewart got up and I followed him as he raced down the stairs. He talked over his shoulder at me as we went into the living room. "Because of who my daughter married, I've been on a list. Big deal. Half the county is on a list of some sort, especially those of us who fed or hid refugees from the cities when the shooting started. But we tend to know each other and we try to keep track of what's going on. And part of keeping track is giving out a warning when the militias are on the move. Jerry."

The boy looked up from the television. He didn't say a word.

Stewart said, "Red alert, son. Take the dog and go down into the cellar. All right? You know the drill."

Jerry nodded and said, "Tucker." The English springer spaniel leaped up and followed him out of the room. I heard the noise of feet and paws slapping on wooden stairs.

Stewart said, "Poor guy's seen more crap in his nine years than some people have during their entire lives."

"I'm sure," I said.

"And I'm sure of one other thing, and that's that we've got to get you out of here," he said. "C'mon, not much time to waste."

We went into the kitchen and Stewart filled my water bottle, which he passed over to me. I put on my coat and slung my blanket roll over my shoulders. He said, "Sorry it can't be dusk. OK. Here's the directions. Back past the barn, go over the electric fence. Don't worry, it's not turned on. By the fence is an old bathtub. Used it for a while as a watering trough. From there, head up the hill. You'll see the path. Get up the hill, keep on going straight. The trail will widen some. When you start coming down the opposite slope, you'll spot the highway in the distance. Maybe ten, fifteen minutes away. Just try to keep moving in a straight line. You can't miss it."

I held out my hand. "Thanks. I owe you a lot, Stewart, a hell of a lot."

He ignored my outstretched hand. "Remember we're out here, OK? See if you can't do something about that. And one more thing."

Stewart brushed past me, went to a closet beside the door leading outside. He opened the closet door, reached up and pulled something down off an upper shelf. Then he brought it out and presented it to me.

A scoped rifle with a leather sling.

I shook my head. "I'm UN. I'm not supposed to carry—"

"Yeah, and our Declaration of Independence promised us life, liberty and the pursuit of happiness, and see where we are now. Look, you said this morning that you didn't want to go back to the militias. Fine. But for God's sake, man, take something so you can defend yourself."

It took about a second for me to make up my mind, a second filled with memories of the Aussie television crew and Sanjay and the dead German pilot and Gary, the executed schoolteacher. "OK. You've convinced me."

"Fine," Stewart said. "Listen up, 'cause we don't have much time. This is a Remington .22 semi-auto." In his other hand he held a small box of ammunition, which he now popped open. He undid a screw assembly under the barrel and said, "Simple way of loading. Tube magazine, here beneath the barrel. Takes twelve rounds. Load them in like this, sliding in, one right after another. Then replace the tube."

Which he did before handing the rifle over to me, along with the cardboard box in which the cartridges rolled around like tiny marbles. I put the box in a coat pocket and continued listening. "Little knob there by the trigger guard, that's the safety. If you see red, it means the safety is off. Action there on the right. Snap it back once and you're ready to go. Then just keep on pulling the trigger. Savvy?"

I shouldered the rifle and went outside to the gray-green and muddy lawn. I felt someone tap me on my shoulder. Stewart was smiling and now his hand was extended.

"OK. Now that you're on your way, good luck," he said.

I squeezed his hand, feeling the roughness of his skin. "Thanks again. And I certainly won't forget you. Not for a moment."

"I know," he said. "Now get your ass in gear before the bad guys show up."

He went back inside and closed the door. I moved as quickly as I could, slipping my way through the mud. I went past the barn and reached the wire fence. I hesitated to touch the wire, seeing how it was secured to each post by an electric insulator. If it was on, it sure could give me a tingle, I thought.

Too late to doubt Stewart now. I grasped the fence, felt nothing except the coldness of the metal strands, and I climbed over. Nearby was the old rusty bathtub, just like Stewart had described, and there was the path, leading up to a hill, a hill nearly covered by pine trees and a few oaks. I started up the path and began huffing with exertion, the rifle bouncing on my back, the rolled-up blankets tugging me a bit off-balance, the spare cartridges rolling around in the little cardboard box. I puffed some more and then the path leveled out. Almost there, the top of the hill. And what had Stewart said? From the hill, on the other side, the highway would be in view. And from that point, about ten or fifteen minutes to reach the road. Ten to fifteen minutes away from being picked up by a convoy, from being saved and having a good meal and a hot shower, and being able to tell somebody, anybody, what I had seen and what I had done, and to get a world of hurt to descend upon the traitorous Peter Brown—

I stopped and moved to the left, past some low brush, which I pulled aside. I heard the sound of engines. I dumped my blankets, pulled the rifle off my shoulder and, remembering again what Stewart had said, snapped back the bolt. And then I checked the safety. No red showing. Safe, then. I placed my arm through the leather sling and brought the scope up to my eye, and the house and buildings and muddy field below me came into close-up. A pickup truck and minivan with every window busted out were parked by the house. I breathed in and out, watching what was going on through the small rifle scope, the black cross-hairs sight superimposing itself over everything I watched.

Five guys in fatigues and carrying weapons were milling around the yard, and one of them started pounding repeatedly at the kitchen door from which I had exited just a few minutes ago. Stewart appeared soon. I could see that they were talking back and forth and Stewart was shaking his head. He stepped out into the yard, talking some more. Two of the guys were leaning against the fender of their pickup truck, ignoring the discussion going on between Stewart and the man I guessed was the leader. The rifle scope shook some as I recognized the guy. One of my escorts, back at the militia camp. Swell.

The door to the house opened again and Stewart turned round, his face screwed up with anger as Tucker barreled out of the house, followed shortly by Jerry. Stewart pointed to the house but Jerry ignored him and went over to the militia guy, tipped his head back and said something to him. For some reason, the fellow looked embarrassed. Tucker the dog went over to the two guys resting against the pickup-truck fender. One of them bent down, picked up the spaniel's tennis ball and tossed it down the driveway. The dog went after the bouncing ball with joyful enthusiasm.

"Careful, Tucker," I whispered. "You're playing with the enemy."

The militia leader seemed now to be talking louder to Stewart, jabbing his finger at Stewart's chest, and Jerry was beside him as well, tugging at the militia leader's coat. My mouth got dry and I thought of the water bottle that I had inside my coat. But I dared not move, not while I was watching what was going on. Now the militia guy was poking Stewart hard, forcing the older man to step back.

And then it went to the shits.

The militiaman—by now looking seriously irritated—pushed Jerry away with one hand, causing the kid to sit down hard in the mud. Stewart rushed forward but the militia guy had already unslung his rifle and now he swung it at Stewart, catching the older man in the jaw with the weapon's heavy stock. Stewart fell down to lie splayed out in the mud as Jerry sat there, bawling. Even Tucker had stopped playing and was looking around him quizzically, as though he could not believe the stupidity and hatred in the human race.

When the militiaman raised his rifle and aimed it at Stewart, I flicked the little knob on the side of the Remington with my thumb. And shot him.

I COULDN'T TELL you who was more surprised. Me, the militia guys or Stewart. The report was quite loud and since the Remington was a .22 the recoil was nonexistent. I wasn't even sure if I had hit the son of a bitch, but I kept on firing, aiming at the running and hiding members of the militia group and then popping a few bullets into their vehicles for good measure. I kept on firing until the trigger suddenly got stiff and unyielding, and I realized that I had blown through all twelve rounds. I did another quick scan of the scene through the telescopic sight and saw Stewart and Jerry and Tucker racing back into the house. I moved the rifle, the view shaking some now as I realized what I had just done. I couldn't make out any of the militiamen, not at all. Then came a flicker of movement, and gunfire crackled and stuttered from the yard down below me. I moved back into the brush, breathing hard, remembering the quick lesson I had gotten from

Stewart. The magazine tube came out with a snap and a twist, and I took the cardboard box of cartridges from my pocket. Two of them fell on the ground and, swearing, I scrabbled among the leaves and dirt to retrieve them. This was no time to waste ammunition.

Counting slowly—I wanted to make sure I put in the correct number—I reloaded the magazine tube, replaced it in its position beneath the gun's barrel, and put the few remaining cartridges back into my coat pocket. I snapped back the action and then squirmed my way back to my shooting spot. Through the scope I saw movement down below: a line of militiamen were coming up the hill toward me. I fired three times more and then ducked and crawled out of there as they returned fire in a rapid sequence of loud booms, punctuated by the frightening sounds of rounds coming in over my head and slamming into branches and tree trunks. They sure as hell weren't firing .22s.

I paused, just long enough to gather my thoughts and an extra breath or two. Then I resumed running.

I GOT BACK on the path quick enough. A small rational part of me understood that this wasn't a good idea, being out in the open like this, but I knew I had no choice. My goal wasn't to sit in the woods and play at being sniper. My goal was to haul ass to the highway, and if that had been my only intention, I wouldn't have shot at those clowns back there. That had been stupid. That hadn't been rational. I should have gone quietly on my way. But, damn it, I was *glad* that I hadn't been rational. I was glad I had stayed and had shot at them. And as I'd been shooting, I'd wanted to shout at them as well: "How does it feel, being on the receiving end of gunfire? How does it feel to hide and cower? How does it feel?"

Somehow, I think they were pissed.

There were distant shouts back there, and some more gunfire, and I ran hard, branches and brambles snapping at my face and hands. For the first few minutes I was at an advantage, slight as it was. They couldn't be sure if I was up on the hill, hiding and waiting, trying to snipe at them. So they had to take their time coming up that rise and keep their heads down. I stopped and fired off a couple of rounds into the air, hoping the noise would slow them. My breathing was racing so hard that it felt like I had little razor blades inside my lungs that lacerated me with every step. Then I fell flat on my face.

I rolled over, saw the exposed root that had tripped me up. I got up from the cold ground and winced. My right ankle was sore. Damn. Time to slow down, just a bit. I picked up the rifle and continued running at a more cautious pace, making sure I took a few extra seconds to dodge the rocks and tree branches that were now threatening to kill me by tripping me up and offering me to the militiamen I had just been firing at.

Some more shouts and shots behind me. The path widened as it passed a knoll of gravel and rock, and below me, in the distance and beyond another line of trees, was my Holy Grail, my Place in Paradise, the Prize of Prizes: the stretch of asphalt and concrete that was the interstate highway. To celebrate what I had just seen I turned around and fired a couple more shots into the woods, just to let my pursuers know I was still alive.

And I kept on running.

ABOUT TEN MINUTES later I slogged through a drainage ditch at the side of the highway, soaking my legs up to my knees, flailing through some cattails growing in long brown stalks beside the muddy water. I went up the grass embankment, breathing hard again, the rifle slippery in my hands. The highway: two lanes right in front of me, then a grass median strip, then another two lanes.

And bless every one of us, some distance toward the west were three Toyota Land Cruisers, parked by the side of the road, all painted white and one with the UN flag flapping from a radio whip antenna at the rear. There seemed to be someone standing beside an open door. I actually choked up for a moment, as if I was seeing the familiar red and white maple-leaf banner out there in the distance, offering me safety, offering me sanctuary from the murderous men behind me. I stood, took a couple of deep breaths, and—

Whee, whee! Rounds went blasting over my head, followed immediately by the sharp cracks of gunfire. I had been spotted, and then some. I ducked and ran as fast as I could across the pavement, dodging back and forth, and I made it to the grass median. More gunshots and then my feet were slapping on the pavement of the second stretch of highway, and I didn't try to make it fancy or pretty as I flopped to the ground and rolled down the other embankment, right into another drainage ditch. My breathing was harsh and spit was running down my chin. I dumped the blanket roll and edged up to the edge of the embankment, peering through the tall grass. Across the way I saw uniformed and armed men heading out into some sort of skirmish line. I put the rifle to my shoulder, aimed through the scope at some guy with a gun, and pulled the trigger.

Nothing happened. I looked at the bolt. Wide open. Out of ammunition.

"Shit," I whispered, slithering back down into the cold water of the ditch. I fumbled through my coat pocket, took out a now-soggy cardboard box of .22 cartridges. Some shouts came at me from across the highway. The box felt dangerously light. I popped open the flap and poured out the tiny cartridges into my dirt-covered hand. Six. Just six shots left. Not even one more, to make it a lucky seven?

I went to work, trying to ignore the yells from the militiamen scant meters away from me across the lanes of the deserted highway. Deserted—except for those three vehicles waiting for me. I spared a quick glance up the highway, but the UN Land Crusiers were hidden by brush from this angle. I could barely make out the blue and white UN banner. I reloaded the tube magazine, put it back into the Remington with shaking hands, snapped the bolt back in and then squirmed my way back up the embankment. Still some movement, heading off in both directions. For a militia, these clowns weren't half bad. I snapped off two shots and then ducked again as return fire went whistling over my head.

I stayed bent over, started moving as fast as I could, my feet slopping through the mud and water of the drainage ditch. More gunfire, and then a shout, heard clearly: "Might as well give up now, UN man! We've got you smoked!"

I decided it was time to start talking as well, but not to them. If I was lucky, the three UN four-by-fours up ahead were guarded by cousins of Charlie, our Marine escort from such a long time ago. I didn't want any misunderstanding as I blundered my way toward them, carrying a loaded rifle in my hands.

"UN coming in!" I yelled. Then I remembered a code phrase I had learned back when I'd thought I could make a damn difference in this damn country, a code phrase of identification. "This is Geneva, Geneva, coming in!"

Finally the brush gave out and there I was. The three Toyota Land Cruisers were all parked on the side of the road, in a row. And if I could have cried, I would have started weeping.

For all three vehicles were abandoned, shot up, tires flattened and glass shattered. Even the UN banner was torn and burned, and judging by the rust around the bullet holes and shrapnel gashes, these Land Crusiers had been here for a while. What I'd earlier thought had been a person was just a coat, hanging from the side of an open door. The place was deserted.

Abandoned. Just like me.

CHAPTER TWENTY

But I wasn't ready to give up, not yet, especially since those fine fellows out there who were hunting me probably had plans for my capture, trial and sentence. Plans that all ended up with me getting shot in the back of the head on this stretch of American highway in about five or ten minutes.

I kept my head down, looked through a Land Cruiser's smashed windows and open doors, hoping I could find something, anything, to help me out. Perhaps a radio with its batteries still working, maybe even a weapon left behind by one of the military escorts. I peered through the open doors and rummaged among the wreckage, trying to ignore the rusty stains on the torn upholstery, the remnants of bandages and some torn clothing.

Nothing.

More gunshots, and a *thonk!* as a bullet struck metal. I got behind the middle vehicle and fired off a shot in reply. How many left? I counted back. Just three. Damn it, just three.

"Hey, UN man, we're gonna get ya! Just a matter of time!"

Another shot, coming from further up the highway. Damn it all to hell. They had me surrounded. I looked at the only path remaining open for me, to the right of the vehicles and leading away from the highway. But there were no woods or shrubbery there, just a knee-deep swamp of cattails and other growing things. If I started slogging through there, they would—

Thonk, thonk! More incoming gunfire, and by instinct I fired three more times—and then felt the stubborn weight of the dead trigger.

Empty.

I squirmed away toward another vehicle that had its rear door hanging open. Crazy, random thoughts were galloping through my mind, everything from simply hiding under one of the shattered Land Cruisers to trying to jump-start one of the engines and maybe make my escape that way. But I didn't think I would have the time to learn the intricacies of how to jump-start a shot-up Toyota four-by-four.

I looked into the rear compartment. More bloody bandages, an open first-aid kit, and attached to the side wall, above the tire well, a bright orange plastic box, secured by straps. I unsnapped the box and sat down on the ground, with a rear tire against my back. I opened the lid—and nestling there was a flare gun, with three cartridges. I pulled out the gun, popped open the barrel, and slid in one of the fat flare shells. I snapped the damn thing shut, looked at the instructions pasted into the lid of the container—which looked to be about twenty paragraphs of fine print with illustrations in orange and red. Sorry, no time. There was a hammer just above the gun's handle, which I pulled back.

I wiggled my way below the Land Cruiser's undercarriage, holding the flare gun out in front of me. The shooting had stopped for just a moment, and across the other lanes I saw figures scurrying forward, coming up the embankment. Somebody yelled out something and a line of about six or seven militiamen came up from the other side and started trotting across the asphalt lanes. I closed my eyes and pulled the trigger of the flare gun. There was a *pop!* and a loud *whoosh!* as the flare, bright orange and red and almost too bright to look at, shot out from the wide-mouthed barrel and went across the highway, trailing sparks and smoke. The approaching gunmen scattered as the flare actually bounced twice on the asphalt before burying itself into the far woodline and brush.

Then I heard something.

More shots, and a couple more yells. I was breathing really hard now as I squirmed my way back out, banging my head against a piece of the four-by-four's transmission. I tried to listen even harder, but all I could make out was the pounding of blood in my ears. I sat up, looked about me. Samuel's Last Stand. If my father was lucky, maybe he'd find out in a week or two. Maybe.

What now?

Trust, I thought. Trust in what you heard.

I reloaded the flare gun and this time, instead of pointing it at my pursuers, I aimed it straight up into the sky. Another satisfying *pop!* and *whoosh!* and the orange-red flare went way up, almost as bright as the sun to look at. It seemed to go up a couple of hundred meters before arcing over and falling back to earth. Another couple of *thonks!* and some glass from a side window fell into my lap.

One more time with the flare gun, and even though the cartridge was as fat as a child's fist my hand was trembling so hard that I could hardly put it into the barrel or breech or whatever it was called. I spared another quick glance, saw more figures coming my way, less than a hundred meters, closing in from both sides. Again, I thought I heard something.

No time to think. Just time to act.

Pop! and *whoosh!* My last flare went up into the sky, and this time, oh, this time, before the flare sputtered out and fell back to the bloody ground the noise was louder—much louder.

Helicopters, heading this way.

"C'mon, boys, c'mon," I said. Then, louder, I yelled, "C'mon!"

Oh, what a sight. Three helicopters were racing toward me. Two of them peeled off as the other one came closer in and then spun to the side. There was a harsh rattling noise and I saw what looked to be sparks coming from the side of the 'copter, and I realized it was a door gunner, chewing up the scenery. And there sure as hell didn't seem to be any return fire coming from the scattered militiamen.

"There you go!" I yelled. "Hose those bastards!"

But then I thought, shit, they might think *I'm* one of those bastards. I made sure I was well away from my discarded rifle and then I half-crawled, half-ran back to the last Land Cruiser in the line and tugged at the torn UN banner there, pulling it free. Now one of the helicopters was over the swampy area to the right, and I waved the flag at it. A gunner in the open door at the side waved back, and the helicopter came forward, touching down just ahead of the vehicles. There was a national flag on the tail, red and white and blue, just above the black stenciled UNFORUS. The gunner and another guy in a green jumpsuit and helmet were waving at me and I ran toward them, dropping the flag on the ground and shielding my face and eyes from the dust and gravel being tossed up. The roaring noise from the engine hurt my ears and the prop wash was pushing me back, like in one of those nightmares where you're trying to escape the knife-wielding madman and your feet seem stuck in taffy.

Yet I kept on running, smelling aviation fuel now, and came up to the doorway where the machine gun rested on its mount. I tried to lift myself in and a couple of strong hands grabbed my shoulders and pulled me aboard. And even before I got my feet into the open cabin the helicopter was up and away, gaining altitude. I rolled over on my side, breathing as hard as before but feeling as light as a feather, and exhilarated. I had made it. I was going to live. No more bad guys. No more nights on cold ground.

Standing over me was one of the crewmen, with his visor up. He had a thin mustache. He asked me something in a language I didn't recognize and I shook my head. "Sorry, I don't understand."

He smiled. "UN?"

"Yes."

"*Engländer*? American?"

"No, Canadian," I said.

He grunted, smiled again, moved his head closer.

"Canadian!" I yelled over the roar of the engine.

"Ah," he said, now comprehending. "Canada! Canada good!" and he gave me a thumbs-up with a gloved hand.

I closed my eyes, breathed out, breathed in. "Yes," I said. "Canada good."

And we flew on, rising ever higher.

WE FLEW INTO a town outside the state capital, Albany, and the helicopter crew must have radioed ahead because when I got to the hospital the medics were quick and efficient. By the time we landed I had found out that the crew was from the Czech Republic, one of the NATO contingents of UNFORUS, and I shook everybody's hand as I got out. I had walked maybe two or three meters across the parking lot of the hospital when a running crew of medical personnel grabbed me and, against my protests, bundled me onto a gurney and brought me into the hospital's emergency room.

The next hour was a blur. I was stripped, examined, checked out and asked a couple of dozen questions—all medically related—and had my feet and teeth checked. A couple of scrapes and cuts on my face and hands were treated. Then I had an embarrassingly erotic sponge bath from two young French nurses—who murmured and giggled among themselves as they dried me off—and raced through eating an apple, a banana and a crunchy-peanut-butter sandwich—which tasted so good that my mouth was full of saliva just from thinking about it, even minutes after I had finished it. Then some clerk came by and issued me with new dosimetry—my old TLD was decaying in a ditch somewhere—and it was like I had gotten back my identity badge for my secret little club.

And an hour later, I was lying in a bed in a curtained-off area in the emergency room, being debriefed by a smiling older woman with black-rimmed glasses and a knitted pink sweater who said she was with the governing board of UNFORUS for the surrounding four counties. Right from the start, she reminded me of my grandmother on my father's side, which was to the UNFORUS woman's disadvantage, because I never could stand Grandmother Simpson. My father's mother had none of his good qualities—what few there were—and many of his poorest qualities, including a hot-blood temper. She also had an urge to pinch my cheeks whenever I got within a meter of her, and a need to smoke a pack of cigarettes a day and drink a highball before dinner.

"I'm Cecile O'Ryan," said the woman in a soft Irish accent. "You've had quite the few days, Mister Simpson, haven't you?"

"Sure," I said. "The rest of my section, how are they?"

She looked down at her clipboard. "I'm sorry—I have bad news about one of your comrades."

"Sanjay Prith," I said. "Yes, I know. The others?"

"Oh," she said brightly. "The others? The latest I heard they were all fine, though not out in the field. The armistice having failed . . . well, our field activities have certainly been restricted."

"Hold on," I said, feeling a lightness in my heart that I could barely stand. Miriam. Safe. Since that wonderful night in the tent, sharing our quarters and each other, and the bloody morning that followed I had tried not to think of her, tried not to wonder if something horrible had happened to her. But it hadn't. She was safe. She was alive. She wasn't stuck in some school-bus prison somewhere deep in the woods, trembling, waiting to be shot or raped when some armed man's mood struck him. Safe. I took a good, long breath.

Now to the business at hand. For example, one Peter Brown, that bastard Brit. I wanted to tell Ms O'Ryan about Peter, about his meeting with the militia units. But I wanted to get one even more important piece of business taken care of before anything else.

O'Ryan said, "Well, I'm sure your colleagues will be glad to hear you're back. Now, though, we have a number of questions that we'd like answered."

"Sure," I said. "But first things first."

"Oh?" she asked, putting about a ton of irritation into that one-syllable word.

"Yes, 'oh'," I said. "There were a man and a young boy. Grandfather and grandson. They fed me and protected me. I want them to be picked up and brought somewhere safe. Here, if that makes sense."

"Their names?" O'Ryan asked, irritation still showing in her tone.

"Stewart Carr. And his grandson Jerry. Plus a dog called Tucker."

"Ah, a dog. Well, perhaps after we're done here, we can file a report and—"

"You don't understand," I said. "This isn't a request."

"What is it, then? An order?"

I shifted my bare legs under the blankets. "Call it what you will. All I'm saying is that I will gladly be debriefed, tell you what I know about things, tell you the best guess I have for the location of one of the main militia camps. But I'm not saying a word until I see Mister Carr and his grandson. And their dog. In front of me."

"Do you know how many refugees and terrorized people we're trying to secure, trying to process out there?"

"I don't know, and I don't particularly care," I said. "I only care right now about that guy, his grandson and their dog. Tucker."

O'Ryan's eyes got icy, just like Grandmother Simpson's. "You're in no position to demand anything, young man."

"Maybe not," I said. "But what kind of position I am in is to contact my old friends back at my old employer, the Toronto *Star*, and tell them what kind of cluster-fuck—excuse my language—is going on here in the States. How my unit in particular spent most of its time driving in circles, trying to uncover war-crimes evidence, including the famous Site A, and how we found shit."

"You've signed a confidentiality agreement," O'Ryan snapped.

"Right. And let's see who'll try to enforce *that* if I resign from the UN's service. All right?"

She continued glaring at me, and then tried another tack. "We have a report that you were using a firearm just before being picked up."

"So?"

"That's in violation of a number of agreements between UNFORUS and the local authorities. A noncombatant such as yourself is strictly forbidden to bear arms," O'Ryan said. "You could find yourself in a county jail for a very long time, Mister Simpson, if we decided not to defend you against any local prosecution."

I wiggled my toes. "Prosecute away," I said. "I can hardly wait to see the coverage *that* would generate: a young man—myself, in this instance—defending himself against a half-dozen or so paramilitaries with a .22 rifle, a weapon designed for hunting squirrels rather than shooting human thugs. Being a former newspaperman myself, I can see how that would make a hell of a story. Wouldn't it?"

Now O'Ryan was in thoroughly pissed-off mode, another familiar attitude of the not-so-dear, departed Grandmother Simpson. She got up suddenly and stalked out of my little curtained-off cubicle, without even bothering to draw the curtain behind her. I guessed that Peter would have to wait. I looked out into the bustling emergency room, saw a man in a uniform of some sort, groaning and moaning as an ER crew worked on him. Bloody bandages were on the dirty tiled floor. I couldn't tell if he was paramilitary or UNFORUS, the poor guy, so I turned my attention to a plastic cup of ice water, which I sipped through a straw. It tasted wonderful.

As the wounded man was wheeled away another uniformed man came into my little cubicle. He was a beefy-looking German with a name tag on his heavy shirt that read HORLENGER. A blue UN beret, folded over, was stuck under his shirt's shoulder loop.

"Simpson?"

"The same," I said.

Horlenger grunted, produced a folded-over topo map. "This house, the one that has the man and the boy. Can you show it to me on the map?"

I said, "Can you show me the highway where I was picked up? By the three shot-up UN vehicles?"

"*Ja*, I can," he said. He pushed aside my ice water on the little side table and unfolded the map. He oriented me by pointing out the stretch of highway where I had been rescued. I recalled the hill and my little run, and I said, "On the other side of the hill. Right here. A farmhouse, a big barn and a pickup truck in the front yard. There's a field over here that should be a good landing place."

Horlenger just nodded, folded the map up. "I hope you know what you're doing," he said.

"How's that?"

He shook his head. "In a few minutes I am going to ask two, maybe three crews to risk their lives, *ja*? Not to mention the equipment, which we don't have enough of. All is being threatened this afternoon. All for an old man and a boy. And a dog. When we could do much more, elsewhere, with what we barely have. You understand?"

"Yeah, I understand. But it's personal. They saved my life, and I promised them."

He nodded. "Then maybe *you* should go. Hmm?"

"If I could, I would."

"Bah," Horlenger said, and he stalked off. I rolled over on my side, pulled up the blankets, and despite the lumpiness of the mattress and the noise in the ER I fell right asleep. As far as I could tell, I didn't dream of a damn thing.

WET. COLD. WET. Cold. I woke up with something slathering against my face, and I looked into sad brown eyes and a furry face. I coughed and sat up. The dog called Tucker got back down on the floor, having been up on his hindquarters, licking my face. I heard a boy's laugh and sat up and rubbed at my eyes.

"Well," Stewart said, smiling at me, his arm round his grandson's shoulders. Jerry had a little blue knapsack in his hands and his nose was still running. Behind them, smiling like she had arranged the whole damn thing, was Ms. Cecile O'Ryan.

"Hey," I said. "You guys OK?"

Jerry piped up. "We flew in a helicopter! And Tucker peed on the floor!"

"I'm sure he did," I said. "Flying like that can be scary."

Stewart came over, offered me his hand, which I gladly shook. He said, "Good for you, Samuel. You didn't forget."

"Not for a moment," I said.

Then he choked up some, started stammering, "You have no idea what we owe you, what it meant to see . . ."

Cecile O'Ryan stepped forward and started tugging at Stewart's elbow. "Now, I'm sure you'd love to talk some more to Mister Simpson, but he's still under treatment and needs his rest. If you come this way, I'll have someone from the nursing staff check you both and get a hot meal into you. All right?"

So they went away, Tucker pausing just to look back at me. Jerry did the same, giving me a little bye-bye wave with his hands, which I returned. They turned the corner, by a nurse's station, and then Ms. O'Ryan came traipsing back, clipboard held up against her chest like a little shield. She came into my area, pulled the curtain shut and said, "Ready to get to work?"

"I thought you told the Carrs that I need my rest," I said.

She smiled unpleasantly at me. "I lied."

I folded my arms. "Fair enough. Ask away." I decided then that I still didn't like her one bit, and that the matter of Peter could wait until I saw Jean-Paul.

I ANSWERED CECILE O'Ryan's questions for the next hour, and then another German officer came in, a blond-haired guy with SCHNEIDER on his name tag. He spread a big topo map over the top of my hospital bed. From the ambush site of a few days back—and *Miriam's alive, Miriam's alive*, came the singing voice inside my head—I did my best to reconstruct my travels, though I wished I had a better idea of where that damn militia camp was located. Schneider's face darkened some when I told him about the soldiers

I had seen shot and the Luftwaffe pilot's body I'd seen hanging, and he made a series of marks on a little notepad he was carrying. He asked me about the camp's defenses and the number of militiamen I'd seen and the weapons they'd carried, and I told him about the netting overhead and the spread-out nature of the place. He said, "Five minutes. Just five minutes with one of the American spy satellites and I would know where that place was. Just five minutes."

Eventually he left and Cecile O'Ryan said, "Would you like to go home?"

"Now?" I asked, shocked.

She laughed. "No, not now. Maybe tomorrow or the next day. But I think you deserve a trip home, after all you've been through."

Sure. Head on out. And I still had a bit of business to attend to, a bit of business that required me to talk to somebody other than Ms. Cecile O'Ryan, from the large UN bureaucracy that was running things.

"Jean-Paul Cloutier," I said.

"Yes?"

"My section leader. Is he still around?"

She made a notation. "I believe so. Why? Do you want to talk to him?"

You better believe it, honey, I thought. I have a little tale to tell him, about Peter and hidden radios and betrayal. Aloud I said, "Yes, as soon as I can. I just want to see . . . Well, I just want to see how he and the others in my section are doing."

O'Ryan nodded, still smiling. I guess she was now my new best friend. "All right. I'll see what I can do. In the meantime, why don't we move you out of here into someplace more comfortable?"

"Sure," I said.

Which was what they did.

ABOUT TEN MINUTES later I was in another part of the hospital, maybe a part where family members could stay while their loved ones were under the knife. I was in a tiny hotel-like room, and I shivered as I remembered that unheated and unlit motel we had all stayed in. It seemed such a long time ago. I was surprised to see two muddy duffel bags on the floor and I opened them up. I felt my throat get thick. My old gear, including my Sony camera stuff and my computer terminal, all in one place. Even some old clothes—though laid out on the bed was what I had been wearing when I had been picked up, freshly laundered.

I went over to a small window and looked outside, feeling calm and peaceful from just looking at all those brilliant electric lights around me, bright lights forcing back the darkness. There were vehicles of all types in the parking lot—civilian trucks and passenger cars, military lorries and even a couple of armored APCs and it was just pleasurable to see them on the move. I looked out and in the distance, on the horizon, was a small orange glow. A fire of some sort. I only hoped that the polite German who had aided in my interrogation had located the camp where I had been kept and was busily blasting it off the face of the earth.

Before I gave myself the luxury of a thorough cleansing I took a small chair from in front of the writing table and shoved it under the main doorknob. Then I made sure that both locks were secured. Only then did I go into the bathroom. I looked at the mirror and saw red-rimmed eyes, a scabbed-over face that had been swabbed with some sort of disinfectant, and nearly a week's worth of beard that still looked like I had been growing it for all of three days. But behind me was a shower. I turned on the faucet and hot water came out, lots and lots of hot water. Believe it or not, I spent a whole hour in that hot and steamy little room, finally getting myself properly cleaned up.

CHAPTER TWENTY-ONE

When I was done with my shower I took an elevator to the basement of the building where a cafeteria had been set up. I didn't expect room-service standards but I was pleased by a little cardboard sign on the room phone—in English, French and German—that advised me that hot meals were served three times a day in the cafeteria and cold meals were available at any time. Checking the little clock by the bed stand, I saw that I had a half-hour before the last hot meal was served.

In the cafeteria there were what looked to be nearly a hundred people, plus a virtual Babel of voices and accents. There were civilians, doctors and nurses, and even some patients, either in wheelchairs or propelling themselves around by metal walkers or canes. Scattered throughout the crowd were the military uniforms of maybe a half-dozen different countries, and their only similarity was the UNFORUS arm patch and brassard on the left arm and the TLDs hanging off lapels. I stood in line and grabbed a plastic tray, still damp and warm from having just been washed. My stomach growled cheerfully at the prospect of hot food coming by for a visit.

I looked around the room. When I got back to looking at the line of people I was in it had moved forward and somebody up ahead was leaning back, looking at me.

Peter Brown.

I dropped my tray, ran forward, and tried my best to kill him.

TRIED MY BEST.

Another way to put that would be "utterly and abjectly failed," but I sure did a little damage. I made some noise, and there were a ruckus and some shouts and then we were grappling on the floor. Peter managed to roll me over after I had hammered him with some weak punches, and eventually he had me pinned, screaming up at him. Then a couple of bruisers—fellow Brits, it sounded like—helped Peter pick me up and drag me out of the cafeteria where we went into a little office with a small desk and two chairs. After he'd slammed the door shut, Peter said, "Samuel, look, just shut your trap for a moment. All right? Talk some sense. I'll give you five minutes to say anything you want, and after those five minutes you listen to me. Then you can take your best shot. Fair enough?"

"You fucking bastard," I said, breathing hard.

Peter smiled, leaned back in a swivel chair. "Not very original, mate. Sorry. You're going to have to do better than that."

"Where do you want me to begin, you traitorous shit? Sanjay's dead because of you. *And it's your fucking fault that I nearly got killed too.*"

That got his attention. He let the swivel chair snap back to its upright position and his ruddy face got even redder. I felt emboldened and went on. "Is *that* better, more original? Got your attention this time?"

Up on the wall behind Peter was a nutrition chart, with dancing slices of bread, grains and vegetables in some kind of food pyramid. It looked ridiculous but my attention was focused entirely on Peter who said, "Have you told anybody this yet?"

I wanted him to be scared of me for a change so I said, "Yeah, I have. And there are others to follow."

"Such as?"

"Jean-Paul, to begin with, when I catch up with him. And then my friends back at the Toronto *Star*. Oh, that'll be a good front-page story, once I resign my position with the UN and get my old job back. I'll even send them a few nice photos of you working in the field. Working for the militias, though—right?"

"Where's your proof?" Peter asked, his voice flat.

Again, I felt emboldened. I was expecting denials and put-downs and the usual abrasive response from Peter, who had picked on me from the very first day I had come to New York state. I was enjoying the discomfort I was putting him through.

"Sure, all in good time," I said dismissively. "But let's begin at the beginning, shall we? From the very start when we went out in the field we were going in circles, weren't we? We had bad intelligence, our communications gear was being jammed, and we found evidence of war crimes only by literally stumbling over it. Am I right?"

Peter just nodded. I went on, speaking quickly. "Then we hooked up with the Aussie television crew. Remember one of their questions? All about saboteurs, working within the UN field groups to block their progress—anyone's progress—in finding Site A. We all thought they were making it up."

"Proof, Samuel," he said. I felt a tiny thrill of victory at finally having this man call me by my right name. "You said you had proof."

"OK," I said. "Let's try this. Four days ago, we went looking for that Aussie TV crew. You tried to give us bogus directions, tried to keep us away from them. Hiding evidence of your mates' activities, were you, Peter? Then, a day after that, I was out in the woods, looking for you. You were out pissing against a tree—or so you said. But I saw something different, Peter. I saw you either losing your mind or talking to someone by radio, because I saw you talking into your wrist. Mentioning grace . . . oh, yeah, somebody's name. Grace. Who was she? Your Stateside contact? And since you seem stable enough—even though you're an arrogant traitor—I think you were relaying information to someone. Your paymaster, no doubt."

"Anything else?" Peter asked in the same flat tone.

"Sure," I said. "One last piece of evidence and then you can give me whatever bullshit you like. Two days after the ambush—and don't you feel guilty about what happened to Sanjay?—I was captured by a militia unit, kept captive in a hidden camp a fair number of klicks away from here. I was being held inside a school bus, and just before I managed to escape I saw the militia leader get a visitor. You. All by your lonesome, all inside that camp, getting smiles and slaps on the back. Like you belonged. Like you were their friend. And I saw you just before I got out. So there you go. Time for your reply, you shit."

Peter actually smiled at me. A very happy and cheerful grin. I said, "Thinking of killing me and then walking out of here? Sure. Try that, with a hundred or so witnesses outside that door. You go right ahead."

Peter kept smiling. "Tell you what, I told you that I'd give you a good answer, once you were done. But I'd like to go one better, if that's all right. Permit me to make a phone call?"

"Sure," I said, now feeling not so confident.

"Fine." He turned the chair and looked over the small desk, picked up the phone and dialed a four-digit number. "Hello, love. Peter here. I need to speak with Lawrence. Right away. Well, of course it's urgent, or else I wouldn't say 'right away.' Correct?" He looked over at me and made a big thing of shrugging. "Secretaries. God help us if they ever—Oh, hello, Lawrence. Sorry to disturb you but I have a bit of a situation. I was wondering if I could borrow you for just a few minutes." There was a pause, and Peter said, "Well, I know it's short notice. But trust me, it was important enough for me to make this call, now, wasn't it? Yes, I understand . . . Very well, I seem to be in the manager's office of this dreadful cafeteria in the basement. Thank you, thank you very much."

Peter hung up the phone and turned around again to face me. "There you go. All will be revealed very soon—if you can be patient, Samuel."

I said nothing, just kept on staring at his confident face. We didn't say anything for a couple of minutes. Through the door I could hear the sounds of feet moving on the tile floor, plates being set down on tables, and the rattle of silverware being used. Surprisingly enough, I didn't feel hungry at all.

"Still angry?" Peter asked, his hands folded across his belly.

I said, "I don't think it matters much who's coming down or what he's saying. All I know is what I saw. Including Sanjay, dead because of you."

Peter ignored that little shot and said, "I saw Miriam an hour or so ago. She was very pleased to hear that you'd been rescued. I imagine your reunion will be wonderful indeed."

Before I could say something sharp in reply, there was a knock on the door, and a man dressed in military fatigues entered. He was tall, well built, and his white hair was cut short. He had the usual UNFORUS brassard and the blue beret through a shoulder loop, and his name tag said HALE. But I also noticed his insignia of rank. The room suddenly seemed a lot colder, because I suddenly realized I had seen this older man somewhere before.

Peter stood up, shook the man's hand, and turned to me. "Samuel? I'd like to introduce you to General Sir Lawrence Hale. He's head of the British contingent for UNFORUS—but of course, since you claim to be a newspaperman, I'm sure you already know that. General, may I present Samuel Simpson, formerly of the Toronto *Star*, currently assigned to the field investigative unit that I've been working with."

I stood up too, feeling now like I was living through that dream in which you're in class and called upon by the teacher to stand up and speak and you know right away that you have no clothes on.

"General," I said.

"Simpson," he replied, grasping my hand for a moment and then ignoring me. He turned to Peter and said, "Captain? How can I help you? And can we make this quick?"

Captain . . . The man I'd thought was a former London cop had this gracious look on his face and said, "General, I just need you to verify something for my friend Samuel here."

"Is that all?" Hale said with a touch of irritation.

"I'm afraid it's necessary. Samuel needs to know my background and what I've been doing here. It's vital for the success of my mission."

Now the general looked at me, his pale blue eyes frosty. "I'm concerned about security."

"You have my assurance that everything will be kept confidential," Peter said.

"Very well," Hale said. "Simpson, Captain Peter Brown is here working in this country for our foreign intelligence service, M16. He has been detached from his own regiment, the SAS."

"Special Air Service," I said, no doubt unnecessarily.

"Indeed," Hale said. "Anything else?"

I couldn't think of a thing to ask him. Peter smiled. "No, sir. Thank you very much."

Hale just grunted and left the office. Peter closed the door. We both sat back down and I said, "What's your mission been? Or is that part of the secret?"

"Oh, it's a secret, all right, but I've decided—entirely on my own—that you deserve to know."

"And why's that?"

Peter said, "That's a rather stupid question, don't you think?"

"Indulge me," I said.

"Back at the campground Charlie told us later what had happened. You went out to make some hot water for morning tea and coffee. The rest of us were getting up when the gunfire started. Sanjay and Miriam, they wanted to go down the trail to see if they could find you. Jean-Paul and Charlie and myself—well, sorry, we thought it was too late. We managed to get the hell out of there but Sanjay thought he saw you, coming through the woods. He got out of one of the Land Cruisers and that was when he got hit. There was a lot more gunfire but we managed to get out of there, just barely. So you saved our lives, Samuel."

"How do you know that?"

"A day later, Charlie and a couple of his Marine buddies came back to retrieve Sanjay. Charlie went down the trail, saw the stove, saw where a metal pan had been dumped, maybe halfway down the trail. Charlie figured that you surprised the militia column, maybe splashed the boiling water on a guy or two. True?"

"True," I said.

"Then they started shooting earlier than they wanted," Peter said. "Which gave us the time to bail out. So there you go."

"Sanjay," I said, feeling my hands get tingly in shame.

"Yes?"

"You said he left to find me?"

"That's right," Peter said. "He wanted to make sure we didn't leave you behind."

"Oh," I said. "It's just that, well, I didn't know him that well and, um . . ."

Peter said, "I can't say that I knew him that well, either. And he was cheating on his wife, and he was a shitty driver, and he complained about my cooking, but in the end he was a brave one. Maybe the bravest of us all, except for you. I mean, going after a militia column with just a pan of hot water . . ."

"I wasn't brave," I said. "I was scared out of my gourd."

"Perhaps," he said. "But that's why you deserve to know. Ask away, but ask away quickly. Your free access to my secrets is only good in this little room."

I thought of a few things, and blurted out, "So, acting like an asshole. Was that you or part of the mission?"

"A mixture of both, I suppose," Peter said, smiling. "I had a role as a cranky Metropolitan police officer to play. I didn't want to get too friendly with the team. It wouldn't have matched my cover."

"And what was your job?"

"A number of different things."

"Tell me, then."

A shrug. "First of all, to let my government know what was really going on in the field. The UN bureaucracy can be thick and slow, and my people wanted to know what was going on in real time, without having to wait for information to muddle its way to Geneva and then to London. That was job number one. Job number two was to gather intelligence about the militias on the ground, to find out if they are as loosely organized as they claim to be or if they are linked to certain factions in Washington. You see, it's in our interest back home to have this country get back to its senses, the quicker the better. And knowing what influence the militias and their supporters might have in DC will make our job that much easier. And job number three . . . well, no offense to Charlie, but job number three was to keep me and everyone else alive. Too bad you seemed to have other ideas."

"The Australian television crew," I said.

"How true. I knew that there was a militia unit working in the area, and that if we had just kept still after that newshound got himself killed a UN convoy was going to make its way down the highway. But the stupid git managed to say something that both of us heard, about where his pals were located, and I didn't want us to have to poke around and look for them. I mean, really, Charlie is a wonderful guy and a Marine and all that, but he could barely keep us together long enough to get the hell out when the shooting did finally start."

"But we found the bodies of the cameraman and producer," I said.

Peter shook his head. "So bloody what? Excuse me for being so blunt, but two more bodies in this place? I mean, really. Here we are, running around, trying to find Site A and keep those militia generals in custody at The Hague, and we're going to waste our time on dead reporters who should have stayed home in the first place? Samuel, please, at least you can see the logic there."

"Maybe, but I don't want to look that hard," I said. "So how did you end up at the militia camp?"

Peter actually laughed. "I was there to get you out, Samuel."

"How?"

"How? By the tried and tested nature of paying a bribe," he said. "Look, we—and I don't mean the UN—had received word of your capture. We were also told about a ransom to be paid, which included ammunition and drugs. So I was there to check on you, to make sure that you were alive and healthy, and to pay up and get out. And let me tell you, that so-called colonel—Saunders, I think his name was, what a perfect idiot—went apoplectic when he realized you had scarpered. I thought he was going to shoot the men who had been guarding you, and then me, for good measure. About the only way I got out of there fair and clear was to pay them off with about half the bribe."

"Ammo?" I asked. "You gave those bastards ammo?"

"I most certainly did," Peter said. "Four cases of standard NATO-issue 7.62-millimeter rounds. I even tossed in some medical supplies for good measure."

"You did, did you?" I said. "Christ, that ammo is going to come back and—"

"I don't quite think so," he said. "You see, concealed in the frame of those crates was a tracking device. When I was sure that you weren't in the camp and when I was safely out of the militia's area of control I activated the tracking device. Some time later that camp was obliterated. Not a particularly good way of building repeat business with the local militias, but since it was their choice to break the armistice I didn't lose any sleep over it."

I remembered seeing the bombing strike when I'd been on the way to find a place to sleep at Stewart Carr's farm. "But there were women there, and children . . ."

"True, and many others who have terrorized their refugee neighbors, and who kept you captive, and who were happily going to kill you if you hadn't escaped or if I hadn't got there in time to buy you out. I'm sure you've figured all this out, but let me remind you. We're in a dirty little war here, a dirty little war that's going to determine what kind of planet we'll be living on for the rest of this wonderful new century. A place where innocents can be slaughtered and nothing can be done about it, or a place where somebody with some authority and force of arms can halt this kind of killing. Killing that can take place even in the homeland of the world's sole remaining superpower. And that's my job. To help bring peace and stability here."

"I see," I said. "And are there any other jobs that you're involved with that you'd like to tell me about?"

"Just the overarching one, of course."

"Site A," I said.

"So right, Samuel," Peter said. "Site A, the site of a massacre where up to two hundred refugee men, women and children were killed and their bodies destroyed or hidden. And our deadline expires in less than two days. If Site A hasn't been found by the time that deadline expires, then a number of bloody men with bloody hands will be released from The Hague."

I thought about what he had told me, what I had seen, and I said, "Sorry. Don't buy it."

"Excuse me?"

"I said, sorry, don't buy it. You're on detached duty from one of the most elite military units in the world, working for one of the most elite intelligence outfits as well. You can summon the general in charge of the British UN contingent to come down and speak to you—and not the other way around. And all this to keep a bunch of militia leaders behind bars at The Hague? Sorry—like I said, I don't buy it. There's more. And what's that, Peter?"

Peter's expression suddenly went blank, as though his good-humored earlier appearance had been carefully removed and put away.

I said, "Come along, Peter. What is it? What's really important about Site A?"

Peter spoke slowly, as if he was choosing his words with care. "Samuel . . . I think you know quite enough for now. I don't think any useful purpose will be served by discussing this matter further."

I thought about what he had just said, about the job he was doing, gathering intelligence in the field, finding out the truth, learning about the militia units and their organization and trying to get this battered country back on its feet and—

The truth.

Looking for the truth.

Looking for Site A. Looking for answers.

But answers to what?

And like a flash—oh my, what a choice of words—it came to me.

I said, "Site A . . . it's more than just a place where bodies are hidden. Evidence is there as well—evidence about the attacks last spring."

No word, no expression, nothing. Peter just sat there.

"That's been one of the biggest questions out there, hasn't it, Peter? Who was behind the suitcase-nuke strike on Manhattan and the EMP balloon strikes that crippled this country? Nobody knows. There's been claims here and there, but nothing concrete. But *you* have an idea. You and your bosses . . . There's evidence, and it's at Site A. Right?"

More silence.

"Peter . . . either you're going to tell me and trust me or we're going to leave here and then I'm off to the *Star* to break this story. So, one way or the other, a choice has to be made. Up to you."

"You fucker," he said sharply.

"Probably, but I've had a rough few days. True, isn't it? Site A and the balloon strikes and the bombing of Manhattan. They're connected."

There seemed to be a struggle going on behind that neutral expression on Peter's face, and he said, "If ever a word of what I'm about to say leaves this room, I'll hurt you."

I smiled. "The usual and customary threat is to *kill* me. Why the difference? Taking mercy on me?"

"Hardly," Peter said. The grim smile that was back on his face had a touch of nastiness about it. "Killing is easy. Hurting you, now . . . I could smash your knees in such a way that no corrective surgery would ever ease the pain, so that you'd have forty or fifty years of hobbling around in agony to look forward to. All because you let word get out about my business. Understand?"

I swallowed. "Yeah. I understand."

"Good." He exhaled loudly before continuing, "Prior to the attacks last spring, we had assets—as they're known—working here in the States, evaluating and gathering intelligence about a cell that was of concern to us because of bits of information we'd been able to secure about a possible domestic attack here in the USA. We had someone who'd managed to reach the upper levels of this cell . . . but her information didn't get to us on time and hence it didn't reach our American cousins. The strikes happened—and then, chaos. Communications were cut off: our asset had been in Manhattan and she got caught up in one of the refugee streams, heading north."

"The refugee stream that got ambushed—and ended up in Site A."

"Exactly. She had managed to leave word through a dead-letter drop that she had the evidence that we had so desperately been looking for . . . and we managed to trace her movements up until the time the column she was with had been ambushed. Then . . . nothing. And so the hunt continues."

"The whole thing about keeping those militia leaders behind bars in The Hague . . . just a cover story?"

"Yes, but a good one. Gives us an excuse to snoop around the countryside with some sense of urgency."

I thought through what Peter had just told me and said, "All right—who were they?"

"Who?"

"Don't play me for an idiot, Peter. Who were they? The cell you infiltrated. The ones who bombed the United States last April."

Peter smiled again and said, "To get to that little gold nugget of information, you have to ask yourself an important Latin question. *Cui bono?* which translates as 'Good for whom?' or—another way of saying it—'Who benefits?' Immediate answer, of course, are those usual collections of malcontents and ragheads from the Middle East who have such miserable lives that they're compelled to blame somebody else—which, of course, means the Great Satan. But really . . . those nukes were taken from an old Soviet Union storage facility, transported here to the United States and, save for the one used in Manhattan, were suspended from high-altitude balloons and then detonated within seconds of each other. Hijacking a plane and driving it into an office building is one thing. Something this complex means a much greater collection of skilled personnel."

"A government, then," I said. "But which one?"

Peter shrugged. "You're a newspaper reporter. Supposedly smart. Run through them and remember what I said: *cui bono*?"

"Britain and France and Germany—I'd eliminate them for obvious reasons. They may not like the United States all that much but I can't see them being behind such a crippling attack."

"Very good. But those three were easy. Continue."

"China . . . But China loves the markets here. Take out the United States and China takes a major hit with all those Wal-Marts out of business. Even Russia had started cooperating with U.S. corporations on gas and oil exploration in Siberia. They wouldn't want a crippled America, either."

Peter's smile was back. "Doing better. Continue. Who benefits, Samuel? Who benefits?"

I ran through other countries in my mind. Japan? Hardly, not with a growing Chinese threat in their neck of the woods. They'd want a strong United States to act as a buffer. North Korea? One or two attacks, maybe, but all these strikes, coordinated like they were? One of the Middle Eastern states . . . But no, that didn't make sense either. Maybe one or two nukes smuggled in a shipping container . . . But something this complicated, this important, couldn't have happened without somebody knowing what was going on, somebody here in the States and—

"Holy shit," I said. I had heard the rumors, of course, but that type of rumor always popped up after a disaster like Pearl Harbor or the JFK assassination or the second World Trade Center attack. Such paranoia couldn't really be taken seriously, but . . .

But . . .

"Congratulations," Peter said. "I do believe you've figured it out."

"The *government*? The *United States* government—they did it?"

He shook his head. "No, not the government. At least, only *part* of the government, a loosely knit organization that we were concerned about, that we had learned of last year. We called them the neo-isolationists, the ones who wanted to pack it all in and retreat back behind the USA's borders and the oceans. No interest in spreading democracy, no interest in making the world safe for globalization. Just interested in minding their own business. Among this group were some military leaders who saw the armed forces they loved being chipped away, day after day, week after week, in car bomb after car bomb, killing their very best and brightest and most dedicated who were trying to give democracy to cultures that didn't want it and probably didn't deserve it."

Peter looked at me and continued. "Then there were some of the defense contractors, the ones who make their money designing missiles and tanks and jet fighters. They *don't* make money designing better body armor or ways of detecting roadside bombs. They saw decades of shrinking profits ahead. Combine that with the true believers in DC, the ones who thought the United States should have left Hitler and Tojo alone more than a half-century ago, and then you have an interesting mix."

"But . . . but the devastation. The cities being emptied out. The food shortages. The refugees being gunned down . . ."

"Sure. And what happened? You know what happened: it's taking time but the troops are coming home. Not only from the Middle East, but from Japan and South Korea and Germany and elsewhere. They wanted a crisis so widespread, so deep, that the President and Congress would have no choice but to run for home. That's what they wanted and, so far, that's what they're getting."

I felt sick to my stomach. "And you have evidence of this . . ."

"Not me. Our asset, lost after leaving Manhattan. Oh, the poor dear's dead, no doubt about it, but we're hoping that her body's in Site A, along with a computer diskette or two. A computer diskette that outlines who belongs to this group, how they smuggled the nukes here, and how they arrived at the decision to set them off. So sorry, but *that's* the importance of Site A. Not the dead refugees. Our asset and those diskettes."

"And once you get that information . . ."

"Decision's already been made at Ten Downing Street. The information, all of it, gets publicized the moment we can secure and verify it. So the people here will know what happened. They'll know that these militias—some of which have received support for supposedly keeping order—were killing their fellow citizens because of a lie. Don't get me wrong, Samuel: this country is known for its blundering way of doing business and for being obstinate and unilateral, certainly. But, all in all, the world needs a United States that's engaged with the rest of the world. Not one hiding in fear, skulking behind its borders and the oceans. And we need those diskettes to make things right. To show the Americans that no *overseas* enemy did this to them. That some of their own people did it."

I rubbed at my face. Lots of stuff to process, I thought—and then something struck me.

"Your asset?"

"Yes?"

"You keep on calling your asset 'her.' Was her name Grace?"

A simple nod. "That it was."

"Sounds like a brave woman."

"She was," Peter said flatly. "Very brave, in so many ways."

"Like what?"

And his expression changed once again, this time to despair. "For once agreeing to be my wife."

THE AIR IN the room was cold and still. I said, "The armistice breaking down like it did, just before the deadline: a hell of a coincidence, right?"

Peter seemed to shake off his dark mood. "Yes, one big coincidence, I'm sure. And it seems to be working in favor of the militia units and their puppet masters, the neo-isolationists."

"Do those people . . . do they know what evidence might be at Site A?"

"Beats the hell out of me. But still . . . I just had the feeling that we were getting close, at least in this county. We *must* have been getting close to finding Site A, considering how viciously the militias were attacking us, sniping at us and making the lives of the UN forces here miserable. So there you go. When the deadline passes, the militia boys go home and the hunt for Site A and one particular body is finished. Oh, we'll poke and prod as best we can, on the outskirts and fringes, but it'll be over, Samuel. The truth will remain hidden for quite some time to come. Maybe long enough so that we fail, and these battered United States ignore the rest of the world."

"Damn," I said.

"Yeah, damn. Nothing much else to say, except I now have one more job."

"You're a busy man," I said.

"Oh, yes, but not as busy as somebody else is going to be," Peter said darkly. "You see, that Aussie television crew was correct, entirely correct. There *are* traitors at work among the UN field teams, traitors who made us go in circles, exposed us to being wounded and killed, and prevented us from doing our jobs. Especially my job: to find those diskettes and Grace. And there was a traitor working in *our* group, Samuel, of that I have no doubt."

I looked at him, at the cool and composed operative who was working behind the lines in so many ways. I said, "Yeah, you're right. We were one screwed-up crew."

Peter nodded. "Yes. We were. When and if Site A is taken care of, as well as everything else, I'm going to focus my attention on finding our group's traitor. I have suspicions but no evidence, and if it takes years to get the evidence together, then so be it. I won't let the matter drop."

I thought about something and said, "You have an idea of who it might be?"

"I do," he said.

"Care to tell me?"

"Why?"

"Because I might be able to help you," I said.

Peter seemed to ponder that for a moment. Then he mentioned a name.

I felt a chill on the back of my neck, and my stomach lurched.

"Yeah," I said. "I think I can help you."

Peter said, "Good."

CHAPTER TWENTY-TWO

I'd been back in my room for about a half-hour when there was a knock at the door.

When I opened it, I was nearly bowled over by a blonde-haired woman smelling of fresh soap and wearing a clean white blouse, tan skirt and a tasty lipstick. She pushed me back into the room and slammed the door behind her, saying, "Oh, Samuel, Samuel . . ."

I was intoxicated by the feel of Miriam in my arms, and also sickened by what was going to happen in the next few minutes. I kissed her back, again and again, and I looked at her bright face, at the tears in her eyes. "Oh, Samuel, I was so scared that you had been shot. I was so frightened that I wouldn't see you again . . . Oh, your face, your poor face . . ." She traced the scabs and scrapes along my skin and I touched her as well.

"You . . . I thought you had died back there, too," I stammered out. "I found your nightgown, all torn up and bloody."

Miriam pushed herself against my chest again and I hugged her. "We barely got out . . . Oh, God, it was so scary, all that shooting . . . One of the Land Cruisers got shot up and Sanjay and I, we wanted to get to you, but Charlie and Jean-Paul said no, no, we couldn't risk it . . . I'm so sorry we left you behind."

I stroked her fine blonde hair. "No apologies. None at all. You did what was right, what was the smart thing to do."

Miriam moved her head so that she could look up at me. "It felt so very wrong, Samuel. And it was even worse when Sanjay thought he saw you. He got out of the Land Cruiser, thought you were running away from the woods . . . and that was when he got shot . . . Oh, God, I hope he didn't suffer, I hope that—"

The door to the bathroom swung open, and there was Peter. Miriam turned her head and said, "I'm sorry, Peter. What are you doing here?"

Peter's face was once more expressionless. "I'm afraid you'll probably find out rather quickly."

Miriam gently pulled herself away from me and said, "Samuel? What's this?"

I couldn't think of what I could say and then there was another knock at the door. Peter looked at me and went over to the door. When he opened it a very happy-looking Jean-Paul came in, bearing a dark bottle of cognac and two snifter glasses. He had on gray dress slacks, black polished shoes and a black turtleneck shirt. "Samuel!" he said. "How good, finally, to see you! Ah, it's been so long, and I'm so happy to see you here, smiling and happy as well."

He was weaving slightly, as though he had been drinking. He looked around him and said, "My, this is quite the party. Miriam and Peter as well. It is too bad that Charlie and Karen are not here."

"And Sanjay," Peter said quietly.

Jean-Paul slowly nodded. "Ah, yes, poor Sanjay. We cannot forget him, eh? His service to us and the UN. What he did and—"

"Actually, Jean-Paul," Peter said, stepping over to him. "I'd like to talk a bit about what you did."

"Excuse me?" he asked. "I don't understand—"

"How much?" I interrupted. Miriam made as if to say something and I talked over her: "How much were you paid? How much?"

Jean-Paul grinned. "How much? You want to know my salary? In Canadian dollars or euros—which are you asking?"

Peter said, "It's not the currency you're paid in that we're concerned with, Jean-Paul. It's what you were doing in exchange for the payment."

Although Jean-Paul's face was still wreathed in smiles, I could tell that there was something going on behind those merry eyes. "I'm sorry, my friends. Perhaps you have started drinking before me, because none of what you are saying is making the slightest sense. I think I will go now and bid you *adieu*, until tomorrow."

Then, moving so fast and smoothly that it amazed me, Peter positioned himself in front of the door, muscular arms folded, his biceps pushing out the fabric of his sweater. "I'm afraid you're here for a while, Jean-Paul.

Like I said before, I don't care what you were paid. I just want to know what you were getting in exchange for betraying your supposed friends."

Miriam looked at me. "Samuel, what is this?"

"What's going on is a little follow-up from the work of those poor dead Aussies," I said. "They were doing a story, and part of the story was whether or not traitors were sprinkled throughout the UN investigative units, sabotaging their work. Units like our team. Right, Jean-Paul?"

He said nothing, still smiling. Miriam said, "Our team? What do you mean?"

Peter said, "What he means, missy, is that any idiot could see that we were compromised. Any fool could see that we were running around in circles, almost getting killed on a couple of occasions. And for what? Some dead cows—no offense, Samuel—and the dead Aussies, who practically fell into our laps. No Site A, not even a lead for Site A. Just us blundering around in the countryside while the clock ticked down for those war criminals at The Hague."

Among other things, I thought. But I remembered my promise to Peter, to keep things secret.

Jean-Paul said, "It's late at night. We're all tired. And you're not making sense."

"Oh?" Peter demanded. "Who was the only one talking to regional headquarters? Who was supposedly talking to them and receiving leads about where to go next? Who *was* that person, Jean-Paul?"

Jean-Paul's face was starting to redden. "All my work, I did in the open. You all heard me, every one of you."

Peter shifted his weight from one foot to the other. "Correct. And all we heard was *you* talking. We never did hear what was coming in on the other side of your earpiece—never heard if, in fact, you were really talking to anyone at all. Maybe you were just talking to static. Who knows? All I know is that you were passing along awful directions to us, directions that didn't help us find anything, except a chance to get killed. Like Sanjay was."

Jean-Paul shook his head, looked at Miriam and then at me. But not at Peter. "My friends, surely you don't believe this, do you? There's no proof, is there?"

"Sorry, Jean-Paul," I said. I went over to an open duffel bag on my bed and pulled out my little laptop. It had already been powered up and I punched up a file. Then I brought the laptop over to Jean-Paul and said, "See this?"

Miriam moved around so that she could see as well. Jean-Paul didn't say anything, so it was up to Miriam. "It looks like a message log, or something."

"Sure does," I said. "Thing is, every time I sent along an information or photo packet to Geneva, there was a receipt mechanism to ensure that it got there and to the right person in time. Every photo packet I sent has a receipt listing, shown here with a time and date stamp. Every single one, except for the last set that was transmitted. The one that was transmitted over *your* laptop, Jean-Paul. The one showing those militiamen driving up to the farmhouse. I never got a receipt for that from Geneva, confirming that the photos had arrived."

Now Jean-Paul's bantering demeanor was gone. "Perhaps you erred, young one. Or perhaps the system didn't send the receipt to you."

"Sure," I said. "Good excuses—and that's just what they are, Jean-Paul. Excuses. I gave the photo packets and information to you because you said you could send them quicker to Geneva. But they never arrived. I made a phone call a while ago, got the night desk at the information sector. They never arrived, Jean-Paul. You took them and probably dumped them, right? What were you doing? Helping out the locals, making sure that photos of their faces didn't end up in a UN computer?"

Jean-Paul looked again at me and Miriam, and said, "Then there must have been some sort of technical error, something that—"

"It's finished, Jean-Paul," Peter said, taking a step toward him. "The Inspector-General's been looking into your history all afternoon. You might have forgotten this, old friend, but radio traffic is carefully logged, and they're going to match their log with my personal diary, and Charlie's, to establish when you claimed you were talking to sector headquarters and getting instructions about what to do next. Your bank accounts are going to be searched, too, and if you think the UN can't find any hidden accounts in Switzerland or the Cayman Islands or the British Virgin Islands then you're sadly mistaken. So. Again: answer Samuel's question. How much?"

Jean-Paul put the glasses and the cognac bottle down on a little night stand by the door. "Look, *mes amis*, I'm sure there is something we can work out here—"

Then Miriam walked right up to him and slapped him. Jean-Paul was temporarily stunned but his expression grew dark and angry, and he raised his arm to strike back. I was getting ready to jump in on the fray when Peter—still moving as quick as the wind—got Jean-Paul in some sort of complicated head- and arm-lock, opened the door and tossed him out into the hallway. Jean-Paul fell against the nearest wall, banging his head, bounced back, and then started running. I made to go after him but Peter held me back with a strong arm. "Let him go, Samuel. Let him go."

Miriam was white-lipped. "After all that? After all that, you're going to let him go?"

Peter closed the door. "Where is he going? Out there, beyond the compound, where the local militia will gun him down before he can confess that he's one of them? No, don't you worry. The IG has officers waiting at the stairwells and the elevator banks. In a few minutes he'll be scooped up and put on the first plane back to Geneva."

"To face trial?" Miriam asked.

Peter laughed. "Dear girl, you've been around this business long enough. You know what's going to happen. The UN will complain to the French, and the French will complain that they're being misunderstood, as always. Jean-Paul will be fined, maybe he'll spend a few weekends in jail back in France, and then he'll get a nice little job as a magistrate in some sleepy French village. The UN is a noble, peaceful organization. You know that. Which is why you hardly ever read any stories about UN peacekeepers running smuggling rings, skimming off oil-for-food contracts, patronizing teenage prostitutes, or—in this case—selling out their comrades for cash. Oldest story in the book, am I right?"

Miriam looked like she was preparing some sort of retort, and I said, "Yeah, Peter. Oldest story in the book."

He picked up the bottle of cognac, tossed it over to me, and I caught it with one hand. Remarkable. Peter said, "It's late at night, there's a bottle of cognac and two glasses there. I'm going to leave and let the two of you get reunited. Or would you prefer me to join you with a glass from the washroom?"

Miriam smiled and came over to me. I said, "See you later, Peter."

"Of course you will," he said.

LATER, LIGHTS OFF and blinds open, we lay in bed, the cognac bottle uncapped, the small glasses at our side. The blankets and sheets were crumpled at the bottom of the bed, and I felt tired and drained and sore and utterly alive. Miriam was cuddled up on my left, her chin pressing into my chest, an occasional finger tracing my lips. She said, "What next for you, Samuel?"

"Short-term, I plan to get some sleep. I hope you can join me."

I sensed her smile in the near-darkness. "I think you can depend on that. And long-term?"

"Long-term? Well, I think you and I are going to need a new boss . . . and if that doesn't work out, a UN lady told me yesterday that I could go home, if I'd like."

"And would you?"

"Go home? Well, it's a thought. But only if you come with me."

Miriam shook her head gently. "I don't have the leave time coming to me."

"Then I won't go."

She pressed herself against me, the feel of her flesh on mine exhilarating. The first time, back in the tent, had been magical and wonderful in the rawest sense: coupling with urgency, in a tent in the dark, with the chance of death or injury at any moment. But here we'd had time to take it slow, to take it wonderfully from one level to the next, to explore tastes and sensations, to see and touch and whisper, and I had tried to stretch it out as long as I could, before I just gave in and collapsed in Miriam's arms, drained of energy and effort.

"I am glad," she said. "I am glad you're not going, for I want to be with you, Samuel. As long as is possible."

I squeezed her shoulders. "I hope that is a very long time."

"Me, too," Miriam said, her voice somber. "But times will change. People will change. One of these days the armistice will be reestablished and the work will continue. But I have a confession to make to you, about our work."

"Go on," I said.

Miriam sighed. "I am getting tired of it, Samuel. Of trying to document what bad things have happened, what kind of death has been dealt out to innocents. I am tired of the dirt and the mud and the stench of death, of seeing bodies broken and swollen and burned."

"You've been at it a long time," I said.

"Ah, too long," she said. "And soon, very soon, perhaps, I am going to give it up."

"Go back to Amsterdam?"

She sighed again, her warm breath feeling good against my chest. "Perhaps, for a bit. But not for long. No, I think it's time for me to do something else."

"What's that?"

"*Médecins Sans Frontières*," she said, the French words rolling softly past her lips.

"Doctors Without Borders," I said. "A good group. Let me guess. Tired of working on the dead?"

Miriam nodded, her chin digging painfully into me now. I ignored the discomfort. "Tired of working *for* the dead, Samuel. You see, that's always been a little wordplay for me, in what I do. I speak for the dead. For the dead woman, butchered as she protected her children. For the teenage girls, brutally raped before they were murdered. For the old men and women in the last years of their lives, cut down because of their last name or skin color or because they were hungry and they escaped from a city that was dying. All of these dead people, on almost every continent, Samuel, I have spoken for. And my voice . . . my voice is getting tired. I can no longer speak for them. I can only speak for myself. And no one else."

"And Doctors Without Borders . . . you'll be working for the living."

"In a way," she said, reaching up to tickle my ear. "I'll be working for the wounded, for the survivors. I will no longer have to speak for them. All I will do is heal them. That is all."

I swallowed, my mouth still stinging a bit from the bite of the cognac. "When do you hope to start?"

"I'm not sure. A month, perhaps two."

I moved an arm across her smooth back. "I'm sure they're eager to take you on."

"Yes . . . but my eagerness, well . . ."

"Go ahead."

Miriam raised herself and kissed me gently. "If I may be so forward, do you intend to be with UNFORUS forever?"

I kissed her in return, tasting the lipstick and cognac and her own special flavor. "As a matter of fact, Miriam, I've been thinking of a change as well. These doctors . . . do you think they could use someone to take photos, to write the occasional press release?"

In the dim light I could make out her smile. "It would mean a severe pay cut, you understand."

"So?"

She laughed and rolled over on top of me, and I hugged her close. "Yes, dear one," she said, kissing me again and again. "I am sure they can use you."

"Wonderful," I said, holding her tight, not wanting to let her move, not an inch. "Wonderful."

THE SOUNDS OF the shower and Miriam singing in her native Dutch woke me up. I was considering getting up to join her when she finished, coming out wrapped in two towels, one around her head, the other around her slick torso. She leaned over and kissed me. "Did I keep you awake last night?"

"Not at all," I said. "Why would you?"

She laughed. "My younger sisters, they always said I snored so loud that they were afraid the local dike would be breached. The washroom is free, if you wish."

I got up and headed to the bathroom, and then looked back at her. She was toweling her hair and said, "Is something wrong?"

"No, everything is right. It's just that . . ."

"What?"

"Well, you have both towels."

"Oh, you," Miriam said, tossing me the towel that she had been using to dry her hair.

I caught the damp fabric and said, "I might get awfully wet, you know, and I might need that second one . . ."

She came over to me, making shooing motions with her hands. "You get in there, and right now. I don't want to miss breakfast."

I kissed her. "A deal."

OUT IN THE corridor Miriam pointed to a scuff mark on the far wall. "Look. Isn't that where Jean-Paul struck his head?"

"We can only hope," I said.

She linked an arm through mine. "It was so strange yesterday, seeing Peter asking all those questions."

"Why?"

She tugged at my arm. "Because, that's why. He seemed very knowledgeable, very inquisitive. Like he knew the answers to his questions before he asked them."

Secrets, I thought. And a promise. I said, "You know Peter. Not very friendly, and an ex-cop to boot. Always suspicious of somebody or something. Or he wouldn't have been a cop."

"Still . . ." We got to the bank of elevators and I punched the down button. Miriam said, "How did this all come about? Why was Peter in your room?"

"We talked some yesterday," I said. "Peter came to me with some suspicions of who might have been betraying our unit. He asked me if anything odd had occurred concerning Jean-Paul. And the only thing I had were the missing photo receipts. If Jean-Paul had really sent those in, like he said he did, then they would have appeared on my machine."

"All that, just to protect the identities of some local militiamen?"

I looked at her. She was wearing slightly wrinkled clothing from yesterday, and was still so very desirable. "More than just that," I said. "Peter thought—and I found it hard to disagree with him—that there was a timely reason for Jean-Paul not to have sent along those photos."

"Why would it have been timely?"

The elevator door finally dinged. "Because if we were all killed that day or the next, then Geneva would have had a pretty fair idea of who might have done it, based on those photos. No photos, no direct leads. And Jean-Paul would have been the sole survivor, with a bloody tale of how he alone had managed to stay alive."

Miriam started saying something in Dutch which I guessed was probably obscene when the elevator door slid open. In front of us were three soldiers in fatigues who immediately stopped talking when they saw us there. They were about my age, muscled and hard-edged, and as well as the UNFORUS brassard that they all wore tiny Union Jacks were sewn on their sleeves. The British, back in their old colonial stomping grounds, almost two and a half centuries later.

They made room for us and I saw that we were all heading to the basement. I said, "Is the British Army making us breakfast today?"

There were smiles and one soldier said, "Dunno, mate—why do you ask?"

"I thought that's why the British Army conquered the world," I said. "They were looking for a good meal."

They laughed at that. Then the door slid open, and out we went.

THERE WAS A line snaking out into the corridor, and I talked with Miriam as we slowly made our way in. I found out about the desperate hours after the shooting that had left Sanjay dead and me missing, and how Charlie had gone back with a few of his comrades to retrieve the body and look for me. I guess that little mission had ticked off the higher-ups in Albany, because with the armistice breakdown all UN-assigned forces were supposed to withdraw to the compounds and refugee camps, to await the outcome of negotiations.

According to Miriam those negotiations were still going on. Not much had happened in the country since I had caught the beautiful tones of the CBC on Stewart Carr's radio, telling listeners about the armistice still not being back in place in Michigan, New York, Vermont, New Hampshire and other states as well.

As we finally got into the cafeteria, into the large room with the cooking smells and the sounds of about a half-dozen languages bouncing off the low tile ceiling, Miriam said, "And so it goes. The men with guns try to keep on killing and stealing, while the rest of us struggle to find some kind of peace."

I was about to reply when I noticed, sitting by himself at a tiny two-person table, an older man who was sipping a cup of tea and looking over at us. His white hair was in a crew cut and he had a thick handlebar mustache.

He wore fatigues and black boots, but with no insignia. He looked at me and I looked at him, and I squeezed Miriam's hand.

"Will you excuse me for a moment?"

Her expression was troubled. "Is something wrong?"

"You could say that," I said. "I have to go see that old man over there."

Miriam spotted him and said, "Why? Do you know him?"

"No, I've never really known him all that well," I said. "But I am related to him."

"Really?" she asked. "Who is he?"

I moved out of the line. "He's my father."

CHAPTER TWENTY-THREE

I went over and my father looked up at me. "Samuel, so good to see you. Have a seat."

I remained standing. "Gee, how nice of you to come see me in my room."

He slurped at his teacup. "Don't get your panties in a twist, Samuel. I knew you were up in your room. I knew you were safe. And this is the only place around here that serves breakfast, swillish as it might taste. So I knew you'd be coming along. Just have a seat, all right?"

I pulled a chair out, sat down. Still standing in line was Miriam, who was looking over in our direction. Father noticed and said, "Who's she? A local, perhaps?"

"Miriam van der Pol," I said. "One of the UN investigators I was working with."

"Aahh," he said. "Very sweet-looking thing. A girlfriend, perhaps?"

"None of your business, *perhaps*," I said. "What are you doing here?"

"Well, so much for father-and-son greetings, eh?" he said, putting the cup down on the dirty table. "I've been here in this miserable country for three days, ever since I got word that you'd been reported missing. I tried using some of my old contacts, some of my old friends, to see what I could find out."

"I'm surprised anyone would be seen talking to you," I said.

There was a bright spark of anger in my father's eyes that immediately transferred itself to the rest of his face, where the skin reddened. "That was some time ago," he said. "And I don't need you or anyone else reminding me about it. Don't you think I'll always remember my time in Somalia, and the trial that followed? Don't you?"

I looked at that stern face, remembered all the times when seeing that particular expression would freeze me, would frighten me, would make me do or say anything to get away from that look. But it didn't look frightening, not now, not after the past few days. It just looked tired and angry.

I sighed. "Yeah, I'm sure you will."

"Damn right," he said. "So here I was, fighting the new war, the war of bureaucrats, trying to find out from what department something might be learned about your fate, Samuel. One office passed me off to another office, one unit to the next. Some people thought you were just missing, others thought you might be a prisoner of one of those gangs of thugs. About the only good fella I met was that black Marine assigned to your unit, Charlie something-or-another."

"Charlie Banner," I said.

"Yeah, Banner," my father said. "I could talk to him, you know? Like one professional soldier to another."

I opened my mouth to say something, thought better of it, though my father noticed right off. "Hey, I know what you're thinking, right? A *professional* soldier. Maybe an oxymoron, right? We're just trained killers with no brains, sent in to kill or destroy or blow up things. How can we be trained to do anything except that? But listen to me, young man, it's the trained ones who protect you and your friends. And it's the trained ones who are called in to clean up other people's messes, other people's disasters. Your great-grandfather and grandfather served their country well in uniform. And I did my best as well, despite what happened in Somalia. So there."

I rested my hands on the stained table. "So there. A nice answer, Father. Look, I've heard the lectures about the military plenty of times. And I know you wished I had joined the military instead of going into journalism. Let's just leave it be, all right?"

He stared at me for a moment and I felt a twinge of regret, knowing what was going on inside his mind. His failure as a husband, as a soldier who wanted nothing more than to have the Simpson military gene passed down to another generation. A chance, maybe, to redeem the Simpson family name, which had been burnished at Dieppe and in Korea, and had forever been tarnished in a hot and dusty place called Mogadishu.

I smiled. "Look, Father. I appreciate you coming here. I really do. But seeing you here . . . well, it was just a start, that's all."

He took another sip from his teacup. That seemed to mollify him some, and he looked around. "They don't know how easy they have it here," he said, his voice lower now, like he was confiding in me. "Here they have power, hot water, hot food and pretty safe conditions, if they keep their noses clean. In Somalia we had tents, dirt everywhere, flies and other vermin, and no air-conditioning, no power, nothing. Here they have the militias. Big deal. They're a minority out in the towns and counties. A well-armed minority, but still a minority. Back in Somalia there was no government, no officials. There were clans and sub-clans, with alliances shifting from week to week. Here, negotiation is dealing with maybe a half-dozen clowns with guns. Over there, dozens and dozens of groups of crazies . . . Still, it doesn't excuse what happened, right?"

I nodded. My father toyed with his teacup. I glanced over at the line, saw that Miriam had moved ahead. My stomach grumbled, wanting breakfast, but something was going on here. I wanted to wait.

"We were frustrated, cooped up like that. Day after day, under hot canvas, hardly anything to do. We had warriors there, Samuel, highly trained and eager warriors. You can't keep them penned up for days. I asked, I pleaded, I begged the powers that were to either send them home or to give them missions. Anything to get out of that blasted tent city. But I was turned down, always turned down. Negotiations were at a delicate stage, they said. Local sensibilities can't be offended, they said. So keep your boys confined to base until further notice. Jesus Christ on a crutch. Still . . . no excuses. They did an awful thing, and I did a worse thing, trying to cover it up."

"Why did you do it, then?" I asked gently. We had never had this kind of conversation before, and I was desperate to take it as far as I could.

It was like my father couldn't look at me, so he kept his gaze focused on his teacup. "By the time I got back home, I was exhausted, Samuel. I had some intestinal bug that was chewing me up from the inside out. Our intervention had been a failure, no matter what glowing stories your friends at the *Star* or *Globe* or *Mail* had written. Your mother had packed up and gone to Florida. I felt as though the UN, the all-bloody and all-powerful UN, had screwed us over pretty good. I had argued and fought for my boys, to give them good quarters, to keep them busy, and I had failed. I had failed pretty badly. So when the rumors started that a couple of them had done bad things back there, had tortured and killed a couple of young thieves . . . Well, no excuses, Samuel. No excuses. But what was I going to do? Go out of my way to help those who had screwed us? Give the UN the benefit of the doubt? Hell, no. My first reaction was to deny everything, to protect my boys. That's what I did. And we all paid the price."

I took a breath. "You did what you thought was right."

A brief smile flickered across my father's face. "Thanks—I think. Though the Chief of Staff and a jury and a bunch of newspapers disagreed with you. So here I am, a disgrace and cashiered out."

"So here you are," I said.

He finished off his tea with a satisfied slurp. "When can you get packed up?"

"Excuse me?"

He put the cup down with a loud rattle. "Come along, Samuel. I said, when can you get packed up? I'm not done here yet. I'm here to take you back home."

Our moment of bonding, it seemed, had just passed. "No."

"Samuel, be reasonable. You've been through a lot, right? Captured and beaten up and escaped, finally getting out free and safe. Shit, boy, you've done everything the blue helmets have asked of you and then some. Give yourself a break, get on back home while you can."

"What do you mean, while I can?"

My father looked around him for a second. Then he said, his voice lower: "Look. The Yanks have a real sense of pride and honor. How do you think they're feeling, having the UN and foreign armies trooping through some of their territories? They only got here during a moment of weakness, after the Manhattan bombing, after the balloon strikes, after the uprisings and the killings of the refugees. A good chunk of the country that doesn't have militias, that doesn't have armed gangs terrorizing its people, well, they probably didn't give a crap at the beginning. Anything to stop the killing. But now that most of the killing has stopped, that majority still sees Ukrainians and Germans and Hungarians trooping through the countryside. A lot of people are getting pissed, Samuel. Oh, there may be a new armistice soon, very soon, but just as certain as that is that one of these days the U.S. Army or the Marines are going to take matters into their own hands and kick everybody out. And I know the Americans. When they kick someone out, it's sure to be bloody. So come on home, Samuel. That's where you belong."

I shook my head. "No, I belong here."

"Samuel, you're being unreasonable, you're being—"

"Father, it's over. All right? I'm staying here, doing my job, because it's important. As important to me as being in the army was for you. All right? Discussion over. I'm staying with the UN and staying in the States, if they want me. And if you want to have a discussion you'll have it by yourself, because I'll get up and leave. Right now."

My father's face reddened some more and then he surprised me for the first time in a long time. He actually laughed. "Damn it, boy. Good for you. I can't say I agree with you and I don't, but damn it anyway, good for you. I always wondered if you had the balls my father and grandfather had, and I'm glad to see that you do."

He leaned over the table, gently punched me on the shoulder, which was about as emotional as I'd ever seen the old man. "OK, stay here. Do what you think's best. And if your young ass gets lost again, I'll come back to look for you. Deal?"

I found myself actually smiling. "OK. Deal."

"Hello there," came a lovely voice. I looked up and my father turned round in his chair as Miriam approached, bringing a tray overflowing with dishes and saucers and coffee cups. She smiled at me and said, "It took some convincing the nice servers but I've got all of us some breakfast. May I join you?"

"Absolutely," I said, and my father joined in, stepping up to help her with the tray and then retrieving a chair for her. Smiling all the while, he said, "Young lady, if Samuel hadn't said yes, I surely would have."

She smiled back at that and I said, "Miriam, I'd like you to meet my father, Ronald Simpson, lately a colonel in the Canadian Army, who's been here for the past few days looking for his lost son."

They shook hands and Miriam said, "What a wonderful father you are, to come look for Samuel."

My father just blushed at that. I looked at Miriam and said, "Yes, you're quite right, Miriam."

"Excuse me?" she asked, and even my father looked a bit confused. I went on, looking at them both. "You're absolutely right. He was a wonderful father, to come find me."

Miriam started talking but my father, speaking gruffly, said, "Come on, kids, let's eat, before it gets cold."

Which was what we did.

MIRIAM HAD GOTTEN the three of us bowls of oatmeal, with some toast and sausage links on the side, and coffee and orange juice. As we ate I felt this odd calmness come over me, as though things were finally making sense, were finally coming together. All through breakfast my father was a charming gentleman, something I found hard to believe, though I had memories from my childhood of how, maybe at Christmas time, my father would smile and joke and even sing. He told a few tales of when I was younger to Miriam, stuff about falling down a heating vent when it was open for repairs, or going door-to-door trying to sell discarded cigar butts, and even I smiled at the old stories.

When breakfast was finished, Miriam said, "Colonel Simpson . . ."

My father shook his head. "Please, call me Ronald. Or Ron."

Miriam smiled, nodded. "Very well, Ronald. Can I ask you something?"

"Ma'am, the time when I cannot answer a question from a beautiful lady such as yourself will be the day I'll hear dirt falling on the lid of my coffin. Go ahead. Ask away."

Miriam said, "In the time you've spent here, have you heard anything about the armistice talks? Are they proceeding?"

My father wiped his fingers with a paper napkin. "Yes, they are proceeding." And he shot me a look as though he was reminding me of our previous talk. "And I'm sure they will succeed eventually. Perhaps today. Perhaps next week. But in the long run . . . as I've told Samuel, I don't think in the long run that being here with the UN will be healthy. I sense bad times coming, once the people—everywhere, not just in the states with active militia—once the people decide the UN has been here long enough and must go."

Miriam reached under the table, squeezed my leg. "Thank you. And I'll tell you, in the long run I don't intend to remain in the UN. And perhaps neither does your son."

That got my father's attention. "Really?"

"Truly," she said. "I am considering joining *Médecins Sans Frontières*, and Samuel has expressed an interest as well. One of these days."

"Ah, Doctors Without Borders. A noble group. It sounds wonderful. But a bit of advice?"

I felt like warning Miriam that advice from my father usually had some sort of price tag attached to it, but I let it slide. Miriam said, "All right. Advice I can take."

My father looked at us both. "Don't stay in the States. Go somewhere else."

I said, "All right. Advice taken."

A smile from the old guy. "Fair enough." He glanced at his watch, said, "Time's not waiting. There's a chartered flight leaving for Toronto in the hour. Sure you can't come?"

"Positive," I said.

"A pity." My father got up, leaned over and gave Miriam a peck on her cheek. Then he held out his hand. I gave it a firm shake and he said, "Write more, Samuel, won't you?"

"Of course," I said.

"Good. You two take care, and remember what I said. Get out of the States."

He walked away, past the long line of aid people and soldiers and doctors still waiting for breakfast. Then he was gone.

Miriam said, "He's certainly something, Samuel."

"That he is," I said. "That he is."

WHEN I BROUGHT the dirty dishes up to the washing station, there was a woman standing there, scraping a dirty plate viciously with a knife. I looked, and then looked again. Karen Tilley.

"Hey," I said. "Karen, how are you?"

She looked up at me from her chore, her red hair unwashed and a tangled mess. "I'm breathing, I guess. How the hell are you?"

"I'm doing all right, considering—"

Karen tossed the plate into a gray plastic bin filled with other dishes, making a loud rattling noise. "Hell, I think you're doing just fine, pal, just fucking fine. You're standing here, breathing and living and everything seems to be working right. You're not dead, shot and left behind—shot dead for the crime of being in this hellhole and trying to help people."

I put the tray of dirty dishes down gingerly, started cleaning them as well. "I'm sorry about Sanjay, Karen."

She snorted. "Spare me your fake sympathy."

"Nothing fake about it. Sanjay . . . I can't believe what he did there, toward the end."

"Bullshit," she said, now tossing the silverware into a bucket half-filled with greasy water. "I know what you all thought about me and Sanjay. Slutty American woman, spreading her legs for a little exotic flesh from the Far East."

"Not true. You and he were professionals. I didn't care what you did in your tents at night. And I know what he did when the shooting took place, that he thought I was coming back and he—"

It was as if Karen wasn't listening to a single word I had said, as if this talk had been prepared for days. She said, "Well, the hell with all of you. Sanjay and me, we had something special, something romantic, something to call our own out there, and it's gone. Thanks to you."

I froze, a dirty oatmeal bowl in my hand. "Me?"

"Of course *you*, you moron," she said, wiping her hands on her sweater. "I know exactly what happened, how you had to be Mr. Helpful, Mr. Goodie-Two-Shoes, Mr. I'm-So-Sweet. You had to get up that morning and make some hot water so that your girlfriend and Charlie and Jean-Paul and Peter would all look up to you, would think, hey, this kid's worth it. A little hot coffee to score points. Right?"

"No, I was just boiling the water to—"

"Asshole," Karen said, stretching out the two-syllable word. "If you hadn't gone out like that, to play Boy Scout, we would have skipped breakfast, I know we would. But we had to wait for you to come back, so there we were, sitting out in the open, dumb and hungry, waiting for you. We waited, Sammy, boy did we wait, and you know what happened next, right?"

"I managed to warn you, by—"

"And if you hadn't gone out, there wouldn't have been anything to warn us about, right? No hot water, no breakfast, just a quick pack-up and we're gone. Well, congratulations, Sammy, you got to do a good deed and you got a good man killed in the process. Fuck you very much."

Karen turned and stalked away, and I just stood there. I suppose a hero in a movie or a made-for-television film would have gone after her to plead his case, to try to explain further, but I was tired. Miriam was back there, waiting for me.

And, after all, I was no hero.

Not at all.

I DIDN'T FEEL like talking any more about Karen or Sanjay or anything to do with that day, so I found Miriam and we went outside to a small hillside park near the hospital complex. It was sunny, there was no wind, and it felt more like a pleasant late September day than a late October one. We sat on a picnic table and held hands, and we looked down to the parking lot crowded with APCs, military trucks and a number of ambulances. On a wide lawn on the far side of the parking lot was a small tent city, with some banners flying. I picked out the Red Cross, the UN and one flag that looked German. Wire fencing and guard posts enclosed the parking lot, and there was the steady drone of engines at work.

Miriam leaned against me and said, "Did you ever come here, to the United States, before the troubles?"

"Sure," I said. "Plenty of times."

"What for?" she asked. "Tourism? To do stories for your newspaper?"

"The truth?"

"Of course, the truth."

I looked into her eyes. "It sounds silly, but this is the truth: I used to go to the States like most Canadians did. For the shopping."

"Shopping?" Miriam sounded incredulous.

"Sure, shopping. The prices were reasonable and you didn't have the incredible taxes we Canucks have to put up with to pay for a creaky national healthcare system."

She put her arm round my shoulders. "I always wanted to come here, you know. Had a chance once, as a high-school student, but I got sick and couldn't make it. And when I did eventually come here, well, it was during a very unhappy time. Right after the Security Council resolution authorizing the intervention. I had often dreamed of coming here to the States as a tourist. It never occurred to me that I would be coming here to look for mass graves. Not in my wildest nightmares."

Or looking for evidence of the people behind the attacks. That was extra—God, was that extra.

Miriam looked around at the scenery, squeezed my shoulder. "Such a big, prosperous and unhappy land. I saw a magazine illustration, last year, before the bombings. It showed a county-by-county breakdown of how the vote for President went. A big divide, with lots of hate, mistrust and bad feelings on both sides. And nobody had the will, the vision, to bridge that gap."

I put a hand on her leg, gave it a squeeze. Below us some vehicles were moving around by the main entrance to the hospital parking lot. I said, "We had the same problem for a while, too. Rural versus urban, the west coast versus the maritimes, the Quebecois versus everybody else. Lucky for us, we managed to muddle through."

"Mmm," she murmured. "Muddle through. I like the sound of that. Tell me, Samuel, what do you think will happen here next?"

I was thinking of what to say when the noise level started to increase. Now there were soldiers down there, coming out of some of the tents. Then came the distant sound of approaching helicopters. I shifted and put my own arm around Miriam.

"Something's going on, isn't it?" she said simply.

"Yes."

"A guess?"

"I have no idea."

She broke free from my grasp. "Then come along. I want to know what's happening."

I got up from the picnic table and followed Miriam down to the large parking lot, though I really wanted to grab her and take her back to my room. I didn't like the sudden burst of noise and activity but my old reporter's curiosity was being tickled. Something was indeed going on.

We made our way down the hill and were soon on the pavement of the parking lot. People started moving about, most of them in uniform, and none seemed to be in a mood to talk. Then, luck of luck, Miriam cried out, "Peter!" and, sure enough, there he was. He looked at us both and then at me and said, "You know, Samuel, you are doing much better than I could ever have imagined."

"Well, I like to surprise people. What's going on here?"

Peter looked around, his hands on his hips. "You mean all this moving around, all these soldiers marching to and fro?"

"Yes," Miriam said. "What's up?"

"Very simple, really," Peter said. "You see, the militias are coming."

I felt cold again and Miriam brought her hand up to her mouth. Peter laughed. "Oh, I'm sorry, I didn't mean to frighten you. What I should have said is that representatives of the militias are heading over. You see, the negotiations are almost complete."

"The armistice," I said.

Peter nodded. "So true. The armistice is back on, so I'm told, but there's going to be a very steep price."

"What's that?" Miriam asked.

Peter said, "The militia leaders, the ones being held at The Hague. They get sprung, a day ahead of schedule, before any last attempt to find Site A. And in exchange for freeing those bloody murderers the armistice is revived."

"That's a hell of a price," I said.

Peter nodded again. "True, mate—and I'm sorry to say that it's a price that's going to be paid."

CHAPTER TWENTY-FOUR

The three of us went up by the guarded entrance to the parking lot where there were two columns of armed soldiers flanking both sides of the main gate, the lines stretching into the lot itself. They looked to be Polish troops and I said, "Please don't tell me that's what I think it is, Peter."

"It surely is," he said. "An honor guard, if you can believe it. A guard of honor for a group of men who don't even know the meaning of the word. Not on your life."

Miriam slipped an arm through mine. "I think I'm going to become ill, right here."

Peter said, "Then I just might get sick right with you, dear."

I squeezed her arm and she said, "Do you want to leave?"

"No," I said. "I have to see this. I really do. I can't believe they're treating them like this."

"Who can?" Peter said.

So we waited some more while other people drifted over to where we stood by the main gate. Some ambulances were moved, to make room for the visitors, I suppose.

I turned to Peter. "Any news about Jean-Paul?"

"What kind of news you looking for?"

"Oh, an arrest, conviction, a public confession of his crimes. That'd be a start."

Peter said, "He's in France now, probably getting some tough questioning from some members of the French government."

"Over his betrayal?" Miriam asked.

"Oh, hell, no," Peter said. "They're going after him because of his real crime, which was embarrassing the French. Everything else is secondary."

"Peter, you are such a cynic," Miriam said.

"No, dear, I'm a realist."

The gate was one of those with a sliding fence portion and now it started moving with a rattle of machinery. The Polish troops stood at attention, though I was pleased to see that, judging from the expressions on some of their faces, they would have preferred to point their rifles toward the gate rather than up in the air. Among us were other aid workers, some soldiers not on immediate duty and various nurses and doctors, some of them in their emergency-room garb. One doctor, smoking a cigarette, said to a nurse, "I swear, Gretchen, if those soldiers weren't there I'd take a scalpel and slit the throat of the first one I see."

If Gretchen said anything by way of a reply I didn't hear it. What we all did hear was the sound of engines and some of us moved back, away from the gate. An APC came through the gate first, followed by another. Both were flying UN banners from their radio whip antennas. Then came a black SUV of some sort with a blue flag that looked like the flag of New York state flying from its radio antenna, and that was followed by a black Cadillac with tinted windows. Three more APCs brought up the rear of the little convoy, and then, overhead, four helicopters circled in a wide sweep. All had weapons of some sort, either protruding from the open doorways on the side or in pods slung underneath.

Peter leaned toward me and shouted over the engine noise. "Not a bad little display, eh?"

"Trying to prove something?" I shouted back.

"Sure," he said. "Wanting to let the militias know the firepower that's out there, in case the armistice talks don't finish up. But it's all for show. All for show. By the end of the day, peace will be upon this land once again."

The helicopters hovered for a while and then flew off, lowering the noise level considerably. Miriam's arm was still linked through mine and I said, "What kind of peace? They'll still be digging up bodies and bones for the next decade."

"Sure they will," Peter said. "But this expensive intervention by NATO forces will be over, the United States will be welcomed back into the ranks of civilized nations, and the true business of this planet—feeding the hunger of the transnational corporations, led by the biggest economic power in the world—will resume. That is, if they decide to reengage with the world."

And then Peter looked at me, with a gaze that said much more would go on: that the true story of how this country had been crippled and who was behind it may still stay secret for a long time to come.

Miriam said, "If I stay with you any longer, Peter, I'm afraid I'll become as cynical as you."

Peter smirked, a look that once would have angered me but now just looked right. "Miriam, if you stay with me any longer, perhaps this boy won't interest you any more."

She laughed. "Oh, I doubt that."

I loved what she had just said, and I also loved the look on Peter's face, which was why I missed the first few seconds of the paramilitaries emerging from their two vehicles. The SUV had guards of a sort, but the word must have come down from somewhere, because their guns were slung over their shoulders rather than held at the ready. All four doors to the Cadillac opened up, and as well as the driver four militia types got out, a woman and three men. They had no weapons, and their uniforms were clean and pressed. One of them came around to look at us, a guy in his late thirties with a closely trimmed beard. I looked at him and he looked at me, and I actually felt my knees sag as though the ligaments and muscles there had just turned into taffy.

He smiled and called out, "Hey, Samuel! Good to see you!"

Peter and Miriam looked at me, and Peter was the first to ask: "Samuel, do you know that man? Was he one of your captors?"

I kept on looking at that comfortable-looking and happy face. "No, worse than that," I said.

Miriam asked, "How could have it been worse?"

I shook my head. "He was a cellmate."

And sure enough, walking over to greet me was Gary Nealon, supposed schoolteacher and fellow prisoner, now wearing the familiar militia uniform—with stars on his collars.

THERE WAS A tussle of sorts when some of the Polish soldiers got between us as I went over to see him. But then there was some talking back and forth and I made it to the Cadillac as Gary's three companions talked to a couple of UN suits. Gary was smiling widely, looking me up and down.

"Man, you look pretty good," he said. "How's it going?"

"You bastard," I said.

"Nope, my birth certificate's all in order," he said. "Can you say the same?"

I think I would have taken another few steps forward and started strangling him had it not been for the sharp-eyed militia guards who were keeping watch on me, and the equally sharp-eyed Polish troops keeping watch on the guards.

"Yeah," I said. "I *can* say the same. You son of a bitch, you were a plant, weren't you? A plant to get information from me."

Gary's eyes were bright and shiny. "Very good, Samuel. Boy, you must be a smart one to have figured that out right now, with me standing right in front of you. Tell me, you still make a list each year for Santa Claus? You didn't have a clue, did you, young fella, all those hours in the school bus. I had to put up with a cold mattress and bad food, all to see if I could plumb that eager young idealistic—and eventually empty—mind. The things I do for my people as head of intelligence."

My fists were clenched. "Like killing their neighbors?"

"Like *protecting* them, that's what, when the feds and the state couldn't do a damn thing when the hordes started streaming in," Gary said, looking around him. "Our real neighbors were protected. We took care of the trespassers. Nobody else could do it so we stepped up to the plate and got the job done. Boy, look at all the angry faces out there. You'd think they lived here or something."

"What do you mean?"

He smirked, and even with the armed men keeping an eye on us I wanted to punch out his lights so bad I could taste it. Gary said, "Look at all of them, parading around. Foreigners. Like they belong here. Get a good look, Samuel, 'cause by this time tomorrow this group will be heading out."

"Some of those people are Americans, working for the UN," I said.

"Then they're not true Americans, are they?"

"Jesus, you jerk, what the hell was that all about, back at the school bus?" I demanded, stepping closer to him, even getting a whiff of cologne from him.

"What do you think?" he shot back. "Intelligence gathering, that's what."

"From *me*?"

"Sure," Gary said. "What do you think, anybody's going to believe your story, that you were just a lost, innocent UN worker, wandering around the landscape? Do you?"

"That was the truth, and you know it."

Another laugh, another urge from me to punch him out. "Sure you were, and I was convinced you were something else. You did pretty good with Colonel Saunders and his boys, but let me tell you, if you'd stayed there one more day, then it would have gotten real rough. Think you would have been able to maintain a cover story if they brought out the knives and broken glass?"

I remembered what Peter had done, looking for me, and I said, "I imagine Colonel Saunders and his boys had more important things to worry about. Like a NATO air strike coming down their throats."

Gary laughed. "So your little cover story continues, eh? Not half-bad. Here's a newsflash for you, supposed ex-reporter Samuel. Colonel Saunders and his crew are fine, just fine."

Something acidy burned at the back of my throat. Peter. Had he been lying all along? Even now? But Gary went on and said, "After you bailed out the whole camp was moved. We knew you were there to gather intelligence. Maybe you even had a GPS device up your ass, for all we knew. So after you broke out, Samuel, the base camp did the same, before your brave pilots came in at ten thousand feet to kill men and women and children armed with rifles. Still, I have to admire you for keeping to your cover story for so long."

"And everything about *you* was a cover story too, right? Schoolteacher with a conscience."

"Oh, that part was true," Gary said proudly. "I was a schoolteacher with a conscience, one of the very few in my school who resisted the brainwashing of the teachers' unions and all the little special-interest groups who wanted to teach the latest fad. Oh, they were so smug and arrogant, thought they had everything under their thumb. They made jokes about me, you know. About having done better teaching in caves during the Stone Age. Teaching about a woman's proper place in the home. About America's proper place in the world. All that old-fashioned stuff. So when Manhattan was bombed and the balloon strikes happened and the power went out and outsiders started stripping our supermarkets and Wal-Marts, guess who stopped laughing? Guess who came to me and others and asked for help? So nice to be a liberal softy when you've got three squares a day. But when you and your kids get hungry you want help, even if you do drive a Volvo. You want your neighbors with guns to do something. So we did. Where's the crime in that?"

"And the cover story about your fiancée? That was true?"

Gary's face was no longer so merry. "No, part of that was true," he said. "But her name wasn't Carol Ramirez. Like I'd go out with a spic. Nope, her name was Carol Rockford. A beautiful white Christian woman. She was in a convoy all right, just like I said. She was helping take care of some foster children from some of our county agencies. Not from away. They were our own. Like we'd try to help those refugees. Just like those people streaming out after Katrina. Some misguided idiots were trying to save a bunch of thieves and druggies and welfare cheats then. Why? We looked after our own, that's what we did, and we took care of them."

"Took care of them, or escorted them to be dumped at the Canadian border?"

It was like he didn't hear me. "So there she was, traveling at night. Some militia units—not with our county, that's for sure—were escorting them, to make sure they could go through any state-police roadblocks without problem, when the bombing started. So that part is true."

"I'm not sure if I can believe you about anything, Gary," I said. "I don't even think you butchers are ready for an armistice."

The woman militia member called over to him, and he waved a hand back in acknowledgment. "Who says anything about us being ready? The Europeans and such, they're starting to scream about the cost in money, the cost in seeing coffins come home with UN flags draped across them. They're looking for any excuse to declare victory and go home. Because they know we'd never give up, not ever. Here's a little secret that you can take back to your masters in Geneva or wherever."

I moved to step back but Gary was quicker, grabbing my upper arm, leaning forward to whisper harshly in my ear. "The secret is, it's nobody's business what we do behind our borders. Understand? Killing niggers or fags or liberals or city people, it's our business, and always will be. No matter the body count. No matter what you folks think or do. No matter how long and hard you look for your mysterious Site A."

I broke free of his grasp. "Asshole."

"Sorry, Samuel," he said. "Time for us to declare victory. Site A? Here's another secret, young one. I was there, right from the beginning."

I said not a word.

Gary's voice got low, dreamy. "It was a wonderful thing—a beautiful thing. All those people, trucked in, scared, angry, not knowing what was going on. So many loud voices, so many opinions, so many voices demanding that we let them go, threatening to sue us, threatening to call whatever cops might still be out there. What a laugh . . . and the shooting started, and we shot them, and we shot them, we lined them up and we shot them . . . and after a while it was just so quiet and clean . . . It was wonderful, Samuel, the most wonderful thing I have ever seen . . ."

I tried to keep my voice even. "You're so fucking proud of yourself, why don't you tell me where it is?"

That seemed to snap Gary out of his happy memory, and he smiled. "Hah. Maybe if you'd spent a couple more days out in the woods instead of being in camp you would have fallen into it. See ya. Maybe I'll come look you up in Toronto when this is all over."

"I doubt it," I said. "You'll be arrested."

He winked at me. "In a few short hours, me and everybody else here will be given a worldwide blanket amnesty. Not to mention our POWs over there at The Hague. Just you see."

Gary turned and walked away and I felt this insane rage just roil through me as I remembered the burned buildings, the dead Australians, Sanjay lying there cold on the ground, the German air-force pilot dangling from a tree, the UN soldiers being shot, one by one, and dumped into a pit . . .

A hole. A pit.

Gary looked at me again and waved. I think I surprised him, for I waved back just as enthusiastically. Then I walked past the armed Poles, back into the crowd.

I WAS LOOKING for Miriam, I was looking for Peter, and I couldn't find either of them. There were more aid workers and off-duty soldiers and hospital folks around me, some talking in small groups, others lifting themselves up on tiptoe to see the dreary action taking place over by the tents, where the militia representatives were being escorted in for the armistice negotiations. I looked around, frantic now. Time was slipping away, and I thought about the militia generals, over there in The Hague, getting prepped to go home. Thought about Peter looking for the body of his Grace, looking for the truth about what had happened here, truth that might still be hidden for years to come. I moved around in a circle, looking for Peter's tall build, for Miriam's blonde hair. I bumped into people, moved again, heard the strange mix of languages, from Dutch to Polish to—

A flash of yellow. Over there. Hillside.

I went through the crowd again, using my elbows and whatever else to clear my way, and praise the Lord and pass the good fortune, there was Miriam, talking intently to Peter, standing a little ways up the hill. I ran on the grass and she smiled at me and any other time I would have just stood there for a second and enjoyed the sensation. But not now.

"Peter!" I yelled. "Where's the general?"

Peter turned in mid-conversation. "Oh, there you are. Who in God's name was—"

"Shut up, please, just shut up," I said, trying to catching my breath, trembling with excitement. "The general. Hale. The one we talked to yesterday. Can you get hold of him?"

I think anyone else would have started asking lots of questions, would have tried to dissuade me from doing what I was doing. But for once in our brief relationship Peter managed not to disappoint me.

"Is it important?"

"Yes," I said.

Miriam said, "I'm sorry, who's this general? And how come the two of you know him?"

I held up a hand. "Just a sec, Miriam. Please. Just a sec."

Peter said, "Important. Just how important?"

I took a deep breath. A gamble, but what the hell. What could anybody do? Send me back home? Assign me to the UN to investigate war crimes?

"Site A," I said.

Miriam stood stock-still. Peter stared at me, his eyes ablaze.

"What about it?" he asked.

"I think I—Hell, scratch that," I said. "I *know* where it is. Peter, I know where Site A is."

"OK," he said. "I guess that's important enough."

PETER WORKED HIS intelligence-agency magic while I was put in the very uncomfortable position of trying to explain to Miriam who Peter really was and why I hadn't told her before. I also had to touch on the question of what kind of relationship we were going to have if I kept secrets, and I was fortunate enough not to have to answer it right away because I was still keeping secret the story of the diskettes. Soon we were escorted into a mildewy-smelling canvas tent housing General Hale and two other UNFORUS officers. Hale looked very irritated, almost like my father on one of his better days, and I started right off.

"General, please excuse me, but a quick question."

Hale looked at Peter and God bless Peter but he didn't look awed or scared or overwhelmed. He just looked confident, like he was here to back up a colleague, someone he had worked with and whom he trusted. That look on his face warmed me almost as much as one of Miriam's smiles.

"All right, a quick question," he said.

"In my debrief, I mentioned a German Luftwaffe pilot's body, on a road by a river. Has that body been recovered?"

Hale looked over at the officers. "George?"

The officer called George flipped through a clipboard, looking at a sheaf of yellow message slips. "Yes, sir. Two days ago."

"How was it recovered?"

The officer looked over at me. "Excuse me?"

"How was it recovered? Who went in there and took it out?"

"An SAR unit," he said. "Search and rescue."

"They use helicopters, don't they? Not ground vehicles."

"Not with the armistice in tatters," Hale said. "Look, young man, I should be there with the negotiations, not spending time with you—"

"Site A—it's at the end of that road," I said.

The general paused in mid-sentence. He swallowed. Looked at me—I was so glad I was not wearing the uniform of the British Army. "What makes you so sure?"

Good question. I hoped my answer would be just as good. "At the end of that road is a tourist attraction. I spotted a brochure for it, and one of the locals who helped me told me about it. Bronson's Iron Works. One of the first open mines and forges in this part of the state."

"And?" the general asked, putting about a ton of skepticism into that one word.

"And it's been disguised. The signs showing how to get there have been removed. And the road leading into the mine has been disguised and blocked, with an earth berm and some foliage. Not enough to fool a serious search operation but enough to fool most people. And I just had words with one of the militia people you've been negotiating with. He let something slip about me being out there and almost having found Site A. Something about falling into it. Sir, it just came together. The disguised road. The missing signs. And an open pit or mine."

As I had been talking, one of the general's assistants had been going through a series of file folders, holding them up to his chest like some paper accordion. Hale turned to him and said, "Henry?"

"Sir, records show that the state park called Bronson's Works was investigated almost two months ago. There was nothing to report. All clear."

Hale turned to me, his face showing disappointment and anger and maybe just a little concern for me for trying to come up with something at such a late date. "Sorry, young man, it looks like you didn't quite—"

"Who did the search?" Peter asked, arms folded.

Hale asked, "Excuse me?"

"You heard me, General. A fair question. Who did the search? Who told you there was nothing there?"

Hale said to the aide, "Henry? You heard the man. Who led the search that told us there was nothing at the place called Bronson's Works?"

Another flip-flip through the papers and folders. Then, looking as pleased as a dog treeing a squirrel, Henry held up a piece of paper.

"One of the first investigators on the ground," he said. "A fellow called Jean-Paul Cloutier."

CHAPTER TWENTY-FIVE

Before the UN convoy left the parking lot, the passenger door of a Land Cruiser opened and Charlie Banner, USMC, clambered in, M-16 in his hands, and sat next to Peter, who was behind the steering wheel. Charlie turned, grinned, and held out a hand to me. I was sitting in the rear.

"M'man Samuel, good to see you," he said. "I've been meanin' to look you up, but I had a shitload of things to do once I got back here, after the armistice broke down. You look pretty good."

I gave his strong hand a firm squeeze, and he paid me the compliment of not trying to squeeze back. "Thanks, Charlie," I said. "You're looking good yourself. Thanks for getting everybody out."

"Thanks for the warning," he said. Then he shook his head. "Too bad about Sanjay, though."

Peter started up the Land Cruiser. "You did your very best, Charlie. Sometimes you can't save 'em all."

"Yeah, that's the hell of it," Charlie said, snapping his seat belt shut. "Sometimes the ones worth saving you can't, and the ones that ain't worth keepin' alive make it until they're ninety or so."

Miriam said, "It's nice at least for us four to be together again, don't you think?"

Charlie looked out at the other vehicles gathering in the hospital parking lot. "Where's Karen? In another Toyota?"

Peter said, "If so, it's one in California. She resigned her UN contract and headed back home. Can't really blame her, can you?"

Out by the tent a cluster of uniformed men and one woman was standing. The militia negotiation team. It was hard to tell what was on their faces, but I could make out Gary just fine. I guess it was a bad idea but I couldn't resist. I gave him a very cheerful wave as Peter put the Land Cruiser in drive and lined us up behind another UN vehicle. Gary didn't wave back, but he did lower his head and talk to the militia woman. Oh well. So much for a defiant gesture.

Charlie shifted in his seat. "California. Nice safe place, so long as you live in one of the right cities. I hope she's OK."

"Knowing Karen, she'll be just fine," Miriam said.

Charlie turned his head. "What does that mean?"

Miriam slipped her hand into mine. "It means nothing. Nothing at all."

AS WE DROVE along the state road, Peter said, "Now, this is what I call traveling in style. I wish we'd had this kind of setup a couple of weeks ago. Nobody would have troubled us, not at all."

"Ain't that the truth," Charlie said.

Even with Miriam's hand held in mine, I was still nervous, a trembling anxiety of anticipation, like lying awake in bed at five a.m. on December 25th as a child, wondering what awaits you downstairs in the dark rooms. Charlie and Peter were right: it certainly was a pleasure to be traveling in style. We were in a convoy of about a dozen vehicles, with a couple of APCs up front and another two in the rear, providing security. There were a half-dozen white Land Cruisers, just like the one we were in, and two open-bed tractor-trailer trucks that were carrying a bulldozer and an excavator. Flanking our progress on both sides were two helicopters—gunships, it looked like—and as we went through the countryside I could sometimes spot people emerging from their homes and trailers, looking at us as we went by.

"What do you think the militia are doing, back at the hospital?" I asked.

Peter said, "Probably hoping that in all the commotion they can scarper out and go home. If you're right, Samuel, and Site A is where you think it is, then the generals at The Hague are going to have a rough time of it."

Miriam said, "Maybe the armistice talks will break down for a long while. Have you thought about that?"

Peter kept on looking straight ahead, at the rear of another Land Cruiser. "Most of the militias in the other states have signed up. These guys were trying to play games, trying to get their leaders back. Fine. Let them play all the games they want. By tomorrow, once the media gets a hold of Site A, they'll be even more isolated and marginalized. The armistice will fall into place by default."

Then Peter spared me a quick glance, and I knew what he was thinking. So much more was at stake than the armistice, or the respective futures of the militias and the UN intervention. So much more.

The road rose up and curved to the left, and I caught a quick glimpse of a general store passing by on our right. I swiveled my head, peering at the innocent-looking building with its friendly front porch and inviting doorway. I must have shuddered or something, because Miriam leaned over and said, "You all right?"

"Yeah," I said, turning my head even more as we raced by Coopers General Store. "Just got bad memories, that's all."

"Of the store, that one there? Why?"

I turned around and looked at that beautiful smile, the concerned look in those sparkling blue eyes. "Had a bad meal there once, that's why."

THE AMAZING THING, to me at least, was that it didn't take long, not at all. After stopping at the earthen berm that was blocking the access road to the state park, a group of military engineers looked around, poking at the ground and checking for land mines or IEDs. When they gave the all-clear, the bulldozer revved up its diesel engine, backed off the trailer and then got to work, tearing apart the dirt and trees and brush as though they were made of polyester foam. While this was going on, we stood outside our Land Cruiser while APCs kept watch at both ends of the road, and soldiers—a mix of Hungarians and Ukrainians—patrolled the woods. I still felt jumpy: the memories of having been here a few days ago, on the run, trying to survive, trying hard not to get caught, came racing back.

Peter was leaning against the dirt fender of the Land Cruiser. "Sun feels good, doesn't it?"

I did the same thing, trying not to think of the days I'd spent in that smelly and cold school bus, trying not to think of what was out there, waiting for us.

Peter said, "My dad told me once, in London, that there were never too many sunny days, and if you got one you should enjoy it for as long as possible. Back when he grew up, there was still a lot of coal being burned in and around London. Lots of cloudy days. Not a bad piece of advice, to enjoy those sunny days that come your way. Your dad ever give you advice, Samuel?"

"Yeah, but I never listened to it," I said.

Miriam asked, "What kind of advice was that, then?"

"Never to volunteer," I said.

Even Charlie, up at the front of the Land Cruiser, heard me, and they all had a good laugh at what I'd said.

A dozen or so meters away the bulldozer started back up again on the flatbed trailer and there were some yells. Charlie said to Peter, "Looks like it's time to saddle up."

"We ride again," Peter said.

I opened the door for Miriam, and just like that she reached up and kissed me. Right on the lips.

"I'll remember that," I said.

"Good," she said. I climbed in after her and got the door shut just as Peter put the Land Cruiser in gear and we rejoined the convoy.

THE GOING WAS slower this time, since the soldiers in charge were keeping a close watch on our progress. The helicopters raced ahead and then came back, hovering overhead, at an altitude of what looked like under a hundred meters or so. APCs and a mine-clearing crew led the way, and armed soldiers were again flanking our sides out in the woods. The river came in view to the right, the one I had forded, and I kept looking around on the left, looking for a particular tree, a tree where I had found a volunteer like myself dangling in the breeze. But the SAR unit that had picked him up had done a good job: there was nothing left, no parachute, no parachute lines, nothing.

Miriam squeezed my hand. "What are you thinking?"

"Truthfully?"

"Of course truthfully."

"OK." I was going to say something snappy, like I'd been imagining her in a bubble bath, wearing nothing but a smile, but I decided that Charlie and Peter didn't need to hear something like that. "I'm thinking that maybe Peter will be able to hide me if we get there and there's no Site A. I imagine that general will be very unhappy."

Miriam reached up with her free hand, tickled Peter's scalp. "You'll do that, won't you, Peter? Hide Samuel if there's trouble?"

"He should ask Charlie," Peter said. "I'm just a cop, nothing else."

Miriam sat back. "Oh, I don't think so. I don't think cops can boss generals around, now, can they? Why won't you tell me who you really are?"

Charlie wouldn't let Peter reply, because he said, "OK, we're here. Now the fun begins."

We came up to a wooden bridge spanning a fast-moving stream that no doubt led into the river I had crossed the other day. The wood planks made a clunking sound as we drove across them. In front of us was a wide stream bed, and up ahead was a dirt parking lot. There was a steep hill at one end of it and two low-slung wooden buildings. There were stumps again, where signposts had been taken down. The convoy came to a halt, parking in a semicircle. I stepped out, slung my duffel bag over my shoulder.

Miriam saw me and smiled. "Still on the job?"

"Until I'm sent home, yeah, I'm still on the job," I said.

The helicopters stayed overhead, darting back and forth like dragonflies seeking prey. Soldiers were moving about and I experienced a little taste of shame, remembering all the times I had thought badly of my father, his service, his chosen career. Being a soldier was more than a matter of black and white. Sometimes they were there in the middle, defending those shades of gray.

Peter got out, looked around. Charlie climbed out and stood next to him, his weapon slung at his side. With Miriam with me I felt indestructible, as though this UN team could go anywhere, do anything to protect the helpless and the innocent.

"Where do we start looking?" Peter asked.

"Wherever the mine entrance is, I suppose."

Charlie said, "There's a crowd forming, over there by the hill. Let's take a walk."

We all walked over, each of us—except Charlie—carrying a bag of gear that marked his or her own specialty. With all the other people around and the soldiers as well, I had the feeling that our little inspection group was about to be overwhelmed. But damn it, we were going to do our job, so long as we could.

There was another series of wooden stumps set into the ground, where signs had been removed. General Hale, now wearing a beret, was standing beside a gravel path that led toward the steep hill. There was a cluster of soldiers and UN types around him, and he caught my eye, offering a slight look of "I certainly hope you're right." I turned and looked at the gathering of APCs and earth-moving equipment and white Toyota Land Cruisers. All here because of me. As if she was sensing what was going on inside my mind, Miriam reached over and squeezed my hand.

"It'll be fine," she said. "Just you see."

"I hope you're right," I said.

Peter said, "Enough of that kissy-face stuff. We've got work to do."

Charlie said nothing. He just smiled and led the way up the path. It rose at a slight angle, fairly wide, and I noticed how chewed up it was. Tire tracks, lots of them, making the dirt look torn up. As we got further up the trail Peter said, "Congratulations."

"What do you mean, congratulations?" I asked.

Miriam whispered something in her native tongue and Peter looked back at me. "Can't you smell it?" he asked.

Then I noticed it, right after he said it. A sickly, sour-sweet smell that made my throat swell up and my eyes start to water. Peter said, "You smell it once, you never get it out of your mind, Samuel, no matter how hard you try . . ."

Ahead of us the path widened, leading to an area where the ground rose steeply and where rock was exposed at the side of the hill. A heavy-duty green canvas tarpaulin was secured against the side of the rock and it moved some, as if it were breathing. A mine-clearing crew was there, looking spectral in their gas masks as they finished their work with their detecting equipment. I coughed again, my eyes still watering, trying to take it all in. Peter said, "I hope you're not too fond of what you're wearing, mate, because when we're through here it's going to be good for burning, and nothing else."

Where the path had widened there were some park benches, and a small metal and wood hut that had REFRESHMENTS/SOUVENIRS displayed on a red, white and blue sign overhead. Above the tarpaulin was a rock overhang, and the place was thick with evergreens and brush. Not much chance of air surveillance finding anything out. Miriam put down her bag and started taking some things out. "This will help," she said. "Trust me, I know."

She opened up a little glass bottle of some type of cold cream, which she smeared on my upper lip and in each nostril. Vicks VapoRub rides again. Just like that time—ages ago, it seemed—when we had excavated those cows back at that burned-out farm. The smell was overwhelming, but it was a heavy mint scent that at least overwhelmed everything else. She did the same with Charlie and Peter, and then passed out little paper facemasks as though we were heading into surgery or some damn thing. Lastly, rubber gloves and clear safety glasses. I put everything on, feeling hot and uncomfortable and not quite understanding how the mine-clearing crew could be doing their job. More people were coming up behind us on the path, and they weren't as prepared as Miriam, for most had handkerchiefs around their faces.

One of the mine-clearing crew came up to me and pulled up his gas mask, his face red and sweating, his black hair sticking to his wet forehead. He said in a thick accent, "Things OK here. You want us to open it up?"

I nodded, too stunned to appreciate that he had asked me instead of Peter or Miriam or anybody else. "Yeah, open it up."

He turned and shouted something—in Slovakian, maybe?—and two of the crew went to one side of the tarpaulin. Ropes and turnbuckles were holding down the side of the heavy canvas, and the mine-clearing crew went to work. The ropes snapped free and two men grabbed a corner and started pulling it back. And damn it if there wasn't an awful gurgling, burping noise as the foul air inside the mine entrance was set free. I got dizzy and walked a few steps, took a deep breath, removed my face-mask, and threw up on the ground. My breakfast came up in three heavy spasms, and I felt enormously embarrassed until I stood up, wiped my face with a coat sleeve and looked around. Except for the men with the gas masks and Charlie, everyone else was standing there as well, a wet mess on the ground around their feet, their eyes glassy and their lips shiny-wet with saliva.

WE WAITED SOME more while an engineering crew came up with large round metal blower fans, which they set up at the mine entrance. Another engineering crew went to work with a generator, powering up the lights within the mine shaft. With the tarpaulin gone, I could make out the round entrance fairly well. There were timbers holding up the sides and the roof, and it looked big enough to drive a truck into. The low roar of the fans was swamped some by the sound of the helicopters hovering overhead and that of the vehicles moving around in the parking lot. General Hale came over to me and said, "The air quality in there is about as good as it's going to get. Since you led us here, I think protocol should be damned and you should have first crack at taking a look. That all right, son?"

I picked up my gear and said, "Only if Peter and Miriam and Charlie go with me. They're my crew."

"Of course," Hale said.

The three of them, all dressed like me with face-masks and rubber gloves and safety glasses, joined me as we went up the dirt roadway into the entrance of the mine. The walls and the roof were rough-hewn rock. The blower fans were switched off and a small crowd of a couple of dozen watched us go in. Temporary lights had been set up at the entrance to provide even more light, and I froze as we took just one step in, for I had seen a small child on the ground. Miriam bumped into me and said, "What's wrong?" I just looked down at the tiny figure and then squatted down on the ground. The doll weighed almost nothing, and its long blonde braids and its cloth face were dirty. I looked ahead to the shapes lying there, stretching out into the darkness, and I stood up, the doll in my hands.

"Nothing's wrong," I said. "But everything's wrong."

"Yes," Miriam said.

I looked over at Peter and Charlie, who seemed to be waiting for me to do something. Even with all that was no doubt going on inside his head, Peter stood still, no real expression on his face. So I went ahead, turned round and said, "Welcome to Site A."

AND ONE OF the horrible things, though I'm not sure if it was the worst thing or not, was how damn easy this was going to be. The militia units or rogue state police or whoever had been in charge here had created an efficient system. The mine shaft went in for a couple of hundred meters and there was still enough room to walk down the middle. On each side, lined up one after another, were the bodies, wrapped in green plastic garbage bags secured with twine. The smell was horrific, a deep, thick odor of decay and sweet-sourness that seemed to ooze right into our pores. The light overhead came from single light bulbs dangling from long power lines, and they wavered some in the air flow, making the shadows quake upon the long lines of dead men, women and children. I wasn't sure what was worse: the sight of all those green-wrapped bodies, stretching out, or the sight of the wet stone floor where the bodily fluids had been leaking out. We walked in slowly, using flashlights to help light our way, and I had to look away each time there was a shorter bundle lying next to a longer one.

Peter led the way and Miriam was beside me. She pulled my head close and said, "The hate, my God, so much hate."

Charlie was behind us, his face cold and impassive, and I knew that if we'd been back at the hospital parking lot he would have opened fire in an instant on the militia representatives who were waiting there, hoping for another armistice.

Then the path ended, at an exhibit of rusting old machinery. There were no more bodies. Just the gloom of the mine shaft, now descending at a steeper angle. Peter leaned in, flashed his light down there, and said, his voice muffled, "There might be more, tossed down the shaft. We'll have to send a crew in there with lights and ropes."

Miriam looked back at the little round spot of light that was the entrance to the tunnel. I stood beside her and shifted my duffel bag from one shoulder to the other. I knew we had work to do, I knew my gear was ready to be pulled out and used, but the sheer scale of everything overwhelmed me. It was like trying to excavate a house foundation using nothing more than a teaspoon.

"Two hundred and twelve," Peter announced.

"Excuse me?" I said.

"Two hundred and twelve," he said. "That's how many bodies are in here. Look, we've got work to do. We've got to get that engineer unit in here, make sure the bodies aren't booby-trapped, and we've got to do everything we can before night falls."

Charlie said, "I think you're too late, man. It's already twilight. Can't you see?"

I think Peter was going to say something about it not even being noontime yet, but he looked at Charlie's face and knew what he meant. I could only imagine what it must be like to see so many of your countrymen laid out like that, dead, for the crime of being hungry and being from away and for being different. That was all.

For being different.

SEVERAL HOURS LATER I was on an exposed piece of rock that was getting some late-afternoon sun, near the entrance of the mine shaft. The two helicopters were still overhead, doing their patrol work, making sure, I guess, that nobody was creeping around to steal the bodies. I'd taken off my gloves, safety glasses and mask and they were in a little pile at my feet, and the cream over my lip and in my nostrils was doing its job as best it could. I had a liter bottle of mineral water, which I was sipping slowly. I was into some sort of nutty routine where I would take a gulp of water, swish it around, spit it out, then take another gulp, and then swallow it. I think I was fooling myself into thinking that maybe I was rinsing out whatever bacteria and odors were coming in from the open mine shaft before I swallowed the next gulp of water.

The work had gotten underway after the engineers had determined that there were no booby traps inside. Soon enough, the bodies started coming out. Temporary morgues with refrigeration units had been set up in large canvas tents in the parking lot, and myself and a couple of other recorders went in first, taking photos and writing down descriptions. Then there was the first pass from the forensics investigators who took measurements and other details of each body. That took some time. Then I helped photograph each body as it was removed and brought out to a flatbed truck. It could hold twenty adult corpses at a time. The soldiers who moved the bodies wore full chemical/biological-warfare gear, with gloves and gas masks. Us UN civilians had to make do with the little face-masks and glasses and ointment. Then, with a roar of diesel engines, the truck carrying twenty dead Americans—or twenty-four or twenty-six, depending if children had been brought out—were taken down to one of the tents, where the real horror began.

I raised the water bottle, swished, spat, and then raised it again, swished and swallowed. The bottle shook so hard that its end rattled against my teeth.

"Hey," came a voice.

"Hey, yourself," I said as Miriam came over and sat down beside me. Her hair was matted at the back of her head and her face was bright red. I offered her my water bottle and she nodded gratefully and took three long swallows. No spitting. She was an expert at this, while I was just a kid newspaper reporter looking to do something different.

"We're almost done emptying the mine," she said. "How are you doing?"

"Lousy," I said.

"Why?"

I took a breath and then regretted it. The stench from the mine shaft seemed to come in waves, and I'd got a good whiff that made my stomach do flip-flops. I coughed and said, "Because I haven't done shit in the past few hours, that's why."

"What have you been doing, then?"

"Sitting. Breathing. Letting other people do the work. I should be down at the tents, doing the documentation, but I can't."

"I know," she said. "It is very tough."

Tough. There was a procedure at the tents, too. With each delivery, soldiers would pick up a body and bring it into the cool interior of the tent. It would then be placed on a metal examining table, set at an angle so that any blood or other bodily fluids would flow down to the feet. Then the medical examiners would get to work, gently snipping away the twine and unwrapping the plastic trash bag. I would be there as well, taking photos, trying to stay out of the way. There would be the low murmur of voices, the clinking sound of medical instruments being dropped into trays, the rustling as the plastic wrapping was taken off and tossed onto the dirt floor. And I would be there, taking photos. The very first photo was that of an old woman dressed in a red flannel nightgown. That was what got to me. A nightgown. I imagined her in a tiny apartment, maybe a cat or two at her feet, having a cup of tea, feeling scared and lonely about what was going on after the attacks, not sure of what tomorrow would bring, and then . . .

The knock at the door. Her family has come, or maybe her neighbors. They are leaving the city, joining the others who have given up after weeks of no power and no water and no food deliveries, of no news on the radio or the television. So she leaves her home and departs from the city and maybe there's help out there, friends, fellow Americans who will help her and her neighbors.

Doesn't that make sense?

And then the refugee column is halted, they are yelled at—and maybe they are robbed and maybe the younger women are taken away—and there you are, cold and frightened and not quite believing that this is happening to you, a little old lady, here in the United States of America, at the beginning of the twenty-first century, believing it must all be a mistake, right up to the point where someone—maybe even Gary, the local schoolteacher—places a pistol at the back of your head, right below the gray curls of hair.

That was what I imagined. Seeing her there, on the table, her skin puffy and dark, the exit wound of the bullet having torn apart her forehead. When the examiners got to that point I took a photo, left the tent, tossed my camera gear down and found the rock.

Tough.

"Yes," I said. "Very tough. But only for a few minutes more."

"You're leaving?" Miriam asked.

"Sure," I said. "Aren't you? There's another shift coming in, and Peter and me and Charlie, we're going to get drunk, I think. Please join us."

She rubbed my back. "Later, I will. I just met a woman, a classmate from the university. I want to talk some. But I'll catch up with you at the hospital. All right?"

"Sure," I said. Below us, some horns started honking and it was time to leave. I was going to kiss Miriam, but she was already up, heading back to the mine shaft. She paused, turned, and waved.

I waved back, and then went down to the parking lot.

PETER WAS STANDING near one of the Land Cruisers, his face grimy and his eyes red-rimmed. Other people were inside the vehicle. I went up to him and said, "Did you find her?"

"Yes," he snapped back.

"I'm sorry."

"Don't be. By this time tomorrow she'll be back home, away from this bloody place. And . . . she did her job, right up to the end."

"Got the diskettes?"

"Got the diskettes."

"I'm . . . My heart goes out to you, Peter."

"Thanks."

I looked back, wondering if I could catch Miriam, but she wasn't in sight. I said, "Can I ask a favor?"

"Ask away."

"Someday . . . someday I'd like to tell Miriam what Site A was all about. If it's all right with you."

Peter sighed. "Sure. Go ahead. But not now—maybe later. Like on your honeymoon or something."

I almost smiled, and then I thought of Peter, no doubt just an hour or so away from having identified his dead wife among the body bags. So I just said, "Sure. Later."

Peter wiped at his eyes. "Come on. Time to leave."

We climbed into the Land Cruiser. Peter was driving again, and Charlie was there and another guy I didn't know, a Japanese fellow who nodded and kept quiet. Peter tried to lighten the mood and said, "Another minute, we would have left you behind."

"A chance for a shower and a drink, I wasn't going to miss it, not at all," I said.

This convoy was smaller, just two APCs in front, and we were the second Land Cruiser in the column. I leaned back in the seat, realizing that my back was throbbing. We went over the bridge, the planks making a clunking sound again, and I was about to ask Charlie what kind of drinks he was hoping for when the bridge blew up behind us, rolling us over.

CHAPTER TWENTY-SIX

When the Land Cruiser rolled over the Japanese guy fell on top of me and started yelling. So did Peter and Charlie. I started fighting with the Japanese guy, trying to get him off me. Somebody, maybe Charlie, got a door open. We got out and stumbled around, and then someone yelled, "Down! Down! Down!" I don't know, maybe the Japanese guy didn't understand English or was too frightened, but he started running up the road, away from the now-burning timbers of the bridge. Automatic gunfire cut him down.

I coughed and choked. Then I crawled behind the overturned Land Cruiser. Peter was there, one arm bleeding and hanging strangely, and he was yelling into a hand-held radio. I crawled over to the other side where Charlie was at work, firing at somebody or something. Another explosion. I heard a loud *whoosh!* and looked up, seeing a smoke trail from a rocket waver up into the sky. One of our helicopters was climbing, its door gunner firing away. There was another *whoosh!* and this time the rocket went right into the helicopter's open hatch. The explosion filled the aircraft with flame and smoke and it crumpled into itself, its blades spinning out like a windmill going berserk. It plummeted down into the hillside, blowing up in a big blossom of fire.

The gunfire was rapid and loud, and it seemed to be all around us. The bridge was ruined, and a Land Cruiser was tangled up in the shattered timbers, its windows blown out, two of its doors hanging open. I didn't see anybody moving around in there. One of the APCs was next to us, its turret gun firing into the woods across the stream, to the left of the parking lot, and I could even hear the *pings!* as return fire struck its armor plating. The other APC was on its side, just like us, and the soldiers who'd been inside it had bailed out and were returning fire with their own automatic weapons. I wanted to yell, I wanted to scream, but most of all I had to find Miriam. Had to. She was on the other side of the stream bed, and now the tents where the bodies were being examined were on fire, their canvas walls and roofs peeling back and streamers of flame and smoke rising into the sky. Charlie stopped firing, ejected an empty clip, took out a full one—tapping it twice on the undercarriage of the Land Cruiser—and inserted it into his M-16. He looked over at me, breathing hard, his eyes wide. "You better stay put, buddy, 'cause we are in some serious shit here. Our air cover's now on the ground, burning to beat the band."

I crawled back to where Peter, panting, was leaning up against the vehicle's undercarriage, one arm bloody and limp, radio in his good hand. "Got through to the region," he shouted. "But it's gonna take 'em a while to help us out. Fuckin' bastards. A classic ambush. Wish I had my bag with me."

"Where is it?"

"Inside the—Hey, don't you dare—"

I got up, hoisted myself over the undercarriage of our Land Cruiser and immediately fell through the open door. The inside was a mess, with gear, empty coffee containers, ropes and duffel bags all mixed together. But I knew what Peter's bag looked like—it had red handles—and I found my own bag as well. I tossed them both out of the open door and then followed them, landing hard on the packed dirt of the roadway. The nearest APC was growling as it churned up soft soil near the road, its turret swiveling, firing again. Charlie yelled, "You go, baby—get some!"

Peter didn't waste any time, opening his bag and tossing out clothing and a notebook until he found a zippered black case. He unzipped it, holding it up to his mouth with his good hand and using his teeth, and pulled out an automatic pistol, a nine-millimeter model, it looked like. He thumbed back the hammer and rolled over beside the front tires and started firing, taking care to place each shot precisely. I had never felt so goddamned helpless in my life. I opened my own bag, dug through the camera gear and my notebooks, and pulled out a small pair of binoculars. I raised myself up over Peter's prone body and tried to focus on what was going on across the way, by the mine's parking lot.

The buildings and tents were now all ablaze, as well as a few of the Land Cruisers. A defensive line of some sort seemed to have been set up at the right side of the parking area, where the ground sloped down at a slight angle to the stream bed. Three APCs were hull-down behind the slope, and were firing up at the woods. There were a number of people there, milling about, and it seemed that only a few had weapons of their own and were firing back. I tried to calm my breathing, tried to calm my shaking hands, and tried to look at each person who was moving around there. Although I saw two or three women, I couldn't find the woman I was looking for.

Charlie stopped firing again. I went over to him and said, "You got anything else? A pistol? The grenade launcher?"

He pulled out a fresh clip. "Grenade launcher's back at base. Pistol I've got, but you're not getting it. Sorry."

"Damn it, I can't just sit here and—"

The bolt of the M-16 snapped back. "The hell you can't. You're a civilian, Sammy, and if I give you that pistol, that's just wasted rounds. And we can't afford wasted rounds."

Charlie was right—but, God, I hated him so at that moment. I looked back at Peter, who was successfully reloading his pistol with one hand, and I brought my binoculars up again to focus on the mine entrance. I saw some flashes of light there, as the militia units poured fire down at us and at our comrades across the stream bed. Then there was a place where the brush and trees thinned out and I could actually make out people moving, people with their hands on their heads—prisoners—and the last person in line, moving up the hill, had long blonde hair.

I dropped the binoculars, got back down behind the Land Cruiser, looked to my left at Peter and to my right at Charlie. I was trying to decide which way to go, so I could ford that stream and do something, when the ground seemed to reach up and slap me down with an enormous *boom!*

I WASN'T OUT for very long, just a minute or two, but I was flat on my back, trying to get some breath into my lungs. I stared up at the smoky sky and at the oily undercarriage of the Land Cruiser, and Peter was yelling from what seemed like a long distance away. I got up and rubbed at my face, and Peter's voice was clearer now: "Samuel, the first-aid kit! Now!"

He wasn't at the front of the Land Cruiser and I turned and saw him with Charlie, who had been dragged back to where the rear tires were. The APC that had been returning fire was on its side now as well, burning furiously, its tires shredded and melting, and something that looked like a person was halfway out of one of the hatches, burning as well. I couldn't bear to look at that for another second, so I got back inside the Land Cruiser, again falling down through the open door, and unclipped the kit from a bulkhead. I got back out and down on the ground, moving my jaw and trying to swallow—my ears felt like they were stuffed with cotton.

Charlie was on his back, his face a mess of blood. I opened the kit and Peter got to work, pulling out bandages and tape. He yelled, "Over here, hold this here," and I did as I was told, holding a thick compress to the back of Charlie's head. I kept the pressure up while Peter, working one-handed, used a pair of scissors, cutting up Charlie's left pants leg, which was soaked through with blood. I glanced around. The firing had lessened. The three APCs across the way were still shooting, but it didn't seem like there was much return fire. The tents and buildings of the mine were smoldering, making a lot of smoke but not much fire.

"Keep that pressure up, mate, just keep that pressure up," Peter said, swearing as he worked on one of Charlie's legs.

I just nodded, trying again to catch my breath. I looked around once more, trying to take it all in. The body of the Japanese guy was still in the middle of the road, the soldiers from the undamaged but overturned APC were still firing—slower, just like everybody else—and the other APC was still burning. Charlie was gurgling now, his breathing getting more raspy.

Peter was working as best he could with one hand, and said, "Keep that pressure up, you hear me?"

"Yeah, I hear you," I said.

The bandage I was pressing against Charlie's head was now getting moist, and then actually wet, with blood.

But I kept up the pressure.

ABOUT AN HOUR later I was standing by the destroyed wooden bridge, looking over the stream bed at the smoking ruins of what had been the most successful mass-grave recovery that UNFORUS had carried out as part of their mandate in the United States.

For about half a day, before the militias had attacked.

In the mess of timbers and planking—and the consensus was that it was a well-hidden, command-detonated mine that had taken out the bridge—a medic crew was trying to extricate whoever might be still alive in the crumpled-up Land Cruiser. Helicopters were now overhead, having quickly replaced their fallen mechanical comrades, and the road behind me was a moving mass of ambulances, APCs and soldiers who were going out into the woods, armed and ready to fight the shadows that had come out earlier and had shattered us. It was dusk and the growing darkness made me shiver. But I still stared up at that spot where I had seen a blonde woman being led away.

"Hey, Samuel," came a voice, and I turned around. Peter was there, one arm in a sling, his other hand holding on to a radio.

"You OK?" I asked.

He moved his arm, winced. "Just temporary, until I get to the hospital."

"How's Charlie doing?"

Peter tried to shrug, winced again. "He got dusted off about fifteen minutes ago. He's holding on, but . . . Well, he's holding on. He's a tough Marine. And thanks for your help."

I said nothing, turned back to look over at the camp. It looked like organized chaos as people moved around, either shouting orders or obeying them. Most of the people were heavily armed, and helicopters landed and took off every few minutes. Every now and then I picked up my binoculars, did a scan. Nothing of interest. Nothing.

Peter said, "We should head back."

"No."

"What are you going to do, head on up into the woods after her?"

"It's a thought."

He squeezed my shoulder. "Let the professionals do their work, Samuel. They'll find her."

I looked back at him—in amazement, I guess. "Professionals? What professionals? We just got the shit kicked out of us, or haven't you noticed? And how long before the armistice gets put back in—after all, we all want peace, right? How long before Miriam is just listed as one of the many missing? That's the new professionalism, isn't it?"

Peter let his hand fall away from my shoulder. "I can't answer that, and I don't want to, because you're probably right. Look, Samuel, we need to go. First, you need a meal and some rest. Second, if you try to do anything tonight the UN guys are just going to grab you and prevent you from doing shit. What Miriam needs from you is a healthy and rested Samuel. That's all you can do for her, at this moment."

I thought about something and said, "The diskettes."

"Yeah?"

"They're . . . they're safe? Tell me they're safe."

"Yeah, they're safe. Halfway across the Atlantic at this moment, ready to be presented to the PM tomorrow."

"At least *that* wasn't fucked up," I said.

Peter said, "Come on, we should go."

I brought the binoculars back up to my eyes. It was getting too dark to see anything clearly and I knew the guys over there wouldn't want to set up any lighting, not yet.

I turned. "Yeah, you're right. Let's get the hell out of here."

We went back to our overturned Land Cruiser, and I made out the wet area in the dirt where Charlie had been bleeding. A crew of some sort was at work at the burned-out APC, and I averted my eyes. I had seen plenty today, thank you. Peter went on up ahead to talk to an officer in fatigues and blue helmet, and while he was talking I noticed Charlie's M-16, resting on the ground. I kicked at it and it fell into the weeds by the side of the roadway. I followed and started kicking again, this time at the embankment, kicking and kicking until I'd dug a hole. Then I pushed the rifle in, tumbled the dirt back over it, and went up to Peter and waited to be evacuated.

I refused to look back at the few lights and smoldering fires that marked where the recovery camp had been.

THE NEXT DAY, stiff and groggy from not enough sleep, I found my way to a particular hospital room, a ward, really, where curtains had been drawn around the beds to give the patients some form of privacy. Finding the right bed wasn't a problem: the Marines in fatigues grouped around it made it easy to locate. They looked back at me and their strong faces beneath short haircuts gave me a very disapproving look, because, after all, I was a civilian. And all civilians do is to send in their military to clean up their messes.

But the bandaged man lying in bed saw me and said in a hoarse whisper, "Hey, Samuel, c'mon over."

The men moved aside and I went to him, grasping the hand that didn't have an IV in it. This was the first time I had ever seen Charlie out of uniform, and it was amazing how he seemed to have shrunk. There was a bandage around the back of his head, and his right leg was also bandaged and was hanging from an overhead chain. A tube was running out of his leg and an IV was feeding into his right hand. His face was scratched and bruised but he was smiling, and he squeezed my hand back, strongly. Peter had been right. Charlie was tough.

"Guys, this is Samuel Simpson, from Canada," Charlie announced to the other Marines. "He was in the unit I was assigned to."

The guys stared and a couple of the friendlier ones just nodded. Then Charlie said, "He's a good guy. Gave me backup when I needed it, and gave me good first aid. Probably wouldn't be here if it weren't for him."

With that statement it was as though an iceberg of hostility had just shattered. The guys smiled and came over and shook my hand and slapped me on the back and introduced themselves to me—although I quickly lost track of who was a private and who was a gunnery sergeant and who was a lance corporal—and they said that if I ever needed anything, all I had to do was check in with the Sixth Marine Expeditionary Force and I'd be taken care of, don't you worry about a thing. Then it was, hey, Charlie, we've got to get going.

And like a quick-moving thunderstorm the Marines jostled around Charlie, poking him and punching his shoulder and squeezing his hand, and then they were gone. Charlie said, "Spare chair there, Samuel, why don't you take a seat?"

Which I did. I looked around the ward, saw a pile of yellow and red plastic toys in the corner. Charlie noticed where I was looking and said, "This used to be a daycare place for the hospital staff. But you can see what they had to do after yesterday's cluster-fuck."

"How are you doing?"

"Oh, Christ, I'm hanging in there," he said. "Got a slight concussion, happened when that Hungarian APC got greased. Also got some shrapnel in my leg and the back of my head. Good thing I was wearing my vest. The medics picked up about a half-pound of shrapnel back there. How about you, Samuel? You doin' OK?"

"No," I said.

"Miriam?" he asked.

"Yep. She and about a half-dozen others were captured. No word yet from the unit that took them. No ransom demands, not yet."

Charlie shifted, winced some. "There will be, you can count on it."

"Yeah," I said. "Look, they treating you all right here? Anything I can get you?"

He frowned. "Yeah. A new country. Think you can arrange that?"

I said, "When we're done here I think it'll be a new country, all right. But not the one you grew up with, I'm afraid."

"Yeah . . . Shit, you know what I was thinking, back when we were getting shot at? That I was returning fire against fellow Americans, that's what. Oh, I was under the proper command authority and properly detached to UNFORUS, but still . . . I was shooting at Americans, who were shooting back at me. A hell of a thing. Something like that hasn't happened since the 1960s. Man, when I was in high school I saw some pictures in a history book of when the cities were burning, during some of the race riots. There you had jeeps with machine-gun mounts and APCs and troops with guns in the street. And everybody's forgotten it ever happened, you know? Never thought there'd be another time when we'd be asked to fight in our own country, against our own citizens."

Another shift, another wince. Charlie went on. "Don't hear much news about it, but I guess there's a few hundred guys from all the services who're now serving time in the stockade for refusing to go out after the militias. Can't rightly blame them for not raising a weapon against an American in a domestic situation. Shit, that's what cops are for. Not the military."

"You must have found it hard, too," I said.

"What makes you think that?" he said sharply.

"Well, I don't know, the reaction I got from your buddies there, and . . ."

Charlie shook his head. "Just because I've got a uniform on doesn't mean I don't have a mind, Samuel. Those are good guys who'll follow orders, just like they've been trained. And some of us . . . well, for some of us it's personal."

I waited, listened to the PA system, hoping for a Doctor Matthews to report somewhere. Charlie was staring right at me as if daring me to say something. So I did.

"You want to tell me why it's personal?"

"Not particularly."

"OK."

Charlie said, "But I will. Maybe it's those damn drugs I've got going through me, make me loosen up my tongue. OK. One little talk from me, and then we drop it, OK? No questions from you. Then we talk about the weather or politics or whatever. That's my deal, Samuel. All right?"

"Fine," I said.

He took a deep breath, shuddered again from the pain. "My mom, she worked for an investment firm, as an admin aide. She was good, a good worker, brought me and my brothers up well after Dad died. A good mom. And she had the rotten luck to be working at an investment firm that had its offices near the World Trade Center construction site in Manhattan. Savvy?"

I couldn't say a word. I only nodded. Southern Manhattan, and the third time it had been the target of hate. And this time the haters were not from overseas, they were from the home territory. And they wanted to outscore and out-terror the first and second times. No truck bomb. No hijacked airliners. Just the power of the split atom, splitting this country apart along old lines of hate and suspicion.

"So that's why it's personal, and why I don't mind trying to keep the peace, even if I am in-country. You know what I mean . . . ?" Charlie said.

I nodded. We sat like that for a bit.

Charlie coughed and said, "You're not saying much."

"You asked me not to."

He started laughing at that, until he winced again from the pain. "Shit, yes, you're right, Samuel. You are fuckin-A right. OK. We can talk now, but let's not talk about Lower Manhattan or balloon strikes or yesterday's shit storm. You got anything else you'd like to chat about?"

"Yes," I said. "I'm looking for your help."

"Me? Man, I'm one fucked-up cat. I ain't going anyplace soon."

"But you've got your friends, just like those Marines who left, right?"

Now Charlie sounded a bit suspicious. "Yeah, of course I do. What are you looking to do?"

I looked around, made sure we were alone, and then I told him. He pondered what I said and asked me a few questions, which I did my best to answer. Then he looked out at the ward, at someone in a gurney being wheeled away, a sheet covering the body from head to toe.

He looked back at me, held out his hand. I shook it, gave it a good squeeze.

"OK, friend," Charlie said. "You've got it."

CHAPTER TWENTY-SEVEN

A day after my talk with Charlie I was back at the ambush site. I had hung around the hospital parking lot for a while, and managed to hitch a ride with a small convoy of earth-moving equipment and APCs that was heading back to assist in the clean-up. The word I got, just before I left, was that the armistice talks were resuming and that the attack two days ago had been the work of rogue militia units who were opposed to any peace talks. I wasn't sure if that was the truth or not—who could tell?—but I didn't particularly care. The news from overseas had also been quiet. If Peter's diskettes had made an impact yet with the British Prime Minister the news hadn't gotten back here yet. The APC I rode in was from another Ukrainian unit, and one of the soldiers practiced his English on me, all during the long drive out there.

At the ambush site a temporary bridge of wood and steel had been set up over the stream, and our wrecked Land Cruiser, as well as the Land Cruiser that had been blown up in the bridge mine detonation, were piled at the side of the road, near the burned-out APC. There was still a haze of smoke and fog in the late-afternoon sky, and I watched the work go on from a distance, just standing there, wearing my UN-issue ID around my neck.

I had on new clothes, camouflage gear, courtesy of the U.S. Marine

Corps. Being a civilian UN employee, I was breaking a half-dozen rules or so and I didn't particularly care. On my back was a heavy knapsack, also courtesy of the U.S. Marine Corps, and among the gear they'd given me were just a few of my personal possessions, including a few snack items and my treasured George Orwell book. My collection of Heinlein short stories was probably turning to mud somewhere, maybe a few klicks from here, but it seemed more appropriate anyway to have the Orwell book. This wasn't the time for wonderful speculation about mankind's glorious future, and Orwell's sharp words were going to guide me during these next few weeks. I rested at the side of the road, watched the work go on at the mine entrance and the parking lot. The story I had heard just before leaving was that the rogue militia was desperately trying, one last time, to destroy the evidence of Site A. Again, though, who knew if that was true?

But one thing was true. Not one word, one sentence, one syllable had been uttered by any of the militia units about the prisoners they had taken two days earlier.

I squatted down, played some with the dirt on the embankment, waiting. A helicopter came overhead and hovered, and I looked around. I was alone on this stretch of road, and the people on the other side of the bridge were all watching the approaching helicopter. And I took advantage of that, working quickly, and dug at the side of the embankment until I had freed Charlie's M-16.

I grabbed it and stood up. Then I walked quickly to the other side of the road and it looked like I was going to make it, until the voice came at me from the brush: "Hey, Samuel, where in hell do you think you're going?"

I stopped, shocked at what I had just heard. Then Peter emerged, wearing camouflage gear like mine, his arm in a sling, fresh bandages around his fingers. I looked to see if anybody else was about and then I walked further into the brush, so that it was just him and me.

"I'm going for a walk," I said.

He nodded at what I was carrying. "Some walk."

"Well, I've heard it's pretty dangerous country out there."

"Yeah, right. Look, Samuel, what the hell are you trying to prove?"

"Prove? You tell me. What was the point of everything we've done these past weeks and months, eh? The case against the militia leaders over in The Hague is still up in the air . . . And where are your promised stories about the bombings, the people behind them, the ones who caused all this chaos? You got your precious information. Where is it? I thought that was the whole key. Get the truth out to get this country up and moving again, recognize who did this to them, make them face the lies and the deceit."

Peter looked subdued for a moment. "Governments . . . they can move slowly sometimes. There are debates and positions to be considered and . . . Oh, bugger it. I don't rightly know. But tell me again. What are you trying to prove?"

I slung the M-16 over my shoulder, where it bumped up against my knapsack. "Not trying to prove anything, and you know it."

He came over to me. "Going to look for Miriam?"

"Yep."

"You won't find her, you know."

"But I might," I said.

"The UN won't like having you out here, traipsing around."

"Back at the hospital there's a letter of resignation from me that no doubt is going through the proper channels. In a week or two, they'll figure out that I'm missing. By the way, how in hell did you know I was coming out here?"

Peter smiled. "I didn't. But I did spot you earlier, at the hospital parking lot, dressed up like you are, with a pretty heavy knapsack on your back. I followed you here in the same little convoy, riding with the guy pulling the bulldozer."

"Well, goody for you."

"Samuel, you know the odds are against you, and—"

"Peter, you're not going to change my mind, not at all," I said. "I'm going to find Miriam if it takes the rest of this month and all the way through winter. I don't care if UN units are looking for her and the others. I don't care if negotiations are going on. I don't even care if the truth comes out about the bombings and the bastards who were behind them. All I know is that the woman I love is out there, scared and in danger, and I'll be goddamned if I'm going to sit on my ass and wait for somebody else to find her. You tell me. If you'd had any proof that your Grace had still been alive, and not dumped in Site A, what would you have done?"

Peter replied without any hesitation. "Same thing you're doing. No doubt about it."

"So there you go," I said.

"That Charlie's weapon?"

"Yep."

"You know how to use it?"

"Well enough," I said. "He gave me a little lesson this morning. Drew pictures and everything. And his buddies gave me some food, a stove, a nice bedroll, night-vision goggles, a couple of grenades and a couple hundred rounds of ammunition."

Peter shook his head again. "You and a gun, all alone against—"

"Remember Karen?" I asked.

That seemed to startle him. "Karen? Of course I remember Karen. Why?"

Another helicopter roared overhead, coming in for a landing, and I waited until the noise had died down. I said, "A week or so ago she said that all the world's problems were due to one thing: men with guns. She was right, you know. Most all of the world's heartache and destruction and death are due to men with guns, not jet bombers or missiles or submarines. But she was only half right."

"Yeah, mate, I see where you're going with this," Peter said.

"I hope so," I said. "The thing is, the only thing that's going to stop the men with guns is *good* men with guns. Trying to negotiate with the bad guys, trying to appeal to their better nature, trying to enhance their self-esteem isn't going to work. It's going to take good men with guns who will either overpower or destroy the bad men. Not very PC and pretty simple, but it was the best I could come up with, these past few days."

"Karen and others might disagree with you," Peter said.

"Fine. And they can discuss my shortcomings all they want, but I'm going out there to start looking for Miriam."

I started to walk past him and Peter said, "Wait, just one second."

"Why?"

He looked at me, smiled and said, "I'll come along. Trust me, Samuel. I'm pretty good at what I do."

"I'm sure you are," I said. "But how much can you do with one arm?"

"Plenty," he said.

I turned around. "Sorry, not good enough."

I started into the woods, seeing an overgrown path ahead of me. Then Peter called out, "A week!"

"Excuse me?"

Behind Peter the shadows along the roadway were lengthening. He said, "A week. The docs say in a week I'm rid of this sling. How about then?"

I thought about that for a moment or two, listening to the sound of machinery at work a little distance away, cleaning up so much debris, so much death. "All right. A week. If I don't find her by then, I'll be back here in a week to pick you up. Deal?"

"Deal," Peter said. "My, you must love her something awful."

"I do," I said.

"I envy you," he said.

I smiled and waved. "Peter, that's the best thing you've ever said to me. Ever."

Peter waved back. "OK, I've taken enough of your time. You go in there and find her, you bastard."

"I will," I said. "I will."

So I turned and walked into the darkness, and the little eight-year-old-boy was gone. Not once was I afraid.

Not once.

Miriam, I thought. Miriam.